HER SUMMER AT PEMBERLEY

A PRIDE AND PREJUDICE SEQUEL

SALLIANNE HINES

GRASSLANDS PRESS

Dedicated to Julie, forever our "bright sunshine"

Her Summer at Pemberley

A GRASSLANDS PRESS publication

www.salliannehines.com

Cover design by Sallianne Hines and Rachael Ritchey

Interior design/formatting by Sallianne Hines

ISBN 978-1-7333844-1-4 (paperback)

ISBN 978-1-7333844-0-7 (ebook)

This is a work of fiction. Names, characters, places, brands, and incidents are either the product of the author's imagination or are used fictitiously. Apart from well-known historical figures, any similarity or resemblance to actual persons living or dead, events, business establishments, or locales is entirely coincidental.

ABOUT THE REGENCY ERA

(OR WHY DO THEY CARE SO MUCH ABOUT GETTING MARRIED?)

In the Regency Era, a *gentleman* was a man who had/needed no profession other than managing his estate or wealth, and might include a clergyman or anyone in trade who had enough wealth to be considered "respectable."

A *gentleman's daughter* could not, for the most part, inherit an estate, own land, or have money of her own. Under the early nineteenth century British legal system, "primogeniture" determined that inheritances went from father to eldest son, in whole —estates were not divided amongst the children because that would lessen the wealth and power of the estate. If there were no sons, the estate was often entailed to the nearest-related male relative. This left a widow and daughters and younger sons with little to nothing, wholly dependent on the kindness and generosity of the male who did inherit. Lacking his kindness, the widow and daughters would depend on other relations. Some amount might be left for a girl's dowry if the estate was not heavily encumbered. When a woman married, all her wealth was usually assigned to her husband, to use wisely or gamble away, as he chose. Women in this economic class called "the landed gentry" were not allowed to work. If they did not "marry well," their lives could be unpleasant indeed.

CHARACTERS FROM Austen's *Pride and Prejudice*

Catherine 'Kitty' Bennet—*'missish' fourth daughter of Mr. & Mrs. Bennet of Longbourn*

Mr. Bennet—*known for sharp wit and indolence, father of five daughters*

Mrs. Bennet—*a silly woman determined her daughters will marry well*

Jane Bennet—*soft-spoken & kind eldest daughter, marries Charles Bingley of Netherfield*

Charles Bingley—*inherited wealth his father made in trade, rents estate at Netherfield*

Lizzy Bennet—*witty, lively second daughter, marries Fitzwilliam Darcy of Pemberley*

Fitzwilliam Darcy—*very rich, owner of Pemberley (a great estate in Derbyshire)*

Mary Bennet—*petulant self-righteous third daughter still at Longbourn*

Lydia Bennet—*wild youngest daughter, eloped at age sixteen with womanizer/gambler George Wickham*

George Wickham—*son of Pemberley's steward, grew up with Darcy but turned to gambling & other vices*

Georgiana Darcy—*Fitzwilliam's younger sister, nearly tricked into eloping with George Wickham at age 15*

Mariah Lucas—*daughter of Sir William & Lady Lucas, neighbors of the Bennet family*

ADDITIONAL CHARACTERS CREATED FOR THIS BOOK *Her Summer at Pemberley* (in order of named appearance)

Poppy—*lady's maid to Kitty at Pemberley*

Cara—*Arabian mare Kitty rides while at Pemberley*

Johnny—*Pemberley stable lad*

Riley Connor—*Pemberley stable master*

Lord & Lady Drake of Cedars; *sons Christopher & Benjamin*

Mr. & Mrs. Wyndham of Greystone; *sons Douglas & Owen, stepdaughter Lucy Jamison*

Squire & Lady Stapleton of Swan's Nest; *son Andrew, daughters Julia, Matilda, Emma, Honora*

Earl & Lady Matlock of Thornhill, near Matlock; *daughter Alice*

Alfred Cressley of Oakhurst near Windsor; *sons George (Murielle), Charles, William*

Margaret Mercer Elphinstone of Windsor *&* Charlotte Augusta of Windsor

CHAPTER ONE

*T*here was no hope at Longbourn. Kitty Bennet had fallen into her sister Lydia's shadow long ago. And now, two years later, Kitty was still seen as merely a dimmer version of Lydia. How could Kitty gain respectability and marry well?

Even her own family did not think highly of her. Her father was heartless. Mr. Bennet's rebuke still rang in Kitty's ears: *I have no time for missish girls and their silly notions.* What gave rise to this tirade? Kitty's request for Maria Lucas to visit a few days at Longbourn. Mrs. Bennet was spending much time at Netherfield whilst her eldest daughter Jane prepared for her first lying-in, and Kitty was bored. Not that being deprived of Mrs. Bennet's company was a great loss, but she *was* less dull than sister Mary.

Mr. Bennet's reproof had driven Kitty to seek solace on horseback, an activity that expressly violated her father's will. In light of that, her thundering ride had delivered a dose of satisfaction, but Kitty could not be content at Longbourn if things did not change.

And change was not likely. Mr. Bennet did not care for change. The most recent—the marriages of his daughters Jane and Elizabeth—had not improved Longbourn. Their absence was felt by all. With no gentle comfort from Jane and no witty retorts from Lizzy, Kitty felt her father's rants most acutely. In short, Longbourn could no longer satisfy. She buried her face in the horse's thick mane and sobbed.

With an indifferent education, a less than respectable fortune, and a family estate entailed away, Kitty's prospects were bleak at best. Now, with the regiment removed from the nearby village of Meryton, there were no dashing young men to offer diversion or romance. It was monstrous unfair! She had not the smallest hope of finding happiness in the neighborhood.

If only she could start afresh ... but how? Where? Netherfield, the seat of her sister Jane and husband Charles Bingley, was still in the neighborhood, and Kitty could not burden Jane during her confinement. Mr. Bennet firmly prohibited *any* visits to Lydia. Kitty frowned. Then slowly her face brightened. Perhaps Lizzy would allow her to visit at Pemberley! The more she thought on this scheme, the more it appealed.

She dwelt on it while she groomed the horse, her right hand moving the currycomb in steady circles followed by the brush in her left hand smoothing down the coat. Her efforts were rewarded by the horse's head slung low in pleasure. Most ladies in her sphere—if they rode at all—relegated this task to a groom, but Kitty found it gratifying. This simple farm horse showed his spirit with Kitty in the sidesaddle—or when she secretly rode astride or with no saddle at all.

Kitty was singular in her equine interest; none of her sisters were horsewomen. They preferred a carriage—except for Lizzy, who would rather walk. For Kitty, riding was a passion, albeit a clandestine one. Her father disapproved of young ladies "galloping about the country"—which diminished her joy in the pursuit not a jot. She chuckled. In this, her father's indolence worked in her favor. He had never kept close watch on his daughters. Thus, whilst Mary kept to the house with extracts and music, Kitty was free to pursue her own pleasures with no one wanting an account of her time. In many ways that was a blessing, but her life at Longbourn was a lonely one.

Kitty took a piece of carrot from her pocket and the horse lipped it from her open hand. She handed the now-sleek animal to the stable lad, then slipped into one of the stalls to remove the riding breeches—which she kept hidden in the feed room—

from beneath her skirt. It would be a great scandal if anyone discovered she rode astride. The groom who accompanied her knew of her daring misdeed, but was sworn to secrecy by misdeeds of his own. Kitty patted down her hair, shook out her skirt, and hurried off to the house.

Once in her room she pulled out her writing desk, prepared a quill, and penned a request to her sister.

Dear Lizzy,

I am in agony with only Mary and Mama for company. I long for a change of situation and neighborhood, and I greatly desire to meet new people. Could I visit you at Pemberley? Will Mr. Darcy approve? Truly I will be no trouble—I am not so much like Lydia as everyone believes.

Papa would be vastly happy to see you. I am sure you could convince him to accompany me to Pemberley. Mama visits Jane very often and is in great anticipation of her first grandchild. She is sure it will be a boy. Jane and Bingley are as happy as ever. Mary keeps mostly to herself.

Please reply soon. I am most eager to escape Longbourn and Papa will not allow me to visit Lydia.

Your sister,

Kitty

She sanded and folded the letter, sealed it with a wafer, and tripped lightly down the stairs to place it in the silver tray for outgoing posts. Then she sprinted back to her room to change for luncheon. It would not do to smell of horse. Her secret might be discovered, and Mama was so disagreeable when upset.

With Mr. Bennet off to another part of the estate, the noon repast was a quiet affair but for Mrs. Bennet bemoaning the lack of letters from Lydia. Between mouthfuls of food, Mrs. Bennet also prattled on about Jane's health and approaching confinement. Mary responded with truisms, and Kitty felt more invisible than a ghost.

Her eye wandered idly to the window. It was a fine April day so she proposed a walk to Lucas Lodge. Chatting with Lady Lucas would divert her mother, and Kitty longed for conversation less stilted than Mary's but more sensible than Mrs. Bennet's. Maria Lucas was somewhat empty-headed, but any variation would be welcome.

"A call on Lady Lucas is just the thing for my poor nerves. What with your father off, no one will miss us, and I must tell Lady Lucas all the particulars of Jane's situation." Then Mrs. Bennet frowned and heaved an exaggerated sigh. "And I suppose Lady Lucas will insist on boring me with every tedious detail about Charlotte's new daughter, as if I care anything about the future mistress of Longbourn." She sniffed. "Oh, why must your father's estate be entailed away from—"

"Mama, you know it does your nerves no good to dwell on that," Kitty reminded her.

"Oh, well, if it must be so ... but I *am* delighted with this idea for a visit today. Go now and get yourselves ready. I suppose we can walk—the road is not likely to be muddy," she commented, peering out the window at the unclouded sky.

The young ladies went to fetch their bonnets as the hall rang with the familiar sound of Mrs. Bennet ranting for her maid: "Hill! Where is Hill? If only my feathered hat were mended ..."

After far more to-do than rationally necessary, the three set off for Lucas Lodge. Mrs. Bennet filled the half-mile with her nattering. Mary trudged silently at her side. Kitty alone appreciated the sweet scent of apple blossoms carried on the breeze, and the pungent smell of Hertfordshire soil now fully awakened. She found much pleasure in country life—when not overset by its loneliness.

Hopeful of an invitation from Lizzy, Kitty smiled to herself. Pemberley would be lovely at this time of year.

CHAPTER TWO

$\mathcal{T}$he carriage bowled north towards Derbyshire. Mr. Bennet dozed, chin bobbing on his chest, spectacles perched precariously at the end of his nose. He had mostly read or slept during the journey and made little effort at conversation, so Kitty was left to contemplate the landscape and examine her own thoughts. She knew her father anticipated seeing Lizzy; and was likely more than eager to leave herself in Lizzy's care. She frowned out the window. Could he not see she and Lizzy were not so different?

Kitty had been overjoyed at Lizzy's invitation to Pemberley. This visit would be a new beginning, away from her dull childhood home and the same tiresome people. Kitty was determined to prove herself worthy of a fine future, but she needed assistance. Jane and Lizzy were her best hope. She must earn their good opinions. But Jane could be of little help now. With a new infant to care for soon, sweet-tempered Jane would have little time to spare. Lizzy, on the other hand, would have nothing to do but order the Pemberley servants about. And Lizzy was skilled at putting forth her opinions and working through difficult situations.

Yes, on this visit Kitty would watch Lizzy and learn. Maybe, with them both being from home, they might grow closer as sisters. Kitty had always envied the bond her elder sisters shared.

And who knew what eligible beaux she might meet in such a neighborhood? The Darcys would mix with the best families. Her eyes gleamed at the prospect. Then she grimaced, realizing there would likely be many accomplished young ladies as well. She was pondering this dilemma when a large jolt threw her nearly out of her seat.

It also jarred her father awake. He scowled and removed his spectacles to look out the carriage window.

"Well, Kitty, that rut was almost large enough to get lost in. Regrettably, it wasn't enough to bounce us right to Pemberley's doorstep. These roads are a trial. Are you doing tolerably well?"

Here was her chance to engage him, to prove she was by no means deficient in wit.

"Yes, Papa, I am well. I believe you are right about the roads —winter has left them close to impassable. You have made this trip a few times, have you not? How much longer until we reach Pemberley? I do so long for a cup of tea and a biscuit."

He twisted his mouth into an annoyed expression and cast her off with a wave of his hand.

No, she would not allow that! She gathered her thoughts.

"How can one tell, Papa? Where we are, that is. I've seen no road signs for some time. Does the landscape inform you of our progress? I see such different landforms and trees here. The farmlands have given way to higher, wilder country these last hours. Look how the large boulders pierce the meadows. Are there certain landmarks that indicate the way?"

Mr. Bennet looked at Kitty with a curious eye.

"Yes, in fact, there are. That lone peak to the northwest tells me we are nearing the posting station. After we change horses, we have about two hours more of our journey. I wasn't aware you took note of such things as boulders and trees. I thought your interests limited to bonnets and lieutenants."

The fragile smile fell from Kitty's face. She struggled to hide her trounced-upon feelings, gulped back a sob, and persisted.

"I find the landscape fascinating. I would love to know more about the rocks and trees, and why they are so different here. In spite of the roughness of our journey, I have so enjoyed the views that my book has not been opened today."

"Well, perhaps Mr. Darcy has some books on the history and topography of the area. It would certainly do you no harm to avail yourself of Pemberley's library; it is one of the finest in the kingdom. Although I predict you will be preoccupied, as usual, with gowns and lace and dances and beaux. I wonder what Lizzy has planned for your visit? Oh, well. Be a good girl now and save your questions for later, and preferably for someone else. You may find *your* book of little interest, but I assure you I do not find mine so." He replaced his spectacles and opened his book, closing the conversation.

Kitty narrowed her eyes at him. How could a young lady respond to this? Were he any other gentleman or acquaintance, would his remarks not be rude? At least at Pemberley she might be in more polite society and not dismissed as a troublesome child. Nearly nineteen was not a child. How could he think it?

She sighed and turned to the scenery, noting features she could ask Mr. Darcy about, if she could rally the courage. His presence was formidable. She had rarely seen him smile, and then only at Lizzy. Kitty had never spoken to him on her own. The very thought made her tremble. How would he treat her? She hoped he would at least allow her the use of his library.

≈

The carriage came to a stop at the Red Lantern to change horses. Kitty could not help but feel sorry for the exhausted beasts and was relieved they would get food and rest. Their plight always tugged at her heart. If she were a horse, she would not wish to be a hired carriage horse.

Her father stepped out of the coach, cleared his throat impatiently to gain her attention and, after handing her out, strode off. Should he not offer his arm? She glanced around to see if others had noticed his lack of manners, then shrugged and followed him into the inn. Some lemonade would be refreshing.

They entered the bustling common room and found a table. Immediately her father began talking with the gentleman next to him—as if she did not exist—so Kitty looked about the room to amuse herself. As her eyes came to rest on the table behind her father, a young man there looked up and met her gaze. He smiled and nodded. Kitty blushed and turned her eyes back towards her own table, but could not quell the smile that bloomed from within her.

A tavern girl brought ale for her father and set a small glass of weak wine in front of Kitty. After a disappointing sip, she stole another look at the young man. He was in the company of an older gentleman, perhaps a father or uncle or older brother, although there was no resemblance. His spirited blue eyes sparkled and his dark cropped hair bobbed when he spoke.

When Mr. Bennet's name was called for the carriage and she and her father stood to leave, the young man and his companion rose. As the strangers passed her table, the young man gave her a warm smile.

This time she dared to meet his eyes. He held hers fast until his companion chuckled and nudged him on. A flame of energy surged through her and she could scarce catch her breath.

Once outdoors, Kitty approved how the young man leapt lightly onto a fine bay. She envied the freedom with which men could ride, and admired his adept horsemanship as much as his good looks. He calmly managed his steed as it danced in anticipation of being off. Whilst his companion mounted a sturdy chestnut, the young man looked at her and touched his hat in an unexpected salute.

Her heart pounded and she dropt a slight curtsey, unsure if that was entirely proper as they had not been introduced. She watched until the two riders turned onto the west road and out of sight.

There had been no young men to meet at Longbourn of late. Surely society would be livelier at Pemberley? Diversions of any kind would be an improvement.

Kitty's father handed her into the carriage. They were off with a lurch and soon turned onto the west road themselves.

Landscapes slipped to second place in her thoughts, and the remainder of the journey passed in a twinkling.

CHAPTER THREE

*L*izzy awaited them on the portico, her trim figure dwarfed by the stately home. As the carriage entered the sweep, Mr. Bennet's face filled with joy on beholding his favorite daughter. Everyone knew Lizzy was his favorite. Kitty could be content with that, if she herself were not such an *un*favorite.

Kitty had always enjoyed Lizzy's company, when she could get it. Her older sister was lively and full of wit, although at times her remarks *were* a trifle wicked. Often this was amusing; but sometimes Kitty felt sorry for the person on the receiving end, unless it was Lydia—the opinions of others never bothered Lydia. Kitty herself had no wish to be out of Lizzy's favor, or the target of her sharp tongue. Kitty recalled how Lizzy had often taken long walks at Longbourn, especially when out of humor. Perhaps they could share long walks at Pemberley?

There! It was the beginning of a plan. She would learn about landscapes from Mr. Darcy, and would take long walks with Lizzy. It would make for a fine new beginning.

The carriage rolled to a stop. Kitty gasped when Mr. Darcy himself stepped forward to hand her out. Gingerly she took his hand and stole a quick glance—his expression was more relaxed than she remembered. He was monstrous handsome.

"Welcome to Pemberley, Miss Bennet. I hope you will find

your stay pleasant and rewarding." He gave her a gentleman-like smile and nodded before turning to address her father.

The majesty of Pemberley rose before her. When they first entered the grounds she had admired the rolling hills and groves of timber. She turned to survey the sweeping panorama, dazzling in all the glory of spring—as if the place itself was wrapping her in welcoming arms.

"Well, what do you think?" It was Lizzy's voice behind her. Kitty turned and the sisters exchanged a warm embrace.

"It's so ... enormous! And beautiful," Kitty remarked, finding herself almost at a loss for words. "I am very happy to see you, Lizzy. Thank you for inviting me. An escape from Longbourn is most welcome."

"I was not surprised by your letter, Kitty, and had been expecting—even hoping—for it for some time. Jane and I have had some discussion about your situation and wish to help you in any way possible." Leaning in close, she whispered, "We know there is not much help for you at Longbourn." As she drew back, her eyes sparkled with mischief.

The sisters linked arms and mounted the steps to the grand entry hall.

"Now, I've assigned Poppy as your personal maid—your lady's maid, if you please—while you are with us. I think you two will get on, and she is very talented at hair arrangements. She will show you to your rooms and help you settle in. Once you are changed and rested, come down for tea. Cook makes lovely cakes. I have her cut them in tiny pieces so I can sample each one without doing too much damage to my figure." She kissed Kitty's cheek and then turned to welcome her father, who was still talking with Mr. Darcy about the journey.

Poppy came forward and curtsied. She was a strawberry blonde, about the same height and age as Kitty, with a sprinkling of freckles across her nose. The two exchanged shy smiles and Kitty followed her upstairs.

They entered a sitting room with a large window overlooking a far meadow framed by wooded hills. The walls were papered with a dramatic design of vines and peacock feathers. The room held a small table with two chairs, a settee, and a writing desk.

All this for herself? In the adjoining room stood a large canopied and curtained bed, along with closets and cupboards, a pair of chairs, and a dressing area that included an elaborately mirrored table for her toilette.

Kitty sank into a chair, set her reticule aside, and removed her pelisse.

Poppy stepped up to take the items.

Kitty eyed her, unsure what to say or do.

"Thank you. I have not had a lady's maid before. At my home, five sisters shared one maid, who was also the housemaid. I think you will find me quite independent in my daily habits, Poppy, unlike finer—"

A knock at the door interrupted their discussion. Poppy opened it and instructed the footmen where to place the trunks.

When they had done and left, she asked, "And what would ye wish to do first, Miss?"

Kitty felt a little uncomfortable being in charge. She had never had anyone to bid about. Lydia had been her younger sister, but Lydia was anything but biddable.

Kitty's present desire was clear.

"First I shall remove my dusty traveling boots and clothing and have a glass of water. Then I should like to wash and put on a fresh gown. Perhaps you could pull a few of my gowns from my large trunk?"

Poppy poured water into the washing basin while Kitty removed her traveling clothes. After completing her ablutions, Kitty turned to the bed where three of her gowns were smoothed and laid out.

"Which do you think best for tea, Poppy? I have not spent much time in such a fine house. Oh! Will I be expected to change again for dinner?"

"The sprigged muslin, I think, for tea. 'Twill bring out yer blue eyes. Aye, Mistress always changes for company dinner."

It dawned on Kitty that Lizzy's daily life had changed a great deal now that she was married. Maybe there was more to being mistress of Pemberley than Kitty had guessed.

"I wonder if Lizzy considers me 'company'?" Kitty mused aloud. "I will ask her at tea. I think she will find it diverting."

Kitty laughed, and Poppy hid her own smile behind her hand.

≈

Soon Kitty descended the stairs. Poppy had done a fine job in a short time, brushing and pulling Kitty's soft brown hair back and up, then working it into a figure eight at the top of her head, with fresh curls around her face. In her sprigged muslin with blue trimmings and green overlay Kitty felt like the spring air itself. It was late afternoon and the weather fine. Perhaps there would be time for a walk about the grounds?

As she entered the drawing room, her cheeks filled with color when Mr. Darcy stood and nodded acknowledgement of her presence.

Her father bumbled to his feet, begrudgingly following Mr. Darcy's example.

Kitty dropt a curtsey and stifled a giggle; her father had never acknowledged her entering or leaving a room in her life, unless it had been at his angry order. Her eyes met Lizzy's, which were alight with amusement.

The journey itself was still under discussion and Kitty waited for an opportune moment to ask Mr. Darcy about the different landscapes in Derbyshire. When she put forth her question, her father rolled his eyes and reached for another piece of cake.

Seeing Mr. Bennet's reaction, Mr. Darcy's eyes widened but his countenance concealed any emotion.

Poor Mr. Darcy. Always needing to keep his feelings and expressions in check. Kitty supposed it a necessary part of being master of a great estate.

Mr. Darcy turned to Kitty. "Many of the peaks hereabouts are made of limestone, and that one you saw near the Red Lantern contains a great cave. There are more than a few underground caverns, and even some underground rivers. The River Derwent, which flows past Pemberley here, is the longest river in Derbyshire and forms the backbone of this county."

"We saw the river as we approached the house," Kitty said, delighted with such a detailed reply. "I am eager to explore the countryside and make discoveries. That is, if allowed ..." Her voice fell. Was such enthusiasm too childish?

Lizzy's eyes twinkled merrily and Mr. Darcy's were lit with pleasure.

"I welcome your enthusiasm for exploring, Miss Bennet," he assured her. "You may plan on many outings and excursions during your visit."

Even Mr. Bennet's stormy countenance could not dampen Kitty's keenness now that she had secured Mr. Darcy's support on the subject.

"There are many volumes in the library that you may find of interest," he continued. "Tomorrow after breakfast I shall give you a personal tour, Miss Bennet; and you are welcome to use the library at any time."

"Thank you, I am much obliged. I wonder ... please, can you call me Kitty? I find 'Miss Bennet' so formal in my sister's house." She hoped her request was not impertinent.

"As you wish. And please call me Fitzwilliam or, as my sister calls me, 'brother.' By the bye, Georgiana returns from London in two days and will be in residence here for the summer. I sincerely hope you two will find pleasure in each other's company. Georgiana is delighted to have Elizabeth here." He beamed at Lizzy, then looked back at Kitty. "My sister was overjoyed when I told her you would be joining us for an extended stay." His affection for his younger sibling shone in his face.

Darcy was much less severe here. He was even friendly. Was this due to his comfort at being in his own home? Or was it due to Lizzy? He was certainly less frightening, by any account.

Kitty's shoulders loosened. "I am looking forward, very much, to becoming better acquainted with Georgiana and am quite sure I will cherish her like a sister. She is a little younger than I, but if I am not mistaken there is much I can learn from her about manners and style and accomplishment, as well as about moving in society. I hope we shall be very good friends."

As the others conversed, Kitty found herself relaxing into the rhythm of polite conversation. She had thought it would feel stiff and artificial but discovered that, when surrounded by others who were polite yet genuine, it felt quite natural.

"Pray, Lizzy, how shall I dress for dinner? Poppy says you dress when entertaining company, but shall you consider me company?"

Lizzy raised a brow. "It is true we dress more formally for dinner when we have guests. Whilst you and Papa are both here, I think we shall dress for *company*. But once Georgiana is home, I believe we shall adopt *family dress*. Would you agree, my love?" she asked, looking at Darcy.

"I see nothing wrong with what you propose, Elizabeth. You are the mistress of Pemberley and we shall all follow your commands on dress and dining. As long as I agree with them, of course," he said with a wink.

Lizzy looked diverted. Was it because his answer was agreeable, or because he had actually made a joke?

Lizzy poured tea for Kitty, and when she passed the plate of cakes her way whispered, "Do try the chocolate ones; they are positively sinful!"

After the tea was drunk Lizzy addressed the group. "The weather is lovely, and I greatly desire a walk. Papa, would you and Fitzwilliam accompany Kitty and myself across the grounds? Are you too tired from your journey? I thought we might stroll in the direction of the orchards and enjoy the blooms."

"My dear, I would welcome the exercise after rattling around in the carriage for so long. Let us walk now."

Lizzy sent a maid to fetch shawls, bonnets, and half boots for herself and Kitty. The items were delivered promptly and soon the ladies joined the gentlemen on a gravel pathway. From Pemberley's main entrance, which faced south, the group headed mostly west, although the path meandered in an inviting way.

A light breeze brushed her cheek. Kitty was bursting with curiosity about her new setting.

"I am eager to discover all of Pemberley's beauties, and learn the histories and stories, come to know the trees and rocks and … well, everything," Kitty offered, overcome with delight.

Darcy looked at her with a kind eye.

"I am honored to share stories and facts about Pemberley with those eager to know them. Many seem impressed, but few ask intelligent or thoughtful questions about the place. I hope, in my enthusiasm, I do not provide too much information; whilst we walk, I cannot see if your eyes grow dull."

Lizzy burst into laughter. "We will be sure to tell you, my dear, if you talk to excess—although that is not one of your usual faults." She gave Darcy's arm a squeeze and laughed again.

Darcy turned to Kitty with a subdued smile, but his eyes held a twinkle.

The ground fell away to the south and west as the walkers progressed; farmlands and orchards revealed themselves in the folds of the land as the contours followed the valley of the River Derwent. Behind the house to the north and east, heavy growths of timber covered the rising hills. To the northwest Kitty could make out a large barn and two long, low buildings. Several green pastures opened between stands of trees.

Darcy followed her gaze. "You are looking at my stables. I raise horses here, Kitty, and I am very particular about the lines. My breeding program is founded on my renowned sire. Although I have some lovely mares myself, we also bring in others of fine lineage each season. My trainers are excellent, and I myself ride nearly every day." He looked at Lizzy rather forlornly. "I have been trying to encourage your sister and, although she has a good seat, I believe she lacks the passion to be a truly splendid rider. Do you ride, Kitty?"

"Now you have hit on her true love!" Lizzy exclaimed.

Kitty blushed. She was unaware Lizzy knew of her interest and glanced at her with some surprise. How much did Lizzy know about her unorthodox riding activities?

"Come, Kitty, many times I saw you on horseback as I rambled just as eagerly about the countryside myself—but on my own two feet, as is my preference." Lizzy gave her sister a knowing look.

Kitty raised her eyebrows and bobbed her head towards their father, who was some steps away, gazing off to the south.

Lizzy put a finger to her lips and smiled conspiratorially.

"I do ride, Fitzwilliam, most eagerly," Kitty said in a low voice. "We had only the farm and carriage horses, but one gelding in particular was light and spirited enough to ride about the country on fine—"

"What is this talk of riding about the country?" boomed Mr. Bennet. "Young girls have no business going about on horseback. Do not let her pester you about this, Darcy, or there will be no end to her whining and cajoling."

Kitty gasped.

Lizzy's eyebrows flew up.

Darcy himself lifted a brow at Mr. Bennet's outburst but his calm voice did not betray his feelings.

"There are several very respectable ladies hereabouts who ride regularly, Mr. Bennet. Lady Drake even rides to the hounds. I have always observed that those with the desire usually have a fine seat, and a way with the beasts as well. I welcome a companion who shares my zeal, Kitty."

Mr. Bennet rolled his eyes.

"Papa," Lizzy said, "we must also remember that Kitty is no longer a child. As a young lady nearing nineteen, it is time for her to define her passions and pursuits, and refine her skills. It will do her a service as she moves into society."

"Into society, is it? Balls and parties and such, I suppose. Well, if that is the plan, I wish you luck. But have a care; the Bennet family cannot withstand another ... well, well, just see that she is closely watched. I caution you now, Darcy—my three younger daughters have barely enough sense between them to know the difference between boots and bonnets."

Tears of shame stung Kitty's eyes.

To her surprise, Lizzy stopped and whirled to face their father, her own eyes flashing.

Kitty held her breath.

"Really, Papa, it is highly unfair of you to lump the younger three together like that. Whilst Lydia's behavior did often set propriety at naught, I recall nothing scandalous about Kitty. You have always been a most considerate father to Jane and me. I do wish you would give Kitty a chance to show her quality." She looked as if she could go on, but instead pursed her lips and turned back to Darcy, taking his arm and striding ahead.

Mr. Bennet cleared his throat. "Then you and Darcy may oversee that. Which, I must say, will be greatly to my relief. I believe I am tired of drama and scandal and would much prefer a good book and a finer brandy."

In a steady voice, Darcy said, "Thank you, sir; Elizabeth and I are happy for the opportunity to introduce Kitty into society beyond Longbourn. She will be in good company with my sister Georgiana, and I will offer both of them my guidance and protection. And, as always, my library and my finest brandy are available at your command."

Mr. Bennet chuckled. "Very well, then. Very well. Are we near to the orchard?"

Lizzy sighed. "Yes, Papa. Can you not detect the sweetness on the breeze? Just around this hill are some of the apples."

A sense of relief flooded Kitty's heart. Lizzy had come to her aid! And Fitzwilliam, in his way, had also stood up for her. She could scarce believe it.

Kitty wondered about him. He must be a good man if Lizzy had agreed to marry him. Lizzy was quite particular. The pair did seem amiable and affectionate with each other, by the looks and conversation they exchanged. He was far more personable here than in Hertfordshire. To her surprise, Kitty found she would like to know him better.

Mr. Bennet, having expressed his views, seemed content to listen as Darcy described the various fruit and nut trees and pointed out the new vineyards that could be seen from a promontory as they rounded the bend.

The rest of the walk passed pleasantly, with no more harsh remarks from Mr. Bennet.

CHAPTER FOUR

itty's eyes opened to utter darkness. What was the time? Her stomach prompted her to wonder about breakfast and she threw back her coverlet. After parting the bed curtains, she padded to the window and drew the draperies aside. A pale light drifted in, revealing mists playing about the edges of the house and the nearby hills.

Should she ring the bell? While still deliberating, she heard a soft knock at her door.

Poppy entered, handily balancing a tray with a cup, saucer, and small pitcher.

It had not occurred to Kitty to inform the maid of her morning preferences. She took her tea black; luckily, the milk had not yet been poured into her cup. She smiled and thanked Poppy, then asked about the morning routine in the house.

"Master rises early most days; six o'clock. He takes coffee and then is for the outdoors, often riding his fine horse o'er the fields. Mistress joins him in the breakfast room at eight o'clock. They eat a full rasher—that is, he does. Then Master begins his day of business, and Mistress writes her letters, and talks with Cook. It is seven now, Miss. Ye have time for tea and we can have ye ready before eight. Shall I pour the milk?"

"No. And thank you for not adding the milk. I take my tea black; it is unusual, I know."

Poppy grinned. "I prefer it so meself, Miss. Now, what gown this morning?"

Kitty paused between sips. "Not knowing our plans for today, I think one of the printed muslins will do. The green one?"

"Aye, and some green ribbons for yer hair. 'Twill be lovely."

And so Kitty prepared for her first full day at Pemberley, keeping her plan for a new beginning foremost in her mind.

≈

Lizzy was already seated in the breakfast room when Kitty entered. Darcy sat at the head of the table, reading the newspaper. Mr. Bennet was likewise engrossed. Both men rose slightly as she entered and she dropt a quick curtsey.

"Splendid, Kitty, you are awake early. I will have someone to talk to during breakfast." Lizzy pulled a wry face and nodded at the gentlemen with their heads behind their newspapers. "There is much to be discussed and decided."

As if on cue, Darcy folded his newspaper and set it aside.

"Yes, my dear, there *is* much to be discussed. Kitty, before I begin my business activities today, I would like to give you a tour of the library, if that is agreeable. Mr. Bennet, you are welcome to join us, although I am convinced you know your way around it from your visits last year."

Mr. Bennet peered over his newspaper. "I do indeed, Darcy. And it is large enough that Kitty's presence shall not annoy me too greatly, as long as she keeps quiet and out of my way."

Darcy's jaw tensed and a flicker of anger lit his eyes, but he maintained his countenance.

Kitty's heart crumpled. Her father always spoke about her in this manner. But now, when reflected in the reactions of others, she saw more clearly how improper it was. And how unkind.

Darcy cleared his throat. "However that may be, when we finish breakfast that shall be our first order of business. But I do have an announcement, or rather ..." he looked at Lizzy, "*we* have an announcement. Elizabeth?"

Lizzy's eyes danced with delight and Kitty felt an unexpected rush of excitement.

"As you know, Georgiana arrives tomorrow afternoon. Fitzwilliam and I wish to do something special to honor her return. We also wish to create a special welcome to the neighborhood for you, Kitty." She paused and locked eyes with her sister. "We have decided to give a ball!"

Kitty gasped. Her eyes flew back and forth between Lizzy and Darcy. "A ball! For me?"

Lizzy seized Kitty's hand in excitement. "We thought it a perfect way for you to meet our neighbors, and they you. It won't be a large party. There are half a dozen or so families in the neighborhood with whom we regularly mingle; many have just returned from Town. You and I will write the invitations this morning, Kitty. And there are a few we may deliver in person—"

"Perhaps, Kitty," Darcy broke in, "you can help me persuade your sister that the three of us should deliver those on horseback, eh?" He smiled broadly at Lizzy.

"Oh, Lizzy, can we? It would be a fine way for me to see the countryside, and to get my bearings."

Lizzy gave Darcy a pert smile and patted his hand. "You can be very convincing, my love. I will agree to deliver the three closest on horseback, if we must. Tomorrow morning."

Darcy and Kitty exchanged a smile of victory.

Mr. Bennet sighed loudly, rattled his newspaper, and disappeared behind it again.

Lizzy frowned at him, then continued. "So after the library, Kitty, you and I shall plan the event. It will be held ten days hence, on the nineteenth of May."

"But that is my nineteenth birthday, Lizzy. Oh, how special it will be!"

Darcy just smiled but Lizzy quipped, "So it is. Imagine that! There is much to be done for such an event, Kitty. I have the finest household staff in the kingdom, but it is the duty of the mistress of the house to direct them in their activities. This will be a chance for you to learn about these duties, Kitty, so you are prepared to assume them when the time comes and you are mistress of your own house."

Mr. Bennet snorted behind his newspaper.

Kitty drank her tea and tried to contain her excitement

enough to sample the breakfast offerings. *Mistress of her own house*. That had always seemed so distant, so many years off. But she would be nineteen soon. The time had come.

A vision of the handsome horseman from the Red Lantern formed in her mind and would not leave until Darcy summoned her to the library.

≈

At the conclusion of a most detailed and thorough tour of the Pemberley library, Lizzy appeared and led Kitty into her morning room, a quiet space towards the back of the house. A large window framed a lovely view of the wooded hills behind. The bright blaze in the grate took the chill off the foggy morning. There were shelves for books and other items, a handsome lady's desk, and three sumptuous chairs, each covered in a different floral print.

"This room is very like you, Lizzy. Did you fit it up specially?"

"I did, in part. I had it painted this soft yellow so that even on dreary winter days it feels warm and cheerful. This was Mrs. Darcy's sitting room and I did not wish to make many changes. I do love being in here. I wish I could have known her."

Kitty looked at the art on the walls. The paintings featured woods, fields, and hills—things Lizzy loved—and Kitty wondered if someday these would be joined by artwork made by the hands of little Darcy children.

Lizzy folded her hands on the desk. "First tell me, Kitty, how does Jane do? Her letters are cheerful, but so they always are. Does she look well? I dislike being so far away at such a time."

Kitty was able to put Lizzy's mind at ease. "Jane looks very well. She has a beautiful bloom. She *is* very large. Mama's tales of disastrous birthings wear on her, I think. I wish Mama would not carry on so."

Lizzy rolled her eyes. "That wish is *not* likely to come true, Kitty. But Jane is practical in health matters."

"And Bingley could not be more attentive, Lizzy."

"Good. Then I believe things will go well. Let us hope we have all inherited Mama's strong constitution for childbearing."

The sisters laughed and then directed their thoughts back to the task at hand.

"Have you given a ball before, Lizzy?"

"Well, yes. Actually, the first ball was to introduce *me* to the neighborhood. Mrs. Reynolds and Georgiana handled most of those arrangements, but they did allow me to follow along to learn the Darcy ways of entertaining. The first autumn here we held a harvest ball—a tradition of the Darcys, where all share the success of the harvest. I was in charge of that, but Georgiana was a great help. Then she returned to London and her classes."

"She has been in London for the season but wanted to linger another week. I am not sure why. I know she enjoys her studies, especially her music. She plays the pianoforte beautifully, and is now learning the harp. She is so talented. She puts us Bennets to shame as far as accomplishments. But she is a sweet girl—very much like you."

Kitty blushed at the compliment, and knew not what to say.

Putting her hand on Kitty's arm, Lizzy said, "I caution you now, Kitty. You must become comfortable with compliments. You will receive many, especially now you are in what might be called a 'gentler' society. A nod and a smile, or a curtsey, are all proper responses. Compliments are gifts, and gifts always deserve acknowledgement."

Kitty smiled at her with relief. "Thank you, Lizzy. These are the kinds of things I wish to become easy about."

Lizzy returned her smile. "And so you shall. Now, we must make the guest list and write the invitations. This is rather short notice for a ball, but it is a small affair so I hope we will be forgiven. Then I will introduce you to Cook and we will discuss the refreshments for the occasion. I have also requested a special cake, a birthday cake. Is ginger still your favorite? Nineteen is the perfect age to join society. And the society here is—mostly—very agreeable, you will see. So, let us begin."

CHAPTER FIVE

*W*ith a start, Kitty opened her eyes. This was an important day—the day they would ride out to three special neighbors and personally invite them to the ball. And Georgiana would arrive in the afternoon. Kitty peered at the clock. Nearly eight! Her thoughts ran wild. Of all days to sleep late ... I must instruct Poppy ... oh dear ...

Throwing open the door to her sitting area, she found her maid setting out the tea.

"Poppy, we must make haste. I am late!" Kitty threw off her nightdress and rushed to the basin. "Just a simple gown for breakfast please. Oh, I am to ride out with Lizzy and Darcy at ten o'clock ..." She dried her face and pulled a slip over her head.

"Ye'll be ready in a trice, Miss."

Soon Kitty was sitting at her dressing table, her hair being pinned up.

"Poppy, please wake me every day by seven, unless I am ill or there has been a very late event the night before."

"Aye, Miss. Seven o'clock it shall be."

Her hair was soon done and her shawl fetched. Kitty was coming to realize the value of an attentive lady's maid.

It was a quarter past eight when Kitty entered the breakfast room. "I am so sorry to be late," she said, dropping a quick curt-sey. "Travel fatigue must have caught up with me. I have now instructed Poppy to wake me by seven. I shall certainly be ready to ride out by ten."

Darcy, already standing, merely nodded and downed the last draught of his coffee before kissing Lizzy's hair and striding out to begin his day's business.

"Oh, Lizzy, I am truly sorry. I did so wish to make a good start here."

"Do not concern yourself, Kitty. You have already taken proper action to prevent it happening again. It does take one a few days to recover from a journey, and to become acquainted with the routines of a different household."

"Now tell me, how are you equipped for clothing? Particularly, do you have a riding habit for this morning? I remember the one you wore at Longbourn—when you wore one!—and it was more than a little shabby."

"I fear that is all I have, Lizzy. Papa did not approve of me riding. Indeed, he probably has no idea how much time I spent on horseback. I am sure Fitzwilliam wishes to present a proper image when calling on neighbors. Must I stay back?"

"Stay back? Oh, no. Georgiana is but an inch or two taller than you and about the same size. He sees no reason you cannot borrow her habit for this morning's outing. It will be brought to your room to see if it will suit. Finish your tea. Today, after we return, we will measure you for a new lady's habit and decide on a hat as well."

Kitty's eyes grew wide.

"And here is something else, Kitty," Lizzy said with a playful look. "Fitzwilliam also wishes to gift you with a new ball gown, as *you* will open the ball."

Kitty's head began to spin.

"Oh, Lizzy, I never expected such generosity!"

"At least you—of us five sisters—will have a proper 'coming out' ball. I am very happy for you."

Tears filled Kitty's eyes.

"Fitzwilliam is very surprised, and pleased, Kitty, with your manner and your expressed interests. You have made a good impression on him—and on me, I must admit."

"He was not angry that I was late to breakfast?"

"No. He is very kind. He does not expect perfection of anyone, except possibly himself. And that is something I am trying to break him of." Lizzy laughed merrily, and Kitty was relieved.

"Where is Papa this morning, Lizzy?"

"He has taken his coffee to the library. He will be leaving in a few days and wants to avail himself of the Pemberley library whilst he can." Lizzy's face grew pensive.

Reluctantly, Kitty broke into her reverie.

"Lizzy, am I very wicked to be ... grateful ... that Papa will not be here for the ball? I wish it to be a wonderful affair, but his unkind words hurt me. I don't want anything to spoil it."

"Who can blame you? Even I was dismayed at Papa's remarks, Kitty. And his want of simple courtesy, to own the truth. Proper manners were not revered at Longbourn, as you know. Jane and I spent much time at Uncle and Aunt Gardiner's. We stayed there for months at a time when Mama went through her confinements with each of you younger girls. And we spent other time there as often as we could arrange it. Aunt Gardiner is as courteous as she is kind, and I am grateful for all she taught me. Now I can carry on the favor and teach you. Georgiana has, of course, been raised with very proper manners and will also have much to show you. She is a fine young lady; but I admit, it has been my study to try to loosen her reserve, at least around the family. I am counting on you to help me there."

"Gladly, Lizzy. But please, do tell me if I am straying past the bounds of propriety. I fear my experiences from Longbourn are a poor guide."

Lizzy wrinkled her brow for a moment, then grinned. "I know. We shall use Mama's technique of winking. If I wink with one eye, you are within the bounds of propriety and doing well. If I wink with both eyes, tend to your actions. We shall have a very merry time as you make your way into society, I am sure. And it will be real society, Kitty. Not the artificial kind of the Bingley sisters. I hope you will make some dear and lifelong friends here."

Kitty laughed at the mention of the detestable sisters, and

they both dissolved in giggles when Lizzy made an exaggerated demonstration of winking with both eyes, like Mama.

≈

As she made her way down the hall, Kitty was handed a letter. To her surprise it was from Lydia. Kitty had written to her younger sister about her upcoming journey to Pemberley. Kitty opened the missive that contained a few hasty scrawls.

Dear Kitty,

How lucky you are to visit Pemberley. How long shall you stay? I have not been invited since last year when I spent a fortnight there. My dear Wickham was not included so I had thought Lizzy would provide other gentlemen for my amusement, but she did not. She is, however, very generous with pocket money, and I also got a new silk gown. Be sure to try for everything you want, but you may have to endure some lectures. Since you are not married, perhaps Lizzy will introduce you to some gentlemen. Do ask her if I may visit whilst you are there, otherwise I fear you may find the place as tiresome as I did. Answer soon.

Your dear sister,
Lydia Wickham

Kitty sank onto a nearby bench. This letter was very like Lydia, but somehow she did not find it as amusing as usual. She pondered this a moment, then gasped, remembering the morning's outing. She tucked the letter into her pocket and scurried down the hall.

She did not know why but she was quite sure she did not wish for Lydia's company at Pemberley.

≈

Once in her rooms, Kitty found the riding habit. It was fashioned of summer-weight wool of the finest hand in a deep chestnut with gold braided trim. Kitty modeled it for Lizzy, who had joined her. The habit fit well but for being a little long. The sleeves could be folded under, but Lizzy called for one of the seamstresses to tack up the hem for safe walking. The boots were too narrow, but fortunately Kitty had recently purchased new half boots that would do for the present.

Kitty carefully placed the feathered and veiled silk hat on her head and turned to face her sister.

"I feel like such a fine lady in this hat, Lizzy!"

A smile played about Lizzy's mouth and she placed her hand on Kitty's shoulder.

"Clothes do help us assume the role, Kitty, particularly when we have not been born to it. I can testify to that. I shall go now and get dressed myself. We must be ready to leave for the stables at ten. Fitzwilliam is more punctual than patient. It may be beyond him to forgive tardiness twice in one morning."

≈

Kitty gazed about the stables in awe. They were clean and roomy and bright, more so than any she had seen. The sweet smell of hay filled the air and the horses munched in contentment. The facility was staffed by men of all ages, from young boys to wizened greybeards. She glanced at Fitzwilliam. His pride showed in his face.

"Here, Kitty, may I present the master of my stables, Mr. Riley Connor. Connor, this is Miss Catherine Bennet, Mrs. Darcy's sister. She states she is an equestrienne and today I shall see for the first time how she rides. As she takes great pleasure in the activity, I grant her permission to ride as often as she wishes whilst she is here. I will accompany her myself when I can. Ah, you have selected Cara for her, a fine choice. What do you think, Kitty?"

Darcy gave Cara's tack a thorough check and nodded his approval to Connor.

"She is beautiful, Fitzwilliam. Part Arabian, I would guess, by the fineness of her form and features?"

"Right ye are, Miss," replied Connor, his eyes twinkling. "I see ye know horseflesh. 'Ere, Johnny, lead the mare to the block so the lass can mount and they be acquainted before settin' off."

Another boy brought up a shapely bay mare. "And Mrs. Darcy, here be your Iris."

Darcy checked Iris's tack and assisted Lizzy into the saddle.

A third boy stepped forward and handed Darcy the reins for his thoroughbred, a fine tall bay.

Kitty settled into the sidesaddle and walked the petite grey mare around the yard to learn how Cara moved and to determine the softness of her mouth.

Darcy watched her. "You have fine form and light hands, Kitty. You will do well with her."

Mr. Connor nodded in agreement.

Kitty's heart swelled. She was rarely complimented by anyone, and never by a man. Knowing Fitzwilliam to be a fine horseman, the praise was doubly meaningful.

Darcy turned to his stable master. "Thank you, Connor. We expect to be back by early afternoon or before. We visit the Drakes, the Wyndhams, and the Stapletons."

"We shall await yer return, Sire."

≈

The sky was still hung with grey, but the heaviest fog had lifted. The three riders made good progress across the meadow to the south. Kitty admired how well Lizzy and Fitzwilliam looked together, both mounted on bays and suited in dark green. Kitty reaffirmed her determination to become an asset to Pemberley in both her riding and her manner.

After passing through an open gate they crossed a bridge and took the road that marked the southern boundary of Pemberley. The riders soon turned down a lane lined with large cedar trees and shortly reached a park. There a fine Palladian home nestled in the arms of a great hill behind it, skirted on both sides by groves of cedars. The lawn was well kept and the entrance cheerful with a bright display of early flowers.

"This is Cedars, the seat of Lord and Lady Drake."

The gatekeeper waved them through and as they came near

the house two stable boys appeared to tend their horses. Darcy helped the ladies dismount.

At the door he presented their calling cards and the butler promptly showed them to the drawing room.

"Lord Drake was a friend of my father's," Darcy told Kitty. "He is some years my senior. Cedars has been in their family for three generations. They have two sons."

Lord and Lady Drake soon appeared, smiling their welcome. The usual bows and curtsies accompanied the introductions.

Lord Drake laughed. "Out for your morning ride, eh Darcy? I must say, your companions this morning are far prettier than the hounds that usually accompany you! Welcome, dear ladies."

Lady Drake also smiled a welcome but then her face took on a penetrating expression. "How fortunate you visit now. I imagine your summer at Pemberley will be quite meaningful, will it not Miss Bennet?"

Kitty knew not how to reply and simply nodded.

Lady Drake then turned to the group with a lightened countenance. "Do you care for tea?"

"Thank you, no," Lizzy replied. "We have just finished breakfast at home. I hope we have not inconvenienced you with the early hour of our call?"

Lady Drake shook her head and smiled. "Such close friends are welcome at any hour, Mrs. Darcy."

"You are very good. We come with an invitation. We are giving a ball in honor of my sister's visit, and to celebrate the return of Miss Darcy for the summer. We must be home soon in anticipation of her arrival today."

"A ball! How delightful!" exclaimed Lady Drake, after opening the invitation. "There is nothing like a ball to gather the neighbors, especially when so many are returning now from Town. Benjamin, our younger son, is still there but we look for him to be home later this week. We expected him last week, but he had some reason or other to linger. I do look forward to having him with us again. He is great company for me, and for his father too."

"And does it follow my company is not so, Mother?"

Kitty turned towards the deep voice.

"Oh, Christopher dear, of course not. But you have so many pursuits and interests, and are so often gone here and there with friends, sometimes it seems you are ... well ... here is a lovely new neighbor, visiting at Pemberley. Miss Bennet, may I present our elder son, Mr. Christopher Drake."

A shock of blonde hair flipped over his light blue eyes as he bowed to Kitty in a most elegant fashion.

"*Enchanté*, Miss Bennet. And how do you find our part of the country?"

She dipped a quick curtsey.

"I have been here but two days, and this is our first ride out. I find the landscape very interesting, even dramatic; it is quite different from the flatter fields and softer hills of Hertfordshire."

"You will find things *much* wilder in this part of the country, Miss Bennet, I assure you," he replied, looking her up and down with a hungry eye.

She glanced towards Lizzy in confusion but her sister was turned away, talking with Lady Drake. Darcy was speaking to Lord Drake. Rather than joining the other gentlemen in conversation, Christopher continued to stare at Kitty in an unsettling way that put her on her guard.

Lord Drake then addressed the group. "So, Darcy, when is this ball of yours?"

"Ten days hence, and I apologize for the short notice. It will be a small affair with the usual neighborhood families."

"Very good, very good. We will be pleased to attend, won't we my dear?"

An ethereal smile graced Lady Drake's countenance.

"Certainly. We are especially honored to receive your invitation in person, Mrs. Darcy. How kind. This will be the first event of the summer. What a joy it will be to see Miss Darcy again—such a talented young lady. If I could choose a daughter, Mr. Darcy ... in any event, Miss Bennet, there are several young people you will enjoy meeting. You and Miss Darcy will have a delightful summer together." She stared intently at Kitty again.

"I am sure we shall," Kitty murmured.

There was a fire deep in Lady Drake's darkening eyes that

drew Kitty into their startling depths. She did not feel uneasy, but found it difficult to look away.

Darcy spoke, breaking the spell, and Kitty recovered her equanimity.

"Miss Bennet is an equestrienne, Lady Drake. As you share this interest, perhaps a ladies' ride can be planned—with the proper gentlemen chaperones, of course." Darcy smiled at Kitty.

Lady Drake's eyes returned to a lighter hue.

"That would be a great pleasure. Mrs. Darcy and I—and Miss Bennet—shall discuss the plan as soon as may be."

Kitty nodded. "I should like that very much."

"Well, we must be off," Darcy said.

Lord Drake said, "Bid our welcome to Miss Darcy. We shall see you all very soon."

"I am honored to meet you, and I look forward to seeing you again at the ball," Kitty concluded, dropping a slight curtsey.

Lady Drake smiled at her warmly.

Christopher's stare was still discomfiting and Kitty was relieved to depart.

Lord and Lady Drake walked them to the door and the horses were brought up. When all were mounted they rode back down the cedar-lined lane.

"After the ball, Kitty, I think we must have calling cards made for you. Do you agree, Fitzwilliam?"

"Yes, that will be wise. Georgiana's cards were made once she was out, and the ball will serve as your coming out, Kitty—if that is agreeable?" Darcy turned to look at her.

"Of course. I am honored, and very much obliged—for the cards, and for the ball, and the gown. You are most generous, Fitzwilliam. I had not expected such a welcome."

Darcy nodded, obviously pleased with her response.

"The Drakes have two young men," Kitty observed. "Are there many young ladies in the neighborhood?"

"There are several," Lizzy replied. "And two or three that Georgiana sees quite regularly when she is here. But young ladies marry and move away so it seems there are fewer in the neighborhood. We must get some of our young men married I think. Do we ride to the Wyndham's next?"

"Yes. We will keep to the lanes for our visits this morning, Kitty, but on our return to Pemberley we might take to the hills and woods if you wish?"

"Oh, yes. The land here is so beautiful and wild, so different from what I have known. I am inspired to try my hand at some drawings. I will look up the various trees in some of the books I found in your library last evening, Fitzwilliam."

"I admire your ambitions, Kitty. Very well then. We shall ride on to Greystone."

≈

Kitty judged they had traveled less than a mile when they turned onto a private lane flanked by meadows. Many rocks and boulders lay about the fields and protruded from the ground. Sheep grazed in the field to their right. As they neared the park, she saw a fine grassy swath with several small stands of trees, and more grey boulders. A large rocky crag rose behind the house, which was itself built of stone—the same stone as that in the fields. Kitty wondered how old this house might be.

The last remnants of the morning fog had lifted and the sun shone as they approached. One stable boy came forward to tend their horses as they dismounted.

"This is picturesque, and Greystone is certainly a fitting name for it," Kitty observed to no one in particular.

At the door Darcy lifted the knocker. After a short wait they were ushered down a heavily timbered passage to a drawing room that looked out over a rolling pasture. To Kitty's delight, several horses grazed there. She was admiring their forms and movements when her party was announced to Mr. and Mrs. Wyndham and a young lady. Kitty turned to see a man some years older than Darcy, and two women who were very much alike in person and in manner, though one was clearly older.

Mr. Wyndham had a warm smile and eyed Kitty with curiosity. His rugged face framed knowing grey eyes.

"Welcome, Darcys, it is wonderful to see you. What brings you our way?"

"Welcome to Greystone Hall," added Mrs. Wyndham cooly.

"Good morning to you all," Darcy said. "First, allow me to introduce my sister-in-law, Miss Catherine Bennet. Kitty, Mr. and Mrs. Wyndham and their daughter, Miss Lucy Jamison." The ladies curtsied and smiles were exchanged.

Although not as jovial as Lord Drake, Mr. Wyndham's manner was kind and Kitty immediately felt at ease with him. Mrs. Wyndham's good looks were marred by a haughty countenance that was mirrored in her daughter. Both had light hair and eyes, and a manner of looking down at the company over long elegant noses.

Lizzy spoke. "We are hosting a ball to welcome my sister to the neighborhood for her visit, and to celebrate Miss Darcy home for the summer. We hope you and your family can join us." She handed Mrs. Wyndham an elegant envelope.

Upon opening it Mrs. Wyndham sighed. "This is quite short notice. I will have to consult our social calendar, Mrs. Darcy."

There was an awkward silence amongst the women. Kitty stole a glance at Lizzy, whose face was a serene mask—an expression Kitty had seen when Lizzy dealt with Mr. Bingley's sisters.

Kitty cast about for a friendly subject. "You have some fine horses there in the field," she commented. "Who are the riders in your family?"

"Father and Owen are the horsemen," replied Lucy. "Mama and I prefer a coach or a phaeton, and my elder brother Douglas drives a curricle."

Disappointment washed over Kitty. She had hoped to find a friend of her own age and sex with whom to explore the countryside on horseback.

"Mr. Wyndham and his son are fine horsemen," Darcy proclaimed. "Where are your sons this morning, Wyndham?"

"Douglas is off visiting friends until tomorrow and Owen is, as usual, at the stables. We expect a foal any moment."

"Say, Wyndham, Kitty here loves to ride. What do you say we put together a mounted exploration for the ladies, sometime after the ball? Perhaps the ladies that don't wish to ride would meet us somewhere that day for a picnic?"

"What a wonderful idea, my dear!" Lizzy exclaimed. "I do ride, but a full day on horseback would be far beyond my interest or endurance. A picnic, at a lovely spot with a view, would be just the thing."

The other women made no reply.

"Brilliant, Darcy! Count Owen and myself in. And Douglas, if he is around. We will allow the ladies to arrange the picnic part of the plan, yes?"

"Agreed. And now we must be off. We have one more call before we return to Pemberley and await my sister's arrival from Town. We do hope to see you at the ball."

The group departed and made for their last stop of the day: Swan's Nest, the seat of Squire and Lady Stapleton.

≈

The lane climbed steadily as they rode along. The rolling fields on their left were towered over by the surrounding hills and tall rocky precipices.

Lizzy opened the very subject Kitty was eager to speak of by saying, "Mrs. Wyndham was in high form today."

Darcy frowned but remained silent.

"Fitzwilliam, do you not agree it would be well to put Kitty on her guard concerning the Wyndham ladies?"

He sighed. "Yes, I suppose it would. Wyndham is an honorable man and a very good friend. He and I share an enthusiasm for horse breeding and training, Kitty, as does his younger son. However, I fear Wyndham's eye was blinded by fine form when he chose his new bride, as he forgot to look at temperament. But, as I have not been in his position—and pray I never shall be, that of losing a beloved wife—I cannot fault him too severely. Our friendship goes back many years. Carry on, my love. You and Kitty will deal with the present Wyndham ladies far more than I."

"Present Wyndham ladies? What do you mean?" Kitty asked.

Lizzy explained. "The present Mrs. Wyndham married Mr. Wyndham just four years ago. Lucy is his stepdaughter and so retains her own father's surname of Jamison. His sons are his own, from his first wife, who died several years ago. His young daughter also died then. Fever. So the present Mrs. Wyndham is herself somewhat new to the neighborhood. I don't think she feels very welcome."

Darcy snorted. "That might improve if she did not look down her nose at everyone."

Lizzy arched an eyebrow. "Isn't that rather like the pot calling the kettle black?"

Darcy looked at her with affection and almost chuckled.

"I suppose you are right. Although this 'pot' learnt a valuable lesson from an upstart of a girl—from Hertfordshire, no less."

"We upstarts have our value, don't we Kitty? Especially when we are from Hertfordshire."

They all enjoyed a laugh.

"Just a caution, Kitty. Don't expect much of a welcome from the Wyndham ladies."

Kitty was quiet as she reflected on Lizzy's words.

≈

After winding upwards for half an hour they reached a broad plateau surrounded by towering peaks. When there was a break in the trees, Kitty caught her breath at the view—they were at one of the higher spots in the county. An old timber and stone house stood in a clearing ahead. Nearby a small waterfall spilled into a lake. Its song filled their ears as they approached. A pair of swans glided along the edge.

"How lovely!" Kitty exclaimed, charmed by the setting. "This place feels very ... old. Ancient. Am I right, Fitzwilliam?"

"You are indeed, Kitty. Swan's Nest was here long before Pemberley was established three generations ago. Legend has it this was the lair of a Scotsman during the border wars, though the borders are some way off ..." He furrowed his brow at this anomaly but continued. "Lady Stapleton *is* Scottish. Her half-brother in Scotland has made a name for himself in the field of geology, the study of rocks. The only Stapleton son, Andrew, has taken a strong interest in the same profession. Andrew is also rather bold in the saddle, with a passion for the steeplechase. A nice young man, with several sisters."

"You may find a special friend amongst them Kitty. The

second sister, Matilda, is a particular friend of Georgiana's," Lizzy added.

"I look forward to meeting some young ladies—some *friendly* young ladies."

Darcy and Lizzy exchanged a smile and the group rode into the park. The moment a stable boy came round to tend their horses, Squire Stapleton himself strode out the door and down the steps to greet them.

"Such a fine morning it is, Darcy; made finer by a call from a good friend."

Darcy dismounted and the gentlemen shook hands, and then helped the ladies dismount.

"And Mrs. Darcy, how are you? You look a picture of health and beauty, if I may say so."

"I am honored by your compliment, Squire, and am in the best of health, thank you. May I introduce my sister? Miss Catherine Bennet from Hertfordshire. Kitty, Squire Stapleton."

Kitty curtsied and smiled.

The squire bowed and returned her smile, which carried through to his eyes and crinkled his face. "Delighted to make your acquaintance, Miss Bennet. I hope your visit is long and pleasant, and that our families can spend much time together."

He turned to Darcy again. "And where is Miss Georgiana?"

"She arrives from Town later today," Darcy said. "Which brings me to the point of our visit. In order to welcome Miss Bennet to the neighborhood, and Miss Georgiana home for the summer, we are giving a ball. We have come to personally invite you and your family."

Lady Stapleton was waving to them excitedly from her position at the door.

"Come to the drawing room and let us share this invitation with my wife and daughters. It is sure to be happy news for all."

The squire offered his arm to Kitty. Lizzy took Darcy's arm and they proceeded indoors.

"Ah, Squire, ye be keeping our guests out of doors in the heat," scolded Lady Stapleton, her eyes dancing with merriment.

"Now come to the drawing room, all of ye, come along, and I will call for lemonade. The sun is high and I'm sure ye've worked up a great thirst." An elderly butler appeared and she gave directions for refreshments.

"That would be most welcome," Lizzy replied, exchanging a kiss on the cheek with the tiny, lively woman.

"Lady Stapleton, may I present my sister, Miss Catherine Bennet of Hertfordshire."

"You are most welcome to Swan's Nest, Miss Bennet. I am sure my girls will be glad of another lass in the neighborhood." Lady Stapleton was so friendly that Kitty felt very welcome.

"So Miss Georgiana returns today? Ah, Matilda will be much relieved, although with the many letters that fly back and forth between them, she likely knows more about it than we do," Lady Stapleton said with a wink. "Let me call the girls so we can make the introductions."

Within minutes, lemonade was served and four young ladies entered the room.

"Oh, girls, here ye are. Today we welcome a new young lady to our neighborhood. Miss Catherine Bennet, these are our daughters: Miss Julia Stapleton, Miss Matilda, Miss Emma, and Miss Honora."

Each girl curtsied in turn. The second and the youngest looked very much like their mother, with a diminutive build, lively green eyes, and reddish hair that appeared resistant to taming. Julia and Emma reflected their father's quiet good looks, being taller with brown hair and spirited blue eyes. Julia especially put Kitty in mind of someone, but as she tried to recollect, the squire spoke and it slipped from her mind.

"I regret our son Andrew is not here, Miss Bennet. He has just returned—the day before yesterday it was—from another trip to Scotland. He is thick with my wife's half-brother; they share an interest in geology. They are off this morning to gather specimens for some study or other. I admire their dedication."

Then he turned to his daughters. "The Darcys have come with an invitation. Darcy, do go on."

"Good morning, ladies," Darcy said with a bow. "To welcome Miss Bennet to the neighborhood for her extended stay, and Miss Georgiana home for the summer, we are giving a ball. On the nineteenth of May. We hope you can attend."

Four young faces lit up, skirts rustled, and several girlish voices chattered with pleasure.

"Oh, girls, how exciting!" Lady Stapleton exclaimed. "Ye'll get to know Miss Bennet, and renew your acquaintance with all your friends who have been in Town or at school. And, of course, see our dear Miss Georgiana again."

Turning to Lizzy, she remarked, "I am sure we shall be in a flurry of activity until the ball. It seems all the girls have outgrown last summer's gowns, so new ones must be sewn and adjustments to old ones made. Oh, such fun for us all!"

The eldest daughter, Julia, spoke to Kitty first.

"Tell us, Miss Bennet, when did you arrive?"

Kitty welcomed the offer to converse, and was pleased that the girls seemed interested in making her acquaintance. They moved to a grouping of seats near the window.

"My father and I arrived the day before yesterday; we traveled up from Hertfordshire."

"And what are your interests and pursuits?" asked Matilda, an eager expression on her face.

Kitty smiled. This was new—having others interested in knowing her, without the interference of a dominating sister.

"I dearly love riding horses. I want to learn drawing. And I am fascinated by the landscapes here, with all the rocks and peaks; it is quite different from Hertfordshire."

"Julia likes to ride," offered Emma. Kitty estimated Emma was about twelve; little Honora could not be more than eight years old. Julia seemed near her own age.

"I do enjoy riding," Julia said with a friendly smile. "I would welcome a riding and exploring companion. My brother is an excellent horseman, even if his riding is daring at times."

"Yes, Mr. Darcy did say your brother likes to steeplechase."

"He does. But he is not careless about his horse—he would never risk his horse's wellbeing. Andrew has a wild streak, but he is mostly sensible. And he is a wonderful dancer. He has been described as dashing. You will enjoy meeting him."

"I am sure I shall. Are there many young people in the neighborhood? Are there balls or dances or excursions or exploring parties during the summer?"

Julia and Matilda looked at each other, mentally calculating people and events.

"I believe close to a dozen in our age group, Miss Bennet, from fifteen to eight-and-twenty or so. Everyone is home from school now, and some have completed school, of course; a few are away visiting friends or relatives or on holiday at any particular time. But there are numbers enough to have small dances and card parties, and especially exploring parties and picnics when the weather is fine."

"Oh, this all sounds delightful. And please call me Kitty. I am so excited to be part of such a happy neighborhood."

Julia and Matilda looked at each other again, and then back at Kitty.

Matilda ventured, "It is, for the most part, a happy neighborhood. There are a few rascals about, and a few intrigues and ... well, one or two shall we say 'difficult' young ladies. However, be assured Julia and I shall stand with you and Georgiana as true friends no matter what."

"You honor us. I am eager to see Georgiana later today. It is many months since we were last in each other's company."

Julia spoke again. "Kitty, your sister sets a fine example for all of us. She is so ladylike, but she also has a sense of fun and mischief. We have, with her and Georgiana, experienced a few adventures and intrigues."

"Have you? I shall like to hear about those. Yes, Lizzy has always been lively and I enjoy her company very much. I have missed her greatly since she married and moved away."

Darcy appeared before them and cleared his throat.

"Well, ladies, I am glad to see you getting on in such a fine way, but we must depart if we are to take some of the lesser-known bridle paths on our return to Pemberley."

Kitty rose, as did the Stapleton sisters.

"Then you will all come to the ball?" Kitty asked.

"You may count on us," said Matilda. "We shall all be there and most eager to dance."

The squire chuckled and turned to Kitty.

"Darcy and I have much in common, you see, Miss Bennet.

We both of us are surrounded by fine ladies." He and Darcy shook hands and the party made for the door.

The sun was high when they departed and the cool spring breeze welcome as they rode the downward path. Kitty had much to engage her thoughts—the new families she had met, the homes she had visited, and the landscapes she had seen. Besides being eager to make the better acquaintance of the two elder Stapleton daughters especially, Kitty was excited to see Georgiana again. She hoped they would all become close friends.

≈

"And how d'ye find the neighbors, Sire?" asked Riley Connor when the party dismounted in the Pemberley stable yard.

"All in fine health, Connor; thank you for asking."

"And Miss Bennet—is our Cara a good match for her?"

Darcy turned to Kitty. "What do you say, Kitty?"

"I adore her! She is a fine mare. Very sure-footed on the wooded and rocky paths we traveled on our return. And in the open, she has a smooth trot and a lovely canter. Yes, I like her very much. I hope I can ride her again."

Darcy's face softened. "She will be yours, Kitty, for the duration of your visit, if you wish. She has not had enough use around here, eh Connor?"

"That be so, Sire, that be so. She's a horse likes to be taken out; wants a job and a change of scene, as it were. I am glad ye two got on well, Miss."

"You are very kind. I will take good care of her, and ride her as often as I can."

Darcy offered an arm to each of the ladies, and the three made their way to the house.

Lizzy voiced what they were all feeling after the morning's exertion.

"We have had a lovely morning and much was accomplished; but I, for one, am famished!"

CHAPTER SIX

*T*hat same day a messenger confirmed Georgiana's arrival near teatime. Cook had baked her favorite lemon pound cake. All was in readiness for the young lady's return to her ancestral home.

As promised, Kitty was measured for a riding habit and a ball gown. Fabrics were chosen from those Lizzy had set by. The gown would be sewn in a creamy white silk. Kitty decided to put off selecting trims until she could confer with Georgiana, thinking it would be an enjoyable task for them to share. And Georgiana would know the latest fashions.

To pass the time, Kitty delved into two books from the Pemberley library. Lizzy relaxed nearby with her needlework. Their father was situated in the library with a book and a brandy. Darcy was in his study with his steward, reviewing plans for a new bridge somewhere on the estate.

The books were interesting enough, but visions of all the new faces Kitty had met swam amongst the depictions of rocks and peaks and trees. In surrender, Kitty stacked the books neatly on the side table and walked to the window, taking in the sweeping view of the lake and beyond. This was like a fairy tale —this beautiful place with a kind family, a wonderful horse, interesting new friends, and a dramatic landscape to explore. She was a fortunate creature indeed—but still found it impossible to wait quietly in one place. No one had ever said patience was one of her virtues.

"Lizzy, do you mind if I go for a walk in the shrubbery? I cannot sit still. I am all anticipation at meeting Miss Darcy again. I do hope she likes me."

"Stay close enough to hear the coach, Kitty. It would be considered a slight if you were not on hand to greet her." Then she gave her younger sister a reassuring smile. "I am certain you two will get on splendidly."

It did not take Kitty long to complete a tour of the pathways in the shrubbery. Early flowers were open and the roses were forming buds, but it would be some time before they bloomed. She settled on a stone bench and gazed at the land around her. Fine woods, rocky peaks, and lush meadows ... then her eye strayed to the stables, surely less than a quarter mile off. She would see how Cara was getting on, and could certainly hear the coach from there.

It was a pleasant walk. The steady rhythm of her footfalls was soothing, and gave her a new understanding of why Lizzy had so often walked abroad at Longbourn.

The stable yard was empty when she arrived. Where might Cara be kept? Darcy had not yet given her a tour of the stables. She heard the clink of metal on metal coming from the tall barn and made for the sound.

"Well, g'day, Miss, did not expect ye again. Ye wish to hack out?" asked Mr. Connor. He was supervising a young boy who held a horse as a farrier worked at replacing a shoe.

"Oh, good afternoon Mr. Connor. Sadly, no, there is not time to ride again. Miss Darcy arrives soon. Is it possible for me to see Cara? I just wondered how she was after our ride. I hope that is not too much trouble?"

His face softened. "No, Miss, no trouble 'tall. Johnny, show Miss ... ?" He looked at her with a wrinkled brow.

"Miss Bennet," Johnny supplied.

"Aye, show Miss Bennet where Cara grazes; 'twould be the northwest paddock, with the other mares. There's a good lad."

Kitty followed the "lad"—a boy of about fifteen—along the fence, stepping carefully. She had not donned her walking shoes or riding boots. Her face broke into a smile when she saw Cara basking happily in the sun in the company of two other horses.

"Thank you for escorting me," Kitty said.

The young man touched his hat but stayed at her side. Was this proper? Had he been a child, she would not have questioned it. But he was somewhere between a child and a man, and not much younger than herself. Perhaps it was proper for him to stay and ensure a lady's safety around the horses? Another question to ask Lizzy or Fitzwilliam.

"Hello, girl. Does the sun feel good?" Kitty cooed. At the sound of Kitty's voice, Cara lifted her head.

The mare nickered and swiftly gained her feet, then trotted over to nuzzle Kitty. Flattered by such an affectionate response, Kitty laughed softly and the mare eased over against the fence to be petted. Kitty stroked the fine muzzle and fondled the small ears, then reached for the mane to untangle a few strands.

"She likes you, Miss Bennet. 'Tis said mares are more particular, and she is like. And no steady rider to be devoted to. Your outing, it was good, eh?"

Kitty was unsure if it was proper for her to converse with a stable lad. She did remember Johnny from this morning. They had not been properly introduced but she decided it would be rude to refuse such polite conversation, so she answered him.

"Yes, we had a lovely ride. She is very light in my hands and has smooth gaits. I hope to ride her often whilst I am here." Then she glanced at him and said, in a lowered voice, "At home, I curried my horse after a ride. I don't suppose any of the ladies here do that, or that it is even proper?"

He turned an earnest face to her. "I do not know about ladies, Miss; but Master, he does groom his favorites himself."

"Does he?" Kitty felt a glow of camaraderie for Fitzwilliam. He must have a deeper understanding of horses than many men bothered to cultivate. "I am glad to hear it. I believe horses like such attention from their riders as well as from their grooms."

"Indeed, Miss."

There was a sudden commotion behind them as a young boy ran noisily into the yard.

"The coach is coming! The coach is coming!"

"Oh, dear! I am to be there to greet Miss Darcy!"

"Then ye'd better run, Miss. The other lads and I will catch up. We must wear our jackets to properly receive."

She turned to Cara and gave her a final caress.

"Go!" Johnny commanded with a chuckle, waving her off as he ran the other direction.

Kitty laughed and gathered up her skirt, quickly picking her way back to the stable yard and the path to the house. Then she ran. She could hear the coach herself now and saw it emerge from the trees as she hastened to the front of the great house. The young men who would attend soon caught up with her and touched their hats as they passed.

She arrived, a little breathless, at the front entrance and climbed the stairs. Luckily, the coach had not yet reached the sweep. The lads were lined up and footmen emerged from the house, followed by Darcy and Lizzy.

"There you are! We need not send a search party," Lizzy said.

"Yes, I am here. I am sorry to cause any worry, but I could not resist a quick walk to the stables to see Cara again."

"A worthy cause, Kitty," Darcy remarked, with a hint of a smile about his mouth.

Lizzy looked at her and winked—with just one eye.

Kitty smiled back and they all walked forward to receive Georgiana.

Miss Georgiana Darcy, heiress to a great fortune, stepped out of the coach and took her brother's welcoming hand. Her eyes fondly swept the scene before her and she moved forward to embrace Fitzwilliam, who folded her into his arms.

"Welcome home, dear one," he said. "I hope your journey was not too trying."

"It is worth a great deal of 'trying' to get home to Pemberley, as I'm sure you will agree, brother."

"Most heartily!"

Then she turned to Elizabeth, reaching out with both hands.

"How I have missed you, Lizzy. A great deal has happened that I wish to discuss with you."

Lizzy lifted a brow. "We are so happy you are returned, Georgiana," she said, and then kissed her cheek. "You are truly the soul of Pemberley. You know I will be happy to visit with you for endless hours, but first you must come in and get refreshed and rested. Your favorite lemon pound cake awaits. We also have much to talk about with *you*. And here is my sister, Kitty. As you know, she is making an extended visit."

Kitty curtsied and Georgiana responded in kind, then she reached out to grasp Kitty's hands.

"I hope you and I shall have a wonderful summer full of great adventures. At last I have a companion, a confidante, and a conspirator!"

Kitty blushed. "I will do my best to be all those things, for those are my own wishes as well." The girls looked deeply at each other and then burst into laughter.

Darcy offered Georgiana his arm and they all went indoors.

Mrs. Reynolds, the former housekeeper, stepped forward to embrace Georgiana as she entered the great hall. Tears filled the eyes of both at this sweet reunion after several months apart. Mrs. Reynolds was retired but came to the great house to advise on preparations for holidays and special events. She was on hand to oversee her young mistress's welcome and to advise on the plans for the ball.

Georgiana's maid curtsied and stepped up to manage her mistress' cloak and other accoutrements. As they headed up the stairway, Georgiana called out, "Please send for the tea. I will not be long."

Darcy turned to the butler. "We will take tea in the music room. Please advise Miss Darcy." He offered one arm to Lizzy and one to Kitty. "Oh, and Wilson, do ask Mr. Bennet to join us there. I believe he is in the library."

The butler bowed and moved off.

"I know not how tired she is; but Georgiana does find comfort in playing so I thought the music room best. It is one of her favorite rooms in the house," Darcy explained.

"Are there any special plans for this evening, Mrs. Darcy?" he inquired with a raised brow.

Lizzy raised a brow back at him. "No, Mr. Darcy, there are no plans other than the musical possibilities you propose. We will be served a special dinner at eight o'clock, featuring several of

Georgiana's favorite dishes. The food served at inns is rarely to a lady's taste, I find. I believe that catching up with interests and news, and finding out how Georgiana wishes to fill her summer will keep us all occupied. And then, there is *the announcement*."

Darcy's eyes pivoted to Lizzy's face.

Lizzy gave him a shrewd look. "The ball, my dear. You have not told Georgiana about the ball yet, have you?"

Kitty felt an undercurrent of something unsaid between them, but knew not what it meant.

"The ball. No, indeed I have not. I am sure Georgiana has not tired of dancing, even after attending many balls in town." He frowned. "I cannot fathom why she has not found a suitable young man after being out for a full season."

"Young ladies with such wealth must be especially discerning about choosing a suitor, my dear. It can be difficult to separate out the fortune hunters from the truer hearts. As you might imagine, I had a great deal of trouble winnowing out all the fortune-hunters vying for a place on my dance card," Lizzy remarked with a very straight face.

Darcy swung his head towards her and she burst into ripples of laughter.

He gave a great sigh, then looked at Kitty.

"Your sister is a colossal tease, Kitty. I am forever trying to understand when she is serious and when she is joking."

"It is all part of your training, my dear. You are perfect in every way—well, nearly so. But I admit I am trying to carve out a little more room for joking and humor. Your defenses are so sharp I can only succeed by catching you unawares."

Darcy chuckled.

Kitty felt more and more at ease as she watched the two of them interact. It set her to wondering what kind of man might one day share her own married life. She had always desired to marry for love but had never really thought what that would mean, precisely. She decided to make a study of it amongst the married couples she would encounter this summer. Her own parents were certainly no example. But her elder sisters seemed to have chosen well and she could likely learn much from their amiable partnerships.

"So Miss Darcy has arrived, has she?" Mr. Bennet came up behind the group, and they all entered the music room.

≈

Georgiana was true to her word. In less than thirty minutes she entered the music room looking refreshed, wearing a lovely peach gown that set off her green eyes and dark hair.

Darcy rose and walked to meet his sister just inside the door.

Mr. Bennet managed to find his feet.

Proper greetings were exchanged, and Georgiana joined her brother on the settee as tea was brought in. The refreshments were set upon eagerly and Georgiana laughed with delight as she reached for a third slice of the lemon pound cake.

"This is delicious. I shall ask Cook to make this cake every week!" she exclaimed. "Though I will have to do a great deal of walking, I daresay."

After sharing news from Town and pertinent information about the Darcy household there, Georgiana looked into all their faces.

"You said you had news for me, did you not? Pray, do not keep me in suspense."

Lizzy laughed. "Here it is. We are giving a ball—to celebrate you home, and to welcome Kitty. If it pleases you, it will also serve as Kitty's coming out, so she will open the dance."

Georgiana's eyes widened with pleasure. "How lovely! I should like it above all things. Who is to attend? And will you not like to open the ball, Kitty?"

"I will, very much. But you must advise me on the proper things to do. I have mostly attended just country assemblies in Meryton. I believe this will be much more grand than those, even if we are still in the country."

"Of course, I will be your happy advisor on all such things. Oh, I am excited. Again, who is to come? And when will it take place? Will you dance first with your father?"

"Our papa is to depart before the ball, so no," Lizzy said. "But perhaps ..."

Three pairs of eyes turned on Darcy.

He chuckled. "I will be honored to be Kitty's partner to open the ball," he said. "Then I shall be assured of having at least three of the loveliest dance partners over the course of the evening, yes?"

They all laughed at his joke. All but Mr. Bennet, who had dozed off in his chair.

"As to your other questions, the ball is on the nineteenth, which is also the day Kitty will be nineteen years old," Lizzy said.

"Oh, it gets more and more special!" exclaimed Georgiana, clapping her hands together.

"And," added Kitty, "your brother has been so generous as to offer me a new gown for the occasion. I am so grateful. Lizzy and I chose the fabrics but I thought, Georgiana, to seek your advice on the trimmings as you have seen the latest styles in Town."

"I have. It will be great fun to select the details with you. I am pleased to help."

"We have invited a half dozen of the usual families we keep company with," Darcy said. "Just this morning, we rode out to personally invite the Drakes, the Wyndhams, and the Stapletons. All have accepted. All but the Wyndham ladies ..."

Georgiana looked puzzled.

"It seems," Lizzy explained with an arch of her brow, "that Mrs. Wyndham and her daughter must consult their social calendars before they can confirm with us."

"I see some things remain the same," remarked Georgiana, arching her own brow in response. "And dancing partners? With whom shall we dance?"

"The squire's family will attend, and he has accepted for Mr. Andrew Stapleton. His geologist uncle is also visiting and will join us. I am sure Wyndham's sons will attend. And Lord Drake's older son, Mr. Christopher, confirmed."

Georgiana pursed her lips at the mention of the latter's name but said nothing.

"I do not know about the younger son, Benjamin; they said he was still in Town. Did they say Mr. Benjamin would return in time, Elizabeth?"

"I cannot remember."

"I believe he has just returned," Georgiana said. A blush quickly crept up her neck to her cheeks.

Darcy looked at her with a quizzical expression.

"Oh, he passed my coach today on the road. He said he was going home," she offered, reaching quickly for her tea. She glanced at Kitty with wide eyes as she sipped.

Kitty knew not what the look signified, but felt sure she was being asked for help. To divert the conversation, she blurted out, "The Wyndhams have some fine horses."

The trick worked and the conversation turned away from the Drakes' younger son.

Georgiana gave Kitty a weak smile.

A fine dinner was served, and the evening passed with great pleasure for all. Even Mr. Bennet managed to stay awake and applaud Miss Darcy when she played several pieces on the pianoforte and a new melody she had learnt on the harp.

Georgiana and Kitty had no chance for private conversation during the evening, so Kitty was obliged to set aside her curiosity until morning.

CHAPTER SEVEN

*S*avory aromas beckoned Kitty to the breakfast room. Beverages, cakes, bacon, toast, and eggs were at the ready. Lizzy sat at Darcy's right hand with toast and a cup of tea. She looked up and smiled as Kitty entered. Darcy rose briefly, followed by Mr. Bennet's attempt at the same.

Kitty helped herself to a plate of food and a cup of chocolate and sat down next to Lizzy, thinking her sister appeared a bit wan. Perhaps she had not slept well?

Georgiana soon appeared, radiant in yellow sprigged muslin, looking like summer itself. She greeted everyone merrily, heaped food upon her plate, and then sat across from Kitty.

"Well, brother, what plans are in store for today?" she asked between bites of bacon and toast.

"I am meeting with my steward this morning. In the afternoon, Mr. Bennet and I will tour some of the farms. Remember, he departs soon for Longbourn. I believe *Mrs.* Darcy is the one to ask about plans that may include you ladies," he said with an affectionate smile at his sibling.

"Excuse me," Kitty said, "but sometime—not today of course —might I also have a tour of the farms, with background and history and topographic information? And a tour of the stables too, Fitzwilliam, if that is agreeable?"

"Yes, I too should like that, brother. Whilst I live here, I must assist Lizzy in the work our mother did with the vicar. The needs of our tenants are important," Georgiana stated emphatically. "My schooling is complete now so I need not return to Town at any certain time, although I do wish to continue with my music masters. But we can discuss that after the ball for I am sure I can think of nothing else at present, and there are many preparations to be made, am I right?"

Georgiana looked pointedly at Kitty, much as she had the previous night.

Kitty held her eye but wondered, again, what this meant and guessed it was related to the ball.

Lizzy nodded quietly as she nibbled at her toast, deferring to Darcy on the topics discussed.

Darcy pushed back his chair and held up his hands.

"I have not yet left the breakfast table and the day has granted me two surprises—both welcome if I may say so. I shall be pleased to give a tour of the farms and stables and," he glanced at Kitty, "shall provide topographic information and historical background as I can. However, today I must especially value my male companion, as it appears my future is full of the company of ladies."

"You have my sympathies on that," came Mr. Bennet's assertion. "Excuse me. I head to the library."

"I shall be off, too," remarked Darcy, kissing Lizzy on the forehead and then whispering something into her ear.

"Wilson," he addressed the butler, "please have coffee and muffins brought to my study in one hour; I will be meeting with Mr. Sawyer."

The butler nodded and followed Darcy out of the room.

Kitty looked at Lizzy with some concern.

"Lizzy, are you unwell? You look pale."

Lizzy leaned back but avoided Kitty's eye.

"Oh, I had a restless night. A short walk and tending to this morning's business will set me to rights. I may retire earlier this evening. Would anyone object to dinner being served at six instead of eight?"

"Of course not," replied Georgiana. "Shall we accompany you on your morning walk?"

"No, I think a turn about the garden in solitude will best revive me. Besides, I have scheduled a meeting for the two of you with the head seamstress, so start thinking about your gowns for the ball. Georgiana, you know where the trims are kept. You and Kitty may experiment to see which details you want to add, and if any others need be ordered from Town; and if you have other gowns that need changes or repairs, be sure to let the women know. I have also ordered a new riding habit be made for Kitty. Now off with you!"

Georgiana took Kitty's arm and the young ladies made for the wardrobe room at the far end of the third floor.

"I hope you don't mind I wore your riding habit yesterday, Georgiana? Mine had grown quite shabby as Papa would not approve me getting a new one. He did not approve me riding at all, and I suppose thought that would prevent me."

"Not approve of you riding? Some parents are so old-fashioned! Many ladies ride hereabouts. Lady Drake even rides to the hounds. I can't say I am *that* daring," she remarked, eyeing Kitty, "but perhaps you are?"

Kitty laughed. "You have found me out. I like Lady Drake very much, although she was unusual in a way that I cannot describe. But yes, I would love to ride on the hunt."

"No, I don't mind at all—you borrowing my habit. I keep one here for each season, and one in town for each season, so I am always prepared," Georgiana replied. "What color will yours be?"

"I requested a rich blue," Kitty replied.

"That will look lovely on you. Oh, here we are." Georgiana knocked and then opened the door.

Several large wooden wardrobes lined the walls; some had their doors thrown open, showing gowns and lengths of cloth hanging on rods; others had shelves holding folded cloth and assorted boxes. The room was bright and overlooked the kitchen garden. Two older women and two younger girls were busy with projects. A very large table was spread with a fine blue cloth.

"Hello, Mrs. Jenson. You look well. May I inquire after the health of your family?"

Mrs. Jenson curtsied. "Thank ye, Miss Darcy. We are all of us very well. What a lovely bloom ye have. So nice to have ye back again at Pemberley."

"Thank you. It is always good to be here. Have you met Mrs. Darcy's sister?"

Mrs. Jenson curtsied. "Aye, when I measured her for the habit and a new ball gown. Y'two are near alike in size, but for a few inches of height. Here y'see the cloth for Miss Bennet's habit. It will make up very nicely I am sure. Mistress ordered two styles of hats from Town an' we shall trim your choice, Miss Bennet, as y'desire. Over 'ere's the cloth for the ball gown so's ye young ladies may choose the trims."

Ideas for gowns, hats, and embellishments engrossed Kitty and Georgiana for some time until Wilson appeared at the door to summon them.

"Miss Darcy, Miss Bennet, callers await you in the drawing room: Squire Stapleton and two other gentlemen. Mrs. Darcy will join you there."

"This has been most delightful, Mrs. Jenson. Here are our choices. I cannot wait to see what you create with your fine eye and magic touch. Good day," said Georgiana and they walked towards the drawing room.

Kitty said, "I met Squire Stapleton yesterday when we delivered their invitation. But his son and Mr. Robertson were out gathering some kind of samples for their study. I wonder if it is they who are calling?"

"The squire is a great favorite of mine. And you probably met my best friend, Matilda?"

Kitty nodded.

"Mr. Andrew is very handsome and a great rider, as his sisters probably told you. And a *very* eligible young man. Quite dashing. He will inherit Swan's Nest. We must call on his sisters before the ball. There is much to discuss."

After some hesitation, she lifted her brow and said, "You met the Drakes yesterday?"

Kitty told her they had, but Benjamin was from home.

At the mention of his name, Georgiana blushed again and, taking Kitty's arm, stopped her.

"Kitty, I must confess a very great secret to you, as you will no doubt discover it soon enough: I carry very strong feelings for Mr. Benjamin Drake, and have for some time, as he does for me. I believe we are in love! I find it so difficult to conceal my feelings, as you may have noticed last night. Ooh, I blush so easily! But Mr. Benjamin is only a second son, and I am expected to marry higher. Can I ask your help to draw attention away from me when such a topic comes up? As you did so well last night?"

Kitty did not hesitate. "Of course. And I should like to hear more about Mr. Benjamin. I met his brother. He cuts a dash, but there was something about him that made me uneasy. I cannot say exactly what, but I did not like the way he looked me over."

"Oh dear, I am so sorry, Kitty. He is like that with all the young ladies. The manners of his parents are not like that. Nor are Mr. Benjamin's. I don't understand it. But I will do you a turn and intervene when I can. Mr. Christopher is quite determined to be my suitor, but I am just as determined I will not have him." She grasped Kitty's hands in despair. "I am in the briars. I hardly know what to do. Nor does Mr. Benjamin. We discussed it at length last week in London."

"Ah, now I ... be assured I will help you however I can," Kitty replied, squeezing her arm.

"Good. Then we have a pact. We must include Julia and Matilda as well. Now, let us meet our guests."

≈

"Would you gentlemen care for tea?" they heard Lizzy offer as they entered the drawing room.

Georgiana stepped forward to make the introductions.

"Kitty, may I present the squire's son, Mr. Andrew Stapleton, and his uncle Mr. Robertson of Edinburgh. Gentlemen, Mrs. Darcy's sister, Miss Catherine Bennet of Hertfordshire."

Kitty's mouth gaped and her own surprise was mirrored in Andrew's widened eyes. Here was the dashing young horseman from the Red Lantern! And more handsome than she remembered. She was now struck by his resemblance to Julia.

The others stared at the silent exchange.

"Pardon us, but Miss Bennet and I are not complete

strangers. I saw her on my way home a few days ago, in the public room at the Red Lantern. A young man could hardly forget the sight of such a lovely lady."

He smiled again at Kitty, who felt her cheeks fill with color. Bows and a curtsey were made.

Georgiana gave Kitty a speaking look and Lizzy arched her brow. More information would certainly be wanted once the gentlemen departed.

"No tea, Mrs. Darcy, I thank you," the squire replied, looking at his son with a half smile. "We are on an exploration of sorts this morning—"

A servant appeared at the door.

"Mr. Benjamin Drake is here, Mrs. Darcy. Shall I show him in?"

"Of course, thank you," Lizzy replied.

"Nothing like having a few young ladies in residence to bring the young men flocking," the squire said with a chuckle. "Perhaps Darcy *won't* be surrounded only by ladies!"

Benjamin Drake appeared at the door.

"Good morning, Mrs. Darcy. Ah, I see I am not the first caller. Good morning Squire, Mr. Robertson, Mr. Andrew."

"How nice to see you," said Lizzy. "Kitty, this is Mr. Benjamin Drake. Benjamin, my sister, Miss Catherine Bennet."

"I am delighted, Miss Bennet. My parents spoke of meeting you yesterday. Welcome to our neighborhood." He bowed and smiled. He was blonde like his brother, but his coloring was more like his mother's, with warm brown eyes and a golden cast to his hair. Not quite as dashing as Christopher, but she thought his countenance more pleasing, with a smile that carried throughout his face.

She smiled at him in return as she dropt a curtsey, and then glanced at Georgiana, whose face was flushed with pleasure. Did the others not notice this?

Benjamin immediately moved to escort Georgiana to a seat and took the chair next to her.

"As I was saying," the squire remarked, "we are on an exploration. I wished to ask Darcy if we might visit the red rock area to the north and perhaps take some samples."

"He is in conference with Mr. Sawyer, Squire, but he may welcome an interruption. This afternoon he and my father tour some of the farms so they will be out that way as well. Please excuse me and I will inquire if he can speak with you." Lizzy left the room, her gown rustling gracefully.

"Father, might Mr. Benjamin and I escort the ladies on a short walk whilst you make arrangements with Mr. Darcy?"

Georgiana and Benjamin looked at each other hopefully.

Was Andrew aware of their mutual attraction? Likely; his sister was Georgiana's best friend.

The squire looked around at the young people.

"Why not? But you are not released from exploring that site with your uncle, Andrew, however more desirable the female company may be."

Andrew smiled. "No, of course not, Father. I am as eager as he to find samples. But I am also eager to make the better acquaintance of Miss Bennet." He nodded at Kitty.

"Very well. Thirty minutes."

"Thirty minutes it shall be."

Soon the four were taking in the fresh air and wholesome views of the countryside, although the focus of each pair was not on the distant hills and valleys. Georgiana and Benjamin strolled along, their eyes locked, enchanted expressions on their faces.

Andrew gave Kitty a knowing look. "They are well matched, if I may be so bold. Surely you see it too, if Miss Darcy has not yet confided in you. I secure them time together when I can."

"What a good friend you are," Kitty replied. "I admire such loyalty. It is not so commonly found, is it?"

"Perhaps not at our age. I believe loyalty grows as integrity is tested. Sometimes it is difficult to determine who is worth our loyalty, do you not agree?"

Kitty's lips eased into a gentle smile. "It is also not common to find such philosophical conversation amongst those our age. I must admit I find it interesting." To herself, she added that she also found Andrew interesting. Most interesting.

Remembering what his sister had related, she said, "I witnessed your excellent horsemanship at the Red Lantern. Your sister says you enjoy the steeplechase and are a bold but considerate rider."

Andrew's eyes lit up. "Ah, well, my sister is very kind. Yes, I do love to ride, and some may call my riding bold. Of course, the steeplechase itself is a rather daring—some might say reckless—activity. However, I am careful to ensure the safety of my mount. And I never gamble on the results, as some do."

He looked down for a moment as they walked along, then turned to her again.

"Julia has related that you are also a horsewoman. May I offer my services as one of the escorts for the ladies' ride I understand is being planned?"

By now Georgiana and Benjamin had lagged far behind, which concerned Kitty.

"We should make our way back; it would be best if we all appear as one party when we approach the house. Although I am not in charge of the ladies' ride, we will need more than a few good horsemen to accompany us. Speak with Lady Drake?"

"Good, excellent. She is one of the finest riders I have seen—woman or man—and is very pleasant and kind. Her younger son takes after her in manner as much as he does in looks. And Lord Drake is a jovial fellow. I will discuss it with her."

It was not lost on Kitty that he most specifically did not comment on the Drakes' elder son.

"Will you be able to join us at the ball?" she asked, hopeful he did not have to return to Scotland any time soon.

"Indeed I will. May I be so bold as to claim the first dance, Miss Bennet?"

Regret rushed in. "I am honored, Mr. Stapleton, but I shall dance the first two with Mr. Darcy. The ball is partly in my honor—it is my official coming out—so we will open the ball."

"Then the next? May I claim the next?" he asked with an appealing crooked grin.

A thrill bubbled within her. "You may, Mr. Stapleton, and I am delighted to accept."

≈

Darcy and Lizzy, as well as the squire and Mr. Robertson, awaited the young people. The horses were being brought up.

"Thank you, ladies, for your pleasant company," said Andrew, with Benjamin joining him in a bow.

Smiles shone in both the young ladies' faces, and they curtsied while Lizzy and Darcy looked on.

"Please, sir," Georgiana called out to Andrew, "do tell your sisters we shall come to them tomorrow if the weather allows."

"I am sure they shall be pleased at that," he replied.

The visitors mounted their horses. Andrew's mount was by far the most spirited—a perfect match for his spirited blue eyes. With a last wave, three gentlemen headed down the lane and took a quick turn to the north towards the exploring area. Benjamin made for the south and home.

Georgiana could not hide the love and joy in her eyes as she watched her beloved ride off. Had Lizzy noticed? At present, Lizzy still seemed preoccupied with her own thoughts.

Kitty watched her sister walk quietly beside Darcy as they all returned to the house.

CHAPTER EIGHT

*L*eaden skies and a mizzling rain filled Kitty's view as she peered out the window. Poor Father, such a dreary day to travel.

The breakfast room was deserted. The walnut clock had not struck eight and to Kitty's surprise neither Darcy nor her father were at the table. She helped herself to the day's offerings and was pouring more tea when Lizzy entered the room, followed in the next moment by Georgiana.

"What a dreary morning," Georgiana mumbled.

"I hope Father will be able to stay ahead of the worst of this storm," Lizzy remarked, looking out the window.

"That is just what I was thinking," Kitty said. "By the way, where is he?"

"I just spoke to him on the stairs. He would take his coffee in the library. We can say goodbye in the great hall. I do wish he would stay longer. He does not seem his usual self."

They ladies ate in silence, listening to the tapping of the rain on the window.

Kitty was soon summoned for a fitting of her riding habit. Only minor adjustments were needed. She also tried on the hats and chose the more serviceable one. Then she made for the library to find a book on the species of trees she might see thereabouts. As she rounded the corner she stopped—the door was ajar. Pondering whether to knock first or just enter, she over-heard voices within and inched closer.

"Papa, are you sure you must leave so soon? Your spirits seem much depressed on this visit and your temper shorter than I ever remember. I know you enjoy the restful atmosphere here."

"I do, Lizzy, but I must leave as planned. No rest for the wicked. There are seasonal duties to oversee at Longbourn, though these no longer excite me now it is certain the estate will not stay in the family. As ridiculous as Mr. Collins is, I had hoped he might choose Mary or Kitty for his bride. Ah well, nothing to kick up a dust about."

Kitty drew a careful breath. She had never considered that her father might have affection for the estate that was being entailed away. His life's work would go to Mr. Collins! No wonder he was often in a pucker. Perhaps his barbed humor was meant to disguise his true feelings. She had never thought about his feelings before and flushed with shame.

"Papa, although things may seem final now, we never know what Providence has in store. Please, do not give in to such melancholy. Many things could change in the years ahead."

"You think that Lizzy, if it comforts you. I do miss your lively company at home, my dear. I fear I have not been very kind or patient with Mary or Kitty. I am angry with myself for not taking better care of you all. My only comforts now are books and brandy."

"Well, perhaps when your seasonal duties are done you can return here for a longer visit. Do what you can for Mary, Papa. And if I may be so bold as to advise my parent, do not seek so much solace in brandy. I shall do what I can for Kitty. She has a great deal of promise, in my eyes, and is interested in many things. I fear she was much overshadowed by Lydia. I am sorry Jane and I did not include her more; she is, after all, only a few years younger than I."

"Now, now, do not blame yourself, Lizzy. I think Lydia blinded us all to many things. Such was her large and demanding personality. She delighted in keeping everything astir. It was all I could do to retreat to my library and— looking back—I believe that was not the best policy. I have been a chucklehead. I am sure Kitty will have a wonderful summer here with you and Darcy. I am sorry I had so little sympathy for her plight."

"Then let us make an agreement, Papa. After a few months we shall reunite—either here or at Longbourn—and celebrate the advances made by all."

"Lizzy, my dear, you do lift my spirits. I promise to be off in good humor. Do not worry; I have no intention of putting a period to my life. I am sure I shall still find great solace in my library—and I will try to find less in brandy. Your advice is worth heeding, my dear, as the past has proved. Do write to me often."

"Of course I will."

Kitty quietly backed up and turned away, tears welling in her eyes. She dabbed at them with her handkerchief, then walked to the library door and knocked firmly. "Hello? May I enter?"

Lizzy appeared at the door with Mr. Bennet behind her.

"Ah, Kitty, we were just leaving to gather Papa's cloak and traveling gear. Come, walk with us."

Mr. Bennet turned an unaccustomed kindly eye on Kitty and offered her his arm.

She looked into his face and to her surprise found some welcome there. Taking his arm, she could only think to say, "I hope you can stay ahead of the rain, Papa."

He patted her arm.

≈

The coach bearing Mr. Bennet disappeared into the fog, and the butler was closing the door when Kitty caught sight of a rider racing towards Pemberley. He saluted the carriage as it passed, his cloak flying behind him.

"Who would be out in this miserable weather?" Lizzy asked.

Georgiana gasped.

"Why, I believe it is Benjamin Drake!" replied Darcy. "I hope nothing is wrong ... come in, man, come in. Is everyone well? How can I be of service to you?"

Benjamin glanced slyly at Georgiana as he shook off his cloak and the footman made to hang up his wet garments.

"Thank you, but all is well at Cedars. I had thought to come visit the Misses Darcy and Bennet to break up the long dreary day. The rain is not likely to become worse at present."

Darcy frowned. "That dark sky tells me a more menacing tale but ... well ... you are always welcome here, Mr. Benjamin."

"Thank you, sir."

Lizzy's dimple was bursting forth and she could not contain the sparkle in her eyes as it spilled into laughter.

"Perhaps some tea will warm us all. Wilson, can you have it brought to the music room please?"

"Of course," he replied and turned away.

"I am sorry to be brief but I must meet with my steward. May I leave the ladies in your capable hands, Mr. Benjamin?"

"Indeed, sir, I am honored."

Darcy strode off and the others entered the music room.

"Mr. Benjamin," said Lizzy, "will you be with us for the ball next week? Your parents said you were delayed in Town last week. I hope your business there was concluded."

He glanced at Georgiana and colored. "My business ... oh, yes it is concluded for now, although not finalized." He eyed Georgiana again. "I certainly shall attend the ball. May I take this opportunity to request the first two dances with you, Miss Darcy? Or do you open the ball?"

Georgiana blushed and smiled as he eagerly engaged her eyes.

"I will be delighted to reserve the first two for you, Mr. Benjamin. It is Miss Bennet who will open the ball and will dance the first two with my brother."

"Thank you, Miss Darcy," he replied, momentarily spellbound. Then he shook his head, as if remembering himself and said, "Miss Bennet, may I request the next set with you?"

"I am honored, but I have promised the next already."

"Ah, then surely the third may still be open? Unless you would be too tired?" He looked at Kitty hopefully.

"I have been accustomed to dancing every dance at our local assemblies; I am sure I shall not be too tired. I thank you, and happily accept."

Lizzy gave her sister a perceptive look. "Your card is filling up quickly, Kitty. It seems you will not be unknown in our neighborhood for long."

After pleasant exchanges about news from the area and from Town, Benjamin cast his gaze towards the window. A heavy mist had coated the panes.

"I am relieved Mother did not attempt to travel this morning. I should return now so she does not worry. She is most eager to see you again, Miss Bennet. And is already talking of the ladies' ride."

Kitty and Georgiana exchanged a look and Kitty said, "I look forward to exploring the area round about, and also becoming better acquainted with Lady Drake."

He offered his arm to Georgiana as they all rose.

"I shall see Mr. Benjamin out, Lizzy," Georgiana offered, assuming an air of nonchalance. But the meaningful look the couple exchanged as she took his arm was far more revealing than her words.

Kitty looked at Lizzy, whose eyes danced in amusement as she watched them leave.

Lizzy then said, "I sincerely hope true love finds a way. And I am not above giving true love a little assistance where needed." She gave Kitty a wink and the sisters shared a hearty laugh.

≈

"Do not be surprised if we receive a call from the Wyndhams yet today," Darcy announced after his meeting with his steward. "It seems our stable lads have exchanged news with Greystone's —the Wyndham sons are eager to meet our guest of honor." He gave Kitty a nod.

"There are two brothers, are there not?"

"Yes," Lizzy replied. "Two brothers, very different indeed. I shall say no more; you must form your own opinion."

"So many new acquaintances," Kitty said. "It is just what I hoped for, Lizzy. Thank you again for inviting me to visit here— both of you."

"Well, Georgiana," Darcy said, "our home has become much more lively these past two years, has it not?"

"Very much, brother. I must say I heartily approve, and I too am grateful."

"Kitty, Mrs. Jenson needs a fitting of your gown, so make haste. Our callers may arrive at any moment."

"I shall go with her," Georgiana offered. She took Kitty's arm and, as the young ladies headed out the door, whispered a little too loudly, "I hope it is only the gentlemen calling today."

Kitty glanced back in time to see Darcy shaking his head and smiling.

≈

It wasn't long until the young ladies were summoned to greet the Wyndhams. It was as Georgiana had hoped—only the gentlemen were present.

The girls entered the drawing room, and the gentlemen rose.

Mr. Wyndham bowed and said, "Miss Bennet, may I introduce my sons—Mr. Douglas Wyndham and Mr. Owen Wyndham. This is Mrs. Darcy's sister, Miss Catherine Bennet, from Hertfordshire."

Kitty curtsied gracefully and smiled at the two young men before her.

"*Enchanté*, Miss Bennet," said Douglas, the elder, sweeping an elaborate bow.

The younger said, "Good morning, Miss Bennet," with a simple bow.

The two were quite different in appearance. The elder had light brown hair and eyes and a stocky build; the younger looked much like his father with dark curls, a lean build, and the same steady grey eyes.

"I am pleased to meet you both," Kitty said.

Douglas turned to Lizzy. "Our mother and sister send their regrets this morning, Mrs. Darcy. Too muddy by half. And they are quite occupied with gowns and other endeavors."

"Oh, I am pleased they will join us, as I assume you both will?" Lizzy inquired.

"Certainly, Mrs. Darcy, we very much anticipate the first social event of the summer," replied Douglas smoothly. His eyes roamed from Georgiana to Kitty and back again. "And may I have the pleasure of requesting the first dance with you, Miss Darcy?" he beamed, appearing sure of a positive reply.

Georgiana looked down. "I am sorry, the first is promised, Mr. Douglas."

"Then the next, perhaps?"

"Certainly. I would be delighted," Georgiana replied with a small smile.

"And Miss ... Bennet, is it? May I have your promise for a dance as well?"

"I would be honored, although—"

Lizzy came to her rescue. "My sister, as guest of honor, will open the ball with Mr. Darcy. Then, I believe, she has already promised the second and third sets. Can you be satisfied with a fourth position, Mr. Douglas?"

His eyes widened in surprise but he recovered quickly. "It will be my honor."

"Thank you," Kitty replied.

"Now, Owen, we've not heard from you," his father said.

"As you know, Father, I am no great dancer. But I would be honored to stand up with both Miss Darcy and Miss Bennet, if they will have me. Perhaps the dance after my brother?"

"Yes, of course, Mr. Owen," replied Georgiana.

"I shall be delighted, Mr. Owen," Kitty said with a kind smile, curious about his manner. She saw a slight flush in his face. Very different indeed. He displayed none of the swagger or dash of the other young men she had met thus far in Derbyshire.

"Well, there we have it; the evening is all set," Mr. Wyndham pronounced with a smile.

"These cakes are delicious, Mrs. Darcy. You certainly do have a marvelous cook."

"Thank you. I shall pass on your compliments," Lizzy said.

As the conversation continued, the elder brother dominated all exchanges, often looking at Miss Darcy for a reaction.

The younger brother said little but had an unspoken awareness to him and keenly watched all that occurred. Kitty could easily believe he had a way with horses. She felt him aware of her as well, though he did not meet her eye.

Not, that is, until they were departing. The ladies accompanied the gentlemen through the front door as their horses were brought up. Kitty observed how Mr. Wyndham and his youngest son related to their mounts, whilst the elder brother focused his efforts on amusing Miss Darcy.

"Good day to you then," called Mr. Wyndham.

Then the younger brother looked directly at Kitty and saluted. Their eyes locked with a powerful resonance that set her tingling. Only the resurgence of the rain broke the spell and she scurried into the house.

CHAPTER NINE

The next morning Kitty and Georgiana set out for Swan's Nest.

"I have never ridden in a phaeton, Georgiana. What an excellent driver you are. Would you teach me to drive?"

Georgiana laughed merrily. "Of course. It will be simple for such an accomplished horsewoman."

The ball was a few days hence, and Georgiana had not yet seen Matilda due to wet weather and muddy roads. There was much to say before dancing could begin. Messages had been sent back and forth and it was arranged the young ladies would picnic in a clearing at the farther end of the pond—secrecy was vital for their frank discussion.

The squire's stable boy stepped up to hold the ponies. Whilst the footman handed the young ladies out, the squire himself approached. His face was weathered and his dark hair now more than half white but there was an uncanny resemblance of his countenance in his son Andrew and in two of his daughters. The spirited blue eyes were the strongest feature. He offered an arm to each young lady.

As they approached the house, Lady Stapleton emerged, twittering with joy.

"The girls will be down at any moment. Julia ran back to fetch her sketchpad and a few supplies," she explained. "My dear

Georgiana, my heart has ached to see you, lass." She grasped her by the shoulders and beamed at her. "You look as lovely as ever." Then she paused, eyeing her carefully. "Do I detect a special bloom? Are you in love?"

Georgiana blushed furiously. "Fie, Lady Stapleton, do not tease me so!"

"There is no fooling this woman," the squire said with a gleam in his eye. "Her heart can penetrate the thickest fog. Perhaps all will be revealed at the ball?"

Kitty scrambled for a way to rescue Georgiana.

"Lady Stapleton, you mentioned a sketchpad. I did not know Julia was an artist."

The strategy was successful and diverted the intrusive if loving questions away from a trembling Georgiana.

"Ah yes, Julia has quite the talent ..."

Just then Matilda and Julia emerged from the house.

"Georgiana!" exclaimed Matilda, and the two friends embraced, rocking and giggling. At the moment, they looked more like schoolgirls than proper young ladies who had already come out.

"I have so much to acquaint you with!" cried Georgiana.

"And I, you," answered Matilda.

"Good morning, Miss Bennet, it is wonderful to see you again," Julia said, her serenity a great contrast to Matilda's wild enthusiasm. It put Kitty in mind of her sister Jane's composed countenance and quiet wisdom.

"Thank you, and do call me Kitty. I am delighted to see you again before the ball. I have so many questions. And I was just told that you draw. I am interested in learning myself. We had no drawing masters anywhere near Longbourn. I would very much like to see your work."

Julia's face brightened at Kitty's interest.

"Let us be off!" cried Matilda, and the young ladies promptly turned down the path towards Cobe's Clearing.

The path meandered alongside the pond through stony meadows and stands of trees, detouring around larger outcroppings of rock. Georgiana and Matilda chattered noisily the entire way, whilst Kitty and Julia both were immersed in their surroundings, listening to the trill of the waterfall and the calls of the birds. Soon the young ladies emerged from a stand of cedars into a sunlit alcove sheltered by rocks. The footman and maid had spread a blanket on a grassy sward and set out their food-stuffs and cushions in the gently dappled light. Julia dismissed them with thanks.

Georgiana eyed each young lady and then began.

"Friends, I have confided in Kitty about Benjamin and she has agreed, like you, to help me avoid the determined pursuits of Mr. Christopher and ..." here she cast Julia an uncomfortable glance ... "and Mr. Douglas, though I am sure his feelings are not at all engaged. I believe it is his stepmother who ..."

Julia's brow knit and she looked down at her lap.

"And please, draw attention away from me even when Benjamin is spoken of. If only I didn't blush so easily! I fear everyone will know. Even this morning ... Kitty, thank you for the rescue when Squire and Lady Stapleton were roasting me—"

"Georgiana," said Kitty with a laugh, "I think I should warn you: I believe your secret was revealed the morning Mr. Benjamin rode through the rain simply to call on you, and to secure the first dance. I know my sister well, and I believe she is aware of your mutual attraction. She even said she is not above giving true love a little help."

"Oh dear," Georgiana fretted. "Well ... yes ... how kind of her. But, oh, do you think she will tell my brother?"

"I do not know. I doubt she keeps secrets from him; but she may delay for a time if she thinks it best."

Julia had gathered her equanimity. "The ball is just days away. Perhaps we should see what transpires at that happy event?"

"Yes, yes!" cried Matilda. "We can still keep our pact to protect each other from unwanted suitors. However, I believe we will all be obliged to dance with each young man more than once that evening."

"I am sure you are right," Georgiana replied, consternation written on her face.

"Can you not put on a cold demeanor with those two? It is not as if you might injure them—they only pursue your fortune," said Matilda as she bit into a sandwich.

"Some might think that Benjamin, as a second son, is also pursuing my fortune," Georgiana mused.

"Do you think there is any truth in that?" Julia asked.

Georgiana stared at the pond in contemplation while the others chewed thoughtfully.

"No, I do not believe so. He has been such a kind friend for so many years. He has given up his own comfort for mine many times. What ... truly, do any of you think I may be blind to less honorable intentions he may have?"

Julia spoke with reasoned calm. "Again, let us be careful observers of what transpires at the ball. I suggest we meet afterwards, like this—away from home and listening ears—where we may speak frankly."

After a pause, Kitty thought it a good time to ask a question that could be crucial to her acceptance in the neighborhood.

"May I ask if either of you have an interest in any young man hereabouts? I do not wish to tread on your toes unknowingly, or allow myself to become attracted to a man that one of you has hopes for," Kitty said. "Nor do I wish to intrude on any young lady's interest."

"My hopes are for a *new* young man—someone's cousin or friend—to be brought to the ball and sweep me away!" answered Matilda with a giggle. "I was once besotted with Mr. Owen Wyndham. I still think him madly attractive in looks, but his abiding fascination with horses—an interest I do not share—led me to be bored with him. Anyway, he showed no real interest in me. I fancy no one in particular at present, nor do I know of any other involvements. Julia?"

Her sister sighed. "No, I do not."

Julia would speak of no one so Kitty felt free to ask, "What about Andrew himself? Does he court a lady here ... or elsewhere?" Those spirited blue eyes had also spent much time in Scotland.

"Andrew is kind and attentive but I am not aware of any abiding interest in a young lady hereabouts. He has certainly never spoken to me about anyone in particular," Julia replied, giving Kitty an amused, sidelong glance. "Again, let us see what the ball brings."

Georgiana clapped her hands together. "Very well then, let us strike hands to protect each other's best interest and to meet as soon as possible after the ball."

Laughing, they joined hands in the bargain.

"To a romantic and revealing ball!" cried Matilda.

CHAPTER TEN

$\mathcal{A}$t last the evening of the ball arrived and Pemberley was abuzz with excitement. Candles blazed and flowers filled the entry and the ballroom.

Poppy was nearly finished adding small blooms to Kitty's hair when a knock at the door announced Lizzy. Adorned in cream silk with green trimmings, Lizzy looked like a young queen. A mix of emeralds and diamonds sparkled in her hair, at her ears, and at the neckline of her gown.

Kitty drew a quick breath.

"Lizzy, you look so beautiful. You are glowing, and your color has returned. I had thought the last few days that you might be feeling unwell?"

"Thank you for your compliments, Kitty. I feel very well tonight, and all preparations seem to be in order. Your hair looks lovely! Poppy, you have done a splendid job."

Poppy beamed as she tucked in the last few blossoms.

"I have something for you, Kitty. Actually, it was Fitzwilliam's idea. As I looked through the Darcy jewels for tonight, I came across these pieces of amethyst. Fitzwilliam remembers his grandmother wearing them long ago. I had them reset with diamonds when we married, but they do not flatter a woman of my coloring, nor of Georgiana's. They will look lovely with your lighter hair and eyes. Should you like to wear them this evening?"

"Truly, Lizzy? Oh, yes! They are divine. I have only my simple cross; I love it but it is quite lost in the splendor of this gown. These jewels are just the thing."

Lizzy came around behind and fastened the necklace whilst Kitty attached the ear bobs. When she faced the looking glass, her whole face shone.

"Perfect!" the three women pronounced at once, and then laughed together.

"We shall meet Georgiana in the music room in a quarter of an hour, Kitty. The guests will begin arriving in half an hour and we must be on hand to greet them."

Kitty rose and gave her sister an affectionate hug.

"Oh, Lizzy, this is all so ... so unbelievably kind. It is beyond my dreams. I have made new friends—both gentlemen and ladies—and am learning new information and skills, and I just ... well ... I feel like I am living a fairytale. I don't know how to express my thanks."

"Your radiant glow is enough," Lizzy replied. With an affectionate squeeze of Kitty's shoulder, Lizzy quit the room.

≈

Kitty and Lizzy had been only minutes in the music room when Georgiana floated in. Her elegant lavender gown trimmed in green set off her features. She looked every inch an heiress.

"Well, isn't my brother a fortunate man tonight!" Georgiana's eyes twinkled. "He shall dance with three of the loveliest ladies at the ball."

"We must take care not to let it swell his head too much, girls," Lizzy replied, her dimple peeping out. "But perhaps it will help him better appreciate a ball—tonight, *and* in the future. Balls are not a favorite of his, as you may know."

≈

Lord and Lady Drake were the first to arrive with their sons. Benjamin's eyes immediately sought Georgiana's and widened at her beauty. Her delight in seeing him was equally obvious. Kitty wished the two of them could just dance away together in a cloud of happiness.

And what did she wish for herself tonight? Before she could formulate an answer, a deep voice interrupted her thoughts.

"*Enchanté*, Miss Bennet. You truly outshine your jewels." Christopher Drake swept a stylized bow before her whilst his eyes roamed up and down her figure.

His manner had not improved. She masked her discomfort with a general reply, then moved her focus to the next arrivals.

How would she ever keep all the names and faces straight? Her head swam as she greeted the various families and guests. Georgiana was at her side, eloquently making the introductions.

The Stapletons were the next familiar group to arrive, and Kitty found comfort in their talkative friendliness. She wished she could break free of the line and join Julia and Matilda, but knew that must wait until later.

"Thank you so much for inviting us," said Andrew with an elegant bow, looking directly at Kitty. "You are radiant tonight, Miss Bennet. You shall have more offers of partners than you can possibly accommodate. Pray, do not forget me for the second set." He smiled at her warmly.

"I look forward to it, Mr. Stapleton. I shall not forget."

Two more family groups new to Kitty followed, after which she found herself suddenly lost in the grey sea of Owen Wyndham's eyes; he was the first of his family in the line.

"Miss Bennet, I am honored," he said, with a simple bow.

She caught her breath and could not speak for a moment.

"I ... we are ... so happy you could all join us," she said, recovering her composure. Why did his gaze discomfit her so? It held not the leer of Mr. Christopher's nor the friendly warmth of Mr. Andrew's. It was not offensive or unkind, yet she was quite undone and all aflutter.

Lucy's stilted voice broke into her thoughts.

"Miss Bennet, I look forward to this ball, and to us becoming better acquainted." She made an elegant curtsey.

"Hello Miss Jamison, we are honored to have you with us."

The musicians began tuning their instruments and the guests gathered around the edges of the ballroom.

Kitty looked towards her sister. "Oh, Lizzy, what do I do?"

Darcy offered his arm and a smile. "Come, Miss Bennet. Let us open the ball."

He was so elegant. Kitty felt flustered and out of her depth.

He smiled at her warmly. "Do not be uneasy. You look charming, Kitty. Just follow my lead."

The instruments joined in a swell as Darcy led Kitty to the center of the floor.

"Do we dance alone?" she asked in a faint voice.

Before he could answer, the music began. Her chest locked. No breath moved in or out. The room was a swirl of light and sound. Somehow she stayed on her feet. At the edge of the room she saw Lizzy, a beacon in the blur of faces and colors. Was that a wink?

Kitty took a deep breath and allowed happiness to flow through her, like moonlight moving through a vase of water.

Soon other couples joined the formation. A sigh of relief escaped her on seeing Georgiana and Benjamin at her left.

Darcy's dancing was elegant, and many curious eyes followed Kitty on the floor.

"You are an excellent dancer, Kitty. I could not be more proud of you."

Kitty thought she would burst from happiness at such a kind remark. Her radiance was genuine and drew admiring looks. How blessed was this happy chance!

When Darcy led her from the floor to where Lizzy stood, Andrew Stapleton immediately appeared and escorted her back to the set. His attention was focused on her alone and his face was animated. She felt the envious glances from other young ladies as Andrew led her through the movements and complimented her grace.

Kitty's next set was promised to Benjamin, who proved a cheerful partner with much to say. He was lively and kind, and Kitty thought what a perfect match he was for Georgiana.

As the music ended, Douglas Wyndham joined her on the floor, saying not a word. Her attempts to engage him in conversation garnered only the shortest of replies so she gave up the effort and immersed herself in the music.

After four sets, Kitty was parched and desirous of a rest when Christopher Drake arrived with a pretentious toss of his blonde hair. Placing her hand on his arm he said, "At last I may claim my turn with this divine nymph."

"Sir, I have promised—"

He laughed and led her to the set as the music began.

"I have had my eye on you all evening, Miss Bennet. Tell me, Hertfordshire must hold many fine balls for you to be so elegant a dancer."

She had not moved much in society but Kitty had experience enough to recognize hollow flattery and strove to turn the conversation to more general topics.

"We did not have many *fine* balls, sir, but enjoyed regular assemblies in Meryton, the village near my home. With four sisters, I had much practice at dancing."

To her surprise, his gaze wandered over the room as they danced. Was he hunting for his next partner? Looking to see who was watching him? Whichever it was, she was not impressed. It was soon apparent he was watching Georgiana, now partnered with Andrew. Kitty was relieved when the dance ended and looked to see if Georgiana might need assistance to divert Christopher's advances.

She could not see her friend.

The next dance was announced and Owen Wyndham approached, eyeing her carefully.

"You look positively parched, Miss Bennet. May I bring you some refreshment before we dance?"

His awareness surprised her and she was happy for the chance to catch her breath.

"Thank you. You are most kind. My first partners have kept me very busy indeed."

He nodded thoughtfully and offered his arm, which she took gratefully. After procuring lemonade and a biscuit, he led her near to the doors that opened onto the terrace and a big starry sky.

"The candlelight is nice enough," he mused, "but for myself, Miss Bennet, I prefer the stars." He looked up at the sky and then into her eyes.

Again a small thrill chased through her body but she could not fathom why.

"I have watched you on the floor tonight. I compliment you on your fine dancing. You are graceful. Athletic even. I imagine you sit a horse well."

She stared at him in surprise. Did he know of her love for riding? Or was this a lucky guess? Curious, she was emboldened to speak.

"Thank you, Mr. Owen, but pray, how did you know I ride?"

His face flushed and he looked at her with a sheepish grin.

"Lady Drake informed me. She came to see our new foal and mentioned how pleased she was to have another equestrienne in the neighborhood. She spoke of an upcoming ladies' ride, and I readily offered my services as a guide."

Kitty was amused and flattered.

"You honor me, sir. Riding is my passion, more so than for many women; although Lady Drake may be one to share my level of enthusiasm. I am excited for the ladies' ride. I like exploring nearly as much as riding."

She looked out the door, momentarily self-conscious about sharing so much so quickly, but then recovered herself.

"I am pleased you will escort us. Mr. Darcy speaks highly of your expertise with horses. I value his judgment above all."

Her partner flushed. The present dance was nearly finished.

"May I still have the honor of dancing with you, Miss Bennet, if you are now refreshed?"

"I should like that very much."

Owen Wyndham proved a fine dancer in spite of his protests. Kitty was sure he must be a superior rider as well. He led the dance with power and grace, and kept his eyes on her but not in a way that made her uncomfortable. They did not have much conversation, but somehow that was not awkward. It felt right; almost as if the conversation took place on a wordless level, as it might with a horse. The partnership of the dance itself was not unlike riding horseback, and Kitty delighted in the sensations and was sorry when the set concluded.

During the next interval the four young ladies gathered together—with Benjamin, who would not leave Georgiana's side.

In order for the ladies to speak in confidence, Georgiana made him a request.

"Might you fetch me a cup of punch, sir? I find I am still thirsty." He bowed and was off.

Then she turned to Kitty. "You opened the ball with such elegance; you were a fine match with my brother."

"Thank you. It was a little frightening at first, but he is a strong partner. The whole world seemed to light up like magic. I am so grateful ... such a memorable night ... I cannot express ..." she paused, breathless.

"I saw you dance with Mr. Benjamin at least twice, am I correct?" Julia asked.

Georgiana blushed. "Three times. Do you think anyone is counting? I hope to partner him at least once more, preferably for the final dance; that always seems the most romantic."

Julia laughed. "I doubt anyone here is counting. This is not Almack's, after all. We are a friendly neighborhood and, if one is to dance every dance, one must partner with some gentlemen more than twice. Besides, several of the older gentlemen who *were* dancing have now retired to the card room. No, I think you are safe, Georgiana; at least from counting. I must say though, your regard for each other is quite apparent to anyone looking for such a clue."

"Even to those not looking!" chimed Matilda. "Do not ever choose to be an actress, Georgiana; your performance would be poor indeed."

Their laugh was interrupted by a sultry voice.

"What delicious gossip amuses you, ladies?"

They turned to see Miss Lucy Jamison, radiant in an elegant gown the color of the morning sky.

"And does this evening's ball please you, Miss Jamison?"

"Oh, most assuredly. Mr. Drake claimed the first two with me, of course. He cuts quite the dash. He and my brother are very good friends, you know. My brother Douglas, that is. They are both so worldly—always riding off to Town or to some watering hole or other. As elder sons, they have social reputations to keep and business connections to make."

Lucy smoothed her skirt before continuing. "I did notice,

Miss Darcy, that Mr. Benjamin favors your company. Of course, younger sons must look to their fortunes as well. I believe he is studying the law, am I correct?" She lifted an inquisitive brow.

Kitty watched in fascination as a neutral mask slipped over Georgiana's features, similar to what Kitty had seen on Lizzy in certain social situations.

"I cannot tell you. He and I are not on intimate terms; we are merely neighbors of long standing. I imagine the law, or the church, or the Navy would be suitable options for him, as for any second son. Pray, what are the professional plans of Mr. Owen?"

Lucy tittered. "Poor Owen. I believe he would prefer to be a stable boy above anything. However, the church is the likely profession for him. He lacks the swagger of an officer, in my opinion. And what of your brother, Miss Stapleton? As eldest, he will of course inherit."

Matilda scowled. "Our brother is dedicated to science, and schools himself in Edinburgh with our uncle, a well-known geologist. Of course Andrew will inherit. But he will accomplish much in his field as well."

"Very true. The men have so many choices. Do you have a young man in the neighborhood that you prefer, Miss Matilda?"

Matilda's scowl deepened.

"Oh, I fear I am too impertinent. I do beg your pardon."

Christopher's deep voice intruded on the awkward silence left in the wake of Lucy's comment.

"Such a bevy of beauties. How shall I choose only one? The next dance begins soon. May I solicit your hand, Miss Darcy? And, if Miss Stapleton is not already engaged, might she save the next for me?"

Both ladies curtsied their consent.

Lucy huffed. Angry blotches burst out on her pale complexion. She glared at Christopher, turned up her nose and flounced off, leaving confused expressions on the faces of the other young ladies and a knowing smirk on Christopher's.

"Some ladies enjoy a game and a challenge," he quipped. He made a little bow in the direction of Lucy's departure. "Checkmate, Miss Lucy." Inexplicably, he failed to notice the wide-eyed shock expressed on the countenances of the ladies surrounding him; or perhaps he noticed but did not care.

With the ball being in her honor, Kitty enjoyed the attention of dancing with nearly every gentleman present, including Squire Stapleton, Mr. Wyndham, and Lord Drake. Georgiana introduced her to four other young men and three other young ladies from the neighborhood.

Kitty looked about her. Did the neighborhood families wonder about her fortune? Did they think Darcy might dower her? Lizzy's elegance as hostess certainly disguised the reality of the Bennet sisters' more modest upbringing. No one would guess a refined lady like Lizzy would have filial relations of questionable reputation and poor judgment.

Kitty danced two more sets with Andrew Stapleton. She had never known a gentleman more charming. The officers from Meryton whom she had found so fascinating in the past—mostly at Lydia's suggestion—now seemed common and dull. Except for Captain Carter. She had held serious feelings for him, but he had planted his affection in the more lucrative garden of Miss Amelia Grange when she inherited twelve thousand pounds. They married some months ago.

Whilst Kitty's heart had been broken for weeks, her head understood that many officers—often being younger sons—also desired or needed to marry well. The rules of society created nearly as dismal a reality for them as for young ladies without fortune or connection, like herself and her sisters.

But Jane and Lizzy had risen, and so would she—it seemed not so impossible in company such as this.

Jane and Lizzy had been lucky enough to fall in love with men of good fortune. Lydia had followed baser urges and, after much trouble and disgrace, married a gaming feckless fool who did not care a rush for her or their life together. No one knew what sister Mary envisioned; she took no interest in meeting gentlemen or in any kind of social life and spent her time alone or with her dear friend Ada.

Kitty was determined to find a handsome man who could support her grandly, or at least comfortably. If he were an excel-

lent horseman, a good dancer, and had other interesting pursuits
—such as science—all the better.

Kitty wandered towards the terrace doors, which had been
flung wide on the warm May evening. She looked for her friends
again and spied Georgiana down the way, on the arm of Christopher Drake. Her face was contorted. It appeared he was
attempting to lead her onto the terrace—alone.

"Miss Bennet," a calm voice addressed her, "may I ..."

She turned to find Owen at her shoulder.

On seeing her look of alarm, he followed her gaze to the
distressing scene.

"Come," he said in a firm voice, "we must prevent this." He
offered his arm, and they moved hastily in Georgiana's direction.

What would he do? Would he fight? Kitty did not know his
temperament but she soon saw his strategy.

Owen positioned himself so as to directly block the only
access to the terrace, with Kitty at his side. Many small groups
had gathered in the cooler air near the opening. He and Kitty
filled the only empty spot.

"I say, Drake, the evening is quite warm. Perhaps we might
fetch refreshments for the ladies? Do come with me." Owen's
words had a friendly air but his voice strongly suggested Christopher's compliance.

Georgiana's eyes grew large.

Christopher seemed momentarily discomfited. A flush
brightened his face and he looked left and right. There was no
polite way to refuse such a proffered task.

"Thank you," Kitty said, boldly giving Owen's arm a slight
squeeze. "The evening *is* warm, it is not? A drink would be most
refreshing."

"Yes, indeed," Georgiana managed weakly.

"Capital. We shall return shortly."

Owen patted Kitty's hand and gave her a speaking look. His
countenance remained serious, but there was a slight twinkle in
his eyes. The young men walked away and Kitty moved to Georgiana's side and took her arm.

With a trembling breath, Georgiana said, "He has been
trailing me all evening. I don't understand it. I know he does not

care for me. As the eldest son, he will inherit Cedars. There is no reason for him to pursue my fortune."

"Perhaps no amount of fortune is enough for some men?" Kitty mused aloud. "Now, let us get you somewhere less precarious before they return. There, Mr. Darcy and Lizzy are not far off. I wonder that Lizzy has not danced much this evening; perhaps her hostess duties prevent her? Christopher won't try his tricks in Mr. Darcy's presence." The girls walked off arm in arm.

"But what about Mr. Owen?" Georgiana asked.

"Oh, he is in on the scheme," Kitty confided. "When he saw my alarm for you, he took action at once. He has very good instincts," she remarked, half to herself, remembering he had also noticed her need for rest and refreshment before dancing.

Darcy and Lizzy received them happily.

"Well, girls, are you finding enough pleasant partners tonight?" Lizzy asked, her eyes shining. "The dancers appear younger and younger as the night wears on, do you not agree, my dear?" she voiced, turning to Fitzwilliam.

"They are a determined lot, I give them that," he said, looking well pleased with the event. "It is wonderful to be part of such a pleasant neighborhood." He patted Lizzy's hand as it rested on his arm.

"I agree. Oh, I see two younger men headed our way. I am sure they will compete for my hand. Whom do you recommend I chuse?" Lizzy arched her brow at Fitzwilliam.

"Neither, my love, for you will be dancing with me." And with that, he led Lizzy over near to the musicians and spoke to the maestro. A more sedate dance number was announced.

The young men arrived with punch, as promised. Owen first looked at Kitty with narrowed eyes, then handed a cup of punch to Georgiana.

"Miss Darcy, may I request the next dance? Once you have partaken of your punch, of course." He slyly eyed Kitty again.

Christopher was flustered. With a slight bow, he handed Kitty a cup and managed to recover his swagger.

"And Miss Bennet, may I have the honor?"

Kitty curtsied her agreement, silently annoyed at her part in the scheme. She decided she had no patience with any young men who used the word "*enchanté*." But never mind that; she would help Georgiana.

As she reached near Owen to place her empty cup on a table, he whispered, "Will you save the last for me, Miss Bennet?"

His eyes found hers and read her answer.

Owen whisked Georgiana away and Kitty resigned herself to her partner.

"How long is your stay at Pemberley, Miss Bennet?" Christopher asked as the set formed.

"I am not certain. But I shall likely stay most of the summer." The stately dance allowed several pauses for conversation. "And what of your summer plans? What pursuits interest the young men hereabouts?"

"Oh, I travel about a great deal. I have many business connections I must attend to. And many friends in all the fashionable places," he replied with a toss of his hair.

"Do you leave a beau behind in Hertfordshire, Miss Bennet?" he asked, a wicked gleam in his eye.

"Mr. Christopher, that is most impertinent, and I shall not answer you. Please choose another subject." Her eyes flashed. She felt no compunction to protect his feelings. She was sure he had no special *tendré* for her.

Proving her right, he laughed heartily and had nothing more to say for the rest of the set.

Soon the final dance of the evening was announced. Kitty looked about for her friends. Georgiana's face was wreathed in smiles as her most desired partner led her to the floor. Matilda was matched with the cousin of a neighbor. Julia stood up with Douglas, but her countenance was expressionless. Lucy looked adoringly at Christopher as they joined the set. Nearby, Fitzwilliam and Lizzy were together again.

"Ahem. Miss Bennet. May I have the honor?" It was not the voice she expected. Andrew Stapleton's face held an amiable smile. "Pray, has someone else spoken for this dance?" he asked when she glanced about her.

"Oh ... yes ... well, I am so sorry. I did promise this dance, but

I do not see the gentleman anywhere about. I am not sure what to do?" An awkward blush crept up her neck.

"Do not concern yourself, Miss Bennet. May I wait here until he arrives? I cannot imagine anything more important than a dance with you."

It sounded like something Christopher might say, but Andrew spoke with such sincerity that Kitty believed it was not false flattery. He did not seem the kind of man to offer such.

"Thank you. Yes, I should like your company. I would feel awkward standing here alone." Most of the dancers had taken their places but still there was no sign of Owen.

After a few minutes, Andrew said, "Well, Miss Bennet, shall we? If the gentleman does arrive and endeavors to cut in, I shall graciously but unhappily allow it."

"You are very kind, Mr. Andrew."

Andrew's understanding raised him even more in Kitty's estimation, and she turned all her attention towards him and his many charms.

All but a tiny thread that wondered why Owen Wyndham had not kept his engagement.

CHAPTER ELEVEN

$\mathcal{T}$he sun was riding high by the time Kitty stirred the next day. At first she was alarmed, but then remembered Lizzy had said they would all sleep late. The ball had lasted until nearly dawn. The tea at Kitty's bedside could not even be called tepid, but her appetite was strong. It must be nearly noon. She rose and rang the bell.

Poppy appeared in minutes with fresh tea, followed by a footman with warm water for her basin. As Kitty's eyes swept the dressing room, she noted her gown and other items had been neatly taken care of. It felt almost sinful to have someone wait on her in such a way. Had Lizzy become comfortable with this?

While Poppy was in the dressing room chusing the needed items of clothing, Kitty's thoughts wandered back to the night before and the last dance with Andrew. The compliment he had given her then still warmed her heart: *"You are the loveliest lady here, Miss Bennet. Your grace, the kindness in your eyes, your pleasant countenance, and your curiosity to learn are unduplicated in this crowd. I look forward to knowing you better."*

Her thoughts then drifted to Owen. What had become of him? He was attractive, to be sure, but she reminded herself that she sought a partner she could depend upon to provide her with a life of elegance and ease. Perhaps Owen's temperament was too mercurial? And could she be content with a clergyman?

When Poppy returned with a gown, Kitty prepared herself for the day, which would likely be quiet and restful.

The breakfast room was deserted, but she found Lizzy taking tea in the drawing room. There was a basket of muffins and some toast and fruit and cold meat. Kitty took a muffin and sat next to Lizzy on the settee.

"Well, Kitty, did the ball live up to your expectations?"

"Oh, Lizzy, it exceeded all my fondest hopes! I find a private ball far preferable to the public assemblies, at least the ones in Meryton. I still danced nearly every dance, but on my own account and not because I was with Lydia. And of course, being in the Darcy household and opening the ball, well, I'm sure that all helped. But yes, I had a wonderful time. What about you, Lizzy? You did not dance as much as you had used to."

"My duties as hostess come first, Kitty. No, I did not dance more than a few dances. But I enjoyed myself very much, and had many conversations with neighbors I had not seen of late. Some of us move in different circles when we are in Town. And of course, Darcy is not fond of balls in general. I do believe he enjoyed this one—and his role launching you into society."

Both drank their tea and sampled more of the fare on offer.

"I know I was 'out' before I came here, Lizzy, but this feels different. Then, I was always in Lydia's company. Now people are coming to know me for myself instead of as Lydia's sister. It has been difficult to shake her shadow, and I thank you again for inviting me here. I believe I now have a chance to ... well, people here will know me on my own merits."

"Yes, I believe you shall have a far better chance here. I did notice that, other than the first dance to open the ball, your own first and last were with Mr. Andrew." She gave Kitty a mischievous look as she sipped her tea.

"He is dashing, Lizzy. His profession in science is interesting. He is a fine dancer, very handsome, and kind. And an excellent horseman. Nothing is wanting. I enjoy his company very much." She paused and looked at Lizzy. "Curiously, I have also found Mr. Owen Wyndham appealing, in a much different way."

Lizzy arched a brow.

"But I wonder if he—"

Just then Darcy entered the room. "Ladies. What a fine day it is. I have had a refreshing ride. Kitty, I assumed you would prefer to sleep this morning or I would have requested your company."

"You are right, Fitzwilliam, I did sleep. It was a late but wonderful evening. But please do include me on some other morning soon. I am very eager to explore the vastness of the Pemberley grounds. And beyond."

"I shall. This morning I rode to Greystone to inquire about Mrs. Wyndham. She was resting, and Wyndham stated it was nothing serious; she is recovering nicely. Oh, Kitty, I did see Mr. Andrew Stapleton this morning and I have a message for you. He mentioned his sisters will likely come to call today; I assume to discuss all the details of the ball. I also assume you and Georgiana shall be agreeable to that?"

"Of course! Well, perhaps I should not speak for—"

"You know me well enough to speak for me on that topic, Kitty," said Georgiana from the doorway. "Planning before the ball and discussing it afterwards are equal parts of the delight of the event, and I would not miss any of it for the world."

≈

Kitty and Georgiana were donning their bonnets in preparation for a walk when they heard the crunch of gravel beneath hooves and wheels. Georgiana threw open the front door.

"Julia and Matilda!"

Lizzy had already been summoned to greet the coach and was descending the stairs to meet the visitors.

"How lovely to see you Miss Stapleton, Miss Matilda. I am sure you are as eager to discuss the events of last night as Kitty and Georgiana are."

"You are going for a walk?" Julia asked.

"Yes, can we talk whilst we walk this morning?"

"Let's do. It is a fine day," Matilda said, echoing Darcy's earlier comment.

"Lizzy, do you wish to join us?" Kitty asked.

"Thank you, no. You have enough minds here for a variety of

opinions. When you return, I shall have tea ready; and then you may apprise me of any tidbits you wish me to know. Will that do?"

"Thank you, Mrs. Darcy. You are very kind," Julia replied.

Nimble hands tied bonnet ribbons and the young ladies were off.

≈

"We slept very late today. Did you also?" Matilda asked.

"Yes, and I the latest," said Georgiana. "Let us walk towards the orchards. The blooms and scent will not be with us long."

Kitty waited for someone to begin.

Julia took the lead. "Georgiana, as you were the main focus of our pact, do tell us how the evening went for you. I saw you dance several times with Mr. Benjamin, and you looked very happy then," she said. "But when he was not lucky enough to be your partner ..."

The group stopped momentarily and Georgiana looked at each of them in turn.

"Perhaps you are not aware of the immense help our pact provided me during the course of the evening. I was grateful to each of you for intervening on my behalf. We might even say coming to my rescue. I would not change my life for the world, but I shall be much more at peace once I am married—hopefully to the man I love—and no longer hunted for my fortune."

"Georgiana, do enlighten us. I know about my help to you, but I was not witness to other incidents," Kitty said.

"Yours was the first, Kitty. Let us walk on as I explain." They headed down the walkway, now two by two as the pathway narrowed on approaching the orchard.

"While I danced with many young men, and most were kind and gentlemanlike, two were impertinent and persistent. I am trying to decide if I should inform my brother. But that will bring into his view the subject of me finding a match, and I am not sure I am ready to discuss my true feelings for Benjamin yet. Hear me out, and then, please, tell me your opinions."

"The two young men of whom I speak—I shall not call them

gentlemen!—were most determined; not only in monopolizing me for dancing, but in trying to lead me outdoors or away from the crowd to be alone with them. Mr. Douglas Wyndham and Mr. Christopher Drake are the two. No one knows the value of reputation better than I, or could take more precautions against giving the slightest appearance of scandal. I believe that is what these two are about—making it appear I have been compromised to force a marriage—though I cannot apprehend why. Both are eldest sons. Both will inherit. I also understand they are good friends, which makes it more puzzling why they would compete with each other when neither cares a whit for me."

"After one dance with Mr. Christopher, he would not let go my arm. He tried to propel me onto the terrace, alone. I was desperate in my mind—trying to decide if I should make a scene —when Kitty and Mr. Owen came to my rescue. Mr. Owen actually blocked the doorway and then insisted on the gentlemen fetching us drinks. Luckily, Mr. Christopher acquiesced. Mr. Owen's demeanor was almost severe, and I think Mr. Christopher may have been a little in fear of such a challenge."

"Mr. Owen would certainly win in a duel," claimed Julia. "His fencing and shooting skills are well known. And he is very resolute, when he wishes to be ..." A pensive look appeared on her face as she trailed off.

Georgiana continued. "Later, as I was quitting the ballroom to refresh myself, I was followed by Mr. Douglas. Luckily, Julia had observed my leaving and followed me to the door. When she saw him catching up to me in the deserted hallway, she called out. Then she and a nearby footman came to see what was happening, and Mr. Douglas retreated."

"How shocking!" exclaimed Matilda.

The others shook their heads.

"Dear me!" exclaimed Kitty. "The ball must have been agony for you with problems such as these."

"Well, the rest of the dance was pleasant—especially when I was dancing with my Benjamin—until the end."

"That's where I came in," Matilda said. "This time it was Mr. Douglas trying to take her out of doors alone. I was panicked and not sure what to do. Luckily I was near Mr. Darcy and heard

Mr. Owen speak to him in an urgent tone, saying, *'My stepmother has taken ill and we leave at once. I must find my brother. And may I beg you send for the apothecary to meet us at Greystone? I have already called for our carriage.'* Mr. Darcy obliged instantly, of course. I indicated where Mr. Douglas was, near the terrace door with Georgiana, who looked distressed. Mr. Owen scowled fiercely and strode across the floor. I followed. The men departed at once and I remained with Georgiana. When the last dance began, Mr. Benjamin appeared for her, and then Mr. Fuller asked me again."

Kitty stared with wide eyes.

"What is it, Kitty?"

"I did not wish to say until I heard this, but Mr. Owen had asked me, earlier in the evening, to save the last for him; and I had agreed. But he did not appear. I wondered greatly at him breaking his word in such a way. Now I see there was an urgent need to do so."

"But you danced the last with my brother," Matilda said.

"Yes, he came to *my* rescue, you might say," Kitty replied. "I suppose it would not do to have the guest of honor sit out the last dance. Your brother is very kind."

Julia had become withdrawn since the talk turned to Mr. Owen and his brother. Kitty glanced at her as they walked side by side, but Julia's eyes hinted that another time would be better for further explanation.

"I think it must be obvious to the two troublemakers," mused Matilda, "that you are certainly not alone and that, as your friends, we are aware of their attempts at impropriety. If you do not wish to tell your brother yet about Mr. Benjamin, we can continue to assist you. But I, too, share your puzzlement at why these two, who will inherit, are so determined to secure you. Of course, I did not mean—"

"Oh, I understand," Georgiana replied. "To me—and probably to you, my friends—it is quite apparent they are not enamored with me, but rather with my fortune."

Julia cleared her throat and stopped so the group could all face each other.

"There is something I must say that may shed some light here. I have heard, from a reliable source, that some of the young men hereabouts are involved in a group, a sort of 'investment club' as they call it. There are rumors it involves gambling and horses," she said in almost a whisper. "While these two will inherit someday, they do not at present have a great deal of money at their disposal. They are both often from home, in Town or at watering holes and such. Betting and gaming debts can make men desperate, and dangerous."

Silence hung over the group. Kitty thought back to Mr. Wickham and his gaming debts, which the Bennets eventually discovered. He had reportedly stooped to some very low behavior. Aloud she observed, "Our group may be entering treacherous ground."

"I say we add a new task to our pact," stated Matilda emphatically. "Let us try to discover facts about these rumors—to see if there is any truth to them, and to learn if these two particular men are truly involved."

"But how shall we discover such things?" Georgiana wondered aloud.

Matilda narrowed her eyes. "We listen. We become more aware. We might even bring up the topic of such rumors, in a general way, to our father and our brother; and Georgiana, you and Kitty to Mr. and Mrs. Darcy."

They looked at each other with a mixture of fear and confusion, then drew strength together.

After consideration, Kitty spoke. "I agree we must gather more facts. But if we discover anything of import we must involve Mr. Darcy at once—he being Georgiana's protector—since the two possibly involved in this scheme seem to be after her. Have we an accord?"

All clasped hands and then walked on, lighter of step and unburdened enough to gossip about the more trivial details of gowns and appearances and pairings at the ball.

But in spite of their brightened demeanors, they were now conscious of a darker undercurrent in Derbyshire society.

CHAPTER TWELVE

*L*ady Drake handed Lizzy a cup of tea. "I thought it best we meet in person to plan the ladies' ride."

"Quite right," Lizzy agreed. "And there is also the exploring party and picnic. Or perhaps we might combine some of these?" she wondered aloud. "What do you think, Kitty?"

"I'm sure I don't know. How many ladies will wish to ride horseback, Lady Drake?"

"Well, let me see," she mused. "You and I of course; Mrs. Goode; oh, and Miss Julia Stapleton. Then there's Lady Richards and her daughter—no, I remember now they are gone to Town for a fortnight. But the weather is favorable at present and I do not wish to wait that long. Miss Darcy, would you wish to ride?"

Georgiana pursed her lips. "Do we have gentlemen to assist us and act as guides? I admit I am not fond of exploring new areas on my own. I prefer a familiar mount on familiar trails."

"I wonder, shall we make a day of it?" Lady Drake pondered. "Those seeking more adventure might ride out early in the morning with our guides. We riders could explore some of the splendors along the river and the cliffs and the dale, then all can meet near Nob Cave at that high clearing that is accessible by coach. The views are splendid, Mrs. Darcy. It is an excellent picnic spot. The old Benwick castle ruins are nearby for exploring. That would make a lovely walk."

"Mr. Andrew has offered himself as a guide, as has Mr. Owen," Kitty said.

"I believe Mr. Darcy will wish to ride with you as well," Lizzy added. "Especially if you were to go, Georgiana," she said, turning towards her for a response.

"Well, if my brother guides us, I shall feel safe; so yes, I will ride then. But what about you, Lizzy?"

"I am no horsewoman. I have never been one to ride for much distance," Lizzy replied, reaching for another piece of cake. "I shall be content to come in the coach for the picnic."

"What say you to Wednesday next? Do you have any encumbrance, Mrs. Darcy?"

"No, I believe that day will be convenient."

"Excellent. I shall have notes delivered to the Wyndhams and the Stapletons and the others so that all the arrangements can be finalized. Perhaps it will be best for each family to provide their own refreshments and servants?"

"Yes, that would seem the simplest," Lizzy agreed. "Now, to hope for good weather!"

≈

That evening at dinner, Lizzy shared the plan with Darcy.

"I would be delighted to guide the ladies on such a ride," he said, with more enthusiasm than Kitty had ever witnessed in him. "There are several worthy places in the area—places not amenable to coaches—that we might explore to advantage on horseback. And both you young ladies will ride?" he inquired, looking particularly at Georgiana.

A laugh bubbled out of her. "Yes, brother, I will go if you are there. Other gentlemen have volunteered as well, but none other would make me feel so secure."

"Thank you, my dear. I am delighted we shall have the chance to ride together. It has been some time, has it not?"

"And with that in mind," Kitty interceded, "might you have time to take us on a shorter ride before the appointed day? I have ridden often since I arrived. Georgiana, if you have not ridden in some time, it might be wise to exercise your muscles."

"You are right, Kitty. What do you say, brother?"

"I have business appointments tomorrow, but I could arrange a ride for the next morning. Would that do?"

"Yes. Oh thank you. Is he not kind and caring, Kitty?"

"Indeed he is. And I would not have guessed him so when first we met him at the Meryton assembly," Kitty said with an arch of her brow, hoping Darcy would take her comment lightly, as meant.

"I cannot take offense, Kitty, when I see merriment in your eye. But let that be a lesson to all of us. Things and people are not always what they seem on first encounter. Even me."

They all laughed and went through to the music room.

≈

On the chosen morning the grooms brought forth the horses. Cara nickered when she saw Kitty and was rewarded with affectionate petting.

"She is happy to see ye, Miss Bennet, no denying," remarked Johnny as he handed Kitty the reins, giving her a knowing glance out of the corner of his eye.

Kitty looked at him with slight alarm, but Darcy was checking Georgiana's tack and unaware of the exchange. She pursed her lips and shook her head at him, although her eyes held a twinkle.

"Miss Bennet, are you quite ready?" Darcy asked, proceeding to give her tack a final inspection.

"I checked it carefully myself as well, sir," remarked Johnny.

"Good lad. A broken strap or loose buckle can bring down the best rider." Darcy assisted Kitty into the saddle and then mounted his own rangy gelding. "Well, ladies, which shall it be? A ride along the river valley? Or winding up through the rockier peaks? Each has a stretch where we may let the horses have their head for a gallop."

"I say the rocky path, brother. It has been some years since I was up there. I should like to see the view again."

"And I," seconded Kitty.

"Very well then. Connor, we shall return within three hours."

"Aye, Sire, ever at yer service."

Johnny tipped his hat at Kitty and she nodded and smiled. Her secret was still safe. She would tell Fitzwilliam the truth at some point, but the time was not yet ripe. There had so far been only one event at which she could prove herself—the ball. It would be best to have her position as a proper lady more firmly implanted in his mind and in the minds of the others before she challenged that by admitting to riding astride in jodhpurs. Perhaps after the picnic, if all went well?

It was a glorious morning in the English countryside and the sky grew brighter as they climbed. When the view allowed, Kitty could see tendrils of mist lingering yet along the distant river, and was pleased they had chosen this sunny path today. As they mounted a tall ridge, they saw a small body of water to the west.

"That is the lake at Swan's Nest," Darcy said. "We see it here from the northeast. There are many streams and rills about, and also many caves. I spent much time as a boy having make-believe adventures in the caves. We especially enjoyed imagining pirates to be hiding there," he said with a laugh. Then his face clouded, and he looked at Georgiana. His sister gave him a sunny smile and he appeared at ease again.

"Below, you see a great swath of green—that is where we will have our gallop if you are equal to it. But first we have a winding downward path to travel."

The gallop across the meadow was refreshing. The turf was springy and the smell of the spring soil and the woodlands stirred a heady draught. Kitty filled her lungs. The ladies stayed on the green whilst Darcy directed his mount closer to the wooded border, jumping fallen logs and small streams.

How she envied Darcy! If she were riding astride, she could easily follow him. How Cara loved the low jumps!

Darcy wheeled back to join them, looking pleased, and gave his horse a hearty rub.

As they turned onto the narrow road they saw two riders moving their way. Kitty focused her eyes and thought she recognized the fine bay and the sturdy chestnut. Yes, it was Andrew and his uncle. Whatever were they doing here?

"Fitzwilliam, are we still on Pemberley land?" she asked.

Darcy was gazing at the riders as well.

"This road is the boundary between Pemberley and Swan's Nest. It is an ancient road that leads to the higher peaks and deep into the Lake Country. It is seldom used now, being suitable only for riders on horseback or those drawing small wagons or driving carts. I do believe that is young Mr. Stapleton and his uncle."

"Hail, and well met!" cried Darcy, nodding to the gentlemen.

"Well met, indeed!" responded Andrew Stapleton.

Mr. Robertson nodded in acknowledgement.

"And what brings you gentlemen out this far? Is the pleasant morning the only attraction?" Darcy asked.

"It *is* a pleasant morning, but for us also a good time to gather more samples for our studies," Andrew replied. "There are some interesting specimens near a grouping of small caves yonder," he indicated.

"Mr. Darcy, whilst I greatly esteem my uncle's company, I cannot help but envy you your riding companions this morning." He touched his hat in salute to the ladies.

"We are conditioning ourselves for the upcoming ladies' ride and picnic," Georgiana said. "Do I understand you will be one of the guides?"

"Yes, I have gallantly offered my services, if I may flatter myself," he said with a smile.

"Good, good," Darcy said. "I also will accompany them. And now, we bid you good day."

"And to you, sir," Andrew said. "Ladies, I look forward to seeing you at the ride." Although he had said 'ladies,' he had looked only at Kitty, and saluted her again as he had done when leaving the Red Lantern just a few weeks ago.

She flushed at the memory and burst into a smile that did not let up all the way back to the stables.

≈

Shortly after the ball Kitty had written to her sister Jane, and also to her family at Longbourn about the memorable event, but not to Lydia—she knew not what to say to her wayward sister. Jane sent a timely response.

Netherfield Park

 My dearest Kitty,

  How I enjoyed your description of the ball! What a delightful coming out for you. Lizzy and I were sure you would find great benefit and pleasure in spending time at Pemberley. I hope your new acquaintances grow into cherished and lifelong friends. I do miss your company. And you were so helpful at diverting Mama when her stories about lying in became frightening. But do not worry, I am determined to focus on the joy of holding my baby in my arms and I am sure all will be well. Charles is most attentive and I want for nothing, except the company of you and Lizzy. I hope you may find as much happiness as I have been so fortunate to enjoy. Please write again and tell me more about your friends and your doings at Pemberley.

  Your loving sister,

  Jane

Kitty folded the letter carefully and placed it amongst her things. Jane was such a comforting person. One could rely on her for the most hopeful outlook in any situation. Kitty was grateful for her two older sisters. She felt valued by them. Far different from how she had felt with Lydia. Sister Mary kept a distance from all her sisters and Kitty wondered if she were lonely or if she preferred solitude and reflection? She had only Mama for company now. Kitty would not wish to trade places with her.

≈

"Come, ladies, the carriage is here," Darcy called as Kitty and Lizzy donned their bonnets and picked up their shawls. "We mustn't keep the Wyndhams waiting."

The moon had risen early. The sun hung low in the western sky, gathering clouds around itself as if preparing to paint its own portrait. The evening was still and warm, and Darcy had ordered the carriage top be lowered so they could better appreciate the countryside awash in pink clouds and ivory moonlight.

"What a beautiful evening," Lizzy murmured, looking back at Pemberley.

Just as Kitty followed her gaze the sun struck all the windows, setting them ablaze.

"We are most fortunate, indeed," Darcy replied, taking his wife's hand and bringing it to his lips.

Kitty had been in Derbyshire only a few weeks, but had yet to see any of the acrimonious exchanges she had witnessed daily at Longbourn between her parents. She found the possibility of such a pleasant partnership very comforting. It left her hopeful she might find the same. And that put her in mind: she had not seen Owen since the ball. She anticipated a renewal of their budding acquaintance this evening at dinner.

The pact she had made with Georgiana and the Stapleton sisters was also on her mind. She was determined to listen carefully to conversations this evening—including those she might usually not find interesting—to do her part in gleaning information about the 'investment club.' As for the other part of the pact—that of protecting Georgiana from unwanted advances—Kitty knew Georgiana had reservations about this evening.

Kitty reached for Georgiana's hand and squeezed it in silent support, eliciting a weak smile. "For making helpful discoveries," she whispered.

They were shown into the drawing room to await dinner. Mr. Wyndham greeted them warmly. Douglas Wyndham bowed elegantly, but the satirical look in his eye was off-putting and aimed particularly at Georgiana.

Kitty glanced around the empty room.

"Oh, the ladies shall be down momentarily," Mr. Wyndham explained, looking a little chagrined. "Something about a last minute gown change."

"And where is Mr. Owen this evening?" asked Darcy.

"I regret he has gone to Windsor, Darcy. I thought he would return today but he has not. We are contracted to breed a few of the royal mares. I was to have gone, but my wife desires me nearby, fearing she may have another spell like she had at the ball. Owen, of course, knows everything about our operation and I trust him implicitly."

"Your trust is well placed, I am sure. I have great admiration for his knowledge and skills. My cousin lives down that way—his estate is just west of the royal mews—and he has written to me concerning some breeding with my stud. It is something I intend to pursue. Well, I am sorry to lose Mr. Owen's company tonight. You, Mr. Douglas, shall be burdened with entertaining us," Darcy said, smiling at the elder son.

Douglas nodded and held up his glass. "I shall do my best, sir," he said, casting one eye at Georgiana, who blinked and stared out the window.

A brittle voice at the doorway said, "My dear Darcys, please excuse our late appearance. We are honored to have you join us for dinner this evening." Mrs. Wyndham smiled as she and her daughter came gliding into the room. The smiles of neither carried to their eyes.

Dinner was immediately announced. The formality kept at Greystone surprised Kitty. Appearances exceeded that of Pemberley in some ways. But as they went in to dinner, Darcy kindly offered Kitty his other arm rather than allow her to enter alone. She again appreciated what a true gentleman her sister had married.

Georgiana was awkwardly seated between Douglas and Mr. Wyndham. Fortunately, the group was small enough that conversation could take place across the table. Even so, Douglas attempted several times to engage Georgiana in whispered talks. She deftly engaged Mr. Wyndham or Lizzy in any questions posed by Douglas.

He managed to mask his frustration and found solace in repeated glasses of wine.

"Speaking of horses and royalty," Mr. Wyndham began, picking up the earlier conversation, "I have heard talk about some kind of gambling group to do with race horses, even involving folks from hereabouts. Have you heard of this, Darcy?"

Kitty pricked up her ears and caught Georgiana's eye.

"I have. It involves not only betting, but also altering the performance of certain horses by use of medicinals," Darcy related with a scowl. "I abhor anyone tampering with the health of a beast as honest as a horse," he said with fervor. "I hope the scoundrels are discovered and receive their just desserts. Things like this come to light sooner or later."

"Sooner, I hope," said Wyndham. "I join you in being repulsed by such actions—harming our esteemed beasts for money. No punishment can be adequate, in my opinion."

Kitty interjected at this point. "How cruel! And the horses so helpless against such an attack. We must all come to their aid."

Douglas gulped at his wine.

"Greed is at the root of much evil," commented Mrs. Wyndham, and her sentiment was echoed around the table, followed by silence.

The conversation did not flow easily. Lucy and her mother made attempts to talk about pursuits and styles in London; but the gentlemen, having no interest in such things, repeatedly turned the conversation towards topics of more general appeal.

"Shall either of you be joining us on the morning ride before the picnic?" Darcy inquired of Mr. Wyndham and Douglas.

Mr. Wyndham's eyes lit up until he looked at his wife.

"I had hoped to join you, Darcy. But Mrs. Wyndham prefers I ride with her and Lucy in the coach."

Douglas added, "I, too, shall ride in the coach, Mr. Darcy. It seems you have enough guides, if I hear correctly?"

"Yes, that appears so. We have Squire and Andrew Stapleton and Christopher Drake. Mr. Owen has also offered to accompany us. Lord Drake has business in town and cannot join us. Yes, we have gentlemen enough. I regret you cannot join us Wyndham; it is a ride you would enjoy."

"I am sure I would. Hopefully another time," Mr. Wyndham answered in a strained voice.

"Mrs. Darcy, will you ride that morning?" Douglas asked.

"No, I shall join them later by coach. I am not one for long exploring rides. Short rides visiting the orchard or nearby friends are more palatable to me. But I do know Georgiana and Kitty look forward to the outing and will have Lady Drake and Mrs. Goode as well as Miss Stapleton with them."

Douglas perked up at this information. "Miss Darcy, I did not know you cared for riding."

"I do not care for it as much as my brother would wish," Georgiana replied, nodding at Darcy with a grin. "But yes, I shall join the ladies this time."

"After we picnic, we can explore the ruins of Benwick Castle," Kitty added with enthusiasm. "I understand it is an easy walk from the picnic area to the castle site."

"Such gadding about the country!" exclaimed Lucy. "I find such outings boring when the landscape is the only attraction. But I do like a mystery. I have heard there are barrows near the ruins, and some say the castle site is haunted," she said, hoping to engage the other young people in her fascination.

"Haunted?" Kitty asked. "By whom?"

"That story has been told since I was a child," Georgiana said. "I set no store by it. But do tell it, Miss Jamison. I still find it entertaining."

"More than entertaining, I should say. Legend has it that Captain Benwick, a soldier, spent many years away at war, leaving behind his young bride, Cassandra. Finding life very lonely, Cassandra took up illicit relations with a nearby duke. When Captain Benwick returned unannounced, he is said to have found the two together and challenged the duke to a duel. As Captain Benwick aimed the fatal blow at the duke, Cassandra rushed in front of her paramour and both were beheaded in one fell stroke. The captain, in his sorrow, took his dagger and ended his own life as well. And all turned to stone. I have not seen the place myself but am very eager to explore it."

"Mr. Darcy showed us a stone circle on our ride the other day," Kitty said. "I should be glad to explore more of these. But what about the haunting?"

"It is said Captain Benwick haunts the site in search of a new bride. And that any young lady entering the castle grounds may be spirited away by him."

Laughter rippled around the table, but it was an uneasy sort of laughter.

Kitty was intrigued by this legend and thought more favorably about Lucy as a companion on adventures such as these.

The ladies went through to the drawing room whilst the gentlemen stayed behind to enjoy port. Mrs. Wyndham silently poured tea for the ladies.

Lizzy tried to break the awkwardness by continuing the conversation from dinner. "Georgiana, all of us are newcomers here but you. Pray, are there other such sites and legends?"

All eyes were on Georgiana. "Yes, the peaks are full of such stories—and actual sites of barrows, castles, caves, cairns, and even a lovers' leap. My brother knows more about these than I do. I always found them unsettling. But Squire Stapleton is the one to ask. Not only is he well informed about these histories and legends, he also has a dramatic way of telling it. We must remember to ask him for some tales at the picnic."

"Oh, yes, that would be exciting," Lucy said, her eyes wide. "I wonder if any young ladies have gone missing from the castle site? Has the captain found his new bride?" She let out a slight cry, followed by laughter.

"Likely the squire will know," Georgiana said with a wicked little smile.

It was not long until the gentlemen joined them. Darcy and Wyndham conversed genially as they entered the room. Douglas appeared somewhat unsteady and Kitty wondered about the amount of wine he had imbibed. She glanced at Georgiana, who gave a small shudder. Douglas made directly for her, landing heavily on the settee, causing both young ladies to move aside to avoid being squashed.

Kitty was appalled. She looked at Lizzy, who simply stared into the teacup in her hand.

Mrs. Wyndham sniffed and glared at her husband.

Douglas spoke in a loud, boorish tone to Georgiana, teasing her more about the legend. He seemed bent on frightening her. Discomfort, growing into alarm, marked Georgiana's face.

Noticing this Darcy said, "Wyndham, what say we gentlemen take a turn outdoors? I feel the need for some air."

"Capital idea!" Douglas slurred. "Come, Miss Darcy. You are not afraid of the dark, surely."

Wyndham took control of the situation, and of his son.

"Douglas, you will join us outdoors. The ladies are not shod for walking, and I believe some fresh air is an excellent idea."

The gentlemen quit the room, much to the unspoken relief of all the ladies.

Lucy snickered. "My brother is in his cups again."

The gentlemen had not been gone long when a servant summoned the guests to their carriage. Mr. and Mrs. Wyndham and Lucy said their farewells at the door. Douglas was nowhere to be seen.

"Ladies, I do apologize for my son's behavior. I shall take him to account severely in the morning; and I beg your forgiveness for any discomfort he caused, especially to you, Miss Darcy."

The ladies simply curtsied, then were handed into the coach, but Darcy said, "Thank you, Wyndham, you have done all that is called for. Let young Wyndham take action to make amends."

"Thank you, Darcy. You are a true friend."

The men shook hands, and Darcy entered the coach.

≈

The next morning found the Darcys together in the break-fast room.

"Don't forget, we are invited for tea at Swan's Nest this after-noon," Darcy reminded them as he rose to take his leave. "I have ordered the coach to be ready promptly at three." He bent to kiss Lizzy on the forehead, bowed quickly to the young ladies, and strode from the room.

"What do you ladies have planned until tea time?" Lizzy said.

"I should like to practice my music," Georgiana replied. "I have been neglecting it of late. There has been so much more to do"—she grinned at Kitty—"and I must not let my discipline lapse too greatly."

"Cara is on my mind," Kitty said, "and I hope to have a good ride today. What about you, Lizzy?"

"I plan a stroll in the near garden as soon as I finish my tea. After that, I have a delicious novel beckoning, although I may set up to read outdoors in the shade as it is such a beautiful day. Shall either of you wish to join me on a walk in the shrubbery?"

"Certainly!" they both chimed at once.

"One more piece of toast and jam for me first," Georgiana remarked, reaching for the basket.

Kitty did likewise. She would need some stores for her ride.

≈

Cara raised her head and nickered as Kitty approached the paddock. "And good morning to you, girl," Kitty said in reply. The mare trotted over to the fence and Kitty held out one of the pieces of apple she had gleaned from the kitchen.

"Hallo, Miss Bennet!" Johnny called as he emerged from the barn with a halter in his hand. "Allow me to bring Raleigh here in for his trim. Then I shall catch Cara."

"Thank you."

"Will this be a singular ride, Miss?"

She knew what this meant. They had created a code for the times she wished to ride astride, wearing jodhpurs she had hidden in the barn.

"Yes, I should like that very much, if it is convenient?" This was also part of the code, to determine if others were around who might notice them leaving if she were not in a sidesaddle.

"'Tis most convenient. Others are groomin' and trimmin'. I shall ask to accompany you. We tack up at the far end."

"I shall meet you there directly."

Kitty entered the barn from a side door and stealthily retrieved her jodhpurs. She snuck into an empty stall and pulled them up under the skirt of her habit, then removed the skirt and hid it. On summer morning rides she never wore the jacket and tall hat of the habit, just a vest over her blouse. She tucked her hair under the round hat she kept with the jodhpurs and met Johnny at the far end of the stable yard. Her heart pounded with excitement. Now for a real ride!

Kitty bridled the mare as Johnny saddled her, and then he tacked up his own mount. Within minutes, they were out the gate to the south and east, in the direction of the river valley.

"Fine mornin' for a ride, Miss," Johnny commented, beaming. "And a ride is a far piece finer than groomin' or trimmin'."

"I agree. Don't you, girl?" Kitty added, petting Cara's neck.

The mare nickered.

"And how is your plan coming along, Johnny?" His great passion at present was a lovely mare owned by one of the nearby estates. Kitty's monetary tips for his accompaniment—and for his secrecy—added to his coffers.

"Agreeable," he replied. "I did pay some to the 'pothecary. Me sister been sick and needed a draught he brewed specially."

"How is she now?"

"Mendin'. Out of bed. Eatin' again. Thank you, Miss, for askin' about her."

"I have four sisters, Johnny. One is very difficult and one barely tolerable, but I love them all. You must be an admirable brother. I always wished I had a brother."

"Think of me as yer brother then. We be bound by our love of horses—and by our secrets." He chuckled.

"I like that. I shall. Thank you, little brother."

They were approaching a flat meadow that ran parallel to the riverbank until it met a road from the nearby village.

"Ready to gallop?"

"Yes, but let us stay off the road. It would be best for me not to be seen."

They were off, horses and riders floating over the springy turf. As they neared the road Johnny turned his horse into a wide circle at seeing a rider coming out of the trees from the far side of the road. Kitty checked Cara and guided her into a wide arc as well. When she and Johnny turned to face the rider, he hailed them with a wave.

"Must be trouble. P'rhaps we can help," Johnny said.

As they trotted closer, Kitty gasped. She knew that great grey horse. And its rider—Owen Wyndham.

CHAPTER THIRTEEN

"*A*h, Johnny my lad, I am in need of help. My wagon's wheel has broken and I have royal mares to deliver to Greystone. Can you and ..." Owen's glance strayed to Johnny's companion and his mouth fell open.

"Wha ... why ... is that you, Miss Bennet?"

Kitty's mare was circling nervously.

A wide smile spread over Owen's face. "I would know your eyes anywhere."

Johnny flushed and looked between Kitty and Owen in confusion.

Kitty's own eyes glanced at Owen in alarm and then down at Cara. What should she say? What could she do?

Owen burst into uproarious laughter.

Kitty stared at him.

Johnny looked at her; then a smile broke over his face and he shrugged.

"So my disguise is poorer than I thought," Kitty said, breaking into laughter herself.

"This is rich, Miss Bennet. But I do sympathize. I have always wondered how ladies managed to feel secure on horseback with their bodies twisted so. I admire your courage."

"Sir—" Johnny began.

"Do not worry; this secret is safe with me," Owen said. "Why should I reveal it? In fact, I wish you might sometime include me on such a ride. It would be far more exciting than the usual rides with ladies." He chuckled.

In their short acquaintance Kitty had not seen Owen this merry or this comfortable. She could now relax in his company—and found she desired more of it.

"But about my wheel and my horses ..." Owen paused in thought. "Pemberley is nearer than Greystone. Johnny, can you return to Pemberley and request two more lads to help me pony these mares? And ask that a message be sent to my father so he can send help to the wagon; it is just across this road and past the fork about a quarter mile. Luckily, I am not too far from home. The wagon has been troublesome all the way. Miss Bennet can stay here and help manage the mares."

Seeing Johnny's doubtful face he added, "Do not be concerned. Old Scoville is here with me, and a proper enough chaperone."

Johnny looked to Kitty and she nodded her approval.

"A bit of unexpected adventure today, Miss," he said, touching his hat.

"Yes. We rarely meet with anyone on our rides."

Owen added, "Oh, and Johnny, when you return with the other lads, do halloo. That will be Miss Bennet's cue to disappear into the trees with Cara. You know the path through yonder trees that crosses the rill in a northward fashion? The two of you can meet there. It is within shouting distance, Miss Bennet, should you encounter any trouble."

Johnny wheeled his horse and was off to Pemberley.

Owen extended his arm in the direction of his wagon.

"Shall we?"

Kitty smiled and urged Cara forward.

"Are you just now returning from Windsor, Mr. Owen?"

"I am, but how did you—?"

"Ha! Now I may surprise you. We were dinner guests at Greystone last evening."

His expression clouded. "I am sorry to have missed that. I hope we may dine together at another time soon."

Kitty's cheeks flushed. "I should like that very much."

Then she frowned. "But what about the wagon driver? How shall I conceal myself from ...?"

Owen gave a throaty laugh and reached up to help her dismount. He lowered her slowly and their eyes locked. His arms were strong and steady, as if she weighed no more than a feather.

She shook herself free and gave him a fierce look.

"You must not make light of my situation, sir."

"I do not, Miss Bennet, truly. Old Scoville, my wagon driver, is a kindly soul, but his vision is not as keen as it once was. I doubt he will pay you any mind; he will assume you are just another stable lad in those clothes. Take care not to speak around him though—your melodic voice will give you away."

She pursed her lips. "You have an answer for every predicament, Mr. Owen."

He gave her a steady look. "That is my duty as a gentleman, Miss Bennet. And as a horsewoman, you know the value of thinking ahead, fine instinct, and quick reactions. Have no fear. Your honor and safety, and your comfort, are my priorities."

It was a pretty speech and she relented.

"You are very kind."

"I also find it delightful that we now share a secret," he said with a wink.

She stared hard at him. "You have found my weakness. I hope, before long, to discover yours."

"I have but one, Miss Bennet, and I am surprised you do not know it already." He looked deeply into her eyes, then made a slight bow.

Color burst onto her cheeks again and she looked quickly away, but a growing smile had already brightened her expression.

They approached the wagon. Old Scoville was leaning against a nearby tree stump, his pipe in his mouth. Apparently dozing.

Kitty was careful not to speak within earshot.

Owen moved the three mares from their tether on the wagon to trees at the edge of the woods in the shade. He filled a bucket from the noisy stream and watered them, then filled the bucket again to water the wagon horse, Cara, and his own mount.

"What are your plans for this fine day, Miss Bennet?" Owen inquired whilst he held the bucket for his horse.

"We are for tea at Swan's Nest this afternoon. Oh, I hope I am not late for luncheon. What will I tell Mr. Darcy if I am tardy? I doubt I could convincingly tell a falsehood. He has been so kind to me."

"There are shortcuts to Pemberley from here. I have gone back and forth on many errands. Johnny will return in less than an hour so you may yet be in time for luncheon. Certainly in time to be ready for tea."

"Mr. Darcy is punctual. If I am not ready to step into the coach at three, I fear the reproaches I shall hear. And I do not wish to bring trouble down on Johnny's head. He is so obliging."

"Johnny is a good lad. I trust him."

The day grew warmer as they waited. Their own mounts, which they had been grazing in hand, were now tied up so Kitty and Owen could graze the royal mares. Kitty looked them over with interest, but as time passed she began to fret.

"You are restless, Miss Bennet, and likely parched. I have beer in the wagon, along with bread and cheese. May I offer you some? It is not fine fare, but it will satisfy."

Kitty looked towards the road expectantly, but neither saw nor heard riders. She sighed.

Owen took the lead line from her and tethered the mares again, then indicated a fallen log in the shade.

"Sit here, Miss Bennet, whilst I fetch food and drink."

All around her the birds chattered and sang. The air was pungent with the smell of fresh soil and springy patches of moss. Newly-leafed trees brightened the woods. Early wildflowers peeped through emerging grass and the stream chattered over its rocky bed. Surely here was heaven itself.

Her eyes were then drawn to Owen as he leapt handily into the wagon, opened a large basket behind the driver's seat and secured two small bags and a bottle. He was agile; each move was dynamic yet measured. She found his person very pleasing.

He vaulted out, retrieved the supplies, and walked towards her with a look that spoke of being pleased with what he saw before him.

She fidgeted and stared up at the trees.

He sat next to her, put the bottle on the ground, then carefully placed one bag on his lap and handed the other to her. He drew his knife from his belt and unwrapped the cheese, cleaning his blade on the cloth before cutting several chunks off the partial wheel of Sage Derby.

"Do you mind tearing the bread and passing some to me, Miss Bennet? This meal has not the elegance that our picnic next week will boast, but it is no matter. I feel quite pleased with the world at this moment." He looked over at her, his countenance expressing the same.

His words described her feelings perfectly—pleased with the world—and she looked at him with appreciation. She tore a handful of bread and passed it over. As their hands touched, she again felt the small thrill that being in his presence seemed to elicit. A feeling not at all unpleasant, she decided, as they feasted happily on the bread and cheese.

"I regret I have no cup to offer you, Miss Bennet. When we travel, we each have a bottle for our use." He uncorked his bottle and wiped it with the cloth from the cheese, then held it up. "To a surprising morning," he murmured.

Kitty looked at him, then burst out laughing.

"I have never drunk beer or ale from a bottle before. I guess one who rides like a man must be prepared to eat and drink like one as well." She tipped the bottle to her lips and enjoyed the rich brew on her parched tongue.

Owen chuckled and devoured another piece of cheese.

"And that makes one more secret I now possess," he said in a lowered voice, with a sly grin. "As we dine, Miss Bennet, tell me of your home. I wish to learn where such an unusual young lady—"

"Unusual? I fear you think poorly of me, sir," she said with her brows knitted into a frown.

"Poorly? Oh, no. I find you quite remarkable. You are as fresh as ... as the spring. Like a young foal. You do not put on airs or engage in coquetry; and I have seen your loyalty to your friends. My esteem for you grows by the minute. Perhaps faster than ..." He trailed off and stared at the ground.

Kitty was torn. She dared not look at him, yet she longed to see his face. Was he heaping false praise upon her? Roasting her for some mischievous reason of his own?

Then again, how *could* he praise her? She had broken all the rules. Perhaps Papa was right; she did not behave like a proper lady and would never find a place in good society—or an honorable partner. It was all hopeless.

And now this young man had the whip hand over her, knowing two secrets that could ruin her. She stole a glance at him as he continued to stare at the ground. A fine hole she'd dug for herself. Darcy said Owen was honorable, but that was with horses and business and men. Was he honorable as a friend? In affairs of the heart?

Her voice wavered as she asked, "Do you have a timepiece, Mr. Owen? The sun is past its zenith."

He looked up, his countenance now serious—almost troubled —and pulled a timepiece from his pocket.

"Half past one."

"Oh, dear. I *have* missed luncheon. Lizzy will worry. Why did I not tell Johnny to send word to the house? Fie! I wonder, shall I leave on my own? I dare not be—"

"No, Miss Bennet, my honor will not allow that. Personally I see no scandal or sin in a lady riding astride, but it *would* be unacceptable for her to ride alone. Out in these woods? Near the road? No, indeed. Too many dangers might befall her. Johnny has a bit of wit about him. He may think to send word to the house even though you did not direct it. Let us wait another quarter hour. If he has not returned by then, we shall concoct a different plan. I cannot command you, but I pray you will agree?" he asked, his eyes even more beseeching than his words.

Kitty could not refuse such an honorable request.

"One quarter hour. No more," she replied softly. She wrapped the remaining bread and handed it to him and took another drink from the bottle.

"Here, Miss Bennet. Have one more bite of bread. As you may not often drink beer"—he smiled—"you may not know the smell can linger on one's breath. You need no false scandals."

He tore off a piece of bread and held it near her mouth. Her lips parted in surprise and he gently placed it upon them. She took it in, unable to look away until he turned to wrap the loaf.

After a few minutes of silence, Owen said, "My previous inquiry was sincere, Miss Bennet. I have not traveled in Hertfordshire. Is society there like it is here? Do you have sisters and brothers, other than Mrs. Darcy? And what of the land? What do you see when you hack out? I would be grateful to learn, if you would oblige me."

His sincerity made her want to talk to him, even confide in him. But something tugged at her. Wickham had possessed this same uncanny ability. She should be more guarded until she knew Owen better. And could ask others about him. So she talked in general terms about Longbourn and Meryton, and about her family.

He listened with interest. "So you have no brothers at all?" he asked. "Your father must have felt greatly—"

Hooves! They leapt to their feet.

"It is he!" Kitty cried.

Owen gathered up their food items and made for the wagon.

Kitty moved towards Cara, eager to be off.

"Wait," he cautioned. "Let us see what has been done and learn the plan. Johnny has brought three lads with him."

"They must not see me," Kitty whispered. "I will be in the shade by the stream."

"Yes. Go now. Stay where I can see you," he directed. "And stand on the distant side of Cara so she can block any view they might have of you."

As she led Cara behind the wagon and into the trees, Kitty was struck by Owen's quick thinking and his attention to every detail. Nothing escaped his notice.

Johnny arrived in an instant.

"Mr. Owen. I requested a message be sent to Greystone to inform them of yer situation and of needin' a wheelwright and another wagon. If 'tis agreeable, I best accompany M ... the other rider ... back to Pemberley. Two of the lads can help you pony the mares on to Greystone, and one lad can stay 'ere with Old Scoville till help arrives for the wagon." His eyes darted about. "The other rider waits ... in the shade?"

"Yes, at the designated place. You have done well, Johnny, and you have my gratitude."

"Obliged, Mr. Owen. Always at yer service. I want to admire these mares but there is no time; we must return with haste." He touched his cap and entered the woods whilst the others prepared the mares to travel.

Kitty had found a fallen log, and when Johnny approached she mounted Cara.

"Miss Bennet, I sent a message to the great house of our delay, and that you would miss luncheon but would be ready for the coach at three. I hope I have not misspoken?"

"Indeed not. It is just what I would have wished. You are very good; and you have managed to keep my secret?"

"Yes, Miss. No one's the wiser. Excepting Mr. Owen."

CHAPTER FOURTEEN

On her return to Pemberley, Kitty rushed up the stairs and into her chambers. To her surprise, Poppy had two gowns and all the extras set out for her choice and was fetching shoes from the dressing room.

"Poppy! You are divine! How did you … ?"

The girl curtsied and a smile washed over her face. "Johnny, it was, sent me word of yer delay. I knew ye would need to dress in a trice. I aimed to be helpful."

"Indeed you did. And indeed you are. Thank you!"

The basin was ready for washing. "Please send word to my sister that I am here dressing for tea."

"Aye, Miss, at once."

≈

Refreshed and ready, and most appreciative of Poppy's skill and assistance, Kitty descended the stairs and found Lizzy in the hallway speaking with a servant.

She turned and searched Kitty's face.

"What is it, Lizzy?"

"Thank you for sending the second message, but I must say the first message about missing luncheon concerned me. Can you explain what it was that delayed you?"

"Certainly. It was nothing so severe ..." Darcy was coming down the hallway. "But Lizzy, can we talk about it later?"

"Of course. But it must be later today."

When Darcy reached Lizzy, he brought her hand up for a tender kiss.

"My darling, you are so beautiful," he whispered, his expression warm with tenderness. They held each other's eyes, and Kitty again felt pleased her sister had found such love.

After a minute he turned. "And Kitty, you look as lovely as this fine summer day."

Kitty curtsied her thanks and smiled.

Georgiana joined them, looking elegant as always.

Darcy smiled. "Now let us be off."

He seemed unusually keen about today's visit. The squire must be a most particular friend.

≈

Squire and Lady Stapleton greeted them. Mr. Andrew Stapleton was also at hand. Although he performed the appropriate greetings to the others, Andrew seemed to have eyes only for Kitty. He offered his arm to escort her to the drawing room. He, too, seemed unusually eager. The very energy swirling about portended more than tea and idle conversation.

The large windows of the drawing room were thrown open on opposite walls, allowing a delicious breeze to waft about. Andrew walked Kitty to the window that overlooked the pond.

"Such a fine day. And you, Miss Bennet, are as dazzling as the sun, and as welcome. There is much I wish to say to you."

Kitty colored but did not know how to reply. She turned as Julia and Matilda entered, followed by their younger sisters. Julia's sensible presence was calming. Georgiana and Matilda were already chatting amiably.

"Let us join your sisters. Have you shared your news with them?" Kitty said brightly to Andrew.

To her dismay, some of the sparkle drained from his face.

"Mr. Stapleton, have I offended you? Are your sisters not already in your confidence?"

"No, they are not. What I have to say is for your ears alone. Can we have a private conversation after tea? It is a fine day for a walk." His eyes implored her.

She agreed to a walk but her heart was reluctant. He was handsome and interesting, to be sure. But they had spent little time together, and none of it in serious conversation. How would she respond if he ...

"Kitty, Andrew, do sit and have some lemonade. Cook has outdone herself again—such an array of biscuits!" Matilda exclaimed, piling three into her palm.

With all parties settled and enjoying refreshments, Kitty was surprised to see Darcy rise and move to stand behind Lizzy's chair. She had rarely seen him so pleased. Lizzy looked up at him with a glow.

"We have some news to share with our dearest friends—you, who are like our family," Darcy began.

Kitty's eyes bolted to Lizzy's face, which was a picture of serenity and joy.

"Oh, my!" escaped from Lady Stapleton.

"This year, before Christmastide, we shall welcome the first of the next generation of Darcys!" he exclaimed. He bent to kiss Lizzy's forehead.

"Lizzy!" Kitty gasped, and was answered with a knowing wink. She rushed to her sister and hugged her. "Oh Lizzy, such happy news!"

"Great news indeed!" the squire said, moving to shake Darcy's hand as Georgiana ran forward to embrace her brother.

"Praise be! About time this neighborhood sees some bairns again! This is the best news in the land, I declare," Lady Stapleton cried as she came over and grasped Lizzy's hands. Kitty would not have been surprised to see the little woman leap for joy.

"Will this truly be the first baby hereabouts in some time?" Lizzy asked.

"Aye, it will. The youngest Nelson is nigh on seven years now. We must discuss the things you will need and how I can help you prepare—if you would welcome my help, that is," Lady Stapleton added, seeming to become aware of propriety again. "I have found no greater joy than in being a mother," she admitted. "Next to being married to the squire, of course." She gave Lizzy a conspiratorial wink.

General laughter and good wishes filled the air, and Lizzy was offered as many cakes and biscuits as she could eat.

The meaningful looks and exchanges Kitty had witnessed, and Lizzy's occasional spells of being unwell, were now explained. Look at the pair of them, so very happy. And to think, Lizzy would have missed all this had she accepted Mr. Collins. Let that be a lesson to me—to listen to my heart.

Kitty looked up to see Andrew offering his arm.

"The time is ripe for our walk, Miss Bennet. Will you do me the honor?"

She was not inclined to leave the happy atmosphere of the drawing room but the pleading look reappeared in his eyes and Kitty could not say no, in spite of her misgivings about what he might say. Surely he would not be offering—

"Miss Bennet?" he repeated.

"Yes, a walk would be lovely." She turned towards Julia. "Will your sisters accompany us?"

"Certainly; we must honor propriety. I have asked Julia if she would stay behind us for a bit, as there is something I wish to speak to you about in confidence, if you will allow it," Andrew said in a quiet voice, close to her ear. He seemed happy yet anxious. The whole situation was puzzling.

Kitty rose and took his arm. With Julia on his other arm, the three made their way outdoors to the path around the pond. The late afternoon light cast a golden glow on the leaves, and the air was heady with the perfume of budding peonies.

Once out of direct view of the house, Julia dropt back, claiming she wished to watch the swans on the water.

"When do you return to Scotland, Mr. Stapleton?" Kitty asked, to give the silence a direction.

"Scotland. Yes, well, my heart is there, indeed ..." he trailed off, looking wistful.

Kitty made another attempt. "You take your studies seriously, I see. I can understand that. I myself find the land here most interesting, and I have not nearly the depth of knowledge you must hold by now. It must be a fascinating field. But how shall you ... or perhaps it is impertinent of me to ask?"

His look encouraged her to go on.

"How shall you work as a scientist in Scotland and yet be master of Swan's Nest?"

"Miss Bennet, since meeting you, I have been struck not only by your beauty, but also by your intelligence—as shown by your interest in my work—and by the sense of honor you demonstrate in social situations," he said, looking at her sidelong. "I have something to confess, in confidence, and a question to ask. I must speak to someone—I cannot speak to my family, not yet. I had hoped to confide in you. Can I depend upon your secrecy?"

Kitty's voice caught in her throat. Secrecy? Did she wish to be bound by Andrew's secrets? Her thoughts flew back to Owen, the man who now possessed two of *her* secrets.

Andrew's face was clouded with concern.

"You may unburden yourself to me and be assured of my secrecy—unless someone is in danger; in which case I must warn you I will consult my sister."

"Thank you. No one is in danger. But you have in fact already touched on one of my concerns. I *am* torn. I love Swan's Nest, of course. It is home. But I also love Scotland, and especially university life. There is much to learn, and I am so eager for it! I believe I can make a worthy contribution to my field. My uncle assures me my ideas are quite forward and encourages me to pursue them. I hope to continue my work in Scotland as long as possible. But my father is not a young man. I have a mother and *four* sisters who will depend on me. You can see my dilemma."

"Indeed." Kitty pursed her lips. "There is a gentleman in my old neighborhood, in Hertfordshire, who travels a great deal. He has a fine estate and is said to rely heavily on his steward. Would that be possible?"

"You think quickly, Miss Bennet. Sadly, my father's steward is old, older than my father himself. A steward *could* look after the land; but not after my mother and sisters."

"True. You have been gathering specimens here. Can you not continue some discovery in Derbyshire?"

"The caves round about and the areas with stone circles are

of great interest. Many of the stones are ancient. There is one site in particular where the findings so far are remarkable. I should like to explore it in more depth. So yes, there is some work to be done here. But the testing must be done at university." He paused, seeming to weigh these ideas.

"I must speak of another dilemma, which more nearly concerns you. May I continue?"

Kitty's pulse quickened. She hesitated, then said, "You may."

"There is another part of my heart that resides in Scotland, and did so very happily until recently."

Kitty's heart thudded to a stop.

"But I must explain. I have always kept young ladies at a distance. As heir to Swan's Nest, I have been pursued by many, but mostly for my fortune. For my part, my mind was on my studies, and I took little interest in society other than considering it a pleasant pastime. As you noticed, I do enjoy dancing."

They exchanged a smile.

"For many months—perhaps years—it has been hoped by both our families that Miss Darcy would be my wife. My father is like an older brother to Mr. Darcy; perhaps even like a father, especially since old Mr. Darcy died. I am very fond of Miss Darcy; but she is like a sister, so close she is to our family. She and Matilda are thick as thieves. And Miss Darcy's heart lies elsewhere. The young man who has captured her heart also returns her feelings. I wish them well and hope their match will be accepted. So I had not taken much notice of young ladies— well besides Anna, who is in Scotland, and there are difficulties ... so I felt there was nothing here for me until such time as I must consider residing at Swan's Nest permanently. Nothing, that is, until you came into the neighborhood, Miss Bennet."

Kitty's heart was pounding and her breath came in quivers.

"I have met no one like you before. Yet I do not wish to be false with you. I shall return to Scotland shortly and know not the length of my stay."

He paused and looked at her, almost through or beyond her. "I can offer nothing at present to any young lady. So what about you, Miss Bennet? Have you left your heart in Hertfordshire?"

They walked on in silence, with Julia still trailing them at a distance. The breeze had stilled and the mingled smells from the water and woods wove amongst Kitty's tangled senses.

"Miss Bennet?"

How much should she tell him? Who was Anna? She sighed.

"Mr. Stapleton, clearly your heart is troubled, and I am sorry for that. I have little experience regarding romance or courtship, and even less wisdom about such matters. I have had no serious attachments myself. Oh, there was one officer with whom I was enraptured for a time. But he married a lady with more fortune than I. My heart was broken, but my mind understood."

She drew a deep breath and continued. "Fortunately, you are free to marry where your heart leads, and that you must sort for yourself, Mr. Stapleton. I think I understand what you are saying, but I cannot help you other than to say this: I do not wish to be unkind. Yet neither do I wish to cause confusion or heartbreak for another by being unclear."

He turned to face her. "You are right, of course. Your insight is admirable, Miss Bennet, and I thank you for sharing it. You have shown yourself a true friend by allowing me to unburden myself, even if I was bold or impertinent. Forgive me. I can see now that you are correct—I must know my own heart first. But how does one do that?" His brows knit together.

Lacking this answer herself, she passed by his question.

"Time itself may lend some clarity to your situation. May I ask, why do you not talk of these things with Julia?"

He looked into her eyes. "Julia is much like you in temperament and wisdom. Perhaps that is part of your appeal to me. But she has her own sorrows of the heart, and they are deep; I do not wish to burden her further at present."

Kitty looked at him with some surprise. So her own impression of Julia being in turmoil was not unfounded.

"I cannot speak of her feelings. I hope she will confide in you before long. I believe it would comfort her."

Julia waited as they approached, then took her brother's arm and the three returned to the merriment of the house to see Lady Stapleton already knitting a tiny hat of the softest wool.

CHAPTER FIFTEEN

*T*he day of the picnic dawned cloudy and cool, perfect for the ladies' morning ride. Tendrils of mist curled round the trees and clung to the fence posts as Darcy, Kitty, and Georgiana made their way along the edge of the field. Wearing her new habit, Kitty felt as elegant as her companions and sat tall on Cara. All the riders would gather at the crossroads where the estates conjoined except for Swan's Nest, which met Pemberley further to the northwest. Darcy dismounted to work the gate, which he could not budge from his position in the saddle. Once they were through and the gate secured, they rode on to the crossroads and saw the others approach.

Lady Drake looked smart in her deep ruby habit. Her son Christopher Drake was maddeningly attractive—if only his character matched his handsome mien. Mrs. Goode was a plain but cheerful lady dressed in a green habit. Mr. Wyndham and Owen emerged like ghosts from the mist, the footsteps of their horses heard long before they could be seen.

"Why, Wyndham!" Darcy exclaimed. "I thought you were meant for the carriage today."

"As did I, my friend. Mrs. Wyndham came to decide that Douglas would be companion enough for herself and Lucy—so I was free to join you on horseback."

"Excellent news indeed!"

Squire Stapleton, along with Andrew and Julia Stapleton and their uncle Mr. Robertson, met the group at a spot down the road—the squire's jovial laughter being heard before the Swan's Nest party physically appeared. Kitty could imagine his voice lifting in song and it would not seem at all odd, such was his character.

At first the ladies rode together—Georgiana with Lady Drake, followed by Kitty and Julia with Mrs. Goode. Kitty observed with pleasure the affection between the two in front of her and hoped Georgiana's dream of marrying Benjamin would come to pass. Christopher Drake, Owen Wyndham, and Andrew Stapleton rode in front, and the four older gentlemen brought up the rear.

The riders first kept near to the bank of the River Derwent as it wound its way through the valley and the oak woods, but soon the bank began to rise.

"Andrew, take the next path to the right," the squire directed.

"The high pass to the Edge?"

"Yes. We will follow that to the top and then work our way down to the bridge at Little Longstone. After two more climbs we shall meet the others near Nob Cave for the picnic. The view of the dale from that spot is unsurpassed."

"The fishing in these parts is also good," Darcy added. "Perhaps next we shall make a fishing expedition, eh?"

The older gentlemen agreed heartily with this idea.

The mists evaporated as they climbed towards the Edge, and the sun glinted off the water. Owen rode up beside Kitty, close enough to speak quietly.

"How very *ladylike* you look in your saddle today, Miss Bennet." He arched a brow at her, and she felt a blush cover her cheeks. He smiled and motioned for her to ride ahead of him as the path narrowed.

The river fell away on their left. Kitty dared not look down and was grateful for Cara's talent at picking her way along the rocky path. The area was rough and craggy, not unlike the rocky land around Greystone and the stony hills behind Swan's Nest. They paused at the top of the Edge to appreciate the view for miles around, staring until the boundary between earth and sky melted into mist. They rode the crest for some little time.

The direction of the descent went to and fro until the riders reached the level of the river again, where a stone bridge spanned the waterway. Two of the horses were reluctant to cross with the water swirling beneath. Darcy led Georgiana's mount across, and the squire assisted Mrs. Goode. Once across, the riders regrouped.

As they readied for another climb, Kitty observed a look of significance pass between Julia and Owen. She sensed a degree of discomfort on both their parts. Julia was melancholy when Owen or Douglas were nearby or discussed. The group moved out and the climb claimed Kitty's attention. The ride was demanding and she was grateful she had been in the saddle several times of late. She hoped Georgiana would not be too sore.

After a time, the squire announced, "Ladies and gentlemen, we have arrived." The sweeping view stole Kitty's breath. The valley was a brilliant green and the river sparkled like the stars. The sun was now gaining in the sky.

Andrew rode up beside her. "Beautiful, is it not?" he said, taking in the view with her. "Much study can be done here, on either side of the river. The rock on one side is composed of limestone, and on the other side of gritstone. Some areas are thought to be old coral reefs, once part of an ancient sea."

Kitty looked at him with admiration. "There is so much to be known about the world. My desire to read and learn is greatly increased after visiting a place such as this. Thank you for sharing some your knowledge."

"Nearby are caves that beckon one to explore. There are many such in the limestone formations."

"I have never seen a real cave up close," Kitty mused.

"We have no time for cave exploring today. Perhaps another outing can be arranged at a cave that has been examined and deemed safe. Caves are not to be explored lightly. Some lead nowhere. Some are an endless maze; explorers can become lost. Some are underground waterways. Caves are always flooding or falling in on themselves."

Kitty shuddered. Like a horse, she feared being trapped in any enclosure—or underground.

"Perhaps cave exploring is not for me," she said with a dubious expression.

Andrew chuckled, then changed the subject.

"The day grows warm. The cool of the oak woods will be welcome before our climb towards Nob Cave, where we will picnic. Near there are castle ruins. We will find some mysterious stone circles as well." His eyes sparkled.

"No wonder people recommend touring the Peaks!" Kitty exclaimed in rapture. "So many beauties and mysteries."

"Indeed there are, Miss Bennet," he said, looking at her with a sly smile. "Indeed there are."

Kitty pondered Andrew's remark as they began their descent to the woods.

The coolness found in the shade of the oaks was exceedingly welcome. The riders stopped for the horses to drink and took their own refreshment whilst they admired the cliffs and ridges looming above. Fishermen could be seen here and there at points along the river. Darcy watched them with great interest. Andrew was showing Kitty the patterns of how moss grew on trees when Christopher spoke to the group.

"I have developed a great appetite. Let us make haste up the hill and finish this ride." His horse danced with impatience.

"No!" Darcy said emphatically. "We have ladies with us, Mr. Drake. We shall arrive in good time, and it is best we all arrive in safety, on uninjured horses. Take another drink and cool off."

Lady Drake frowned at her son. "It is never wise to put others, or horses, at peril. You know this."

Christopher scowled and turned his back on the group.

Andrew, still beside Kitty, shook his head.

Kitty wondered about the friendships between the five young men she had met. By her observation, they seemed none too cordial. Even those who were brothers were markedly different in attitude and manner. Perhaps Julia could enlighten her about the men and their backgrounds. More than castle ruins and stone circles now piqued Kitty's interest.

≈

Three coaches and three wagons greeted the morning explorers when they gained the summit. Further on, rugs and cushions were set out in the shade of an obliging beech. Servants gathered at the wagons, filling the food trays.

Lizzy waved gaily at Kitty and she waved back. There were stable lads to see to the horses, but Kitty would tend to Cara herself.

Lady Drake was of the same mind and greeted Kitty with a smile as she situated Cara nearby.

"You are a true horsewoman, Miss Bennet. I, too, personally ensure that my dear Seraphin is happily situated before I seek my own comfort."

"They depend upon us, do they not, my lady?"

"Indeed they do. And we must honor that trust, no matter the cost, I say."

Kitty and Lady Drake walked arm in arm towards the picnic.

Darcy joined them after also seeing to his mount.

"You do me proud, Kitty," he said with an approving nod. "You will have Cara's lifelong devotion, I am certain of it."

He seated himself on one side of Lizzy so Kitty settled herself on the other.

"You look exhilarated—and exhausted!" Lizzy exclaimed.

"Indeed, I am both. But Lizzy, have you seen this country yourself? So many wonders and mysteries, such dramatic scenery. The rolling hills of Hertfordshire have their own kind of beauty, of course, but this land is so ... surprising! At every turn there is an expansive view or a great formation to be wondered at."

Lizzy looked at her fondly. "I am glad you are finding so much to enjoy. The first year of our marriage, Darcy gallantly guided me on many such outings and I, too, was awed by the drama this landscape affords. This love of the land appears to be one that you and I share more deeply than I was ever aware. I wish I had included you on more of my rambles about Long-bourn. Although I must own that a solo walk was sometimes my only course for preserving my peace of mind. Our household was often in uproar."

They laughed together at those memories.

"How well I remember. Often it was some disagreement between Lydia and me. She seemed to get her way with everyone around her," Kitty finished quietly, noticing others were now joining them. "I wonder if she is pleased with her way of life?" Kitty whispered, more to herself than to anyone else.

Lizzy pursed her lips and cocked her head.

Lady Stapleton and her three younger girls descended onto the picnic rugs, and many happy conversations began at once. Georgiana and Matilda Stapleton sat together, of course, with a delighted Benjamin Drake at the side of his undeclared beloved. Not an avid horseman, he had accompanied Lizzy in the coach. Christopher Drake sat next to his mother, but kept a roving eye on the young ladies surrounding him.

Mrs. Wyndham made a dramatic production of settling upon multiple cushions under a large propped parasol, fanning herself and complaining of the heat. In contrast to her mother's puckered countenance, Lucy Jamison's face was bright and her eye ranged eagerly amongst the young gentlemen, pausing on Christopher more often than not.

Servants with laden trays were nearing the picnickers when the sound of approaching hooves caused all to look up. Owen shot to his feet, followed by Mr. Wyndham. A look passed between them after which Owen reluctantly resumed his seat, which was straight across from Kitty.

Mr. Wyndham exchanged a look with Darcy, then said, "My son has arrived. I shall help him see to his horse." Douglas had not traveled in the coach with his stepmother and stepsister, as had been arranged. Kitty saw a speaking look pass between Owen and Julia—a look of presage—but the food was being served so questions would have to wait.

Mr. Wyndham and Douglas Wyndham returned presently, and the picnic began in earnest.

The variety of sandwiches and fruits and cold meats was especially welcomed by the morning riders. Therefore, the bulk of the early conversation was left to those who had arrived by carriage, and they had little to say for themselves about a carriage ride. Some did ask questions of those who had been on the morning adventure.

When the intensity of eating had lessened, and fruits and cakes were being nibbled upon, the conversation brightened.

"The best way to know the land is to travel it on horseback," declared the squire, bringing out his pipe but not lighting it.

"While horseback is certainly preferable to a carriage for exploring, I am a great advocate of coming to know the land by my own two feet," Lizzy opined.

"I do remember hearing, whilst in Hertfordshire, that you were known as a *great walker*, my dear," Darcy teased.

"Indeed I was, and proud to claim it!" Lizzy cried, holding up her glass to cheers and laughter. Lizzy was as well-liked here as she had been in Hertfordshire. Kitty's heart filled with gladness for her sister to have found such a congenial neighborhood.

Still fussing with her cushions, Mrs. Wyndham was neither conversant nor congenial. Her complaints about the heat did lessen when some clouds drifted in and gave periodic relief from the intensity of the sunlight.

The servants came round with wine and ale. Douglas instantly held up his glass for more, but at a withering look from his father lowered it unfilled.

Julia looked uncomfortable. As a diversion, Kitty voiced a request.

"Squire, before we begin exploring, might you tell us some of the stories about this area? I have been informed, by a very reliable source"—she looked pointedly at Georgiana—"that you are famous for imparting great life into the old legends."

Georgiana, with a mouthful of lemon pound cake, tittered and covered her face.

The squire roared with laughter.

"Miss Georgiana has been spreading my reputation as a bard, has she? And I always had to take such care, when she was a wee one, not to make the tales too frightening as she was such a skittish little thing." He laughed again.

Lucy piped up. "I have told Miss Bennet the tale of Benwick Castle. But tell us, Squire, has Captain Benwick ever found a new bride? Have any young ladies gone missing from the site?" she asked, her eyes afire with her relish for mystery.

"I am not the only one who knows these tales," the squire replied, looking at Mr. Darcy and then at Mr. Wyndham.

"But I believe my sister is right, Squire," Darcy countered. "You have a gift for imparting such drama to old stories. Do regale us with a tale."

"Ho! My circle of fame widens. Very well. Now, Miss Jamison, you ask of Captain Benwick and his search for a bride?" He gazed off in the distance for a dramatic pause.

"It seems Captain Benwick learnt his lesson and is most scrupulous in choosing his next bride. He seeks a young lady of honor, and of course great beauty. Any of ye young ladies present might do. They say that when the captain catches sight of such a young lady as he desires, the ancient gods pull the clouds over the sun in approval of his choice. Such a young lady might then be caught unawares in the diminished light and lose her footing. Should she fall, and her hand come in contact with Benwick's signet ring—which was cut from his hand in the fray, but never found—she shall come under his spell and will be deemed his betrothed, soon to join him in the nether world."

Just then a cloud drifted across the face of the sun and there were many gasps from the squire's enthralled listeners.

The squire's mouth twitched at the corners.

"Yes, Miss Jamison, young ladies go missing every year hereabouts. There are many dangers, natural and otherwise: lovers' triangles and betrayals, elopements, and even Lovers' Leap. Who can say if one of the missing has become Captain Benwick's bride?" He began to fiddle with his pipe, his eyes twinkling with merriment at his audience's rapt attention.

After a few moments of silence Matilda said, "Papa, please tell us, what of the barrows?" She grasped Georgiana's hand in a glee of fearfulness. "Who is buried in them? And the cairns? Who made them? And why?"

He looked around slowly at each face in the group.

"The cairns are mostly waymarks, left by ancient or recent travelers—some earthly ... some not."

Matilda gasped.

"Whilst some stone piles do point the way, some send travelers astray, to who knows what end? As for the barrows—now those were made by ancient peoples; a tradition that some say simply grew out of the need to bury loved ones on such rocky ground as this. But," he said as he studied the pipe in his hands, "some say the barrows signify far more. Sites of burial, yes; but also sites of possession, or of healing in the old ways ... and in other, unexplainable ways. There are rumors of treasure buried within the barrows, guarded by malevolent wights. Some say such tombs mark the entrance to the faerie realm. Who knows? None can tell, for those who have gone there do not return ..." His eyes held a mischievous spark.

But suddenly his mien changed, turning uncharacteristically serious.

"However ... I *do* believe there is a power in the very stone here—an ancient power for good or ill. It is not to be trifled with. Some hereabouts, who know the old ways, can draw great power from the stone." He looked intently into each pair of eyes that watched him.

"And this also I caution you—do not move the stones from the entrance to a barrow, nor step over any such stones yourself. For my part, I do not wish to parley with faeries or wights."

For a moment, no one spoke.

Then Mr. Wyndham's voice was heard. "And take care to pass a barrow only on the west. I heard this warning as a lad, and thought it only an old wives' tale. But since then I have seen it done—consistently—by horses at liberty. They pass the barrows only on the west, even if inconvenient. They must have a reason for doing so. I regard their wisdom."

The softer melody of Lady Drake's voice came forth with another caution.

"And pray, never circle round a barrow, or a church—especially not *widdershins*, you know, counter the clock. Evil events await those who do. In the ancient tale of Burd Helen, that was how she accidentally opened the door to the spirit world."

Scattered clouds again passed over the sun, and the group fell silent. An unexplained chill caused Kitty to tremble, and she cast her eyes to the ground.

After a few moments Lizzy said, "I did not know you were learned in lore, Lady Drake."

The squire and Lady Drake exchanged a subtle glance.

Then Lady Drake spoke again. "Signs may be read by any whose eyes are open, Mrs. Darcy. Assistance may be summoned on many levels. Knowledge is a tool of particular benefit to those who do not easily wield a sword."

An eerie feeling passed amongst the group. They looked at each other uneasily. No one offered up other conversation, and the silence shrouded all those sheltering under the great beech. Kitty sought Owen's face and found some comfort in his steady grey eyes.

Mrs. Wyndham broke the mood with an imperious sniff. "Well, in my opinion, we have been sitting far too long. Let us walk under the sun and sky whilst we may."

Clouds were congregating far to the west. Kitty noticed Darcy watching them too.

"Then let us make for the castle site," urged Lucy. "I have heard much to thrill me; now I wish to see for myself."

Matilda and Georgiana joined her, and Benjamin quickly caught up to them. Followed by Christopher and Douglas, they all hurried off. Kitty and Julia followed more slowly, accompanied by Andrew Stapleton and Owen Wyndham.

The older gentlemen attended their ladies, with Lady Drake and Mrs. Goode partnering for the excursion. The sun had again escaped the clouds, and the squire's tales seemed to dissipate like the mist.

CHAPTER SIXTEEN

The walk to the site took the explorers through small copses and sunny clearings. A freshening breeze dispersed the heat of the afternoon. Soon the ruins were visible. Parts of three outer walls remained of the structure, none of substantial height except the north wall. A few crumbling lines of stone indicated where some rooms may have been situated. The entire area was strewn with rocky debris. A short distance to the west, three barrows marched from south to north.

"A somber bunch we are," Andrew observed as the four settled on one of the lower walls. "Were my father's tales too frightening?"

"I am sure the tales were new only to me," Kitty said. "And I have heard such before. We have our own of Hertfordshire, such as the headless horse at Burnham Green and the hauntings at Minsden Chapel. Tales of mystery are not new to me, although the squire does have a way of spinning the yarn, making it more frightful yet more enticing at the same time."

Owen chuckled. "That he does. He has an entertaining way with tales and songs."

"How lucky you are to have such a father," Kitty said, glancing at Julia.

Julia looked at her curiously.

Kitty faltered a moment. "Oh, I mean he seems such a fun

father, and so kind. My own father boasts a sharp wit himself, but he often directs it in ways that are ... less generous," she mused, almost to herself.

To her surprise, Owen covered her hand with his and gave it a light squeeze.

Then Andrew spoke. "I did observe your father at the Red Lantern, Kitty, if only for a short time. I had wished him to be more attentive to you in such a place. It was almost as if you were alone. I had a small battle within myself to abstain from coming to your aid and comfort."

Kitty turned to him in surprise. "I had no idea I had been in your thoughts to that extent, sir."

"How could a gentleman not think of you, Miss Bennet?"

Owen's grip tightened on Kitty's hand.

"Hear, hear, Stapleton. On that very subject we are in strong agreement. But sometimes our fathers have burdens of which we know naught. They may not mean to slight us," Owen offered.

"Indeed. And sometimes those burdens *are* known, or are suspected by others, even if not divulged," Andrew remarked thoughtfully.

Julia looked over at Owen, and then at her brother.

"I am sure you two have burdens of your own, even now as young men, do you not?"

Andrew looked at Owen and then at Kitty and Julia.

"We do indeed. And our burden at present is to be sure we promenade on the west side of those barrows so as to avoid any encounters with wights. I am willing to defend you ladies from any human foe, but with wayward spirits I possess no wisdom and claim no power," Andrew said with a brighter attitude.

The other young people nearby were bent to the ground.

"What is this about, Matilda?" her sister asked.

"We search for the signet ring. So as to avoid it, of course!"

Christopher leapt onto the lowest of the walls and began to walk it like a tightrope.

"I wonder how high these battlements were at one time? High enough to afford a view of the far-off sea?" He laughed uproariously at his own joke. "Ah, to have been a knight in the days of old!" He feigned swordplay, then began to scramble up the side of the high north wall.

"No, Christopher!" Lucy cried out. "The stone … it is crumbling and unstable. It is a long way to fall."

"Nonsense. A knight of old knows no fear; especially when there are foes to be fought, or a charming damsel in need of rescue." He spun around on the span to demonstrate his courage —or his foolishness.

"Miss Jamison is right. This stone is very old," Andrew said. "Were I a bird I would not trust it, Drake. Do come down and spare the ladies a bloody spectacle."

"Oh, very well … when you put it that way. And I would not wish to alarm my mother, with my father in Town these two weeks. Let us wander down a path I have espied leading into the woods. My mother spoke of a stone circle in a clearing that way."

Both groups turned to set off. Andrew looked back and called out to Douglas.

"Wyndham, are you coming? Mr. Owen, what is your brother up to?"

Owen shrugged.

"Come, man. Leave off there and join us for a walk to the stones."

Douglas had been leaning against the edge of the west wall. He turned away and took a drink from a flask, then clumsily slid it into his waistcoat.

"A circle of stones … wouldn't wanna miss that," he said with a slur.

Julia scowled. "Come!" she hissed to Andrew, and strode off as he grabbed at his hat in an effort to keep up with her.

Benjamin and Matilda had commanded both Georgiana's arms so Douglas offered Lucy his unsteady arm.

She sighed loudly. "Oh, Douglas, do find your self control." Though obviously irritated by her stepbrother's unrestrained imbibing, when Christopher took her other arm her mood recovered. She whispered something to him and giggled into his shoulder.

The older members of the party had preceded the younger to the stone circle and were standing in small groups talking quietly.

Lizzy gazed contentedly at the surrounding woods as the sun dappled the leaves. The bucolic setting belied the attested violence of the legend.

Several stones, none more than knee high, formed a semi-circle with an opening that faced down the path towards the castle ruins. These were a few strides apart, as if standing in perpetual vigil. Some were nearly obscured by the flush of new grass. Five or six strides from the semi-circle, two taller stones—nearly waist-high to a man had they been upright—lay on the ground with the smaller ends touching, both pointing towards the semi-circle of guardian stones. And then, a sword's reach away, stood a single stone, nearly Kitty's height, divided at the top, with the shorter protrusion aimed at the fallen stones. It remained upright but leaned precariously. Kitty recalled Lucy's tale with a shiver.

The sunset was still hours off but the orb had traveled halfway down the western sky. Kitty suddenly felt more than eager for everyone to be delivered safely home.

"Human actions immortalized in stone," wagged Andrew. "Which of your actions would you wish immortalized?" he asked the group.

No one replied.

"It is sobering to think how one small action can change the course of a life, or many lives—even the course of history," Owen said, staring at the site.

"Bah! You lot are dull indeed," Douglas said, stomping away with an unsteady gait. The other followed in a pensive mood.

Once the group returned to the picnic site, final refreshments were enjoyed and traveling bottles refilled. The breeze had stilled and the clouds in the west were building; it would not be many hours until the clouds devoured the sun as it dipped lower in the sky.

The servants began to clear the site and pack the wagons whilst those family members riding in the coaches made ready to leave. Horses were harnessed or bridled and saddled. The group of horseback riders would travel with the coaches on the return trip; all were weary from the challenge of the morning.

"Ride with me, Kitty," Julia urged, leading her horse up next to Kitty's. Julia's face held an intense expression.

"I should like that," Kitty replied.

Georgiana chose to return in the coach with Lizzy and Benjamin, which Kitty deemed wise considering Georgiana's lack of recent riding. Her horse was tethered behind the coach and could happily walk or trot along.

Mrs. Wyndham's plaintive voice was heard.

"Those clouds are menacing, Mr. Wyndham. It's violence will be unleashed upon us soon, mark my words. Do stay close to the coach, my love."

≈

Once the coaches and riders descended from the picnic site, the road rolled gently and meandered easily around rocky outcroppings or large trees. The party crossed a few bridges over gurgling rills swollen with late spring rains.

The canopies of the coaches had been lowered for easier conversation. The day had been pleasant and the group amenable, until Kitty overheard Christopher goading Douglas,. Christopher's loud guffaws carried on the breeze. For two gentlemen who traveled often together, they got on poorly.

The breeze rose and the clouds crept up behind the party. Kitty glanced back but felt sure they would be home long before the rain reached them.

At the rear, Douglas was scowling at Christopher. Near the middle coach, the squire and Andrew were in conversation, but Kitty could not hear their words over Matilda's incessant chatting with anyone who would listen.

Julia was quietly studying the landscape and Kitty settled comfortably into her own saddle to enjoy this easier ride along the road, being at leisure to take in the many beauties of the greener land in the serene valley. Estates and farms dotted the countryside; some nestled in the folds of the land, others perched boldly on a high point to command a view.

"That one, over there," Christopher shouted.

Kitty turned to see him pointing to the steeple of a church.

"A betting man unwilling to wager on himself? Ha! Now I've heard it all." Christopher's sneering tone caused several in the party to turn their heads.

Douglas' face was red and strained.

"You know I can beat you, Drake, blindfolded even," he said, his voice rising in anger.

Kitty was startled at the wrathful tone.

Julia did not turn. Her face was set and her eyes hard, but her lip quivered.

"Julia, whatever is the matter?" Kitty asked.

Her friend continued to stare straight ahead.

The loud voices also drew Andrew's attention, and he rode back to quell the disturbance.

"Here now, gentlemen. We are committed to seeing our ladies safely home. Mr. Drake, perhaps you can ride near Miss Jamison's carriage and carry on a more pleasant conversation there."

"The devil take you, Drake. The wager is on!" Douglas pulled his horse out to the side.

Andrew protested. "Wyndham, no. Come, man, ride with me, or the squire ..."

"Pull out, Drake!" Douglas hollered. "To the steeple and back. On your mark, ready, go!" He leaned forward and was off.

Julia gasped.

Squire Stapleton jerked to attention at the commotion.

The other horses in the party danced and pawed.

Christopher bolted after Douglas and, at a nod from the squire, Andrew urged his horse to follow.

"Squire, what is this?" Darcy called back, directing the coaches to halt.

"Hopefully, a very short steeplechase." The furrow in his brow belied his playful words.

"A steeplechase?" cried Lucy, her eyes wide. "How bold!"

Darcy frowned at her. "How foolish I should say. These horses are already tired, and none have been in training for jumps so early this season. The ground is boggy. Wyndham, what can we do?"

Mr. Wyndham's face was flushed in mortification.

"Ride by my carriage if you will, Darcy. Owen and I shall go out to meet them on their return. Pray, keep the party together."

"I too will meet them," said Lady Drake, pulling out to the side. "This is most ill-advised. My son shall know my feelings on his return, be assured." Her face was stony as her eyes followed the progress of the steeplechasers, who had become mere dots in the landscape. Only the most far-sighted could see them as they neared the steeple.

Kitty turned to Julia, whose face was ashen.

"You care for him, do you not?" she whispered.

A tear rolled down her friend's face.

"I did, so greatly. I still do. But he is in such a state. I have lost him to his pain and sorrow. There is naught I can do." She sniffed and pulled back her shoulders with an effort. Another tear escaped and trickled down her cheek.

Kitty knew not how to comfort her friend.

Meanwhile, the source of that sorrow was circling the church steeple ... *widdershins*.

CHAPTER SEVENTEEN

"The riders are returning," cried Lucy, "but I cannot tell who is in the lead."

As they drew closer, Douglas reeled in the saddle, throwing his horse off-balance. Both went down directly in Christopher's path, causing his horse to swerve madly and fall, tossing him out of the saddle. Andrew was coming from farther behind and had time to check his horse by arcing widely. Mr. Wyndham and Owen raced to the scene. Some of the females in the carriages screamed and covered their eyes.

Lady Drake was off, riding hard to her son. Darcy followed.

The squire rode to the front of the group and stayed the carriages.

"We may need transport for the injured," he said to no one in particular.

Both of the downed horses regained their feet, but one limped badly. Christopher was up now, walking well enough to get hold of his horse. One arm was pinched to his side. All that could be seen of Douglas was a lump on the ground.

Kitty looked wildly at the squire, then caught the motion of a rider speeding towards them. It was Owen.

"It's bad, sir," he reported to the squire, breathless. "Douglas is unconscious. His horse fell on him and both his legs are askew. We must have help at once!"

"We have only women here, son. I cannot ride away and leave them unguarded on the road. There is only Benjamin and myself."

"I cannot leave my brother." Owen's eyes flew to Kitty.

Instantly she knew his mind.

"Send me, Squire!" she offered in a bold voice. "I know the direction from here. Pemberley is closest, is it not?"

The squire looked hard at her. "Send a lady across country? Alone?"

"I can ride astride, sir, and like the wind."

His brows lifted at this admission, and he looked in Lizzy's direction. When Lizzy quietly nodded her assent, the squire gave his approval.

"Miss Bennet, take my horse," cried Owen. "You can manage him. Ride to Pemberley. Tell Connor what has happened. Give him our direction. Have someone ride for the nearest surgeon—Wilson will know best."

As he spoke, she slipped from her saddle and handed her reins to Julia, whose face was stricken. Kitty looked from Lizzy to Julia and back. *You must help Julia!* she communicated wordlessly to her sister.

Lizzy nodded her understanding.

Owen gave Kitty a leg up onto his great grey gelding.

She adjusted her skirts as best she could and looked around to fix the location in her mind.

"I will manage Cara," he assured her. "Ride fast, Miss Bennet. May God go with you!"

After a last look into Owen's eyes, Kitty and the great grey were away like a phantom.

≈

The ride cross-country was a blur. What if Douglas were dead? Poor Mr. Wyndham. Poor Julia. Owen's horse had a long stride and flattened into it, covering ground more swiftly than Kitty had ever done before. The crossroads soon appeared, as did the gate Darcy had struggled with that morning. It was closed. She gulped and aimed the horse directly at the gate. He seemed to know her intent and gathered himself for the jump. Kitty felt his muscles bunch under her and with a powerful thrust from his hocks he left the ground. They sailed over the gate, horse and rider flying as one, and she instinctively leaned forward to give him his head. He had done this before. He stretched out for the landing and continued on as if the gate had been only a small log. They flew across the field and were at the stables in minutes.

"Mr. Connor! Mr. Connor!" Kitty cried, gasping for breath. A young lad appeared, followed by Johnny.

Her face was ablaze and Johnny ran to her in alarm, grasping the bridle and circling the horse calmly.

"Mr. Connor, help is needed!"

Riley Connor came trotting around the corner. His eyes widened at the sight of her, and at the horse she was riding.

"What's this?"

Kitty was still breathless but managed to impart the severity of the accident and the location.

Mr. Connor barked orders, and the whole stable yard mobilized in a trice.

"Mr. Owen says to send Johnny. And for Wilson to send for the surgeon or ..."

Mr. Connor nodded to Johnny, who sped off.

"Can ye ride yet to the house, Miss? Tell Wilson. He will know who to send for and will make the note. Bring it here and young Lucas will take it. Then we shall see to you and the horse. Mr. Owen's, is he not?"

Kitty nodded and turned for the house. A footman emerged at the first sound of hooves, and she cried for him to summon Wilson, who appeared in a moment. After hearing her need, he ran in and returned with a note. She reached for it and wheeled to make for the stables again. Her breath was slowing but her heart still raced. She delivered the missive, and young Lucas leapt onto a readied horse and was away.

"There, Miss. Our lads have gone. I sent lads also to Cedars and Greystone with a report. Help shall be on the way from many quarters. 'Tis in the hands of Providence now. Let me help ye down." A stable lad took the grey's reins.

Mr. Connor set Kitty on her feet, but her legs collapsed under her. He caught her in time, scooped her up, and carried her to a bench between two trees where he gently set her down.

"Do not move," he said and rushed to the barn whilst she reclined, trying to steady her heart.

Mr. Connor returned with a warm blanket, a bottle, and an apple.

"Like a horse after a race, Miss. A nice blanket, a little rest, something to drink, and a sweet treat—ye'll be good as new."

Kitty smiled at his analogy, and did not object being compared to a racehorse. After a drink and a few bites of the apple, she was improved and sat up to finish them.

Mr. Connor sat beside her in silence. He was old enough to be her grandfather, and she appreciated his kindly ways.

"Now ye must walk, Miss. A cool down, aye?"

When she nodded, he called out, "Roger! Roger, here, lend us an arm. A walk will be good for ye, Miss." Leaning on the two of them, she walked slowly to the house. There two footmen helped her up the stairs where Poppy was ready to attend her. Her riding habit was removed, along with her half boots, and she stepped into a readied bath. Once wrapped into a warm robe, she returned to the sitting room.

"Do you wish for tea, Miss? Something to eat?"

"Tea would be wonderful, Poppy. And something light, perhaps a sandwich? I shall dine when the others return."

Poppy had propped the pillows just so and Kitty leaned back, sinking into the comforting softness. Her body was ready to rest, but her mind fretted about the others—those who had been hurt, and those who loved them.

Soon Poppy appeared with a tray, and Kitty moved to the small table and chair.

"Why, Poppy, how thoughtful. You have also brought my favorite biscuits. Thank you."

"Yer welcome, Miss." Poppy sat with her whilst she ate, and Kitty appreciated her watchful eye, although she had now regained almost her full strength.

"I fear I may be quite sore tomorrow, Poppy. Not just the race for help. But also the morning ride, it was challenging. Some very rough terrain, but so beautiful. Do you know the area around the Edge above the River Derwent?"

"Aye. Me sister lives over that way. Very lovely it is with the high peaks and the green river valley. Her husband greatly enjoys the fishing."

Kitty chuckled. "I saw Mr. Darcy watching the fishermen, and he looked quite envious. He even proposed a fishing expedition to be the next outing." She took another sip of tea and a last bite of biscuit.

Less pleasant thoughts took hold again, and her worries for the others returned.

"Oh, Poppy, I believe Mr. Douglas is seriously injured. The whole episode was ... well, I'd rather not speak of it. There's nothing to do now but wait, I suppose."

A knock at the door produced a servant who announced the carriage had returned. Minutes later Lizzy and Georgiana burst into the room. Poppy curtsied and left, taking the tray.

Georgiana rushed to Kitty's side and took her hands.

"Oh, Kitty, how brave you were. Are you all right? You look a little pale."

Lizzy scrutinized her sister. "Are you injured?"

"No, not at all. I am well. Please, sit. And tell me what happened after I left. Are all alive? Will all recover?"

"There is mostly good news," Lizzy reassured her. "But not all. Christopher has injured his shoulder in a most painful way; but other than that, he is well. Darcy says his horse pulled a stifle but will recover with treatment. Andrew was not injured, nor was his horse. The extent of Douglas' injuries is not yet known. He is being taken to Matlock, which is the nearest surgeon. Pity that; it is some way off. He did regain consciousness a few times but could not move on his own, or speak. Sadly, his horse paid the gravest price and had to be destroyed. Darcy said his leg was shattered beyond mending, and suspected an injury to the spine as well. It angers Darcy when a horse is harmed by such carelessness. He is furious."

"And what of the Wyndhams?" Kitty asked.

"I will not address the female Wynhams as there is not much to tell beyond hysteria. But Mr. Wyndham is understandably distraught. His eldest son has been struggling with some severe problems of a mental and spiritual nature. It seems he has never been the same since his mother died. He was the first to come down with the fever that took her and his little sister. He himself recovered, but he shoulders the blame for their deaths, and for his father's loss. In addition, we believe he and Mr. Christopher have taken up with a fast crowd and may be involved in some questionable activities. The Drakes are not happy about that."

Lizzy paused a moment, looking both girls directly in the eye.

"All this of which I speak is of a most confidential nature, and is not to be revealed to anyone or spoken of at all, except to me."

"Of course," Kitty replied.

"Yes," said Georgiana.

"As I'm sure you became aware during our dinner with the Wyndhams, Douglas has been drinking to excess. This has clouded his judgment and he is angry most of the time. Liquor can be a demon once it takes hold. His choice today was care- less. If he survives, it is likely he will never walk again."

Both girls gasped.

"Whatever the outcome, we Darcys are in full support of the Wyndhams—Mr. Wyndham and Mr. Owen especially. Mr. Wyndham and Darcy are very thick. Oh, it is all too much to contemplate." She shook her head, then looked closely at her sister again.

"Kitty, how are you feeling now?"

"At first, I was exhausted. Mr. Connor was most helpful, providing me with drink, a blanket, and an apple. He even carried me to a bench to rest! Then he and one of his lads walked me here to the house. Darcy's staff is exemplary; everyone knew exactly what to do. I am so grateful."

"And we are all grateful to you for making that daring ride," Georgiana said. "But how did Mr. Owen know you could do such a thing? He seemed so sure ..."

Lizzy lifted a brow. "Does this have to do with the delay the other morning, Kitty? I had forgotten to ask you more about that."

Kitty looked at the two of them and took a deep breath.

"Now is *my* turn to swear the two of you to secrecy. Lizzy, you may, of course, enlighten Fitzwilliam if you think it necessary. But I do not wish to cause trouble for Johnny; he has been most kind and helpful—and honorable." She proceeded to tell them of her secret rides astride around Pemberley, disguised as a boy, and her pact with Johnny. Then she told of their accidental meeting with Owen and the broken down wagon.

Georgiana's eyes grew large. "I am incredulous, Kitty. I don't even know what to say. Not only are you brave, you are most determined."

Lizzy did not appear so shocked. "I had no specific suspicions of your riding style, Kitty, but I am not wholly surprised to hear this. You have a great deal more spirit than anyone around Longbourn or Meryton might have guessed. And now Mr. Owen knows your secret, and the squire will guess it. He appears jolly on the surface but he is shrewd, and wise. I admire him greatly. You risked not only your safety, but also your reputation by making this ride to Pemberley. We shall see what becomes of it." She looked at Kitty soberly. Then she winked, with one eye.

"Oh, Lizzy, thank you. Then I can count on you to stand behind me?"

"Indeed you can."

"And I," Georgiana declared.

Another knock came at the door.

"Mrs. Darcy, if you please, Mr. Darcy has arrived and requests your company, and that of the young ladies, in his book room. If Miss Bennet is able?"

"Thank you. Please tell him we shall all come directly."

The three exchanged expectant looks. Kitty changed her robe for a frock. Then they left to discover the master's opinion concerning the day's events.

≈

The room was subdued when they entered, lit only by a small fire and the rosy hue of a cloud-filled sunset through the window adjacent to Darcy's great desk. The other walls were covered with books. Kitty had been told these were estate books and books of a personal nature to the family, not for public perusal.

"Come in, ladies," Darcy said, motioning for them to sit. Standing at the hearth, he once again seemed a formidable figure as he stared into the fire. Kitty and Georgiana settled onto the settee. Lizzy chose a wingback chair. No one spoke for some little time.

Kitty's heart pounded. Was he angry with her? Would he send her away? How much had he learnt of her secret? How much should she tell him? She twirled and untwirled her handkerchief until it was damp and shapeless.

Darcy walked to the window and stood looking out for a time, then chose a chair and turned it away from the fire to face them. His face was shrouded.

"Kitty," he began in a measured voice, "however did you manage that gate?"

Her mind reeled. This was not the question she had expected. There was nothing for it but to tell the truth. She swallowed hard to steady her voice.

"We jumped it. I remembered your difficulty with it when we departed and judged haste to be crucial. Owen's horse, being long-legged and rangy and very athletic ... well, I determined it would be best."

"That blasted gate!" he muttered. He stared long at her, and she looked down in confusion.

"And the horse? How did he manage it?"

She jerked her head up at this second question, also unexpected.

"Very well. He sailed over it with ease and continued on the run up to the stables. I detected no unsoundness in him as the lad walked him out after I dismounted. I hope I have done no harm."

"And you? How do you fare after all this?"

"I was only exhausted for a short time. After the attentive care from your stable and house staff, I am now very well."

"Good, good. That is just what I hoped to hear—no harm done. Connor says Owen's horse is well after—"

"Cara? Is she all right?"

Darcy smiled at her concern. "Yes, Cara is settled in with a flake of hay and some mash."

He then looked at Lizzy with concern. "And you, my dear wife? Has all this uproar caused you any discomfort? Any illness? Do you need to rest?"

"No, my dear, I am also very well." She smiled at him warmly. "And very proud of my sister. She has risked much in this daring ride."

"She has indeed," he said thoughtfully. He rose and poured himself a brandy. "Do you ladies desire a tot of brandy after this trying day? Georgiana, please ring the bell."

Darcy lit the table lamp and poured the brandy. In moments a tray with light fare was brought to the room. As Lizzy poured herself tea, Darcy turned to her.

"And have you apprised Kitty of the events after her winged departure?"

"I have, in brief. Is there further news?"

"No, not yet. I shall ride to Greystone early tomorrow unless we have news by messenger." He swirled the brandy in his glass and took a drink. "Mr. Wyndham accompanies his injured son to Matlock. Mr. Owen will stay and care for his stepmother and sister, and the estate."

Darcy turned his focus to Kitty again.

"I am pleased to hear your compliments of Pemberley's staff. We train rigorously for such emergencies and are grateful Providence has spared us the need to test our readiness often. One thing puzzles me, however. That is, why you have felt the need to keep a crucial secret from me? To bear it alone? What can you mean by this, Kitty?"

Kitty's eyes darted to Lizzy, who was studying Darcy's face and thus imparted no counsel.

"Truly I meant no disrespect to you, Fitzwilliam. I did not wish to burden you with my passionate—but socially unacceptable—habit and thought it likely beneath your notice as long as it was kept secret. Please do not think ill of Johnny. He is such an honorable lad and quick to help—first Mr. Owen with the broken down wagon, and now the accident. He is saving the tips I give him towards the purchase of a beloved mare; that is, when there is money left after paying for his sister's medical needs. Oh, please ..."

Darcy held up his hand. "Enough. I have been apprised of the wagon incident. Johnny will be well rewarded for his quick thinking and fast action then and today. And I will fully fund his sister's care. I hope to someday make Johnny the stable master of Pemberley. He has been honorable and kept your secret. But Mr. Connor is not so easily fooled and was aware of your 'habit' from nearly the beginning. He informed me at once, but in a manner of such kindness that I allowed it to continue. His heart holds a soft spot for you, Kitty. He had a daughter, who would be about your age now, or a little older. She had a passion for horses, as you have. She died in childbed a few years ago. The youngest lad you see around the stables, little Ike, is Connor's grandson. So your secret has been known for some time by a privileged few. I shall neither condone it nor forbid it, but I advise you to keep it under wraps. You have my permission to carry on."

Tears of relief spilled from Kitty's eyes. "Thank you," she murmured.

Darcy looked now at Lizzy, almost as if for support, and then at the girls.

"I would wish," he began, "that both of you—Georgiana and Kitty—would not keep secrets from me. I am your brother, not your father, though my position is sometimes awkwardly poised between those. I may sometimes miss the mark. I have been told, on very good authority," he again looked at Lizzy, whose eyes danced with merriment, "yes, been told *most* affectionately, that I might at times appear ... well ... formidable." His expression conveyed surprise at this.

Kitty and Georgiana glanced at each other, trying to suppress their mirth.

"It is so then? I am seen by you as formidable? Well, however I may choose to present myself to the world, I do not wish to be formidable to my wife or my sisters. My wife, of course, does not allow such nonsense." He looked at her with a grin. "I wish you would not hesitate to come to me with your concerns. I shall try to be wise, and—if needed—impartial. And to help you in any way I can."

He took another drink of his brandy whilst looking steadily at Georgiana.

She squirmed under his steady gaze. At last she spoke.

"What is it, brother?"

"This brings me to an issue with you, little sister. I have eyes, and sensibility enough I think. Is there something you wish to tell me? Something you have, perhaps, been reluctant to share?" His eyes now held a satirical expression.

Georgiana's eyes grew large. She glanced at Kitty, who could only raise her eyebrows.

"Do you refer to a matter of my heart?"

"I do," he replied coolly. "Come, tell me more."

Twisting her ring, Georgiana took a deep breath.

"I have attempted to be most discreet. I know you are likely to disapprove. He is a second son. Not a first son nor wealthy nobility, as I am sure you have hoped." Her voice quavered. "I made some poor judgments in the past. I do not wish to repeat such errors or cause you further pain."

Darcy sighed. "My most fervent desire, dear sister, is for your happiness. I have learnt that happiness, especially domestic happiness, can sometimes come in unexpected packages," he said, with an affectionate smile at Lizzy. "And I *do* commend you. You *have* been discreet. However, young Mr. Benjamin has not. His affection for you is obvious, even to a dull stranger. He honors you, he protects you, he flourishes in your company. He even rides through the rain on the flimsiest of excuses to be near you. No, even if your behavior did not tip your hand, his has laid all the cards on the table."

"How long have you known?"

"It is hard to say. For many months now, at least. But even when younger, you had an affinity for each other's company, which I read as friendship. I will say to you what I said to Kitty. Whilst I think him a most upstanding young gentleman, I will neither condone nor forbid this blossoming romance. You have had a full season in town, and I was surprised you did not find someone in that time. Your seeming lack of interest in the whole matter puzzled me. This sheds some light. No, I only beg you to take a little more time before committing yourself."

He sat up in sudden alarm.

"Have you promised yourself?"

His intensity did not unnerve her.

"I have not. Neither has Benjamin formally declared himself. But we have long known each others' hearts."

"Be that as it may, I would wish you to wait—at least until Christmastide—to make a decision. That is time enough. Will you do that?"

"I will. Oddly enough, it is the same timeline I had set for myself."

Darkness was thick outside the window and raindrops now pattered against the pane.

"Well, Mrs. Wyndham was only slightly off in her weather prediction," Lizzy commented.

Kitty spoke. "And what of Mr. Christopher, Fitzwilliam? How is his injury? Lady Drake seemed quite severe on his behavior, and most displeased."

Darcy threw back the rest of his brandy.

"I can tell you she was *most* displeased. I would not wish to be Mr. Christopher at this moment. It seems his shoulder was dislocated in his fall. Mrs. Goode and Mr. Owen had experience with such and were able to set it right, though the process looked quite painful. He suffered no permanent harm. His behavior of late has become a thorn in the sides of Lord and Lady Drake. Their son is nine and twenty. He must be reined in, and I do not envy them that task."

With a clear brow, Darcy said, "Now, ladies, it is time for us to prepare for dinner."

As they rose, Kitty was greatly relieved to see Lizzy wink one eye.

CHAPTER EIGHTEEN

"*L*adies, I have a proposition for you," Darcy announced at breakfast one morning. "I must reply to my cousin, Mr. Alfred Cressley. He visited Pemberley last autumn. At that time I promised to come for two of his mares and bring them here for breeding. As we are nearing the end of the covering season, I must do so soon. He lives some miles this side of London, at Oakhurst Lodge."

"Kitty, as you know," Darcy said with a sly smile, "the Wyndhams have three royal mares at Greystone for breeding. Mr. Owen informs me the mares have settled and are ready to be returned to Windsor. In order to help Wyndham—who is still at Matlock with his son— I shall return those mares to Windsor and so answer two situations with one journey. Mr. Owen will accompany me."

"But what has this to do with us?" Georgiana asked as she buttered her toast.

Darcy took a deep breath. "I propose that you young ladies join me on this journey. We shall stay with my cousin at Oakhurst rather than traveling all the way to our own home in London."

"A journey? Oh, yes!" Georgiana clapped her hands in glee.

"Will you go with us, Lizzy?" Kitty asked.

Lizzy smiled complacently. "Not this time. I fear it would be uncomfortable to travel that far in my condition. I would need many stops, and I find the heat of travel in summer makes me ill, even when not carrying a child."

"A journey of our own ... an adventure, Kitty. Oh, please say yes," Georgiana implored.

Kitty stared hard at her sister. "Are you sure you do not wish me to stay with you? With Fitzwilliam gone, who will take care of you?"

Lizzy looked amused. "Fitzwilliam does not take direct care of me when he *is* here, Kitty. As much as I adore his company, I believe I shall be quite safe alone for that short time; you will be gone less than a fortnight. Mr. Benjamin will be at Cedars most of that time, except for some business at school he must attend to. And of course Lord and Lady Drake and Squire and Lady Stapleton are here. I can manage."

Darcy added, "I have also invited Mr. Christopher. As we three gentlemen will be on horseback and you will be in the coach, I thought you might each wish to invite a friend on the journey."

Darcy was ill-prepared for the screams of delight.

"Julia and Matilda!" were shouted in unison.

"A little less enthusiasm, ladies, if you please," Darcy said, taken aback.

Lizzy arched a brow at them. "Take care, girls. If you frighten him too much, he may change his mind."

Kitty and Georgiana each took a deep breath.

"There. We are ladies again. It was but a momentary lapse," Georgiana said with a laugh. "When do we depart?"

"The day after tomorrow. We shall stop in Matlock on the way to pay a visit to my uncle, the earl. We shall also call on Mr. Wyndham there to learn how Douglas gets on, and to deliver to Wyndham his wife and daughter, in their own carriage."

"What about Mr. Andrew?" Georgiana asked, with a glance at Kitty.

"He and his uncle leave for Scotland in two days," Darcy said.

This subdued the girls and they exchanged a glance. Would Andrew call and take his leave? Kitty thought he must but was puzzled he had not informed her of such plans.

"It seems a well-thought-out scheme, my dear," Lizzy said. "I shall invite Lady Stapleton and Lady Drake for visits whilst you are all gone. I will walk in the garden in the mornings, then get lost in novels during the heat of the day. I think we shall all find pleasure in our doings. And now, you young ladies should begin to pack!"

As Kitty and Georgiana made for their rooms, Wilson handed Kitty a letter.

"It is from Mama," Kitty said.

"You had best read it now, and answer if you will, before we depart. There may not be much time for writing on our journey." Georgiana made for her own apartments and Kitty for hers.

Kitty sank into the chair by her window and found she was a little reluctant to open the letter. She had never been apart from her mother and so had never received a letter from her. Would Mama's written words hold more comfort than those spoken?

Longbourn, Hertfordshire

Dear Kitty,

I have been so busy with your sister Jane that it nearly slipped my mind to answer your letter. We were all entertained by your description of the ball. I would like to have seen you open the dance, what an honor. You have always been a fine dancer. But why are you waiting to secure one of the young men? It appears there are several to chuse from. You would best make your interest known before they are snatched away by young ladies with greater fortune. In this world we must go after what we want.

I hope Lizzy is introducing you to eligible young men. Has she provided you with gowns and bonnets enough to draw their attention? I am sure the company at Pemberley can boast of high incomes and elegant lifestyles.

Your sister Mary continues her musical studies but I must say her practicing tears at my nerves. Thankfully I can travel to Netherfield nearly every day and share my confinement experiences and those of others with Jane so she is prepared. I hardly know how to wait any longer for her baby to arrive.

Lydia asks me to remind you that she desires to visit Pemberley while you are there. Did you not receive her letter? She would be sure to help you find a suitable husband.

Your papa requests I tell you that he will write when he has completed his spring tasks and gathered his thoughts. I cannot imagine what he finds to keep himself so busy, he rarely leaves his library except when he is gone on estate business. I shouldn't devote much time to that as it will all go to Mr. Collins anyway, but your father will do as he wishes I suppose.

Do write again and tell us all your news.

Your devoted mother

Kitty folded the letter, set it in her lap, and gazed out the window. Longbourn seemed far removed indeed. Her mother cared only with matrimonial results. It mattered not what Kitty herself felt or thought, about the young man or about anything else. Having been so unknown and unvalued at Longbourn, she was more grateful than ever for her visit to Pemberley.

She frowned at the thought of returning to Longbourn. Then she pushed that aside. Right now she had an exciting journey to prepare for that would be shared with her new friends. She was most fortunate indeed, and rose to ring the bell for Poppy.

≈

Rain poured down all the next day, so the distractions of packing and planning were welcome. Neither the Pemberley nor the Swan's Nest young ladies braved the rain, but servants were sent back and forth with notes about plans and gowns. None of these notes contained any greetings or good wishes from Mr. Andrew for Kitty. Would he leave without saying goodbye?

One caller did brave the rain. The afternoon before their departure, as the clouds were dispersing, Benjamin Drake arrived to take tea. Although Lizzy and Kitty were also present, he and Georgiana had eyes and conversation only for each other. Their farewell was private, and suspiciously long.

Later that day, the sun showed its full face at last. The green of the countryside was nearly blinding when the Pemberley ladies managed a stroll in the garden. Kitty then walked to the stables to see Cara and bid her farewell.

"I know you will take good care of her, Johnny," she said as they leaned on the fence and watched the horses stretching in the sun.

"She will miss you, Miss Bennet. I will keep her in form with some short rides. Shall you ride at Thornhill Manor at Matlock, or at Oakhurst Lodge?"

Kitty looked at Johnny blankly. "I do not know. Likely we will not have time at the earl's at Thornhill as we stay but one night each way. I do not know the plans at Oakhurst; but with such a breeding business they must have many horses. I hope they are not all race horses, and that we may hack into the countryside." She pursed her lips in thought.

"Shall you ride in your habit? Or in your disguise?" His eyes danced in fun.

Kitty laughed. "I shall be prepared to do both!" she cried. "One never knows who might need to be rescued."

≈

The carriage left Pemberley early the next day. Kitty received no message from Andrew. The clear skies promised a fine day so she tried to leave her disappointment behind.

"I hope it will not be too hot," Georgiana worried aloud. "I get so fatigued if I become overheated."

"The only thing to fatigue me shall be jostling around in the carriage. I would much prefer to be on horseback," Kitty said, looking with envy at the men as they rode beside, ahead of, or behind the carriages, just as they chose. The Wyndham carriage had joined them now.

"Nothing shall fatigue me," Matilda asserted. "It has been many months since I have been on a journey of any distance. I am ready to see new places and new faces, especially *handsome* new faces!"

They all laughed merrily except Julia. Since the accident, she had been even more subdued. Kitty hoped for a chance to talk with her alone, and that the trip itself might prove a pleasant diversion for her.

Kitty had been introduced to the Earl of Matlock and his family at the joint wedding of her older sisters. Other than that, she had no direct experience with anyone of title except Sir William Lucas, who was anything but formal.

Kitty turned to Georgiana. "Are there young people to be met at Thornhill?"

Georgiana knit her brow. "I seem to remember a little girl, some years younger than myself. I have heard nothing of her recently." She called out to Darcy. "Brother, is there still a young lady at Thornhill?"

Darcy rode closer to reply.

"Yes, I believe so, unless she is traveling. She is about five years your junior, Georgiana."

The young ladies then retreated to their own thoughts.

The trip to Matlock was accomplished with no difficulties and no drama, except when in Mrs. Wyndham's company. Her antics put Kitty in mind of her own mother, although Mrs. Wyndham did have a more elegant way of fretting. At least she traveled in her own carriage so the drama was not continuous. Kitty pondered the oddity of the match with Mr. Wyndham. What would have drawn them together?

A different drama—one much more welcome—was found in the landscape. Kitty marveled at the lofty cliffs that rose boldly above the River Derwent as they made their way south. A skirting of fine woods covered the lower parts of the crags. She sometimes dropt out of the conversation around her, mesmerized by the sights as they journeyed to Thornhill Manor, the seat of the Earl of Matlock.

After passing through the manor's impressive woods, they emerged into a fine park where a staff of attendants greeted them when their carriage stopped. It was past teatime, but Kitty held out hope for refreshments before the late dinner hour common in many grand houses. The butler greeted Darcy congenially, and the entire party was ushered into the drawing room and announced.

Earl and Lady Matlock rose to greet them and introductions were made.

"Cousin Alice, I am so pleased to see you again," Georgiana said, with a graceful curtsey. "It has been many years since we have met." Alice was tall but with a youthful fullness of face.

"Indeed it has," the earl said. "Alice here was but a moppet when last you two were together. Why has it been so long? And you, Miss Darcy, are now a gracious young lady. You remind me so much of your dear mother. I can almost see my sister's smile in your eyes," he said, gazing at her fondly.

"We are honored to welcome such a large party," said Lady Matlock. "Preparations and accommodations are all in hand. Are you sure you can stay only one night?"

"I am afraid it must be so. The royal mares are expected at Windsor; and the sooner I deliver them, the more relieved I shall be. Perhaps on our return journey we may be able to honor your kind invitation to stay for more than one night."

"Agreed. Now let us postpone further conversation until after you rest. We dine at nine, so I gather substantial refreshment may be welcome as soon as may be?"

"That would be most kind," Darcy said, anticipating the desires of his party.

≈

The teatime offerings were ample and delicious, and adequately dulled the travelers' sharp appetites. The group that gathered in the drawing room—after a brief rest and a change of clothing—was varied enough to break into smaller groups after general news had been shared. When the men turned to talk of hunting and politics, the ladies gathered near Lady Matlock to discuss social events, entertainments, fashions, and some news from the royal court. Kitty was enthralled by the information about royalty, especially Princess Charlotte. She had heard of her, but mostly negative comments about her lack of beauty and want of grace. Lady Matlock seemed to have a soft spot for this princess, whom she said was a great favorite with people high and low, and her eventual ascent to the throne was happily anticipated.

"Why, she is very near our ages!" exclaimed Georgiana, looking around at her friends. "I don't suppose we shall ever meet royalty in our social circle. I wonder what a royal princess does with her time?"

Lady Matlock answered. "She is said to have a passion for horses and is described as a fearless and bold rider."

"We have one such here with us!" exclaimed Matilda. A nudge from her sister reminded her to subdue such information. She ended with, "Miss Bennet is an expert horsewoman and hopes to ride to the hounds with our Lady Drake some day."

Alice turned to Kitty. "How fascinating! And how long will you stay in Derbyshire, Miss Bennet?"

"I do not know," Kitty replied. "I believe I shall stay most of the summer. Perhaps this princess will open the way for more active riding by ladies? I would welcome that. Even my own father disapproved of me riding about our manor."

"And what of these horses that you return to Windsor?" asked Lady Matlock.

Lucy responded in a carefully modulated voice. "While I do not know much about their breeding program or ours, they were covered by our stallion at Greystone, Lady Matlock."

"I see. My husband has deep interest in horse husbandry, especially the thoroughbred lines. I confess I do not pay much attention to the details, but I have wondered at the practice of sending out or importing mares or stallions."

"If I may, Your Ladyship, it is a way of bringing 'fresh blood' one might say, into the bloodlines," Kitty offered. "It can introduce new traits, strengthen strong features, lessen weak tendencies, and improve the overall health or disposition of a line. Repeated in-line breeding can eventually cause weaknesses. From what I know, there is quite an art about it."

Lady Matlock nodded graciously whilst the others looked at Kitty in astonishment.

Alice piped up. "I should like to see you ride, Miss Bennet, and hear of your horseback adventures. Mama rarely rides. I would so enjoy talking with someone of your knowledge."

Kitty had never known a young person to look up to her. It was a new and welcome experience.

"Do you have a horse of your own, Miss Matlock?"

"I have two. A sweet little mare for hacking about, and a more athletic gelding that I hope ..." she looked towards her mother "... that I hope may someday be a hunter."

Her mother appeared not to hear.

Talk then turned to fashions and balls, to the distinct pleasure and relief of Mrs. Wyndham and Lucy, until dinner.

During the lengthy meal Kitty watched Georgiana closely to ensure that her own manners satisfied the formality of the fine dinner. She had never dined in such high company. The other girls also looked to Georgiana to lead the way. It was the most elegant meal Kitty had ever been privileged to enjoy.

After dining, the ladies went through to the music room to prepare for entertainment. Georgiana was asked to play, and Alice showed her the selection of sheet music available whilst the ladies sipped tea.

The return of the gentlemen enlivened the conversation and there was more mixing and moving about the room. Christopher Drake paid his respects to Miss Alice. Lucy, unable to be content with Alice enjoying all his attention, joined them.

Kitty had not forgotten their mission to listen for comments about the 'investment club.' Towards the end of the evening, her vigil was rewarded when she overheard some talk between Darcy and his uncle about the problems the scoundrels were causing at the racing stables.

"Why can they not bet like honorable gentlemen?" the earl demanded. "Let racing remain an honest sport."

"Any time wagering becomes part of a sport, some of its beauty dies, in my opinion," Darcy said. "It becomes, for some, about the money rather than about developing great talent. If ever I caught someone drugging a horse, I would personally whip him within an inch of his life!" Darcy exclaimed vehemently, silencing the room.

He turned with an apologetic bow.

"Pardon me, ladies, I was overwarm in my words. Let us have some music to soothe those of us who may need it."

Kitty could not be sure, but Christopher seemed to avoid Darcy and the earl after this.

While the musicians determined who would play what, Mrs. Wyndham held forth about her plan to stay in Matlock until Darcy's return from Windsor. She began with great drama to describe her stepson's injuries when Darcy intervened with a sensible explanation of the accident.

The earl was moved and offered his sympathies.

"The waters at the Matlock Bath have been a powerful cure for many."

"That—plus the availability of the surgeon—is why Mr. Wyndham has taken lodgings there," Darcy said. "I am eager to see how his son gets on. I have had a few notes from his father, but I understand the young man remains confined to a wheel-chair and his spirits are greatly dampened."

"The waters may be of help there also," Lady Matlock said. "When the spirit is cured, the body heals."

Kitty was struck by this wisdom.

Julia stared hard at Lady Matlock.

As the music was performed, Owen stood or sat near the older gentlemen. Kitty wondered at his lack of sociability. He certainly had not Andrew's easy affability or charm. He kept a watchful eye on his stepmother and stepsister, as his father would wish. He also kept vigil over Julia. Did he and Julia share a past? There seemed some connection between them—an uneasy or sad connection.

Kitty longed for Owen's relaxed and witty conversation, like they had enjoyed the day of the wagon breakdown, but Owen did not meet her eye all evening.

CHAPTER NINETEEN

*K*itty tossed and turned. How could she be so restless? Here was a fine bed, excellent attendants, the best of food. She could not determine the source of her disquiet. Was she not accustomed to travel? Her journeys had been only to the homes of family, and with family, so perhaps that was it. She was now with others she knew, and some she felt close to, but it was not as if Lizzy were here. No, on this journey she must depend on herself alone.

Some of her party were in the breakfast room the next morning when she entered. The gentlemen rose and Darcy gave her a welcoming smile.

"Sit here," Georgiana indicated, seeming quite at home.

Darcy advised them of the day's plan.

"Please remember, we must leave for Matlock by noon. We will all lunch with the Wyndhams there and afterwards will proceed to our next stop while the Wyndham ladies remain."

"Oh, must I?" cried Lucy with a frown. "There is nothing I can do for Douglas. I would sooner go on to Town."

Darcy gave her a critical look. "May I remind you, Miss Jamison, we do not go into London. We will lodge at Oakhurst, seat of my cousin Alfred Cressley, several miles west of London. Mr. Owen and Mr. Christopher will travel on to Windsor with my cousin and myself to deliver the royal mares."

Lucy flounced in her seat, a petulant look marring her fair features. The others stared at this behavior from a young lady who had grown well beyond the schoolroom.

Darcy cleared his throat and gave her a stern look that did nothing to change her disposition.

"Let us have a look at your own breeding stock, uncle," he said, changing the focus. "Gentlemen?" The men strode from the room.

Mrs. Wyndham had not yet made her morning appearance. Lady Matlock had already excused herself to see to household business. Kitty, Georgiana, the Stapleton sisters, and young Alice remained at the table, still gaping at Lucy.

"Why can I not go? Owen gets to go, and Douglas is his *real* brother," Lucy said, reaching for another muffin. "He should be the one to stay in Matlock."

"There is much beauty to be seen in this area," Kitty remarked, trying to redirect the conversation. "What is there to do hereabouts, Alice?"

"There are waterfalls and caverns, and many beautiful walks and rides," Alice replied. "I hope you can make a longer stay some time."

"Thank you, Alice," Georgiana said. "I should be glad to have a longer visit here at any time I can arrange." The others echoed her sentiments.

A morning walk was taken about the gardens. Julia brought her sketching pad and found a seat towards one side of the area while the other young ladies explored.

"May I join you, Julia?" Kitty asked.

Julia looked up in surprise, then nodded, indicating for Kitty to sit. A companionable silence extended for some time while Julia sketched a scene of trees and rocks. Kitty marveled at her deft strokes.

"Forgive me, I do not wish to intrude, Julia, but you seem ... unhappy. Is there anything I might do?"

Julia sighed, put down her pencil, and looked at Kitty.

"I am sorry to cast a sober light on such a delightful journey. But my heart is not in it."

After a moment, Kitty asked, "Where is your heart?"

"Do you not know?"

"Is it Mr. Owen? Do you and he have a history? I see many meaningful looks pass between you, and afterward you both seem disturbed."

"Mr. Owen? No, Kitty. It is his brother who holds my heart."

"Mr. Douglas? But you have never spoken of him, except at the steeplechase ..."

"And why should I? You see how he is. Even before this accident, he had been in such a state for many months. He and I share a long history, not unlike that of Georgiana and Mr. Benjamin. In the past, he confided in me—of his sorrow in losing his mother and sister, and his belief it was his fault. But then he changed, Kitty. Instead of being sad, he grew angry and bitter. He pushed everyone away, including me. One day on a walk by our pond, he nearly assaulted me. He was drinking secretly. I did not fully understand what was happening. I was shocked when he made to strike me. Mr. Owen happened to see that. It was he who acted the part of an elder brother, Kitty. He intervened and got me safely away. He wishes me to stay away from Douglas. To give him up. To abandon him."

"Oh, Julia! I had no idea you carried so much sorrow."

"There is more. It was after that when Douglas began traveling to town with Mr. Christopher. They became secretive. Douglas then began drinking openly. Mr. Owen was furious. I do believe Mr. Christopher and Douglas are involved in the 'investment club.' There may be others as well. Mr. Owen told all this to my brother Andrew and me. So far, they have not told my father. I dread what he might do if he learnt of it. Probably send me far away from Douglas. Mr. Owen and Mr. Wyndham are so kind and Douglas used to be like them. But Kitty, it is as if the real Douglas died—months before the steeplechase accident."

A teardrop fell onto the lovely sketch, blurring its beauty.

Kitty put her arm around her friend. "This whole tale is so sad. And, are you ... will you see him today when we visit?"

"Mr. Owen says I should not, but I feel I must. I still love him, Kitty. Sadly my love was not enough for him." She sighed. "Yes, I will visit with the group, but if I leave of a sudden, please speak for me? Tell them a violent headache has taken me out of doors to the fresh air."

"Of course."

The others had changed their direction and were returning. Julia took a deep breath and addressed her drawing, though Kitty knew her friend's heart and mind were elsewhere.

≈

Soon the carriages were ready, thank-yous and goodbyes were said, and the group wound down the hillside to the town of Matlock. The Wyndhams' lodgings were easy to find at the Matlock Bath area in the outskirts of town. Kitty did not wonder this was a place of healing; besides its legendary waters, surely the beauty of the surroundings must inspire hope.

Mr. Wyndham greeted his wife and daughter with joy, handing them out of the carriage, then heartily welcomed Owen. A servant unloaded the baggage.

"Owen, will you oversee the horses and carriage at the livery?" his father asked.

"Certainly. I shall return when all is situated."

How nice it must be when the man of a family was so accommodating and so capable. It seemed there was nothing Owen could not manage. Except his brother.

"Please, Darcy, all of you, come in. The lodgings are small but there is a drawing room of sorts. I am so glad for your company," Mr. Wyndham said. He looked worn and haggard.

They all crowded into the small but agreeable room. Mrs. Wyndham ordered tea from the cheerful maid and then looked about her in dismay.

"Really, my dear, are there no better lodgings than this?"

Lucy scowled at the surroundings and whispered under her breath.

Christopher paced restlessly about the tiny room, glancing often at Lucy in commiseration.

"These rooms have been most pleasant and very adequate for Douglas and myself. It will be cozy with you ladies here, but I am sure we shall all get on very well for a short time. Douglas is now with the nurse at the waters and returns any moment. We saw the surgeon this morning. Douglas is speaking well, and his upper body is strong—he has regained the use of his arms to a great degree. But he remains confined to a wheelchair for now."

"I see," Darcy said. "Well, that seems like great progress, considering his condition after the accident."

"Yes, the surgeon tells me the same thing. He says full recovery can take many months."

Mrs. Wyndham looked horrified.

"Surely you cannot mean to stay here for months? How shall Lucy and I survive? Why, it is unconscionable! I cannot find it acceptable."

"My dear, we can discuss it in more detail later," Wyndham said whilst motioning her to calm down. He glanced at Darcy.

"So, Wyndham," Darcy remarked, "shall Mr. Douglas feel comfortable with us visiting him today? What does his surgeon recommend?"

"I spoke to him about that very thing this morning. The surgeon believes a few short visits, with only two in his room at a time, would be beneficial. His spirits remain much depressed."

"Understandable, my man. None of us enjoy being ill or inca-pacitated. We shall keep our visits short and will then be on our way. I shall send you a note by messenger when we are leaving Oakhurst after Windsor, on the return leg of our journey, so you will know when to expect us here again. Is there anything I can get for you or Mr. Douglas anywhere along the way? Something you cannot find here in the village?"

"Thank you, Darcy, but your company and the delivery of my family are the greatest gift."

"I wish I could stay, Father," Owen remarked, having slipped back into the room. "But with three mares to manage, and the conclusion of the business documentation, I must go on."

"Of course, that is as I expected. You do me proud by carrying on the estate business so ably in my absence, son, and by your care for your stepmother and Lucy. I am a fortunate man indeed."

There was noise at the back door.

"Owen, your brother has returned. You and I shall go to him

first. Please, help yourselves to refreshments. We will be only a few minutes." They bowed and quitted the room.

"Your husband is an admirable man, Mrs. Wyndham, to bear so much adversity with such serenity and wisdom."

"Thank you, Mr. Darcy. He is more forbearing than I can say I am. I am quite put out at these miserable lodgings."

Kitty was almost overcome at Darcy's slight roll of his eyes and quickly stuffed her mouth with a piece of cake.

Two by two they visited the injured man, with the Stapleton sisters last.

"No, Julia, you cannot!" came Matilda's cry from the sick room. "Father would forbid it. Mr. Darcy will forbid it. It is impossible!" She burst into the drawing room in quite a state.

Darcy stepped forward. "Whatever is the matter, Miss Matilda?"

"Julia says she will stay here until we return. Mr. Douglas has asked her to, and she agreed. Tell her she cannot, Mr. Darcy."

Georgiana ran to comfort Matilda whilst Kitty struggled to understand what was happening.

Owen did not disguise his agitation.

"He cannot do this to her. No, she must go on. She has suffered enough."

Darcy looked at Owen, and then at his father.

"Wyndham, what is going on here?"

"Darcy, let us retreat to the outdoors a moment," Wyndham suggested. "Come, Owen, you must join us. I can speak only for my family. Darcy, you must speak for the squire in his stead."

How much would Owen divulge?

In a few moments they returned and Darcy walked directly to the sick room to speak privately with Julia and Douglas. Kitty realized she was the only one who had been unaware of the previous history between the two.

Mr. Wyndham spoke in a pained voice. "Douglas called for Miss Stapleton even in his delirium. It seems the bond they had has been sorely tried but not severed on his part. And perhaps not on hers? He claims he cannot live—does not wish to live—without her."

Everyone pondered the situation in silence.

Owen paced the room, an intense scowl on his face, his hands formed into fists as if to fight off a demon.

Which decision would be right for Julia? Could true love triumph? Even lead to a recovery? It seemed Darcy would have the final word, and he soon re-entered the sitting room.

"I was not aware of the intensity of the prior attachment between those two. If you agree, Wyndham—and if you and your wife will provide proper supervision—I will allow Miss Stapleton to remain here whilst we go on to Oakhurst. It will be less than a week until our return here. If there is healing or a reconciliation in their future, it will be apparent by that time. But no matter the outcome, Miss Stapleton must return home with us, and any further visits must be sanctioned by her father."

Wyndham was nodding thoughtfully when Owen's voice burst forth.

"No! How can you allow this? She does not know her own mind—she is swamped by grief. She cannot be allowed to sacrifice herself."

Darcy's face showed surprise at this uncharacteristic outburst from Owen.

"Son," said Wyndham, "I agree with Darcy. You may be better informed on this situation than either of us, but we have the wisdom of years. Miss Stapleton is an intelligent young lady. We must allow her to know her own heart—and Douglas to know his. I believe we must give them this chance."

Kitty, too, was surprised at Owen's vehemence. His burst of anger led her to suspect there was more to be known than what Julia had confided.

Owen drew himself up and faced the two men squarely.

"Very well. I hope you are right. I pray this is a decision we do not all come to regret." With that, he walked out the door, his fists belying the calm demeanor he had managed to compose.

Christopher raised a brow at Lucy.

Her eyes lit up with sudden realization.

"I shall take Julia's place! There is nothing for me here, and Douglas will not miss me in any case. Please, may I go?

Mrs. Wyndham appeared rattled by a problem greater than

that of less-than-elegant surroundings. She sighed and looked to her husband.

Wyndham looked askance. "Darcy, you have enough to manage, do you not?"

Darcy looked from Wyndham to Lucy.

"Miss Jamison, you wish to join the company to Oakhurst?"

"Oh, yes, I sincerely do, sir. What can I do to convince you, Mr. Darcy?"

"That is easy. You must agree to respect me as your full father figure with the same authority over you as I have over the other young ladies. All decorum will be observed. No reputations will be sullied, and there will be no quarreling. I do not know you as well as the other young ladies, but perhaps you, too, deserve your chance?"

CHAPTER TWENTY

*F*resh horses were harnessed and the carriage made ready. Julia's baggage was brought into the lodging, and Lucy's was added to Darcy's carriage. Lucy was all smiles as she joined Georgiana, Kitty, and Matilda.

"Oh, what a merry time we shall have!" she cried. She shared a special smile with Christopher, who tipped his hat to her.

Kitty exchanged a skeptical look with Georgiana, and the carriage pulled away with a jerk.

Saying goodbye to Julia had been difficult. Kitty wanted to believe her friend was making the right choice and that true love would triumph. But could Douglas really love her? Did he really have her happiness in mind?

Kitty's last words with Julia left only a wake of confusion.

"Kitty, you do support me in this choice, do you not?" Julia had asked, grasping Kitty's hands.

"I cannot say, Julia. So much of your affair happened before I ever arrived. I have not seen you two together and in love. I have only seen you sad, and him a deeply troubled soul."

"But I do believe my love can heal him. And the revival of our love will certainly do away with my sadness."

Kitty remained doubtful. "But what of his trying to strike you? How can that be love, in any sense? I worry for you, Julia. Are you sure you would not rather come with us and think about it more—away from his influence—before placing yourself in his power once again?"

Julia drew back. "I thought you were my friend."

Kitty was torn and reconsidered. But after reflecting, all she could offer was, "I *am* your friend. And a true friend offers true counsel to the best of her ability, from her heart. None of us can see the future. What harm would it do to delay this decision by a week? When we return, speak with him again and see if you both feel the same."

"What harm? At best, it will delay his healing. At worst ... he says he does not wish to live without me. I cannot risk that! I love him. I must stay."

"Very well, Julia. You have my best wishes that love will prevail. I shall miss you in our adventures."

"Kitty, I am sorry to disappoint you. But this is something I must do. For Douglas. And for myself."

"I understand. We can talk again on our journey home."

≈

The scenery continued to be a refreshing distraction as the coach made its way south. The weather was agreeable; the food at the traveling inns less so. Soup, bread, and cheese were the most tolerable fare.

With Georgiana and Matilda such bosom friends, Kitty found herself thrown in with Lucy, who tended to prattle on about things in which Kitty could claim only passing interest, such as gossip about others, fashions in London, and trends set by the *ton*. Lucy had no interest in horses, art, or the landscape. It did not take long for Kitty's attentiveness to lag, but Lucy failed to read Kitty's lack of interest.

Lucy was also a stranger to discretion and soon took Kitty into her confidence. She whispered observations about Christopher's merits and attractions and looked to her new friend to agree. Kitty had been aware of Lucy favoring him but now paid it more attention.

"Is he not handsome, Kitty? See how his eyes sparkle when he looks at me?"

"He does seem to pay you special attention, Lucy."

"I do not care for horses myself; but he rides well, does he not? He is bold and daring."

"Much of good horsemanship is invisible, Lucy. It is about understanding the horse's mind and working with the horse's natural ability."

"Pish posh! It is about looking dashing. One horse will do as well as another, I am sure."

Kitty sighed. It was like talking to a turnip. Lucy *was* quite taken with mysteries and legends though, and on that topic they might find mutual interest.

"Lucy, perhaps we may discover some legends surrounding Oakhurst. Shall you be interested in exploring with me?"

"Legends? Oh, yes. I love to be thrilled! And it makes Mr. Christopher's strength and daring even more desirable—having a man look out for you, that is. It makes me feel like a true woman, Kitty."

"Indeed." Kitty sighed in resignation. Would they be able to ride at Oakhurst? At the next change of horses, she would ask Fitzwilliam.

How close was Oakhurst to Windsor Forest? There were many legends of that famous place. Would that she could deliver the mares with the men and see the royal stables!

She looked out at Fitzwilliam, riding along calmly, taking in the sights. Nothing seemed to escape his observation with regards to the coach and the horses and the riders. It occurred to Kitty that Owen possessed many of these same traits and skills. Did Fitzwilliam have the explosive temper Owen had demonstrated? A man's temper could be quite frightening. At least she could say that her father was never violent—she did not fear for her safety when he was angry. She sighed. There was so much she did not know about men. If only she had had a brother.

Her eye was suddenly taken by a particularly unusual rock formation, and she tried to press it into her memory so she might attempt to sketch it later. Perhaps Darcy could purchase a sketchbook and pencils for her somewhere along the way?

Her mind wandered in this fashion as the carriage rolled on, her own thoughts interspersed with comments by Lucy about hoped-for parties and Christopher's endless assets. Anyone could notice Christopher's efforts at exhibiting his prowess riding past the carriage at various paces, attempting to catch the eyes of the ladies.

Whatever were Georgiana and Matilda talking of? She leaned forward to better hear them.

"Please, share something interesting," she whispered. "The conversation grows thin on this side of the carriage."

The two across from her smirked and spoke more loudly of general topics.

"Are there young people at Oakhurst?" Kitty asked.

Georgiana raised her eyebrows in surprise.

"I do not know. I believe Mr. Cressley has at least one son, perhaps more. I shall ask my brother at our next dining stop—if one can call it dining. I find the food rather coarse, do you not?"

By the next day Kitty was weary of the coach, and more than weary of Lucy's insipid company. Travel had always sounded exciting, but the reality was more tedious than she had expected. Although they stayed in the finest establishments, she did not feel at ease. Darcy had procured a sketchbook and pencils for her, and these proved a worthy distraction. She gave her attention to her partial sketch of a tree. Drawing had looked so easy when she watched Julia. She applied the eraser again.

At the stop for luncheon Darcy said, "Later today we shall arrive at Oakhurst. So be of good cheer. Our journey is nearly completed, for now."

"Brother, what shall be our activities at Oakhurst?" Georgiana asked.

"I have not given that much thought yet, my dear," he answered. "My main concern is to get the royal mares delivered safely for Mr. Wyndham. Once that is completed, well ... we shall see what is available and what my cousin has planned."

"Are there any young people in residence?" Matilda asked.

"I do not know. His eldest son married last year. Mr. Cressley has two other sons as well. I assume they all remain at Oakhurst, but I cannot be sure." He looked at the eager faces in front of him. "Cultivate patience, ladies. It is a desirable virtue."

Georgiana made a silly face at him, and they all laughed.

≈

The afternoon had grown warm and all were relieved to enter the large park of Oakhurst. Trees arched over the lane in many places, providing welcome shade.

"Brother," Georgiana called out, "is Oakhurst as great as Pemberley?"

"If you mean in size, yes; the estates are similar in acreage. The house itself is of a different style than Pemberley. It is older. It was once a royal hunting lodge. I admire it very much. Long ago these grounds were part of the great forest. Do remember, Georgiana, Mr. Cressley's wife died some years back. I do not know what, if any, feminine influence remains at Oakhurst. I hope you shall all be comfortable."

They rode some time in the quiet of the woods until at last Oakhurst Lodge appeared in a clearing, set upon a slight hill. Several lanes led off in various directions. Kitty wondered where the horses grazed in so much wooded land.

Upon their arrival, the travelers were immediately attended to and shown into the drawing room. The afternoon sun penetrated the tall windows, glinting on the dark woodwork that was heavily carved. They were announced, and Alfred Cressley stood and strode forward, hand outstretched. His face was rugged but his countenance pleasant. His hair had gone white, but his dark eyes still flashed with vigor.

A younger man also rose and came forward. Kitty saw the resemblance at once—a younger version of the older man, with the same lively dark eyes.

"My dear cousin, how good it is to see you again. And you have brought with you a great and varied company, I see. Excellent! Which of these handsome young ladies is your sister?"

"May I present my sister, Miss Georgiana Darcy."

Georgiana made a lovely curtsey and smiled up at her cousin.

"Yes, on closer look, the picture of my dear aunt she is, Fitzwilliam. A great beauty. Miss Darcy," he said, bowing to her.

"Thank you. May I introduce my companions?"

"By all means. But first, here is my youngest son, William."

"Miss Darcy, I am most pleased to make your acquaintance. My father has spoken much of Pemberley and of your brother. I hope to some day have the honor of visiting there."

"You are most welcome to visit whenever convenient."

He smiled his acknowledgement and bowed in response to her curtsey.

Georgiana began. "Here is my sister-in-law, Miss Catherine Bennet, from Hertfordshire. She visits us for the summer."

Kitty stepped forward and curtsied.

"Welcome to Oakhurst , Miss Bennet." Mr. Cressley bowed.

"I am delighted to make your acquaintance, Miss Bennet," said William, bowing.

"Thank you. I am honored."

Georgiana now looked at Matilda. "Please meet my dear friend, Miss Matilda Stapleton, daughter of our neighbor Squire Stapleton of Swan's Nest."

Matilda's curtsey was quick and lively and excitement sparkled in her eyes.

"I am very pleased to meet you both."

"Welcome to Oakhurst Lodge, Miss Stapleton."

"Miss Stapleton, it is an honor and a pleasure," said Mr. William, delight evident in his face.

"And our friend and neighbor, Miss Lucy Jamison of Greystone Hall," Georgiana continued.

"You are most welcome to Oakhurst, Miss Jamison."

"Delighted, Miss Jamison," replied William, bowing. As he stepped back, his gaze returned at once to Matilda.

Darcy spoke then. "It is for Miss Jamison's father—and Mr. Owen's (nodding at Owen)—that I return the three royal mares tomorrow. Mr. Wyndham and I share a strong interest in horse husbandry, especially in particular lines."

Darcy introduced Owen and Christopher. Kitty thought she saw a spark of recognition in William's eye at the introduction to Christopher, who displayed his trademark cocky elegance.

"Drake is a name I know from Cambridge. Might you be related to a Mr. Benjamin Drake? He and I were acquainted, both studying the law."

"Yes," Christopher answered brightly, "Benjamin is my younger brother."

Georgiana could not hide her delight at the mention of Benjamin's name and exclaimed, "How lucky we share such a connection!"

"He is a most personable young man, well liked amongst his school fellows. I was a year ahead of him there." He glanced with curiosity between Christopher's face and Georgiana's.

Georgiana blushed, suddenly aware of being outspoken.

"Yes, I believe he has just completed his coursework," Christopher responded, tossing his head.

William looked at him again, slightly puzzled, as if trying to make a connection.

Mr. Cressley ushered them towards the door.

"Now, allow my staff to show you to your rooms so you can get some rest and clean off the traveling dust. Tea will be served whenever you are ready. Shall one hour be sufficient?"

"Certainly. That is most kind."

≈

Mr. Alfred Cressley welcomed them back to the drawing room.

"Ah, here you are! I hope you are refreshed and ready for some lively conversation. And pray, Miss Darcy, will you honor us with your musical talent this evening? You were unfortunately from home when I visited last autumn, but your praises have been sung"— he chuckled at his own joke—"far and wide. We do not often have a talented musician in our midst."

Georgiana blushed, but Kitty could see she was pleased as she nodded her assent.

Just then another gentleman entered the room and bowed.

"Charles, you are just in time." Introductions were made all round to Cressley's second son, who looked remarkably like his younger brother, though he had a more serious air about him. "My eldest son, George, and his wife Murielle will join us for dinner."

"You are a houseful of men, Cressley. At Pemberley I am now surrounded by women."

"Darcy, you cause us all to be envious. I have met your bride, and bewitching she is with her lively ways and quick wit. You are most fortunate indeed!"

The conversation continued, touching on family news, tidings from the world, and soon turned to horses.

"Are all your sons involved with your horse interests?"

"To some extent, yes. All are excellent horsemen. George is the most involved with the breeding program and with the estate in general as he will, of course, inherit. George and Murielle live here. William is an attorney and specializes in issues related to livestock —especially horses and racing. As you can imagine, there is much to do there. His office is in Reading. And Charles has just taken the living here at Oakhurst. My sons have all done me proud."

He looked at his guests with a twinkling eye.

"Now, I wonder if you young ladies would have the smallest interest in a party? Dinner, cards, and perhaps a bit of dancing? If you are agreeable, our neighbors enjoy meeting folk from other areas. We are near to Town, it is true; but most of us prefer the quiet life here. And I think the older we get, the quieter the better."

All the female eyes were riveted to Mr. Cressley's face.

Darcy looked at the young ladies with a satirical grin.

"I believe you have hit on just the thing, Cressley. Look at their faces—not a scowl amongst them."

"I have invited two other families—all with younger members—and their summer guests. I believe we will make a lively group," he quipped.

Then he turned back to Darcy. "You return the mares tomorrow, eh?"

"Yes. I have these two gentlemen to assist me, but you and your sons are most welcome to accompany us, should you care to. It may involve an overnight stay, depending on how business is carried out."

"I cannot speak for George, but I am most eager to accompany you, Darcy. Charles? William?"

"Unfortunately, I have a case in the village tomorrow," William said.

Charles shook his head. "I have a parishioner in the last stages of illness. I feel it my duty to be nearby should the need arise."

"Of course," his father replied.

"Would ladies be welcome on this venture, Fitzwilliam?" Kitty inquired breathlessly.

"Ladies? Do we have some horsewomen amongst us, Darcy?"

Darcy smiled at Kitty indulgently.

"Miss Bennet here is an unsurpassed horsewoman and knows a good deal about the beasts. I know she is most interested in this transaction and in seeing the royal mews."

"I should also like it above all things," chimed Lucy. "I enjoy a country ride ..."

Kitty gaped.

Owen's eyebrows shot up.

"... and I would dearly love to see any part of the royal grounds."

All eyes were on Darcy.

"I had anticipated your desire for this, Miss Bennet. Although your interest takes me by surprise, Miss Jamison, I believe it would be pleasant for the ladies to have each other for company. If we leave after an early breakfast, will that allow us sufficient time, Cressley?"

"Certainly. All will be ready by eight."

The door opened and admitted George and Murielle Cressley. George looked much like his brothers but his eyes were a pale blue. Murielle was short of stature with blond curls, and obviously with child.

Introductions were made and congratulations offered concerning the happy event. Alfred Cressley beamed.

"It will be my first grandchild. Ah, that dear Mary could be here. She loved children above anything."

Darcy shared his expectation of a child himself and then dinner was announced. Mr. Cressley offered his arm to Georgiana. Darcy led Kitty through, whilst William hastily stepped up for Matilda. Lucy was happy on Christopher's arm, and Charles and Owen followed behind.

The dinner was long, the courses many, and the candles burned low. At last Murielle led the ladies through. There was much talk of babies and nurseries and the time flew by. The gentlemen entered again and to Kitty's surprise, Owen took a seat next to her.

"You are pleased about tomorrow," he began, looking at her sidelong.

"Indeed I am. That cannot shock you, I am sure."

He turned and smiled; it was a kind, genuine smile.

"I must confess, Mr. Owen, that I was not prepared for your sister's interest. She has said on many occasions that she prefers a coach to horseback. Am I correct that we shall all ride?"

"You are. She likely assumes you two will be in a carriage." He called over to Lucy. "May I have a word?"

Lucy made quick possession of Christopher's arm and the two came across the room.

"You are aware that we go on horseback tomorrow?"

Lucy's countenance failed and she turned to Christopher. "Is that true?"

He threw his head back and laughed out loud.

She glared at him and faced her brother again.

"It is not as I expected but I shan't be one to forfeit. I shall ride with the rest of you," she announced and then flounced off.

Christopher smirked and followed her.

"She is a capable rider," Owen said, "so I have no worries there. But she prefers being catered to over making any effort for herself. It will be an interesting journey." He chuckled.

Here was the Owen that Kitty had come to know during the wagon incident. Did his change of mood mean he was already reconciled regarding Julia and his brother?

Kitty was certain Andrew Stapleton would not have yielded so soon regarding his sister.

CHAPTER TWENTY-ONE

*T*he fog magnified every sound in the cool grey air. The footfalls of the horses echoed around them. Every snort or sneeze was like an explosion. Darcy and Alfred Cressley set the pace to Windsor at an active walk, each leading a mare. Owen ponied the third mare. The party anticipated arriving at the royal mews near noon. A note had been sent ahead, so they would be expected.

Georgiana and Matilda, having no interest in the errand, remained at Oakhurst.

All rode in silence except Darcy and Cressley, who conversed in low tones. Kitty rode between Owen and George Cressley. Christopher and Lucy brought up the rear. The horses in front were skittish, so George rode up to put more space between the two mares.

Kitty and Owen looked at each other expectantly. Kitty searched her mind but all she could think to talk of was the weather, in spite of having many questions she wished to ask Owen. *Please say something* she begged silently.

"I like this." His voice was muffled in the fog.

Kitty looked at him, puzzled.

"What, exactly, is it you like?"

"How it is both quiet and loud at once," he replied. "The

hush around us keeps us quiet, yet the sounds that do happen seem loud and sharp. There is a kind of beauty about it."

Kitty smiled. "At Longbourn, I enjoyed riding on foggy mornings. The world around me would at first be in a hush, as you say. Then, as the sun burned through, everything seemed to wake up and smile. There were some good things about Longbourn."

Owen looked at her curiously.

She frowned. "I find gentlemen do not, in general, understand the struggles of ladies, Mr. Owen. Men have many choices in life. We ladies have few, and even supreme effort or brilliant skill or amazing talent do not change this. It is unpleasant to feel so ... stuck. Locked in."

He said nothing.

She quailed. She had shared too much. Too vehemently. The silence was awkward so she blundered on.

"My summer visit at Pemberley has been so pleasant," she said, changing her direction and tone. "I enjoy my sister's company immensely and have missed her since she married and moved away. And becoming better acquainted with my new sister Georgiana has been one of the best parts of my visit." She stopped abruptly, not knowing what else to say.

Owen was smiling in that calm way he had.

"Miss Darcy is one of the sweetest and kindest young ladies of my acquaintance. I shall certainly agree with you there, Miss Bennet; knowing her is a delight."

They walked on in silence for a time until Owen spoke again.

"Your horse. Do you find him agreeable?"

She reached down to pat the bay gelding from Oakhurst.

"It is difficult to say; we have only been walking. But he has a long, easy stride and is light in my hands."

"He is a jumper. Darcy tells me you managed that gate very well on your wild ride to Pemberley the day of the picnic." He gave her a sly grin.

"Yes ... well ... I knew the gate was stubborn, even for Mr. Darcy, and time was critical. Your horse sailed over the gate as if it were no more than a small log. I did my best to stay centered and let him do the work."

"A perfect strategy, Miss Bennet. A good hunter knows his job. Sultan has been over many hunting courses," he said with pride, scratching his gelding's withers.

"I should like to see the two of you in action some day, if I might," she said, then wondered if that was too bold.

He brightened. "Yes? I would be happy to give you a demonstration. Perhaps we might have a small show at Pemberley or at Greystone. Cara would enjoy it."

Thinking of Cara, Kitty smiled. "She would. She likes to show off. She is another wonderful part of my visit."

Kitty thought carefully a moment, and then said, "Mr. Darcy knows my secret. My riding secret, that is. He knew it before you discovered it. I don't know how much the others know, such as Lady Drake or the squire. But I thought you should know Mr. Darcy neither forbids it nor approves it. I have his permission to continue, but I must keep it as secret as possible. May I depend on you, Mr. Owen?"

He turned to her with a sincere countenance.

"You may always depend on me, Miss Bennet."

Her heart pounded at his honesty and at the implied scope of his promise, echoed by the depth and steadiness in his eyes.

A loud guffaw came from behind them. Kitty turned to see Lucy scowl at Christopher and urge her mount ahead.

"Do ride with me, Miss Bennet," she said, checking her horse next to Kitty's. "I find my previous companion to be most impolitic. I detest swaggering above all things."

Owen checked his horse and nodded for the ladies to go ahead. He raised an eyebrow at Kitty and smiled.

"Mr. Darcy, how much farther? Can we see our destination yet?" Lucy inquired.

Darcy turned, his face unreadable.

"We have been riding just one hour, Miss Jamison. I shall announce when we can see the royal stables. They are, however, surrounded by great woods so they may remain hidden from us for some time. I have not ridden this way for several years. Have you, Cressley? George?"

"I have, Mr. Darcy," George replied. "You are correct. The greatness of the woods keeps even the larger buildings quite hidden. I think your estimate of another three hours is spot on."

"Let us stop at the next likely place for a bite and a sip, eh?" Cressley suggested. "Dismount and stretch our legs. Allowing the mares a few bites of grass may improve their moods."

"A few bites may improve everyone's mood," said Christopher with a laugh, and the others joined in. All except Lucy, who continued to pout prettily.

After crossing a bridge over a rill, they came upon a grassy spot and dismounted. The young men took turns grazing the mares in hand, and all partook of some bread and cheese with beer or watered wine.

The melody of the rushing water was appealing, and Kitty made her way to its edge. How joyful it sounded, gurgling over the rocks like a baby's laugh. She thought of Lizzy and the little Darcy to come. And Jane's baby, expected at any moment. *Perhaps we will have news of Jane when we return to Pemberley?* She was lost in reverie when she felt another's presence.

It was Owen. "The sound gives you joy, Miss Bennet?"

"It is like a baby's laugh. It reminds me that two of my sisters are now expecting. I hope to hear news of Jane's baby when we return to Pemberley."

He looked at her with a smile. "I hope you do. And my best wishes for Mrs. Darcy. Your brother has shared his good news with my father and me."

"Will you be returning with us?" she asked. "Or will you and Lucy stay some time at Matlock with your brother?"

"I cannot say, Miss Bennet. I hope we shall all return at once, and that Douglas' doctoring will be completed for the present. There is much to do at home. My brother has caused so much pain to so many. I do not understand his choices. How can he hurt my father so? After all the loss my father has endured ..."

He slashed at the grasses with his crop.

"Does Mr. Douglas not struggle with his own pain, too?" Kitty asked.

His look betrayed his surprise at her knowledge.

"Miss Stapleton has spoken to you about some of this. I am glad she has been able to unburden herself to a degree. She has suffered long. And my brother does nothing to relieve her. How can he be so cruel? I cannot be generous with him, Miss Bennet. His choices have been reprehensible, and almost all his troubles are of his own doing. The drinking, the gambling ...”

She looked at him with alarm.

“Do not suppose me ignorant of his activities in Town and other places. His need for money has been great and constant, yet he has nothing to show for it. The reason is obvious. I have heard the rumors. I do not know for sure he is involved in those activities, or how deeply. He will not talk to me. He will not let me help him.”

“Perhaps,” Kitty offered, “this ... the accident ... will be a turning point for him. Perhaps he and Julia—their love—can speed his healing.”

Owen stared at the ground. His words were bitter.

“Or perhaps ... and more likely ... he will use her for her money and drain what little spirit she has left, pulling her down with him as he sinks.” With that, he stormed away, slashing at everything in his path.

Kitty pondered his words as she returned to the group and quietly ate her bread and cheese. Hearing laughter, she looked around. Lucy and Christopher had made amends again.

≈

“May I ride with you, Kitty?” Darcy asked and pulled alongside her.

Kitty looked at him in surprise.

“Of course; I should welcome your company above all.”

Darcy looked at Kitty thoughtfully.

“Thank you. Kitty, I could not help observing you and Mr. Owen talking by the water, and his angry retreat. You have been subdued since then. Did he offend or distress you? May I be of assistance?”

Darcy’s face was so sincere, Kitty nearly burst into tears at his kindness. She steadied herself.

“He has not offended me. But the whole situation—the accident, his family being divided, and now Julia’s involvement—has made him very angry. It distresses me also. I have become fond of Julia. Like Mr. Owen, I do not wish to see her hurt."

"Of course not. In my acquaintance—no, stronger than that —my friendship with Mr. Owen over the years, I know him to be a young man to take charge and do his best. He wishes to make things better for everyone. His skills with horses and in the horse business are beyond reproach; they are brilliant. But people are not like horses. A horse's driving desire is to please us and avoid pain. A horse will not punish itself. But sometimes a man will do that very thing if he thinks he's had a part in causing some wrenching sorrow. Sorrow itself can become an illness, breeding more harmful habits such as liquor or gambling or ... I will not go on in the presence of a lady."

Kitty weighed his words as they rode along.

"Surely it is not Mr. Douglas' fault that his mother and sister died. Why can he not see that?"

"Sorrow can blind us to the simplest truths."

She thought of Julia. "Or give us false hope?"

"Precisely," he replied. "Miss Stapleton is two and twenty. I am not sure how many years ago Mr. Douglas began drowning his sorrows, but I believe the two of them had been strongly attached. He was but a boy when his mother died, maybe about twelve. Old enough to wrongly feel blame, but not old enough to understand that tragedy sometimes happens, with no one at fault. And too young to comprehend that no one can repair such a loss. All we can do is go on. Mr. Douglas was away at school for many years, of course, but he left Cambridge before attaining his degree. As an eldest son, that is of little matter if he has good skills in managing the estate. But he takes little interest in Greystone. He does not care for horse husbandry nor for any part of the business or the farming. He has been floundering for some time. Taking up with Mr. Christopher and gadding about the country together—it is too rackety by half and will benefit neither. More likely it will bring ruination." Darcy frowned.

The mare he led was restless; he changed hands on the lead.

Kitty said, "And now the accident. Many would struggle to recover from such a gloomy situation even without all the other history. Mr. Owen fears his brother will use Julia for her money and drag her into ruination with him. I do not know how to help her, Fitzwilliam. Or how to help any of them."

Darcy looked at her with kindness. "There is no help anyone can offer, not really. Miss Stapleton must find her own way, as must each of the others. All a friend can do is be there at the ready. And listen. That is something I learnt from your sister, Kitty. There is great value in sharing one's burdens with a trusted friend. I think we men often don't know this; or don't value it. Yes, Lizzy—and now Georgiana too—have taught me the value of listening, and being listened to. And that I need not always have an answer, or mend things. Sometimes mending cannot be done. Your kindness will help Miss Stapleton in ways you may not yet see."

George cried out, "There! Through the trees. The castle and the long brick building. It will not be long now."

This news rallied the group. Their energy was renewed, along with their appetites. The sun was nearly overhead.

CHAPTER TWENTY-TWO

*a*t the royal mews, business was conducted quickly and the mares taken away by the stable attendants. The stable master had arranged for a luncheon on the grounds to be followed by a tour of the facility.

The head groom and the stable master joined the party at the elegantly-appointed tables under the shade of a spreading oak. Kitty gazed about her, taking it all in. Sleek, beautifully-kept horses could be seen in well-tended paddocks as the sun shone on the bright grass and into the dark forest. Just as they concluded their meal, her eye caught the motion of a small group entering one of the buildings. She rose to follow her own party, which entered the same building from the other direction.

As the groups neared each other, two ladies looked over at them. One was tall and willowy, with dark eyes and auburn hair, dressed in a deep violet habit. The other was much shorter with a fuller figure and blonde curls cascading below her hat. She wore a lovely sky blue habit, but her form and movements lacked the elegance of her companion.

"Sibley! We have guests? Dear Sibley, do introduce us. It is not often I visit here, and even less often I meet other young people." The blonde lady lurched towards them with a manly stride but her eyes were bright and her smile friendly.

"Of course, Your Highness ..."

Kitty gasped. Was this Princess Charlotte? Her eyes flew to Fitzwilliam. He stood by the master and prompted him with names, introducing the ladies first.

"Miss Catherine Bennet of Longbourn at Hertfordshire."

Kitty made the deepest and most graceful curtsey of her life. She flushed with color but met the princess' eyes with a smile. "Your Highness."

All were introduced one by one, after which the princess asked, "And are you here to tour? It is not common."

Owen stepped forward and made a slight bow.

"Your Highness, we have returned three of the royal mares who were covered by my family's stallion."

"All the way from Derbyshire! Your stud's bloodlines must be impressive." She then turned to Kitty and Lucy.

"And do you ladies merely accompany the gentlemen?"

Lucy was struck dumb, so Kitty spoke.

"I take a great interest in horses, Your Highness, and love to ride above anything."

Princess Charlotte looked at her closely.

"Do you? Well, I share your passion. Some call me reckless, but there is nothing I love more than a raging gallop. I am not known for being ladylike. Are you a bold rider, Miss Bennet?"

Kitty hesitated. "Some might say yes."

"Then we must ride together. Do you return to ..."

"Oakhurst, Your Highness," the master provided.

"... to Oakhurst today?"

Darcy answered, "No, Your Highness. We have been generously given lodgings here for this evening and plan to leave tomorrow afternoon."

"Fie, we have just ridden, and I have an appointment later this afternoon. Shall we ride tomorrow, say ten o'clock? Elphinstone, is that agreeable to you? Gentlemen?"

Bows and a nod confirmed the plan.

"Good, then it is settled. Sibley, will you handle the arrangements?"

"Certainly, Your Highness."

Princess Charlotte then added, "I invite you to explore the forest on your own this afternoon if you have not ridden too far today." She guffawed. "Ridden too far—is there such a thing?" She smiled at Kitty. "There are many wonderful bridle paths. The forest is vast. I wager you'll not find such scope or beauty anywhere else in the kingdom. Well, we must be off. Until tomorrow then."

Curtsies and bows were repeated and amazed looks exchanged amongst the visitors.

Kitty looked at Fitzwilliam again.

"To ride with Princess Charlotte—can it be true?"

"A great honor indeed," he replied.

They continued their tour and then enjoyed a leisurely tea. Dinner would not be served until nine o'clock at the guest lodge.

Cressley commented, "They have been most hospitable and obliging here, Darcy. I would not have expected so much."

"Nor I."

Christopher stood and looked at the group.

"Shall we take the princess up on her offer? Who is game? Who will join me for a hack in this magnificent forest before dinner?" He smiled in an inviting way, particularly at Lucy.

Lucy could not resist him.

"I shall join you," she said, forgetting the two could not ride unaccompanied.

The others in the party begged off, claiming to have spent enough time in the saddle for the day, and chortling about the princess's comment.

Christopher eyed Kitty.

"Come, Miss Bennet. Surely you wish to explore?"

The forest beckoned. Kitty was tempted. She looked at Darcy, who merely raised a brow.

"If the ride is short—no more than an hour—and if we stay on the paths, I will go."

"Excellent! I shall tell the groom and be back to fetch you ladies when all is ready."

He returned some time later with a gleam in his eye.

Darcy gave him a cautionary look.

"Do return punctually, Mr. Christopher. The ladies will need time to dress for dinner."

Christopher said nothing, only bowed his acquiescence, and

the three riders were away to the mounting area. Owen and Darcy and the Cressley men left with the stable master to further discuss business.

Watching Christopher lift Lucy into the saddle, Kitty noted a small saddlebag attached to the cantle, and a similar bag tied to his own. What could he wish to carry on such a brief ride? But perhaps the bags had been there all along.

He did not—as a gentleman should—check Kitty's tack, and he allowed the groom to assist her into the saddle. Did his amorous feelings for Lucy cause him to forget his duties? That was no surprise. Kitty had never marked his concern for others or for decorum.

Poor Lady Drake. Her situation with her son was not unlike Mr. Bennet's own trials with Kitty's sister Lydia.

Soon the three were mounted and they emerged from the barn. The sun was approaching the crown of the hills to the west as they swept under the eaves of the great and ancient Windsor Forest. Such tales were told about it! Bold knights rescuing damsels in distress ... exploits of robber barons ... royal stag hunts. Stories flowed from her memory as the party moved quietly through the trees. They seemed to be on a main path, but several other paths wound away in one direction or another.

"Mr. Christopher, do we not have a guide?" Kitty asked.

"Our ride is not long, Miss Bennet. There was no need to trouble anyone," he replied.

"Do you know which path to take?"

"I have an idea, Miss Bennet. Further on this path will fork, according to the groom. We shall keep to the left." He and Lucy dawdled behind.

Kitty's Oakhurst gelding was restless under her.

"My horse wants a faster pace. I shall await you at the fork."

"Very good, Miss Bennet."

Kitty turned to see the young couple plodding along, their heads leaning very close together. Such intimacy made her uncomfortable, and she urged her horse forward.

The canopy overhead was open in many places, allowing the sun's slanting rays to penetrate. She could make out clearings here and there through the trees. The rich smell of the forest filled her nostrils and she breathed deeply. After a brisk trot, she perceived the fork a little ahead, as Christopher had described. She cantered to the spot and then checked her horse.

Wondering how far behind they were, she turned.

The path was empty.

The light was fading. Kitty peered dubiously down the path. Where could they be? The way had curved some, so perhaps Lucy and Christopher were hidden around a bend. Had they stopped to pick a stone from a hoof? The light overhead—when she could see any—was touched with pink. She recalled their morning ride into this valley. The sun would soon disappear behind those tall westerly hills. The tangled boughs overhead competed to block the last shreds of light. The shadows of the trees were playing tricks on her eyes and she called out for her companions.

There was no reply. For a moment she panicked. Would anyone hear her cries for assistance? Would such a commotion summon help? Or draw unsavory sorts? Or attract the beasts of the forest? She grasped a handful of mane and patted the gelding's withers. His warmth was comforting. She must think!

Facing in the direction she thought she had come from, Kitty urged the horse forward at a walk. In the waning light—and viewing everything from the opposite direction—nothing looked familiar. She could not judge if she remained true to the original path or not.

Her lower lip began to quiver. She bit it to keep from crying. She must not alarm her horse. She tried to breathe deeply, but her hands shook on the reins. Perhaps her horse knew the way back; they often did, but that occurred mostly on familiar ground. This horse was from Cressley's stock and, like Kitty herself, had never been here before.

She craned her neck as they moved along, hoping to see something familiar. Suddenly the horse's muscles bunched beneath her. Something raced across the path in front of him and he shied, pawing the air in panic. The reins slipped from her fingers. Kitty leaned forward, clinging to the mane to stay aboard. The frightened horse backed into a low branch and knocked her out of the saddle. Landing with a thud, a biting pain shot through her wrist. The terrified horse bolted into the dark. The poor thing! She prayed he would not hurt himself or get his bridle tangled amongst the branches.

She looked about her. Tears filled her eyes. The darkness was nearly complete. She would not to cry. She would not be missish. Managing to stand, she felt her way to a large tree trunk. She leaned her back against it, but her legs grew weak and, losing the battle for courage, she collapsed to the ground and wept.

Time passed—she knew not how long—and her weeping turned to anger. How could they do this? Abandon her in the forest? They will not wish to face Darcy after this! What are they about anyway? Where would they go?

The saddlebags. Had Christopher planned this? Was it some kind of elopement—or worse? However this had come about, she was now in a predicament. She must not dwell on why until she was safe. She must think like Darcy now, or like a scientist, or like a man. She must solve the problem at hand. Even her throbbing wrist must not distract her.

She was in the forest, in the dark, and lost. Sight was useless. What could her other senses tell her? What did she hear? The coo of mourning doves. The twittering of night birds. The call of an owl. She strained her ears further abroad for any sound of humans or the welcome hoof beats of a horse. Nothing. She sighed. A forest was not familiar to her. Most of her rides had been across the meadows and down the country lanes of Long-bourn. There one could nearly always see the sky and look for the position of the sun or the stars. Here the shadows were deep and the ancient forest blotted out the heavens.

Kitty's only experience of such dense woods had been on the ladies' ride along the River Derwent, the day of the picnic.

Unbidden, something suddenly illuminated her mind; something Andrew had shown her that very day. Dear Andrew! What a fine instructor. Whilst on the high rocky passes and also down by the river, he had showed her how moss grows mostly on the north side of trees.

She reached behind her, feeling the tree's bark. It was rough and fissured. She came to her knees and turned towards the tree, allowing her hands to stretch out on either side, feeling for the textured sponginess of moss. She ignored the stinging pain in her wrist. The tree's trunk was too vast for her to encircle with her arms. Moving to the right, she stretched her hand along the bark until she felt a change. Yes! It was moss. Her hand explored to determine how far the moss grew, and she soon found the other edge. So this side was north. She pictured it firmly in her mind. Her pride in her own resourcefulness buoyed her resolve and momentarily eclipsed her fear.

Leaning against the tree so her back was to the north, she peered into the woods in each direction. A faint shimmer slowly appeared to her left. Silhouettes of some of the trees were visible. The moon. It was rising—in the east. How fortunate it shows its face so early! Now she had some bearings: east and north. But from which direction had they entered the forest?

She struggled to remember the location of the sun during tea, but her mind's eye failed her; she had paid the sun no heed then. Continuing to retrace the activities of the afternoon, at last she recalled shielding the left side of her face as they emerged from the barn. West! They had ridden straight into the forest, so they had been going north. She knew the path had wound its way around but did not remember any particularly sharp turns until the fork.

From these deductions, she concocted a plan and felt a burst of pride at her rational thinking. Even Papa might be proud of her now.

The night noises of the woods came from every direction as she trod silently along the unseen path. Skittering noises, snuffling, chattering sounds, creaking, and the occasional call of some bird. Were there dangerous beasts here? Wolves? Bears? Did they hunt at night? She wished now she had read far more about the world of nature, and vowed to do so if Providence granted her that chance.

The moon had risen high enough for its face to glow through the canopy above. Was she still moving in her intended direction? She checked another tree to confirm, found the moss, and gauged the path was aiming more or less to the south. She squared her shoulders and trudged on, tucking her aching wrist close to her body.

A small light twinkled in the trees ahead. She stopped and blinked. Red it was, not unlike the eye of a beast, and bobbed here and there, definitely approaching. She gasped, ready to call out, but then stopped of a sudden and thought better of it. It could be help, or it could be more trouble. She held her breath but heard no voices. She hesitated. They would see her before she could see them. It would be wise to stay out of sight until she knew if this was friend or foe.

Carefully she moved two steps off the path and hastily reached down for a few sticks and stones to make a cairn of sorts to guide her back to the path.

The light continued to approach, getting larger. It was no beast's eye, but a lantern. A few steps further off the path, she found a large tree and knelt behind it, not daring to breathe. The pounding of her heart filled her ears until her head swam. Touching the tree, she steadied herself.

"Hallo? Hallo?" a voice called.

Could they be searching for her?

"Hallo ... Miss Ben—

At the very moment she heard her name, the lantern illuminated the familiar face uttering it—Owen! Her legs quaked.

"Owen! Owen! I am here," she called, trying to steady her strangled voice as she rose to her feet.

"Miss Bennet? Where are you?"

Keeping her hand on the tree for support, she stepped around it.

"Here. I am here."

Holding up the lantern, Owen rushed towards her, his face lit with joy.

"Thank God! Are you hurt?" Upon seeing Kitty's face, he embraced her with his free arm and kissed her hair. Then he drew back. "Pardon me, in my joy I believe I breached ..."

"Oh, etiquette be hanged!" she cried and threw her arms about his neck. "I am so happy to see you."

His smile broadened. "I can tell you have your wits about you. Can you walk? Are you hurt?"

"Only my wrist. When I fell. The horse ... he reared ... a branch knocked me ... the poor horse, was he ...?"

"He is unharmed. When he returned riderless, Darcy and I flew into action."

"Christopher and Lucy ... ?"

"They have not been seen. How did you become separated?"

Kitty tried to explain in breathless bursts. "They were behind ... it was as if they left a-purpose ... a plan?... the small saddlebags ... I did not suspect ..."

She swayed.

Owen reached around her waist to support her but nearly tripped over an obstacle. "What is here?"

Following his gaze, she laughed weakly.

"My cairn ... to mark the path. Your lantern—I knew not if you were friend or foe."

He laughed heartily. "There is a great story here. Let us get you back to the lodge and tended to. Then everyone may hear the whole of it. Come, lean on me."

Waving the lantern back and forth, he called out, "Darcy! Darcy! I found her! Darcy, this way."

Soon several twinkling lights made their way towards them, and in moments Darcy burst onto the path. Owen took his lantern.

"Kitty! Oh, Kitty, are you hurt? Come, put your arms about my neck. Yes, there's a good girl." He swooped her up in his arms. "We have not far to go."

Brandishing two lanterns, Owen led the way. Others ran ahead to call off the search. When they neared the edge of the forest, Darcy set her on her feet and supported her with his arm. They emerged from the trees into the glowing light of the moon.

Kitty was out of the shadow at last.

CHAPTER TWENTY-THREE

*P*rincess Charlotte herself and her best friend Miss Margaret Mercer Elphinstone were at the guest lodge to receive Kitty on her return. The stable master had informed the princess of the search. A physician had been called. After examining Kitty, he pronounced her in excellent condition other than her wrist, which he splinted and wrapped. Darcy's face expressed his relief.

The princess thanked the physician and saw him out. Then she turned to Kitty.

"We shall stay with you for a time this evening, Miss Bennet, while the searchers go out again. What an ordeal! I have called for tea—a substantial tea—for surely you have missed dinner. Tea, cold meats, cakes, and tales! A fine ending we shall make of this evening of adventure and mayhem."

Then she turned to the men.

"I wish you gentlemen luck in finding the scoundrel who abandoned Miss Bennet. And the missing young lady—is she with him of her own accord? Or has he made her a captive?"

"I do not believe Miss Jamison is a captive of *his*, but perhaps a captive of her own gullible heart," Kitty said quietly. "I think Mr. Drake does care for her, in his way."

Owen remained silent during this conversation, although he and Kitty exchanged a few glances.

"Where might he go? Is this Mr. Drake a newcomer to the area?" Miss Elphinstone asked.

To everyone's surprise, it was Mr. Alfred Cressley who responded.

"I do not believe so, Your Highness. According to my other son William, Mr. Christopher Drake has been observed many times at racetracks, taverns, clubs, and other such events. He appears to be deep within a crowd involved in gambling, especially on the horse races. No, he is no stranger."

"But are you sure it is he?" Darcy asked.

"Quite sure, Mr. Darcy. He is a dashing young man, high-spirited, and has a unique way of tossing his blonde hair about. William recognized him immediately when your party arrived at Oakhurst."

George Cressley then spoke. "I too have noticed him at the track when I was there on breeding business."

Mr. Cressley continued. "We were surprised to find him in your company, Darcy. Some young men who wander astray in their youth *are* able to recover their honor and place in society. Let us hope that may be the case here."

"This is ill news indeed," Darcy said, brooding on the meaning of it all. "Perhaps he is unaware of the dangers of this crowd?"

Mr. Cressley shook his head.

"Unlikely. He and another gentleman who is often with him appear to be materially involved. Most such are in it for the money, to fund their gambling. Those who run these groups appear to have prestige, but it is all a sham. No one has seen the other gentleman of late though," he said.

Darcy glanced quickly at Owen. He then changed the subject by directing the attention of the men to assembling search parties to seek the wayward couple. Messengers and scouts had been sent out earlier but none had returned with news. The stable master would stay behind with a few lads that could be sent out if news arrived or the couple returned. The plan was in place, the searchers ready, and the ladies saw them off. Then Kitty, Miss Elphinstone, and Princess Charlotte returned to the drawing room.

Tea was brought immediately, the fire stoked, and a blanket fetched for Kitty. Miss Elphinstone poured. Her regal bearing and mien made her seem more a princess than Charlotte, whose common jolliness contradicted her royal heritage.

"Your Highness, you are most kind ..." Kitty began.

Charlotte waved her arm.

"Please, call me Charlotte. Let us use our Christian names—it is just we ladies now. It is a rare treat to meet anyone near my own age. I am a virtual prisoner, eh Margaret? Sometimes I am even banned from seeing Margaret, my dearest friend."

Kitty gave her a quizzical look at this but it was not her place to question the princess.

"Please call me Kitty, as my friends do," she said. "How fortunate that it is my left wrist or I should be in danger of spilling my tea with this awkward splinting and wrapping. How can I ever thank you for bringing the physician? I am sure his word set Mr. Darcy's mind at ease as much as it did mine."

Charlotte buttered some bread onto which she piled several slices of meat.

"It is also fortunate that is your only injury, Kitty. And that you kept your wits about you so as not to wander deeper into the forest. Things could have gone very ill indeed. Do tell us all the details now, from the beginning. I should like to hear the story in its entirety."

Kitty smiled. "You are right. My fate could have been much worse. I did plunge into a panic at first, especially after my horse bolted." She proceeded to tell the tale in full, from riding ahead of the whispering couple, to turning back and finding her companions gone, to the horse rearing and bolting.

"You must ride often, Kitty. Where is your home again?"

"I have lived all my life at Longbourn, our family estate in Hertfordshire. But I am spending the summer at Pemberley, the seat of my brother-in-law, Mr. Darcy, in Derbyshire."

"The peaks area?" Charlotte asked.

"Yes. And what beauty and drama are found there! I have a lovely little part Arabian mare I ride—she is Mr. Darcy's. My own father disapproved of young ladies riding." She furrowed her brow. "He disapproved of most everything I did," she said, thinking back.

The princess helped herself to several more slices of meat and nodded in commiseration.

"My father is the same."

Kitty looked up to see a sadness lingering in the face of the princess and felt sympathy for her.

"Fortunately my father did not monitor my activities well and I was able to ride often, on the sly. I even ..." Kitty looked at them both carefully. "May I share a confidence with you? Will you keep it secret?" Both ladies nodded, their eyes lighting up, so Kitty continued. "I even managed to often ride astride, disguised as a boy."

Charlotte roared with laughter.

"A fine picture that makes, Kitty! I can see it in my head. And in exchange, I will share a secret with you. I have done the same! When I was younger, of course. My body now would be more difficult to disguise." She burst into a loud cackle. "This ridiculous notion of riding sidesaddle, when one wants speed or to jump a course ... why, one's balance is so precarious when twisted to the side."

"Precisely!" Kitty enjoined. "I cannot help but think it also throws the horse off balance, having to compensate for such an awkward position."

Margaret took hold of her teacup.

"To a pair of true horsewomen." She smiled and held up her cup in salute, and they met it with theirs.

"To true horsewomen and the secrets they must conceal!" Charlotte proclaimed. They all three laughed and drained their cups.

"After the horse bolted," Margaret asked, "what did you do? Surely it was dark by then, and the paths in the forest can be confusing, even in the daylight."

"That was when I truly panicked. I had hoped the horse would take me back even though he was not familiar with the forest. It is said horses can find their way. But once I lost him, I had to find some way to cope. I admit I wept for a time. Then I told myself I must think like a man."

"Like a man?"

"Yes. Logically. Scientifically. Mr. Darcy was my inspiration; as was a friend from Derbyshire, a Mr. Stapleton, who is a geologist. A few of us had taken a ladies' ride along the River Derwent some time ago. Lady Drake, the mother of the very Mr. Christopher Drake they now search for, organized the party. She is a fine rider, and I'm told even rides to the hounds. Her younger son is quite in love with Mr. Darcy's sister and is the finest gentleman you would ever wish to meet, so very unlike his brother. Anyway, Mr. Stapleton is an excellent teacher, and I was an enthusiastic student of the many rock formations, trees, caves, and other features of the Derbyshire landscape. He showed me how moss can usually be found growing on the north side of trees. It can be relied on, to a good degree, to find the compass direction."

"I was not aware of that. How peculiar," Charlotte said.

"Nor I," said Margaret.

"This memory came back to me, surely from Providence itself, as I sat by a large tree in the dark to gather my thoughts. For some time the darkness was complete. I did not wish to wander in circles or go deeper into the forest by mistake. So I felt for the moss and found it. Thus, I had determined north. But then I had to remember which direction we had taken riding into the forest. Of course, I had not paid any attention at the time, but eventually memory served and I determined we had entered the forest from the south. And then, luckiest of all, the moon rose—in the east of course—so I had some bearings and I could see, though only a little. That was when I began to walk, ever so slowly, in a southerly direction."

"That is brilliant!"

"Amazing! You might have made it out all on your own and been your own hero," Charlotte said, laughing heartily.

Kitty smiled. "Possibly. However, I do admit I was most relieved to see Owen ... Mr. Wyndham ... coming towards me with a lantern. I hid until I was certain the lantern-bearer was friend, not foe."

"Very wise, Kitty. There *are* unsavory sorts about, even in the royal grounds," Margaret commented. "A lady must take care."

"But ...'Owen.' You use his Christian name? He is well known to you then?" Charlotte asked with an arched brow as she chomped on a large piece of cake. "He is a handsome fellow."

Kitty blushed. "By happenstance, he discovered my masculine riding secret. He came upon me and the stable boy one day while we were out for a hack. Mr. Owen's wagon had broken down—actually he was en route to his estate with the very royal mares we returned today—and he recognized me by my eyes. So far, he has kept my secret."

Margaret's brows were knit together. "And what is the name of the young lady who is now missing? This Mr. Wyndham seems mightily concerned for her."

"He is, Margaret. She is his stepsister. She is quite unlike him in character and principles. His real brother was recently injured in a steeplechase. He may never walk again."

Princess Charlotte's face grew sober.

"But Wyndham ... I seem to remember that name attached to the rumors I have heard about a gambling group." Miss Elphinstone looked at Kitty. "I believe they call themselves an 'investment club.' My father is investigating the situation. They not only gamble but also attempt to fix races by drugging horses, or jockeys, or both. There have been several injuries, and at least one horse has died and one jockey is crippled. Was this injured Mr. Wyndham actually Mr. Drake's comrade?"

Kitty frowned. "Mr. Owen's brother did—before the accident—often travel with Mr. Drake, I have been told. I have no firsthand information. I hope you are misinformed about them. Lord and Lady Drake are upstanding people."

"And Mr. Wyndham—at present in Matlock with his injured son—is as fine a man as you will ever want to know. His younger son, Mr. Owen, has shouldered the responsibilities of the estate and especially the horse husbandry program in his father's absence. The family has suffered much sorrow. Mr. Owen's mother and sister were taken by fever some years back. The older son had contracted it first and blames himself for their deaths. His reactions have caused much grief."

Margaret had been listening to this account with care.

"I cannot think that these two young men concocted this 'investment club.' They are merely the pawns of greater criminal minds. Perhaps," said she in a lowered voice, "they could be used —with or without their knowledge or consent—to bring the real culprits to account?"

The princess poured more tea for each of them, chortling as the cups overflowed.

"Now there is a scheme. And that makes sense, Margaret. If these two young men were convicted, the crimes would still go on. Those in control would simply find two more such young men to do their bidding for a small share of the purse."

"Exactly," Margaret said.

Intrigued by this plan, Kitty asked, "Do you mean there might be a way for these two to be released from their crime and so not dishonor their families? For them to have a second chance to do right?"

Princess Charlotte said, "Certainly the injured one will no longer be involved ... unless he has another accomplice. We may have a way to work on young Mr. Drake, to save both his own reputation and that of his lady love, should she wish it. But we cannot know until they are found."

She leaned back in her chair. "We will need to communicate amongst ourselves in the weeks ahead. Kitty, leave your direction with Margaret here; and it would be best to write only to her. Sometimes my mail or messages are intercepted—even changed or falsified. We have no way of knowing who is at the top of this illicit scheme, and who may be protecting them. We must take great care. Fortunes are at stake for the culprits. Let Margaret be in charge of our plan. I will be equally involved, but silent."

Kitty raised her brow, wondering at this.

Charlotte sighed. "Such is the situation, I am afraid. At present, I am ensconced at Cranbourne Lodge in the Great Park. But my father moves me around at his whim and decides whom I may or may not see. You are surprised?"

Kitty's eyes were wide. "I confess I am. I had imagined a sumptuous life of parties and balls and travel and fine dining amongst the royalty. It does not seem like this bears out?"

"No, it does not. I will need to marry to gain my freedom, like any other gentlewoman. Only then will I have my own home to order as I wish. And someday rule as ... well, and so my mind is bent for now on a marriage; and one for love if that can be managed. You see, I am not so different from you or your friends, Kitty. I wish I had friends and could socialize where I wish. Margaret here is my closest and most devoted ..."

A servant knocked and announced that some of the searchers had returned. The trays of tea things were removed and when the servants had quitted the room, Margaret spoke again in a low voice.

"Most of the searchers know only that they seek a young couple who may have eloped. Let us preserve that notion."

Charlotte nodded. "Yes, that is wise. We must speak tomorrow, Kitty, before you depart. Shall you still wish to ride tomorrow morning?"

"The physician advised against risking another fall."

"Best to follow his advice, though I regret losing the chance to gallop about with you. You will be at risk enough during your return journey."

"I am disappointed to not ride with you. But there will be another time, I hope?"

"Of course. Perhaps I may escape to Derbyshire one day!" Charlotte laughed heartily.

Kitty wrote her direction at both Pemberley and Longbourn and passed it to Margaret.

"I believe I shall be at Pemberley for the summer, perhaps a little longer. My sister's confinement will begin in late autumn, and I do not know yet if she wishes me to stay for the birth."

≈

It was not long until Darcy, Owen, and the Cressleys entered. They had little to report. The young couple had not been seen.

"One stable boy did disclose Mr. Drake had asked for directions to nearby inns. Riders will be sent out again at dawn," Darcy said.

Owen stood sullenly beside Darcy.

George Cressley frowned, then asked, "What of our departure, Darcy? Shall we leave tomorrow or delay until they are found?"

"I believe we should leave immediately after luncheon no matter if they are found or not. But it troubles me to leave the young lady in such circumstances."

"Perhaps I may be entrusted to stay and continue the search?" George offered.

Owen protested. "She is my sister; I should stay."

Darcy's face was severe. "Both of you shall stay, but only for two days. Mr. Owen, you must return with us when we leave Oakhurst. It is not known yet if your father and brother will remain in Matlock some weeks longer. You are needed to manage Greystone."

"I will do so, for my father. My brother cares nothing for the estate. Why should I keep it running for—"

Darcy clipped him off—"Good. And Kitty," he remarked, turning to her, "can I assume your gracious invitation to ride with the princess and her party has been ... postponed due to your injury?"

Princess Charlotte answered. "She has already declined, Mr. Darcy. But I have renewed the offer for any time possible in the future. As Miss Elphinstone has advised, Miss Bennet has enough risk on the return to Oakhurst and beyond. Her wrist must not be reinjured."

Owen looked at Kitty with concern, then cast hard eyes towards the fireplace, his mouth grim in a clenched jaw.

CHAPTER TWENTY-FOUR

The return trip to Oakhurst was made without incident although Kitty did have to insist that Darcy not lead her horse as if she were a helpless child. After demonstrating her level of control using one hand, he relented. He and his cousin talked about family affairs and events, horse breeding and the horse market, as well as estate issues and interests. Kitty listened halfway but found her mind straying towards the many events of late. Here was time to try and make sense of it all. Owen's countenance—alternately troubled or smiling—floated amongst her other thoughts and impressions. The journey was not the same without him.

They reached Oakhurst not long after teatime. Georgiana and Matilda greeted them in the foyer with great enthusiasm.

"Oh, Kitty, how we have missed you! Oh, what has happened to your wrist?" said Georgiana, reaching out and taking Kitty's hand gently. Then, looking about, she asked, "Where is the rest of the party?"

Darcy grimaced. "Please allow Kitty to rest before peppering her with questions." Darcy kissed Georgiana on the forehead in greeting. "Perhaps you could see to tea? I am sure Kitty needs refreshment. Just for you ladies at present; Alfred and I will see to the horses and meet with the head groom."

"Of course. I shall arrange it directly with Lady Matlock."

When William saw Kitty's wrist he directed the staff that she be attended to immediately in her quarters.

"You are very kind, Mr. William," she said and the three ladies mounted the stairs.

Kitty turned to Georgiana and Matilda.

"We are a much diminished party, for now. As you may imagine, there is much news to share. Please, grant me half an hour and a spot of tea—black please—and then I shall regale you with all the details."

"And we shall tell you of the party plans!" quipped Matilda. "We have not been idle whilst you were gone."

Kitty glanced at Matilda. Her joy was infectious and helped Kitty's mood change for the better.

"*You* certainly have not, Matilda," Georgiana chided, and Matilda blushed but looked delighted all the same. "Kitty, we shall meet in the music room."

Kitty retreated to wash and change. The maid assisted her in renewing the outer wrap on her wrist, which was encrusted with dust. After a brief rest, Kitty donned a fresh gown and had her hair brushed out and redone, then made for the music room.

"Is it just we three then?" she asked as Georgiana poured the tea.

"Yes. Murielle is resting until dinner."

"William has gone to the stables, and Charles is on vicarage business. So you need not guard your words, Kitty," Matilda remarked. "Now, where are the others?"

Kitty explained the events at Windsor to the best of her memory.

"Missing? How shocking! Do you think they have eloped?" Georgiana asked.

"That is how it appears. However, do you remember our pact? The one about the 'investment club'? We now add two new members: Princess Charlotte and her closest friend, Miss Margaret Mercer Elphinstone."

"The royal princess?" they exclaimed in unison.

"You met her?

"And talked with her?"

"Yes, first in one of the stables, and again after my rescue. She is friendly and approachable, and so very kind."

"But how is she involved in our pact?" Matilda asked.

"It appears Mr. Christopher was familiar to both William and Mr. Cressley before we ever arrived at Oakhurst. He had frequented the racetracks and taverns and is suspected to be part of a gambling scheme, the very one we had talked of. Miss Elphinstone's father is investigating the case, so she had heard of it. I think there may be two reasons for Mr. Christopher's disappearance. First, he knew he had been recognized. And second, Lucy was a pleasant distraction for his escape. Their affection did seem to grow during our journey, though his manner is more teasing than I should prefer for myself. Nothing can be known for certain until they are found."

Kitty took a few sips of tea and a bite of a sandwich.

"So Mr. Owen and Mr. George have stayed at Windsor to aid in the search?"

"Yes. Mr. Owen is furious and his patience grows thin. Mr. Darcy demanded that they both return in two days, whether the couple is found or not. Mr. Owen must manage Greystone should Mr. Wyndham need to stay longer at Matlock with Mr. Douglas."

"Poor Mr. Wyndham!" Georgiana said, shaking her head. "It is so unfair that he has yet another problem to cope with—his stepdaughter eloping, or worse."

"Mr. Owen is quite cast down by it all. He is still upset about Julia as well."

"He was so angry at Matlock," Georgiana remarked. "And none of us knows yet how Julia gets on. I hope love will triumph. For her, and for Lucy."

Matilda broke in. "You spoke of being rescued. Tell us about that."

Kitty related the whole of the incident in the forest, to the amazement of the young ladies.

"My brother will be so proud of you, Kitty, for putting that knowledge to such good use."

"Yes, I imagine he will," Kitty mused. Other than the moss,

she had not thought about Andrew of late. "But he is in Scotland by now. You may write to him about it, Matilda."

They sipped their tea.

Kitty sighed and stared off in the distance.

Seeing Georgiana's worried expression, she said, "Do not be troubled on my account. It is my concern for the others that wearies me. But now, tell me what has taken place here in my absence. If I am not mistaken, an attachment is forming? Or has been formed?" She looked directly at Matilda.

Matilda laughed and joy lit her face.

"Mr. William is divine, Kitty. He is so kind and amusing. He has gone to great trouble to entertain us. I am quite entranced."

"Indeed she is. And from what I can ascertain, so is he," Georgiana said. "I am very happy for you, Matilda. Oh, tell her about the party."

"Party?"

"Yes. Mrs. Cressley and Mr. William, having arranged it with Mr. Cressley prior to his departure, honor us with a party—supper, cards, and perhaps dancing. Two families have called whilst here and will attend. It will be a most pleasant evening."

"I am sure it will. I look forward to it. I have met so many new people this summer. You cannot imagine my happiness at that. How different from my lonely life at Longbourn. I wonder if Mr. Christopher and Lucy will return for the party? Or indeed, if they will return at all."

All three reflected solemnly on the possibilities.

Georgiana and Matilda played and sang duets, and the time passed pleasantly until dinner was announced.

≈

Murielle groused when she found her husband had not returned with the group.

"What can be so important that my *caro spozo* must stay at Windsor? What has he to do with a young couple foolish enough to elope?"

"Mrs. Cressley, I look for them to return in two days at the longest," Darcy replied.

Alfred Cressley placed a hand on her shoulder.

"Now, do not worry, my dear. George will be back at any moment, good news or ill. I understand you wishing him nearby at this time."

"Thank you. He has traveled so frequently this past year. It is quite distressing. I shall rest much easier when he is returned."

General events of the journey were discussed and family news exchanged.

Kitty watched the looks shared between William and Matilda throughout the evening. It seemed love *had* triumphed at Oakhurst.

≈

The next two days were spent walking about the delightful grounds, playing and singing, visiting the stables, and engaging in conversation. Darcy and Cressley rode about the estate. Darcy would not hear of Kitty risking further injury and she was sorry to miss those outings. So she worked at her drawing. She found mares and foals delightful subjects, and her knowledge of equine form served her well.

During a leisurely breakfast the morning of the party, hooves were heard on the sweep. Mr. Cressley excused himself and returned momentarily to announce that a party of four had returned from Windsor.

"They have all of them gone to their chambers to change and refresh but will join us shortly. They left Windsor at dawn. We shall meet them in the drawing room. Morton, please have tea and refreshments for the travelers brought there in half an hour," he said, nodding at the butler.

"Oh, and Miss Bennet, this letter was carried by Mr. Owen Wyndham for you," he said, presenting her with a missive addressed in an elegant flowing hand, bearing a royal seal. "You made some fortunate connections at Windsor."

"Thank you, Mr. Cressley," Kitty said, without further comment. Murielle and William looked at her with curiosity, not having heard about the royal encounter. Darcy merely lifted a brow. When she did not open the envelope immediately, the bustle of breakfast resumed.

Kitty was making for her room to read her letter in private when Darcy caught up with her. His face was stern and his formidable demeanor had returned.

"Do you have bad news about the four that have just arrived?" she asked him.

"I know no more than you, Kitty. But we shall find out soon enough I imagine." He nodded his head towards the letter .

"I shall apprise you of anything of import, Fitzwilliam. I believe the letter is from Miss Elphinstone. Princess Charlotte said she is not always at liberty to write, and that sometimes her mail is ... supervised by others."

"I am not surprised. Her father is disliked by some, and the intrigues surrounding him are many. Princess Charlotte, however, is a great favorite with the people. Some believe he feels threatened by her popularity. Do be careful Kitty. As friendly as the princess appears to be, do not get pulled into any business that is not your own."

"Be assured I shall request your advice on anything that I may question. You are already apprised of the two issues at hand —the 'investment club,' and the attempted elopement—even though some are only aware of one?" she asked with an arch of her brow.

"Yes. And I advise you to consult with me before any involvement."

"I shall."

"Good. Now go. Read your letter in private. We shall meet shortly with the new arrivals and get the news that shall determine the course of action for many. I shall have a private word with Mr. Owen and Mr. George now."

Kitty settled into the chair by the window in her room. She turned the letter over several times, admiring the script, almost disbelieving that this missive was from royalty ... well, the direct friend of royalty. She thought back to her lonely and uneventful months in Longbourn and was grateful for the new and dear friends that were now part of her life. Their puzzling situations presented many questions; there was much to share with Lizzy when they returned. She broke the seal and opened the letter.

My dear Miss B,

I pray your trip was uneventful, in the best sense, and that your wrist continues to mend.

The others from your party will have returned to you by the time you read this. Mr. D. required strong convincing to offer for Miss J. His attitude was cavalier. He appears to care little for the impact of his actions on others. The couple were found at an inn of low reputation near the racetrack. Your other new friend and I cannot like him.

We must be guarded in how and with whom we share information. I am not convinced of Mr. G.C.'s honor. Be on guard there. I believe your Mr. W. can be trusted with a confidence (thus my entrusting him with this letter), although his judgment may be tainted by his anger at the above couple, and perhaps the other situations you spoke of. He has our sympathies.

Please advise of anything you learn in the case, and when your direction changes. We both wish you Godspeed in your travels and will continue to honor our pact.

Yours in friendship,
MME

Kitty pondered this not-surprising news about Mr. Christopher, and this most-surprising news about Mr. George Cressley. Darcy would need to be apprised at once.

When she arrived in the drawing room Darcy was engaged in conversation with Mr. Alfred Cressley. Owen sat near Georgiana, Matilda, and Lucy, his eyes dark and his face sullen. William Cressley was also near, delighting in Matilda. Charles Cressley sat alone, reading. George Cressley was curiously absent, as was Christopher Drake. Darcy caught Kitty's eye and made for the doorway.

"Excuse me, Miss Bennet," a deep voice said from behind her. She turned to see Christopher and stepped back to allow him to enter. All eyes riveted to him.

"Ladies and gentlemen," Christopher said, bowing elegantly, "we all meet again."

"My dear!" Lucy exclaimed. Her beau moved towards her with a conceited smirk.

Darcy spoke in a low tone, turning away from the room so his voice would not carry.

"Did your letter carry news beyond the usual feminine exchanges?"

Kitty eyed him with surprise, then glared at him.

"I am disappointed at your words, Fitzwilliam. At present, our female contingent appears the only one reliable regarding these concerns. Perhaps we should manage them on our own?"

Darcy's brows flew up at the intensity of her reply.

"No, indeed. I am sorry. Kitty, I am not accustomed to feeling uninformed about people and issues for which I am responsible. It has put me quite out of my element." He cleared his throat. "Is there news about either of our concerns of which you wish me to be aware?"

"There is. I would gladly show you the letter; but if we steal away now, I fear it will cause suspicion. Miss Elphinstone says that Mr. Christopher had to be strongly convinced to offer for Lucy, and that she and the princess found his attitude cavalier. They do not like him."

"None of that surprises me."

"Nor I. But what did surprise me was a warning about Mr. George Cressley. They doubt his honor and warn us to be on our guard."

Darcy scowled. "Duplicity?" He composed his countenance and turned back towards the company, carefully surveying each person in it, including George, who had just entered the room.

"I had not suspected that; and in my own family. Perhaps your friends are wrong. In any case, I shall take that recommendation for now and advise you do so as well. The fewer people who know our business, the better."

Kitty squirmed. Georgiana was watching them curiously, so she smiled to put her at ease.

"There are others who are aware of our initial concern, Fitzwilliam. We had formed a pact about it after the ball, and

Julia also spoke to me alone about it after Douglas was injured. She had suspected Douglas and Christopher of being involved in some kind of gambling scheme, as both wanted more money to support the expensive independent reputations they wished to achieve. So Julia, Matilda, Georgiana, and I formed a pact to listen and discover what we could about the 'investment club'."

Darcy's eyes narrowed and he stiffened beside her.

"And this is what you young ladies have been up to? Clearly, I have underestimated you all. Did I not ask you to tell me about things?"

"There has been naught to tell until this trip; and whilst on the trip there has been no time or place for private discussion. Even what we *do* know is mostly hearsay or rumor. I have now shared it, as you wished. We do not merit your wrath, Fitzwilliam. Please honor your promise to refrain from becoming formidable." Kitty lifted her chin and stared him in the eye.

He returned her stare for a moment, then his face softened into a grin.

"Your spirit is not unlike your sister's, Kitty. I cannot fault it, but it takes me by surprise. I had not known the two of you were so alike. Continue listening for now and let us see what is revealed and by whom today. We shall have a discussion before leaving for Matlock to determine a course of action."

"Certainly. At that time, I will apprise you of more details concerning the involvement of our royal friends."

He lifted a brow at her but she gracefully moved away.

Kitty joined the younger group that was more happily engaged in talking about the evening's upcoming party.

Before long, Owen came and stood near Kitty, listening to the group. She could not read his expression, but he seemed less angry. After a time, he took a seat next to her.

"Miss Bennet, may I inquire about your wrist? I was concerned about you riding with the injury."

"It is healing well, but I have not ridden since we arrived at Oakhurst. That has tried me sorely as I long to explore these woods and paths. And I, in my turn, was concerned for you, Mr. Owen." She leaned closer and spoke almost in a whisper. "You have so many challenges before you at present." She nodded towards his sister, who clung to Christopher's arm.

"Indeed. I wonder how my patience shall last, and I pray that the choices I make are for the best. It is at such times one especially values a steady friend, Miss Bennet, and I have longed to speak with you in just that way. You are strong-minded, and I value your insight. I have wished to know your opinions. Pardon me if I am too forward," he said, coloring slightly.

She blushed at the compliment and hesitated as she thought about what he might mean.

"Thank you, Mr. Owen. You honor me. How does your sister do? She appears happy in spite of—"

"Happy? Happy to disregard any blight on her reputation or on that of her family, unfortunately. She has been blinded by her infatuation for Christopher Drake for some time."

"Does he return her affection, do you think?"

Owen looked at Kitty. "In his way, possibly. I have known him to flirt with many a young lady, but he has always returned to Lucy. He thrives on attention and causing uproar. They seem to enjoy their quarrels as much as their happier times." He shrugged. "Some are like that. I hope his motivation is not like my brother's with Miss Stapleton. But Lucy's dowry is small, of which Drake is aware. And that will not matter once he inherits. I believe Lord Drake has him on a tight pecuniary leash at present, which stifles his style. I hope he will not abandon my sister should an heiress happen along. He had to be coerced to offer for Lucy. She can be troublesome and shallow, but she deserves happiness as much as you or I; and I pray she will find it. I merely question if he is the man she should rely upon."

They were both staring at the couple when Lucy became aware. She waved happily at them and convinced Christopher to walk over and join them.

"Brother, did you tell Kitty our good news?" Lucy asked.

Owen stared at her, incredulous.

"There is no news to tell, Lucy. Our father has not been spoken to. Nothing is officially declared."

"It is for us!" she retorted. "Besides, I am two and twenty. I need no one's permission to marry, nor does my beloved." She patted Christopher's arm with affection and pressed her cheek against his shoulder.

Owen scowled.

"My dear," Christopher replied, "your brother is right. We must do things the honorable way or our reputations might suffer." He chortled at his own sarcasm.

Kitty rose to meet him face to face.

"You may not bother about your own reputation, Mr. Drake, but have a care for that of my friend Lucy, and for her family. And do remember, she is only in our party by Mr. Darcy's special permission. He is not charmed by rebellious attitudes or callous actions, so beware!" Her face was flushed in anger, but she managed to control her urge to stomp off and instead made a serene exit.

Desiring both fresh air and privacy, Kitty made for the door. She had hardly been alone since she left the shadow of Windsor Forest. The rhythm of her own footsteps was comforting as she moved across the grass to one of the upper wooded paths. As she walked, some of her scattered thoughts seemed to fall into more of an order. If only she could speak with Lizzy.

The dappled sunlight and the calling of the birds soothed her, and she slowed her pace. The path grew narrow and grasses began to encroach. This way was little used. She sank onto a fallen log and gazed through the trees at the valley below, enjoying the smell of the woods and the subtle beauty of the woodland flowers. Then, amongst the woodland sounds, she heard the quiet footfalls of a horse. She peered in the direction of the sound. Near a distant outcropping of boulders stood two men, one holding a horse.

Was she in danger here? Her heart thumped and her breath grew shallow. Not wishing to be seen, she slipped from the log and slowly made her way back along the path she had come. After rounding a dense grouping of cedars, she risked a look back. One man was heading her way, quickly enough that he would overtake her before she reached the lawn.

Gathering up her gown, she sprinted down the path whilst he was yet out of sight, then slowed to a walk, thankful she had worn a gown of darker green. The lawn was within reach and she breathed a sigh of relief. Pretending to look down the valley, she watched the man's progress from the corner of her eye. He was coming to the house.

Taking a deep breath to calm herself, she sought for logic. But it would not serve; there were too many unknowns. She feigned to wander aimlessly along the edge of the lawn. When she heard his footsteps, she turned.

"Mr. Cressley!" Her astonishment was genuine.

He was equally surprised. "Miss Bennet! What do you do here?"

She dropt him a quick curtsey. "I am enjoying the solace of the woods, Mr. George. I fear I am unused to being in so much company for so long."

His eyes narrowed.

"And how was your return trip? I have not yet heard where the couple were found. They do both seem happy."

His face relaxed somewhat. "Our trip was ... expedient. And how do you recover from your ordeal in Windsor Forest, Miss Bennet?" he asked, nodding towards her wrapped wrist.

"Very well, sir. I thank you. I am sorry you and Mr. Owen were tasked with such a chore in finding the missing couple. Was it an elopement?" she asked, knowing full well the true situation.

"I must talk to Mr. Darcy before I share any information, Miss Bennet, but do not trouble yourself—all involved are safe now," he said with a smile as he offered her his arm.

She did not ask him where he had been or what was of interest up the pathway. Would he notice that? Or just take her for an empty-headed female? She smiled insipidly as she took his arm and began to talk about the evening's party.

After escorting her to the drawing room door, he bowed.

"I must see my wife, Miss Bennet."

"Of course. Please give her my best wishes," she replied with a curtsey.

Turning into the doorway, she saw Darcy's barely-perceivable raised brow. It was not nearly as comforting as Lizzy's wink.

CHAPTER TWENTY-FIVE

*A*fter tea, the four younger ladies met in Georgiana's room. Gowns were discussed and chosen.

"Who shall be amongst the company this evening?" Kitty asked Georgiana.

With a sly smile, Georgiana said, "Perhaps you should ask Matilda. She has been deep in conference with Mr. William, and I believe knows far more about this family and the neighborhood than I."

Matilda gurgled with laughter. "I will not deny it, nor do I wish to!" she exclaimed. "Every minute in his company is happiness beyond words." Her irrepressible delight shone in her eyes and was contagious to them all.

"Then speak! Tell us who will intrigue and delight us this evening," Lucy demanded, dancing about the room with an invisible form that Kitty could only guess was Christopher.

"The Lodge family and the Cavendish family will be the guests. There are several younger brothers and sisters, but of interest to us are Louisa Lodge and her brother Philip, and Martha Cavendish and her brother Lewis. My William and Mr. Lewis Cavendish are very thick. A cousin of one of them—I don't remember which—is visiting and will also join us—a Mr. Graham Waverly from Sussex."

"And have you met any of them?" Kitty asked with interest.

Georgiana smiled. "We have indeed. The ladies have called on us twice, and we have called at their homes with Mr. William. The gentlemen called here once. Mr. Waverly is particularly handsome, and I found Mr. Cavendish most congenial. What is your opinion, Matilda?"

"I confess I hardly noticed. After all, my William was present." She feigned a great swoon and they all broke into laughter.

"It promises to be a pleasant evening," Lucy said. "And it seems you, Kitty, are the only one who might consider herself eligible to meet new men. After all, I am engaged; Matilda confesses she is in love, and Georgiana is all but promised to Mr. Benjamin Drake."

Georgiana started at this.

Lucy sniggered. "I am not blind, Georgiana. Your mutual affection—and most markedly *his* affection—has been obvious for months. Are either of the visiting ladies in love or engaged?"

"Miss Cavendish claims a suitor in Brighton. Miss Lodge spoke of no particular gentleman but she has a fortune of twenty thousand pounds," Matilda said.

"Within our company only Mr. Charles and Mr. Owen are unattached," Lucy said. "So that makes three for Kitty and Miss Lodge—no, five if we count Charles and Owen—to choose amongst. The odds are in your favor tonight, Kitty."

"Except I do not have a fortune of twenty thousand pounds," Kitty said softly. "That may change the odds."

"Not for those who are worth having, I should say," Georgiana remarked. "Plus, you have the Bennet spirit, Kitty, which my brother found irresistible. And he is the most wonderful man in the world ... along with Benjamin, of course."

"Time to dress, ladies," Matilda announced, and all left for their respective rooms to prepare for the evening.

≈

The guests arrived and introductions were made. Cocktails were served, and all were ushered into a room where several tables were set for cards. Dozens of candles flickered invitingly, and the long golden rays of the sun shone through the many-paned windows. Sunset would come late at this time of year.

Murielle Cressley acted as hostess for her father-in-law and so did not sit down to cards herself.

"Please, find your name and take your seat," she announced. The twelve younger people were seated at three tables, and the older members at two tables.

Murielle rang a tiny bell. "We shall play for half an hour; then the gentlemen will rotate tables amongst their set—we shall do that twice—so all may mingle before supper. You may begin when ready."

Kitty was paired with Martha Cavendish, whom she found friendly. At their table were Christopher Drake and Philip Lodge. Mr. Lodge had an elegant manner about him and was reserved in contrast to Christopher's showy demeanor. Philip and Martha had an easy familiarity, having been neighbors for many years, but he did not meet Kitty's eyes. Was he uncomfortable with ladies or with new people in general? Or did he feel himself above his company?

Christopher tossed his hair and aimed his charms at Martha; and when he discovered she had a beau, only increased his attentions to her. Perhaps he felt free to practice his manly arts, knowing he would not be expected to follow through. Whilst he did not look towards Lucy during his time at Kitty's table, Lucy eyed him several times. What a troublesome beau Christopher would be.

Murielle rang her bell. Glasses were refilled. Kitty and Martha were joined by Lewis Cavendish and William Cressley, who were chums and quite jolly. Much conversation and laughter accompanied the rollicking and haphazard game.

Kitty watched William with amusement. He was continually diverted by Matilda's voice and made many poor plays, but these were all laughed away with good nature. *Besotted!*

Lewis Cavendish, as personable as his sister, kept up an animated conversation and asked Kitty many questions about her interests, her visit, and about Hertfordshire, where he had visited once. She was easily drawn in by his friendliness and flattered by his marked interest.

Once again the bell rang. Joining Kitty and Martha this time were Owen Wyndham and Graham Waverly, Martha's cousin. Owen maintained the reserve that Kitty had observed of him when in groups. Graham Waverly was quite bewitching. He regaled them with stories of his training in medical work, sharing only those anecdotes with happy or amusing outcomes it seemed. His eyes twinkled with merriment.

In addition to his own stories, he asked Kitty about herself and her life, and especially her visit in Derbyshire and the Pemberley estate. He sat next to Kitty and often leaned in close to make a point or share a laugh. Kitty was highly aware of the special attention he was paying her and responded warmly to his dimpled smile and blue eyes. His blonde good looks rivaled Christopher's, and were unmarred by the latter's sometimes sneering quality.

As she basked in the charm of Graham's attentions, a flush crept up Owen's face. His eyes flashed at her a few times, and his mouth was set in a rigid line.

Oh, Owen, must you always be troubled? Can you not just enjoy yourself? She wished she could ease his many burdens, but she also wished to feel unhampered in making new friends without upsetting an old friend. In spite of her esteem of Owen, resentment was growing. She was less desirous of his company because it was only occasionally pleasant. His many problems wore on her. She found the sunny charm and affability of a Graham Waverly or an Andrew Stapleton to be more desirable.

The younger people filled both sides of the large dining table, with the older members of the party being honored with places near to the head and foot occupied by Mr. Alfred Cressley and his daughter-in-law Murielle. Kitty was seated between Graham Waverly and William Cressley. Across from her were Matilda and Georgiana, with whom she exchanged many speaking looks but little conversation. Seated between those ladies was the ebullient Lewis Cavendish. Also on that side of the table sat Christopher Drake, next to heiress Louisa Lodge—much to Lucy's consternation. Owen was on the other side of Louisa.

Drawing all eyes to himself, Christopher exclaimed loudly, "I, for one, am famished! What a fine spread we have here." He then leaned over just a little farther than was proper to help Louisa, whilst looking into her eyes and smiling. Christopher's appetite for the fine supper had likely been enhanced by his appetite for Louisa's twenty thousand pounds.

Kitty wrinkled her nose. She did not envy Lucy one jot.

The rosy hues streaking the midsummer sky were diminished by the blaze of candles on and around the table. What was it Owen had once said? Candlelight was nice, but he preferred the stars. Kitty glanced down the table but was unable to catch his eye. He, too, was gazing out the large windows at the sky. Her heart softened towards him once more.

The meal went on for some time. Afterwards some of the younger group preferred to dance, but Kitty's heart was not in it, nor did she wish to jostle her injured wrist. The crowd felt constraining, and the lingering twilight called her out of doors.

Seeing Darcy nearby, she walked over to him.

"I long to walk about the garden alone. May I do so?"

"Certainly. Why not. The evening is lovely. I will station myself here at the terrace door, but do keep within the walls."

"I shall."

The sky's rosy streaks had melted into a mantle of violet with golden stars winking through in clusters like flowers. A crescent moon hung low in the sky. The coo of the doves was soothing, and Kitty walked the perimeter of the garden slowly, savoring the scents of earth, herbs, and night flowers mingled with the nearby woods. She breathed deeply, reflecting on how far she was from Longbourn and that, even when she returned, it would not be the same. It would never be the same, because she was not the same. This visit had changed her. At this critical point in her life, her future depended on her own choices over the next months—and to a degree on what luck brought her way. She prayed that Providence would guide her to happiness.

As she pondered what that happiness might look like, the motion of someone moving towards Darcy caught her eye. It was Graham Waverly. Darcy shook his head and motioned him back indoors. She sighed with relief and began another turn about the garden. She wanted to make the choices about her life, not have them made for her by some scandal. When she looked back,

Darcy was facing indoors, talking with Mr. Cressley and the Cavendishes.

After a time she perceived a shadow along the garden wall, moving towards her. The gait was not familiar and until the silhouetted figure came quite near she could not recognize him.

When his face came into the light, she saw it was Graham Waverly. What was he about? Had Fitzwilliam not stopped him from intruding on her reverie just moments ago? A prickling sensation moved up her neck, causing her to move quickly towards the lighter area near the doors. Fitzwilliam was still turned away.

Mr. Waverly stopped in front of her and bowed.

"Miss Bennet, is it not a lovely evening?" His face looked pleasant and sincere. But a turn alone with him in the starlit garden would give a very wrong impression. Although she found him attractive and intriguing, this disregard of Fitzwilliam's direction cast his character in a less flattering light.

Unsettled by his sudden appearance, she said, "Mr. Waverly, what do you do here? Did my brother not—"

"Miss Bennet, we are not children to be directed. The evening calls for romance, does it not? You are so lovely. You enjoyed my earlier attentions I believe, and I only sought to ..." He faltered, following her gaze.

Owen and Georgiana were speaking with Darcy and, at Darcy's nod, headed towards Kitty. In a trice the other couple had joined them.

With a brief bow, Owen said, "Miss Bennet, Mr. Waverly. Who could remain indoors on such a pleasant evening? Miss Darcy also expressed a desire to enjoy the outdoors."

Georgiana dropt a curtsey and approached Graham.

"Have you ever traveled to Derbyshire, sir?"

Owen offered Kitty his arm. Looking up she mouthed a silent 'thank you.' A smile spread over his face, but he said nothing and led her away a few steps, putting Graham in the position of escorting Georgiana.

"I have not been to Derbyshire, Miss Darcy. Have you been to Sussex?"

"No. I should dearly like to travel more. Do tell me some of the delights of Sussex."

Leaving the other couple several steps behind, Kitty and Owen walked on in silence. It was a comfortable silence. His body had lost its earlier tension and his countenance had smoothed. She glanced back at Darcy, who continued at his self-appointed post. Turning to Owen, she asked in a low voice, "How did you know?"

"That you might need assistance?" He looked long at Kitty and then spoke.

"I would not have you think I keep watch over you—not that I do not wish to—but that is your brother's job at present. I only help when I can. I happened to overhear when Mr. Waverly expressed to Mr. Darcy his desire to walk with you in the garden. Alone. He was, of course, denied. My instincts told me to watch how Mr. Waverly took this refusal. I watched him gulp down a glass of wine then quietly move to a side door. I followed, just to see what he was up to. He went out and, after stopping at a nearby tree, walked around the outside of the house. I stationed myself so as to observe anyone entering the garden area. It is walled in, true enough, but there are three ways to enter. It was not long before he entered through the west gate, but he kept to the shadows near the wall rather than openly walking the path. Naturally, that aroused my suspicion. For someone to disregard your brother's entreaty indicates to me a grave lack of integrity. Miss Darcy came to converse with me and when I mentioned what I had seen, she was eager to accompany me in your behalf. You know the rest."

"I was unaware of my risk until Mr. Waverly was in front of me."

The night sky had deepened and there was a hush about the garden. Owen sought her eyes again.

"No, I imagine not. You are strong and resourceful. Your integrity I doubt not. But women are in a precarious position as concerns their reputations. I do not agree with it, but I do not make these rules. Some small thing can cast a long shadow on a woman's honor. Mr. Darcy's intervention would have drawn undue attention. If Miss Darcy and I simply joined you, all the requirements of propriety would be met with little or no notice by anyone. I hope I have not offended?"

Kitty squeezed his arm. "Of course not." They walked on for a bit, the other couple still trailing them by several steps. "With your honor giving rise to such careful attentions towards me, the predicament of your sister must be most frustrating to you."

He gave her a wry smile. "It is, for the sake of my family, and especially my father. My sister seems oblivious to any ill effects. Whilst I honor her as my sister, she has never been kind to me. Not that she has singled me out; just that she is not ... well, she has only herself and her own desires in mind as she walks through life. I do not believe her intentionally unkind. More unawares, I would say. She lacks insight, but she is not evil. She enjoys adventure—not unlike you—but she wants your wisdom and common sense."

Kitty flushed at his compliment.

Owen went on. "I wearied of the continual drama between Lucy and Christopher Drake this evening. I believe him especially vulnerable to any heiress at present. He is not above leaving my sister in the lurch—especially with the engagement not yet public, nor even known or sanctioned by her father or his. I know not what happened between Drake and Lucy whilst they were missing. She does not take me into her confidence in that way. I wish she had a sister. Perhaps she would talk more with another woman."

Giving this last comment some thought, Kitty saw a way she might help. If Lucy would confide in her, the true danger of her predicament might be found out. If it were possible she could be with child, a hasty marriage would be imperative. If things had not progressed that far, perhaps a more suitable mate might be found. The disappearance of the couple was known only to their immediate group, most of whom could be relied on for confidentiality. Perhaps she could help Lucy make wiser choices than her own sister Lydia had done.

"Mr. Owen, I would be honored if your sister would choose to confide in me. Truly, I do not know what I would do without my sisters and their counsel. I have missed Lizzy greatly on this journey. There is much I wish to discuss with her. I grow eager to be home."

He gave her a curious sideways look.

"I shall make an effort to let Lucy know my feelings in this, and my desire to be like a sister to her."

"Miss Bennet, that is most kind."

He stopped walking and turned to her with knitted brows.

"You are eager to return to Longbourn?"

"No, not to Longbourn." In answering him, her eyes widened. "No, it is Pemberley that feels like home now."

"Pemberley feels like home to you?" asked Georgiana, who had just caught up with them. "I am so happy to hear that. I wish you could live with us always," she said. "Well, at least until we each marry and set up our own homes. I have never had sisters, and now I have two who are most precious to me. It is a delight I am not eager to give up with any alacrity!" The ladies joined hands affectionately.

When the four re-entered the house, space had been cleared for dancing to Murielle's piano accompaniment.

"Come join us!" cried Lucy. She was paired with Christopher of course; and Matilda and William were partnered. Reels and jigs were danced to the delight of the onlookers. Dancing carried on for some time with several changes of partners.

Kitty was not surprised to see Christopher pay marked attention to Louisa Lodge. The drama between he and Lucy continued to play out, to everyone's consternation but their own.

The moon set long before the revelers made for their own bedchambers.

≈

It was a weary group that breakfasted quickly the next morning; all but Darcy. He appeared as alert and energetic as always. It was he who had insisted on an early start, for the longest leg of their return journey would be today. Goodbyes were said, thanks made, and a new trunk added to the luggage. William Cressley would accompany them to Derbyshire. His avowed agenda was to bring the pair of Oakhurst mares to Pemberley. But his true agenda was obvious to all.

"Are you engaged to him then?" Lucy asked the impertinent question as the young ladies settled themselves in the carriage.

Matilda covered her yawn and stared at Lucy.

"Of course not. We have not known each other long, and he has yet to meet my family and speak to my father. But I cannot deny that is my dearest wish. And now, Lucy, my second dearest wish is to get back to my early morning dreams if you will be so kind as to allow me."

Lucy appeared deep in thought. Georgiana began to doze also, and Kitty thought the time ripe for planting a seed of friendship.

"This is the longest trip I've ever taken on my own," Kitty began. "I find I am very eager to talk with Lizzy about all I have seen, the adventures I have experienced, and the people I have met. Just talking with Lizzy helps me sort things out in my mind. With no sisters, are you close to your mother in that way? Do you confide in her?"

Lucy looked askance. "No! Do you talk about intimate things with your mother?"

Kitty had to laugh. "No, indeed. My mother has her own ideas and is unable to hear differing thoughts, much less give wise counsel."

"My mother is the same. Her interests are fashions, the *ton*, appearances, and wealth. And now, especially after almost losing her baby after the ball, I do not wish to trouble or upset her."

"She is with child?"

"Oh! I think I was not to say—"

"You can rely on me. Just before we left, Lizzy announced she and Mr. Darcy expect a new little Darcy sometime before Christmas. I trust you will keep that a secret."

"Of course. Kitty, how long shall you remain at Pemberley?"

"My choice would be to stay until after the baby arrives, or even longer. I should like to help Lizzy and, of course, care for the infant. I am the fourth of five sisters, so I have not much experience with babies or small children. My eldest sister, Jane, began her first confinement as I left Longbourn, and I hope to have news of her baby when we return to Pemberley."

"How lucky for you, Kitty. I mean, having a home to return to. And trusted sisters. After my father died and before Mother married Mr. Wyndham, she and I moved often, staying with family members or friends here and there. I felt close to no one but my grandmother. She came to us when my father died, until we had to start moving around. I have not seen her for many months now. I hope she comes for the birth of my new sibling."

Kitty's heart went out to Lucy. How difficult such loneliness must be. She had felt lonely herself at Longbourn but had suffered neither the loss of her father nor of her home. Although with one would come the other, as Mrs. Bennet so often reminded them.

"I hope your grandmother is able to come. That would be lovely for all of you. When is the baby expected?"

"Late winter or early spring. Mother has lost two since she has remarried."

"I am sorry for that." Taking a different tack, she said, "You are lucky to have brothers. I have always wished for a brother, especially an elder brother. Georgiana is lucky there. I do not know Mr. Douglas well, but Mr. Owen seems kind. How do you find them?"

Lucy sighed. "I would trade them both for a sister. To Douglas, I do not exist. He is wrapped up in his own problems, and now ... well, and as for Owen, he is oh ... he has always been kind to me, but never ... oh, he is not personable, Kitty. He does not like to sit and chat."

Kitty nodded. "He is much like Mr. Darcy that way. Very kind, but you are right—he is not one to chat. I personally do not know many men who are talkative unless one wishes to talk about hunting or war or politics—although I am always eager to talk about horses. I found Lewis Cavendish friendly; he had much to say about many things. I enjoyed his company. He and his sister seemed much alike."

"Yes," Lucy agreed, "he had many amusing stories."

"Rather like Mr. Andrew and Mr. Benjamin in our neighborhood."

"Indeed. But friendly as some are, we cannot talk to men about the more intimate concerns ladies have."

"No, you are right there. If I may, I would be honored to act as your sister. I can be relied on to keep confidences. And you and I are the older of our group in the neighborhood, excepting Julia."

"Poor Julia. I do not know what she sees in Douglas. How old are you, Kitty?"

"I have just turned nineteen. And you?"

"I shall be three and twenty in February. I hope my sibling might be born on my birthday."

Kitty deemed it a good time to delve deeper.

"You and Mr. Christopher seem close, when you are not in disagreement that is. Do you find you can talk with him?"

Lucy pursed her lips and looked sidelong at Kitty.

"I do not know how much to trust him, Kitty. He is dashing and handsome and entertaining. I admit I am in love with him. But he is unpredictable. And he seems to enjoy vexing me. He is a great tease and an unforgiveable flirt."

Kitty could only nod in agreement.

"He has offered for me, you know. At first we were going to elope. But I wished to have my mother at my wedding, not just some strangers from a tavern. When we were found by Mr. George Cressley and returned to Windsor, Christopher made me his offer at the guest lodge there, in front of my brother and Princess Charlotte herself. It was so romantic! The princess looked very pleased and embraced me. Kitty, she embraced me! I felt so honored. She is very friendly, if a bit unusual in style."

"Indeed, she is most kind. She was very helpful to me when I was rescued from the forest by your brother. She and Miss Elphinstone stayed with me until the searchers returned. I enjoy her outspoken nature. I do hope to see her again someday."

"Owen told me about finding you in the forest. I am so sorry, Kitty. I did not think about you at all when Christopher convinced me to ride away with him. I had never imagined you would go through such an ordeal. Can you forgive me?"

"I already have, but I thank you for your apology. How did those few nights go for you? Were you frightened?"

Lucy sighed again and took a few minutes before answering.

"I was not afraid. Christopher had talked about getting a special license because his father is a Lord and all. But he did not have enough money with him. And that was not how I wished my wedding to be." She paused. "Looking back, I did not think at all. Not enough to be wise. He has such a power over me. I am determined to do whatever I can to keep him, Kitty. I hope my father approves and that we can be married as soon as may be. He will inherit, and I will have a secure home. No one need know about our dalliance. And perhaps our child will be born not long after my sibling—how exciting that would be!"

Kitty tried to mask her shock. "And, is that already a possibility?"

Lucy looked at her and then lowered her eyes.

"It is. I could not resist him, Kitty. Please do not judge me. I pray everything will turn out for the best."

"I do not judge you. And I join you in wishing Providence to give you the happy ending you seek, especially for you and any child that may be born. Perhaps Providence can also help Mr. Christopher settle down as an elder son should, and not antagonize you so?"

Lucy giggled. "I will join you in that prayer. I do think he will be more settled once he inherits, but that may be some years away. His lack of money at present frustrates him greatly, and he is always seeking ways to get more. My dowry is small. That is another reason I hope to marry quickly, so he cannot abandon me for an heiress like Miss Lodge."

"Why is he in need of so much money? He stands to inherit a great deal, does he not?"

"He does. Whilst on our adventure we spent some time at the racetrack and with folks from there. Kitty, I believe he gambles and that does worry me. Several of the people around the racetrack also asked after Douglas, but lost interest once they heard of his accident. What do you think it means?"

Kitty chose to keep her own counsel for the present.

"I cannot imagine, Lucy. Do you think your father will approve your marriage? And will your mother? You do not *need* their approval but it would maintain the dignity of Greystone if all was done in an honorable way."

"Yes, my poor father has so many burdens of late. I do not wish to add to them. He has been *very* kind to me, and treats me like a daughter. I am fond of him."

"And I. He is the kindest and best of men."

"I wonder how things will go when we get to Matlock?" Lucy mused.

CHAPTER TWENTY-SIX

*T*he weather had turned rainy, and the entire party was relieved to arrive in Matlock at the Baths. The Wyndhams would stay at the lodgings there, and the Darcy party would ascend the cliff to Thornhill to stay the night. But first there were issues to be faced and plans to be made.

"Oh, how miserable you must all be!" cried Mrs. Wyndham as the young ladies entered the drawing room. Lucy hurried to her mother's open arms.

"Truly, it was not unpleasant for us in the coach," Georgiana said. "The road was not rutted yet and we did not get stuck. We are hardly damp but for our shoes. But do let me near that welcome blaze in the grate for I am chilled." She quickly made her way to the fireplace then looked towards the door in concern. "The gentlemen must be soaked through; it has rained all morning."

"Not to worry, Mrs. Wyndham," said Christopher with a disarming smile, being the first of the gentlemen to enter. "It is but a summer rain. I am not chilled; at least nothing a glass of brandy will not remedy." He winked at Lucy and moved across the room to stand next to her.

"I believe tea will suffice, Mr. Drake," Darcy said, scowling at Christopher as the servant managed their cloaks and hats. "It is too early for brandy."

William Cressley and Owen Wyndham then entered and handed over their rain-soaked cloaks.

Mr. Wyndham emerged from a back room, pushing Douglas in a wheelchair, followed by Julia.

"Here we are," Mr. Wyndham announced; but before he could finish, Matilda ran forward to greet her sister.

"Julia! Oh, how we have missed you. There is so much to tell!" she exclaimed, grasping her sister's hands.

Julia's face lit up at this show of affection and embraced her sister but put a finger to her lips so Wyndham could continue.

"And we have good news today. Douglas?"

Douglas Wyndham did not greet anyone and sullenly looked out the window as he spoke.

"My father refers to the fact that my surgeon recommends I return home for now. I shall see the surgeon again in sixty days or so to decide a further course of treatment. My father is, of course, greatly encouraged by this news. Far more encouraged than I." He struck the wheelchair with the heel of his hand and glared at no one in particular.

Silence settled on the room like a dense fog.

Kitty sought Julia's face. Her tear-filled eyes were on her beloved Douglas. Kitty sighed.

"In any case," Mrs. Wyndham said with a forced smile, "let us have tea. Gentlemen, if you need to change clothing, Mr. Wyndham can show you the way."

When all were assembled again, Darcy introduced Mr. William Cressley.

Matilda stood next to him beaming with delight.

"He is my *very* special friend," she said, her eyes wide.

Julia sought Kitty's eyes and Kitty nodded.

"How long will you stay in Derbyshire, Mr. Cressley?" Mr. Wyndham asked.

William looked at Matilda and colored slightly.

"I have no set plans, sir. I wish to meet Matilda's family, and of course visit my cousin's equine operation. We have brought two Oakhurst mares with us."

The sky brightened as tea was served, but conversation remained dull and strained. There was much news to be shared but no one offered to speak. As the refreshments concluded, Darcy stood and said, "Wyndham, do come with me to the stables. I wish to show you the mares."

Mr. Wyndham lifted his brows but rose and followed Darcy, who gave Christopher a sidelong glance before they quitted the room. Christopher squirmed uneasily and made an intense study of his boots. The mares would not be the only topic of conversation. Lucy remained blithely unaware of the shifting undercurrents in the room.

Julia was now sitting with Matilda and William. Remembering her own feelings when her younger sister appeared so lucky in love, Kitty could imagine how Julia might feel. Although William Cressley—unlike George Wickham—was likely not a scoundrel. But with the questions hovering about his brother, how could one tell?

After a quarter hour, Christopher slipped from the room.

Owen came to sit at Kitty's side and offered her a biscuit.

"Why, thank you," she replied, her eyes studying him.

"I wonder what my father will say," Owen mused.

"I also wondered that very thing," Kitty said. "I am sure we will find out soon. It would be unlike Mr. Darcy to delay an important matter of propriety."

"True," he observed, taking another drink of tea.

Changing direction, he then asked, "And do you think the squire will approve of William Cressley?"

"I imagine so. Mr. William is from a good family and appears to be an honorable man. I have seen nothing to cause me to doubt him, have you?"

Owen sighed. "No, I have not. And Mr. Darcy must be satisfied with him or he would not have allowed him to travel with us. I hope William Cressley is as he appears, for Miss Matilda's sake. If he is, I believe they shall be very happy."

Kitty watched the affectionate expressions exchanged between Matilda and William and smiled at Owen.

"I agree. Our little group could use a happy event, yes?"

Owen sighed again and nodded.

Just then the three gentlemen returned from the stables.

Kitty and Owen looked up expectantly but nothing was said, nothing announced. The couple exchanged a puzzled look.

"Perhaps Mr. Darcy will not speak until Lord and Lady Drake have been informed," Owen said. "I wonder how much he will reveal to them?"

"Or convince Mr. Christopher to reveal, perhaps?" Kitty said.

"Yes." Owen gave her a wry smile. "Mr. Darcy can be most persuasive, I will testify to that. I would not wish to be on the other side of him in a dispute."

"Nor I," said Kitty. She had come to value the ease she felt in Owen's presence at times like this. Unbidden, the memory of her uneasy conversation with Andrew Stapleton drifted into her consciousness, causing her feelings to again hang in uncertainty. She pushed them aside to offer Owen some good news.

"I spoke with your sister during the carriage ride. She did wish for a confidante. I have a better understanding of her now."

"And she of you?" Owen asked, lifting a brow.

Kitty shook her head. "I cannot say. She asked me no questions but was eager to talk about her own concerns. I cannot imagine being without sisters." Should she say more? She had not been asked to keep any secrets but did not wish to betray Lucy's trust.

"Thank you for your kindness to my sister, Miss Bennet. I will not ask you to betray her confidence. It is of comfort just to know that someone of sense is now in her circle."

Kitty thought even better of him for this remark, and also appreciated his trust in herself.

Darcy stood. "We will be expected for dinner at Thornhill, so we had best depart now. Wyndham, we shall leave your family to enjoy a reunion, and we will depart early tomorrow together for the last leg of our journey. I am eager to return to my wife and see how she gets on."

As he made this last statement, he looked particularly at Kitty, who nodded in agreement.

≈

Earl and Lady Matlock greeted them warmly at their return

to Thornhill, as did young Alice. The sky cleared, lawn games were offered for amusement, and a light tea was served. The carriage ride had been time enough to update Julia on most of the happenings from the journey, but Kitty longed to speak to Julia alone. The situation with Douglas did not appear promising. How had Julia borne all this alone? Mrs. Wyndham could not be an intelligent companion.

Pleading exhaustion after a few rounds of games, Kitty found a seat away from the others so as to be alone with her thoughts. More and more she understood Lizzy's long rambles whilst living in the frequent uproar at Longbourn. Embarrassment flooded her sensibilities as she recalled her own role in many of those upheavals, even though Lydia was usually the one stirring the pot.

While watching the others on the lawn, Kitty could not help but notice Christopher Drake's marked attention to Alice. His behavior was highly improper for a betrothed man, acting so the mooncalf. He could not be ignorant of Alice's fortune. Young Alice appeared quite taken by his animated conversation and focused attention. Kitty had no one's permission to divulge the engagement but, knowing she could not rely on Christopher's scant sense of honor, she could not sit idly by.

Christopher was procuring two lemonades when Kitty sidled up next to him and said in a dulcet voice, "Mr. Drake, how kind of you to fetch lemonade for Miss Alice on this warm day."

He nodded, then started at the glare in Kitty's eyes.

"I should dearly love to hear the stories with which you are amusing Miss Alice. I simply must join you."

Christopher looked perturbed but had no proper way to refuse.

"After you, Miss Bennet."

Over the years Kitty had learnt from her talented younger sister how to insinuate herself into situations, and in her heart whispered a quick 'thank you' to Lydia.

"Tell me more about your riding and your horses, Miss Alice," Kitty said with a sweet smile at Christopher. "Do you know their breeding lines?" The talk then turned to such and went on amiably for some time. Christopher was able to contribute on the topic but it was clearly not the agenda he had in mind. Kitty was pleased with her success at foiling his plan thus far. Poor Lucy! The sooner she and Christopher were married, the better for all.

Convinced that he would moderate his behavior knowing he was being watched, Kitty walked towards Julia, who was seated alone sketching.

"Did you make many sketches whilst at Matlock, Julia? I would love to see more of your work. The landscapes hereabouts are so inspiring."

"Indeed they are, and I have sketched many of them. I also found other sources of inspiration, Kitty. But I fear they may not elicit your good opinion."

"Why, Julia, whatever do you mean?"

Julia started several pages back in her sketchbook, first displaying some breathtaking natural scenes. But as the pages turned, the subject matter changed to many likenesses of Douglas Wyndham.

Kitty gasped. They were superb, expressing the agony and the anger in his soul.

"You have captured his very essence."

Julia made no reply, just paged through the drawings until she returned to her present landscape.

"I did not know you drew portraits, Julia."

"Nor did I. But I wished to capture him whilst I had the chance. If only I had drawn him in happier times." A wistful expression filled her eyes. "I plan to sketch each member of my family once I return to Swan's Nest."

Kitty hesitated but had to ask—she might not have another time alone with Julia—"How went your week with Mr. Douglas?"

Julia's face was clouded. "You saw him, Kitty. He has not much improved. Perhaps it is too soon. We talked a little. But he is still so angry about his condition that he cannot see past it. He has no hope. He cannot bear the thought of life confined to a wheelchair."

Kitty frowned. "Is there no possibility then for a complete recovery?"

"Strangely, the physician agrees with Lady Matlock on one

point: that Douglas' body cannot fully heal until his spirit does. His own bitterness poisons him, Kitty. My presence did no immediate good, though it was only of short duration. His father has great hopes that being back at Greystone will inspire further recovery. I have not given up. We have too much history, he and I."

Kitty pondered a moment and then said, "I believe Greystone will inspire either healing or deeper bitterness, but a change nonetheless. I pray that Providence will guide him out of the darkness."

"Amen."

After a comfortable silence Kitty said, "I tried some drawing on the journey. I would value your suggestions, Julia. I especially enjoyed sketching mares and foals. Might I commission you to draw a portrait of Cara?"

Julia chuckled. "You are likely to draw a better portrait of Cara yourself, Kitty. But I *would* like to draw you and Cara together. That is something you cannot do yourself."

"I would cherish such a drawing forever!" Kitty reached over to embrace her friend.

They sat in silence again whilst Julia continued drawing. At one point she asked, "What of our intrigue with the 'investment club'? The updates from Georgiana and Matilda seemed rather vague."

"You are correct, but there are some developments of which they are unaware. Some situations occurred of a questionable nature, and I felt it best for my brother to be informed."

"Mr. Darcy knows of our pact?"

"He does now. As do Princess Charlotte and her dear friend Miss Elphinstone."

"What? The royal princess?" Julia gasped.

Kitty explained how each of the others became involved and also disclosed the suspicions surrounding George Cressley, Christopher Drake, and Douglas Wyndham.

"And what of Mr. William Cressley? Do you suspect him?"

"No. No one does. He seems to have eyes only for your sister at present."

Julia looked over at Matilda and William, flirting and laughing together.

"Yes, I will likely have an additional family member to sketch."

Kitty smiled. "A wedding portrait."

"But, Kitty, what is the truth of Lucy and Mr. Christopher? Did they really try to elope? Do you know—are they engaged? Watching him fawn over Miss Alice today, one would guess not. I cannot imagine him as a husband, can you?"

They both looked over at him, now involved in activities with the larger group. He seemed to feel their eyes upon him and looked their way, giving them a salute, which they both found amusing.

"I did let him know I was watching him with Alice," Kitty said with a smirk. "I cannot divulge anything else at present, but he will not wish to gainsay Mr. Darcy. You can be sure of that." They laughed at that unlikely prospect. "I would not trade places with Lucy, nor wish Mr. Christopher to be mine. But she does seem aware of his faults and loves him in spite of them."

"She has confided in you?"

Kitty nodded.

"I am glad, for her sake. She never seemed to take to me, perhaps because of Douglas. She has no sensible female to talk with, her mother being so ... well ... whatever did Mr. Wyndham see in her, I wonder?"

"Perhaps, as someone said to me, he saw a fine looking horse; so fine, that he forgot to evaluate temperament," Kitty said with a laugh. "But I must be serious. Poor Mr. Wyndham has a very full plate, yet he is so kind to everyone."

"Yes, he is a good man," Julia said softly, then turned to look at her friend. "Kitty?"

"Yes?"

"Whom *do* you wish to be yours? Have you formed a preference since you have come amongst us? My brother appeared to have a preference for you. But he is not the only one."

Kitty looked at her sharply and felt color creep into her cheeks.

"Truthfully, Julia, I do not know. There are a few young men whose company I enjoy, and I may even say I fancy them. Oh, I envy Matilda and her certainty of her love in so short a time. Why can I not be so clear about my own feelings?"

Julia applied her eraser, brushed away the crumbs, and said, "You and I are different from Matilda. I love her dearly; she is so joyful. Perhaps that is why she is easily satisfied. Not that she is settling—not at all. She has simply found someone of equal joy. It seems they both knew immediately."

"Yes, it did seem so."

Kitty wondered about Julia's happiness, and if it would involve Douglas.

Darcy and the earl appeared, and the entire party dispersed to dress for dinner.

≈

Another long and elegant meal tested Kitty's memory of the proper manners for dining in high company. Later, Miss Alice provided music and then Julia and Matilda sang duets; and of course Georgiana performed, becoming more comfortable playing, and even singing, for larger groups. Darcy beamed with pride after her performance.

Kitty was uncomfortably aware that only she and Lucy did not play. Why had their mothers not insisted they learn the skills expected of ladies?

Jane excelled in needlework and flower arranging. Lizzy could play adequately and had a naturally lovely voice. Aunt Gardiner was credited with insisting they learn these arts whilst they stayed with her in Cheapside. Mary practiced often, it was true; but her pedantic style, self-centeredness, and poor voice marred her performance. Lydia's and Kitty's only attempts at artistry had been trimming bonnets.

Kitty was even more determined now to improve her riding skills and learn to draw well, if Julia thought she had enough talent to make the effort worthwhile. Lord knows she should not sing! She would also keep her Windsor Forest vow to read extensively about the natural world around her.

With an early departure anticipated for the next day, the

group did not stay up unusually late. Darcy and his uncle and aunt did remain in the drawing room when the others retired.

≈

Grey clouds troubled the sky and a fine mist surrounded Thornhill when Kitty entered the breakfast room the next morning. Darcy and the earl rose and nodded. Lady Matlock and Georgiana were also present.

"Kitty, I have some news," Darcy announced. "I have a letter here from Lizzy."

Kitty's heart skipped a beat.

"Is she well?"

"She reports she is very well. And that your sister Jane is delivered of a fine healthy boy with a headful of blonde curls. He has been christened Edward Charles Thomas Bingley."

"How wonderful!" Kitty exclaimed, tears coming to her eyes.

"You are Aunt Kitty now!" Georgiana exclaimed.

Kitty looked at Darcy expectantly.

"Yes, I informed my aunt and uncle last night that we expect a young Darcy before November," he said with a broad a grin.

"We are all very excited to welcome a new child to the Darcy clan," Lady Matlock said. "With neither of my sons yet married and Alice far too young, you can be sure I shall come for a visit early in the spring, Fitzwilliam. I dote on babies."

"Where are your sons at present?" Kitty asked.

"Both are in London," answered the earl. "Richard with the horse guards in the service of the Regent; and our eldest, Arthur, attends to business in town. He is a most eligible bachelor."

A servant announced the arrival of the Wyndham coach.

"Very good," said the earl. "Please call for Mr. Darcy's coach and horses. I shall go out to greet the Wyndhams. It will be too arduous for the injured young man to leave the coach."

"And I shall too, my love. A little mist will not stop me from greeting guests. I shall join you, if you will be obliging enough to hold an umbrella."

He smiled at his wife. "Of course, my dear."

When Matilda and Julia entered the room Lady Matlock invited them to partake of the offerings.

"I shall also provide your party with baskets of food for your journey—far superior to what you may find at a posting inn," Lady Matlock added as she left the room.

"Be quick, ladies," Darcy said. "We do not wish to keep the Wyndhams waiting."

Cups of chocolate were poured and drunk. Toast was eaten. Bonnets and pelisses were donned.

The sky remained leaden but the ground mist was lifting. The ladies were handed into the Darcy coach and the riders mounted their horses. Farewells were said and promises made of a visit to see the new Darcy child.

Then the entire party was off for home.

CHAPTER TWENTY-SEVEN

"*D*o you think our father will approve of William?" Matilda mused aloud. "How soon do you think we might marry?"

The other young ladies gaped at her.

"Has he declared himself then?" Georgiana asked.

"I had kept it secret until now, but yes, he spoke on our last night at Oakhurst. He even asked Mr. Darcy about it. But please, say nothing until my father has approved. Mr. Cressley approves, based on Mr. Darcy's recommendation of me and my family. I find I am quite impatient to be married."

Julia frowned. "Matilda, have you truly considered all that marriage will encompass? With Mr. William's law practice in Reading, you will live there. You will leave the country for town, and you will be far away from us. Should you be happy there?"

Matilda stared at her sister. "Of course I realize my entire life will change. But as ladies, we have always expected that change, unless we married an eldest son from our own neighborhood. Georgiana and Benjamin will also live elsewhere."

"Please," said Georgiana with a blush. "Nothing is settled in my case."

They all rolled their eyes.

"But you have known Mr. William such a short time, Matilda," Kitty said. "It is rather like my situation. There are men I think I fancy, that I have met here this summer. But having known them such a short time, I cannot commit myself with confidence yet."

After a few moments of silence Georgiana spoke.

"Your situations *are* alike and yet unlike, Kitty. Matilda has had a season in town where she met and socialized with many eligible young men, none of whom caught her eye. For many years she has known eligible men in our neighborhood. None appealed in that way. But now, Mr. William does. He comes from a good family—the Darcy family!—(here they all laughed), so an adequate history is known. He has an honorable occupation and can provide for a wife and family. She will not lose all ties. Roads and carriages keep improving, so travel will become easier. It is not as if she is going off to Scotland or France, where she knows no one but her betrothed."

"Yes! That is it precisely!" Matilda chirped. "I already feel I know William well. We spent a good deal of time together—properly chaperoned of course—while you went to Windsor, Kitty. I am sure of my regard for him, and of his for me."

"It all seems so ... easy," Kitty mused.

"Sometimes things *are* exactly as they seem," Julia observed. "Our heart speaks. And nothing happens to complicate it."

Georgiana smiled with contentment at those words.

For her—and for Matilda—their hearts had spoken.

Kitty pondered her own confusion, and wondered about the voice of her own heart. Had it spoken? Had she failed to hear?

≈

At their final posting stop, messengers were sent on to announce the pending arrivals at Greystone, Swan's Nest, Cedars, and Pemberley. Kitty imagined Lizzy would be as excited as herself. They had been gone less than a fortnight, but so much had happened. The hired horses were now exchanged for their own carriage steeds. How she wished Cara were here! What a lovely ride it would be back home to Pemberley.

Home. To Pemberley. How odd. Certainly Pemberley was not her permanent home. Might Derbyshire be? Andrew Stapleton had all but offered for her, had he not? Owen Wyndham had shown true friendship and hints of something beyond, but had by no means declared himself. And she had certainly not met all the young men in Derbyshire.

As the horses were harnessed, Kitty walked along the lane adjacent to the coaching inn, side by side with Julia, coaxing life back into their limbs and sharing the silence but not their thoughts. A few wispy clouds skittered by, hiding here and there behind the peaks.

Returning to Longbourn weighed on Kitty's mind. She could not desire it. Would Fitzwilliam and Lizzy allow her to stay until the baby was born? She frowned. She could be of little help. She had no experience with infants. All told, she was a young lady of no experience and few talents. Who would engage himself to such a lady? She cringed. Nineteen and the only talents of which she could boast were trimming bonnets and horsemanship—and that was a talent not much valued in ladies.

This renewed her determination to add to her repertoire whilst still in Derbyshire. She could improve at trimming bonnets. Might Lucy be interested in sharing such an activity? Julia could be her drawing mentor. Kitty had no interest in needlework, but knitting, such as Lady Stapleton did, looked less tedious. Was there something she could make for the baby?

Georgiana was experienced at being mistress of a household. Kitty knew nothing of the matter. She had been acting like a guest at Pemberley. It was time to ask Lizzy and Georgiana to teach her those skills. If she became proficient at running such a great household, she would certainly be successful at managing the smaller one she would likely have. Or at managing Longbourn if her father outlived her mother, though the idea of living there was disheartening.

A young lad ran up alongside her and touched his cap.

"S'cuse me, Miss, I am sent to say the coaches be ready." He smiled and bowed. He could not be more than eight years old. Kitty reached into her reticule and deposited a coin in his open hand. Julia did likewise. His eyes grew wide. "Thank ye, Miss and ... both Misses ... very kind!" He bowed again and skittered off.

Kitty and Julia turned back towards the inn. Owen waved at

them and Kitty waved back.

She most definitely did not wish to return to Longbourn.

≈

As the coach rattled down the road, Kitty thought back to her previous arrival at Pemberley and the goals she had set then to escape Lydia's shadow and her father's diatribes. It was time for a new plan.

Before long, the coaches reached the familiar crossroads. A coach from Swan's Nest waited to take the Stapleton sisters up their winding road, accompanied by William Cressley on horseback. The Greystone and Pemberley carriages rumbled on together until the Greystone lane was reached. Kitty and Georgiana waved to Lucy, who hung out the carriage window to say goodbye. Owen checked his horse and caught Kitty's eye. A smile broke over his face and he saluted her. She caught her breath—he was quite handsome when he smiled.

Christopher then followed the Darcy coach down the road.

"Poor Lucy, how lonely she must be. Let us invite her more often and call more often, shall we Georgiana?"

Georgiana smiled at Kitty. "Of course we shall. You found more good in her in a week than the rest of us have found in—"

"Miss Darcy," Christopher called, "do look out the window."

Georgiana leaned over and let out a little cry.

The coach came to a stop.

Benjamin's smiling face suddenly filled the glass.

"Miss Darcy. Miss Bennet. How glad I am to see you arrive home in safety. I am overjoyed. I shall call on you very soon."

Darcy rode up with a broad smile on his face.

"Follow the carriage, Mr. Benjamin, and join us for tea. Mr. Christopher?"

Christopher looked at Darcy with a serious expression.

"Thank you, sir, but I shall ride on home. Mother will be eager to see me."

"That she will," Benjamin said. "And Father. He returned from Town yesterday."

A look of worry flashed across Christopher's face, but he

quickly switched it for his usual brash smile.

"Ah, then there will be much to discuss."

"I wish you the best," Darcy said.

"Thank you, Mr. Darcy."

Darcy tied the mares to the back of the coach. Benjamin mounted his horse again.

"Chris, please tell Mother I shall be back for dinner."

"Of course, Ben. Enjoy your visit." With that, Christopher cantered off towards Cedars.

Georgiana's eyes and attention were on Benjamin as he rode beside the carriage so Kitty took the opportunity to invent a new plan for herself. She would improve her horsemanship and Lady Drake would be her model. She would spend time alone with Lizzy to sort her own thoughts about the future and learn about running a household. She would make something for the Darcy and Bingley babies, with Lady Stapleton's help. And she would apply to Julia for drawing instruction. And she would read about the natural world around her.

There, the second plan was made. But could she stay in Derbyshire long enough to achieve it? She pondered a plan for romance but was at a loss. Might Lizzy have some advice there?

Darcy and Benjamin galloped on ahead. Georgiana clapped with delight as the carriage turned into the sweep. Kitty's own heart rose at returning to Pemberley.

"Whoa now, whoa!" cried the driver.

As before, Lizzy awaited them on the portico, looking splendid in a light green dress, pressing her hands together in her own eagerness to see them. Darcy leapt the steps onto the porch, grasped her hands, and gazed at her before kissing her with enthusiasm. He then turned to receive the others, but kept an arm around Lizzy's shoulders.

The coach stopped, but instead of a footman, Benjamin's happy face opened the door and handed Kitty out, and then Georgiana. He kept hold of Georgiana's hand until she tittered and nudged him.

Lizzy embraced each of the girls and held Kitty's eyes long.

"I have prepared myself for a lengthy and detailed recounting of this journey," she said, her eyes twinkling. "Fitzwilliam sent me a few very cryptic notes about exciting and mysterious—and even some royal—goings-on, and I simply must have my share of the news."

Darcy tipped his head back and laughed at her mimic of his domineering aunt.

"It is good to be home," he said. "And now, my love, let us have tea."

Servants scurried about indoors and out, unloading the coach, carrying trunks upstairs, and driving the horses back to the stables.

Cara! Kitty resolved to go to her mare directly after tea.

"Is thirty minutes long enough for you ladies to refresh yourselves?" Darcy asked.

"Yes, quite," Georgiana replied as she and Kitty ascended the stairs. "Is it long enough for *you*?" she asked, looking at Lizzy and then back at her brother with an impertinent light in her eyes.

They all laughed when his face colored, and the two younger ladies ran the rest of the way up the stairs.

Even with much jovial conversation during tea, Kitty felt awkward sitting with two couples obviously eager to spend time alone with each other.

"I simply must see Cara. I do not think my company will be missed at present," she said, with a wink at Lizzy.

"Perhaps not at present," Lizzy replied, with a warm look at Darcy. "But do not be long, for there is much to talk about."

Georgiana reached over and touched her arm.

"Would you mind very much if we accompany you, Kitty? I could use a walk after so much time in the carriage, and it is very fine out."

Kitty glanced at Benjamin's face. His brows were raised in eager anticipation.

"Of course, I would welcome your company. Let us call for our bonnets."

More news was shared with Benjamin, who was particularly surprised by Matilda's new love and likely wedding.

"I had always thought Miss Stapleton would marry first, being the eldest. She and Mr. Douglas were together for a long time. Did he return with you? What is his condition?"

Benjamin was brought up to date on the Wyndham situation, although Kitty kept to herself the information about Christopher's pending nuptials with Lucy. Benjamin might be even more surprised at *that* turn of events, and it would be best he hear of it from his own family.

When they approached the stable yard, Kitty ran ahead to the paddock.

"Cara!" she called.

The mare whinnied and came trotting to the fence.

"Oh, my dear, sweet girl, I have missed you so." She opened her hand and sweet pieces of carrot were eagerly received.

"You are such a fine lady, aren't you? And Cara, do you want to know a secret? I think I am now well on the way to becoming a fine lady myself." She smiled as she stroked the mare's cheek and kissed her velvety nose.

"Miss Bennet! How good to see ye. Yer lady has missed ye greatly," said Johnny, touching his hat and making a slight bow.

"And I have missed her even more!" Kitty cried.

"And good day to you, Johnny. When might we ride? Are you available tomorrow? I have great plans for my riding and I must talk to Mr. Connor about them. Oh, I am so happy to be back."

"Tomorrow mornin' will be good to ride, Miss Bennet. The afternoons be quite warm, but that is a good time to talk to Mr. Connor. He is gone home now."

"Excellent. About half past nine then? But I do not leave yet. I must spend some more time with my lovely Cara." She eyed the brush in Johnny's hand.

He chuckled and handed it to her.

Cara met Kitty at the gate, eager for the tender ministrations of a good brushing and loving words. It was a sweet reunion.

≈

A letter was due to Longbourn telling of the journey, and one of congratulations was due to Netherfield, so that evening Kitty sat at her writing desk, prepared her quill, and began.

. . .

Pemberley, Derbyshire

 Dear Mama and Papa,

 I am happy to inform you of the completion of a pleasant journey taken by myself and Georgiana and several others under the care of Mr. Darcy. We traveled by coach and also by horseback to visit his uncle, the Earl of Matlock at Thornhill, then on to visit his cousin Alfred Cressley at Oakhurst Lodge some miles west of London. We also returned three mares to the Royal Mews at Windsor. By a very happy chance, I made the acquaintance of Princess Charlotte of Wales and her friend Miss Elphinstone. Princess Charlotte is an avid horsewoman, like myself. We now correspond. I can scarce believe my good fortune.

 I have met many new people this summer and have become very close with Miss Georgiana. She is like a sister to me now. I am also particular friends with Julia Stapleton, daughter of Squire and Lady Stapleton of Swan's Nest. She is teaching me to draw. There have been exciting excursions, card parties, picnics, and even some intrigues. Life here is most interesting and also holds many opportunities for learning. Can you imagine that my learning how moss grows on trees saved me in a risky situation while riding in Windsor Forest?

 Lizzy seems well and she and Fitzwilliam look forward to the arrival of their baby in a few months. Let us hope she has your strong constitution, Mama. It seems Jane does and I am delighted to hear of the arrival of baby Edward. I shall write to Jane and Mr. Bingley directly.

 Mr. Darcy has allowed me to ride a lovely mare, Cara, during my stay here. I have also made the acquaintance of Lady Drake, a great horsewoman at a neighboring estate. She even rides to the hounds. I hope I may be invited to join the hunt.

 Lizzy and Darcy have not set a time for me to leave Pemberley and I must say I am happy to stay as long as they will have me. Julia's mother is to teach me to knit so I can make things for the Darcy baby and also for baby Edward. I will ask Jane what he might need. Give little Edward a kiss from his Aunt Kitty.

 I am most grateful to Lizzy and Fitzwilliam for inviting me here and to you Papa, for accompanying me. I believe I am becoming a lady, in the best sense, and that you will be proud of me.

 Your loving daughter,

 Kitty

. . .

After preparing that letter for the post, Kitty pulled out another sheet to write to Jane.

Pemberley, Derbyshire
Dear Jane and Charles,

My heartiest congratulations on the birth of little Edward. If only you were closer I could hold him and give him a kiss from his Aunt Kitty. Mama must be beside herself with joy. I hope she does not overstay her welcome too severely so you may have time alone with each other and your precious son.

I am grateful to visit Lizzy and Fitzwilliam for so long. Life here is vastly different than life at Longbourn and I am meeting many people and learning much. My friend Julia is teaching me to draw. I especially enjoy drawing horses. Even Lizzy has been surprised to discover how often I rode in secret whilst at Longbourn. Fitzwilliam, a great horseman himself, has allowed me to ride a lovely mare, Cara, during my visit, and I ride nearly every day.

We have just returned from a journey to Fitzwilliam's relatives at Matlock and at Oakhurst, some miles west of London. We delivered some mares to the Royal Mews and I was so fortunate as to meet Princess Charlotte and her friend Miss Elphinstone. The Princess is also an avid horsewoman and we now correspond. I can scarce believe it! There have been many excursions, card parties, and even some intrigues. Lizzy is as well-liked here as ever she was in Longbourn, which can be no surprise to you.

Georgiana and I have grown as close as real sisters. She has become more lively, especially at home and amongst close friends, and I am sure you can guess Lizzy is behind that. Lizzy and Fitzwilliam seem vastly happy together and are a wonderful example of a marriage based on true love and real partnership, as are you two. I hope I may be as lucky – and choose as wisely. There is nothing to tell in that area yet, but there are some possibilities.

My friend's mother will teach me to knit. Please write and tell me what I might make for little Edward.

Love and blessings,
Kitty

The next morning, after a few schooling exercises in the ring, Kitty set out with Johnny to enjoy the shady paths north of the stables. Her wrist was still wrapped but no longer splinted. It was a quiet, uneventful ride, full of the pleasure of sitting a fine horse, enjoying good conversation, and breathing in the rich, woodsy air. She felt renewed and inspired.

When they returned, Mr. Connor awaited her.

"Johnny says ye wish to speak with me, Miss Bennet?"

"Why, yes, if you are not too busy? I wish to receive more formal training in horsemanship. I am sure Mr. Darcy will not object to my taking lessons. What else might I learn?"

Mr. Connor scratched his head.

"Yer already a fine rider, Miss. I will speak with the master about instruction as might be, eh, suitable for a lady," he said, cocking his head.

Kitty laughed. "I know Mr. Darcy is aware of my less 'suitable' riding style. I shall limit that to the Pemberley grounds. When I jumped that gate on Mr. Owen's horse, it was such a thrill. I should like to learn to jump. I think Mr. Darcy will support this."

"Oh, and Miss Julia Stapleton is to come do a sketch of myself with Cara. I began sketching on my journey—first land-scapes as there were many breathtaking examples; but my true love is drawing mares and foals."

Mr. Connor chuckled. "Ye got the fever, Miss, 'long with the talent, bless ye. We shall do whatever the master approves."

"Kitty," said Georgiana, now come up behind her, "we should return to the house. Benjamin must be at Cedars for dinner, and we must also prepare ourselves to dine."

"Yes. One moment."

She stepped to the fence and Cara swung her head over the top rail and nickered. Kitty kissed the mare's cheek and ruffled her forelock.

"Until tomorrow, Cara."

CHAPTER TWENTY-EIGHT

"*I* do regret you younger girls did not have the time with Aunt Gardiner that Jane and I enjoyed," Lizzy said as she and Kitty walked the winding path towards the orchard. The summer morning shone with the glory of blooms and rich grasses, and the fragrance was heady. Georgiana had a music master attending her, so the timing was perfect for a long walk and an intimate talk. "Even more, I regret I did not make the effort to share what I knew."

"Who could blame you, Lizzy? You are our sister, not our mother. Our own mother taught us few of the skills expected in a lady, and even less of the manners," Kitty said. "None in Meryton displayed the manners of those I have met here, Lizzy. But you fit right into this society."

Lizzy took her sister's arm. "We each fit, but in different ways, which makes society itself so interesting. I am unlike Lady Drake and unlike Lady Stapleton, yet we all find each other interesting. You will find your own unique way to fit into our set —and into your own."

"That is exactly what I wish, Lizzy. But I so feel wanting. My education is no match for that of the other young ladies. The only skill about which I can fairly boast is my horsemanship— and that is not considered the most ladylike of skills. I hardly know how it helps me blend into society."

"True. Might you find Lady Drake a mentor there? She certainly shares your enthusiasm and could guide you in the best ways to develop that."

"I should like that very much. But how can we go about it?"

"We shall ... rather, *you* shall invite her to tea to discuss all the particulars."

"I shall pen a note as soon as we return. I also mean to write to Maria Lucas, and send a thank you to Princess Charlotte and let her know we are arrived safe."

Lizzy nodded in approval.

"But, Lizzy, if you feel up to it, could you teach me two skills that you have mastered?"

Lizzy laughed. "Pray, Kitty, what might those be?"

"You have always excelled at needlework, and I should like to become proficient enough to make a few things for you and Fitzwilliam's baby, and for little Edward."

Lizzy smiled at her warmly. "That is very sweet of you, Kitty. I will teach you what I know. Do consider that I, myself, am learning about what the baby will need from both Mrs. Reynolds and Lady Stapleton. These warmer afternoons are perfect for sitting in the shade and tending to one kind of needlework or another, especially if surrounded by amiable company. But you mentioned two skills?"

"Yes. The other is being mistress of a house. You seem to have mastered running this grand home. Might you teach me some of your ways, that I might run my own home well someday, should I be so lucky? As of now, I know more about running a stables than a home, and that certainly won't do!"

They both laughed.

"Of course. But Kitty, my transition was made much easier by the expertise of Mr. Darcy's kind staff, both here and in Town. Indeed, I think the key to running a great house successfully is to have the best staff and treat them well. I have been most fortunate. Now, let us return. The heat increases, and I wish for a cool chair and a refreshing drink."

They walked for a time in silence.

"Kitty, if you are serious about improving, might you be interested in working with a tutor? Not daily schooling like a child, but someone who could set you on a reading program. I read mostly literature and philosophy. I can guide you in those, but a tutor would know how to fill the holes left by Mama not bothering to provide us a governess. A tutor could work with you in the areas of mathematics and the sciences perhaps? It is never too late to learn. I can speak to Fitzwilliam about it if this is something you would commit both the time and the effort to."

"Truly, Lizzy? Yes, I am serious. But that would, I suppose, involve a longer-term approach, and we have not yet discussed how long I might stay. I should dearly love to help with the baby, even though I have little experience. Georgiana will be here to help with the household, and I could assist her. I am willing to stay for as long as you and Fitzwilliam will have me. I find the thought of returning to Longbourn most dismal, especially with winter coming on." Kitty sighed at the gloomy thought. "I have grown to value interesting people and lively conversation and, as you know, little of that is to be found at Longbourn."

"Let me talk with Fitzwilliam about the length of your stay and the tutoring. Meanwhile, we will commence immediately with a literature program, learning to manage a household, and choosing a project to make for the baby. That should keep you quite busy, Kitty, with your riding besides. How will you have time for socializing—or romance?" she asked with a playful glint in her eye.

Kitty blushed. "Surely I can do needlework in the presence of others. And I have asked Julia to teach me about drawing. She is very talented, Lizzy. You should see the portraits she did of Mr. Douglas whilst they were in Matlock. Her landscapes are excellent as well. And I can surely find others to ride with."

Lizzy looked at her quizzically. "Very well. And what of romance, Kitty? Have you anyone of interest? It seems there are a few who have found *you* of interest."

Kitty frowned. "I am confused about romance, Lizzy. I envy Matilda. She found a man she immediately liked, and he immediately liked her. It was all so simple. I wish it could be so for me. Yet for some it is complicated and wrought with drama, and even pain. I do not envy Lucy's situation with Mr. Christopher. That is not the kind of love I seek. And poor Julia—her love for

Mr. Douglas is tearing her apart." Kitty looked sadly off in the distance for some few minutes.

"As for me, well, as you may have observed, I thought I was quite in love with Mr. Andrew Stapleton from the first moment I encountered him at the coaching inn. So dashing and handsome and spirited, with an interesting occupation in science. There is no other family I would be so happy to become a part of—to be Julia's sister! Then there was a man I met at Oakhurst, a Mr. Cavendish, who seemed interested in me. I found in him the same qualities that I liked in Mr. Andrew—easy conversation and a lively spirit. But there was still something wanting. A magic, or a mystical connection, if you will. Is such a thing real, Lizzy? Or is that just the stuff of novels?"

Lizzy's eyes softened as she looked at her younger sister.

"Oh, no, Kitty, it is not just the stuff of novels. It is a real thing. And most desirable. Some say it appears and grows *after* a marriage, and perhaps it can; but both Jane and I have found such happiness because the men we fell in love with came with a balance of traits—the handsome, romantic parts as well as the steady and kind parts based on friendship and shared values. I think it very important to have a partner you can fancy *and* trust." She looked more closely at Kitty. "Have you met anyone with those magical qualities of which you speak?"

Kitty glanced up and colored.

"I am not sure. He seems unlikely. Not the kind of man I had envisioned. Whilst Mr. Andrew is dashing, for some reason it is Mr. Owen who sets my heart fluttering. I cannot fathom why. He is not so elegant nor so outgoing as the other men. He has a great many troubles at present, with his brother and with Lucy. Some of these he has shared with me, as a friend. He is a great friend—loyal and dependable. It was he who rescued me in Windsor Forest. It was he who kept my secret about riding astride. He is very gallant, but at first does not appear so. He knows what to do in every situation and can be relied on. He has a temper, as well, but it seems to be an honest temper, not foul like his brother's; he does not take it out on others, at least not that I have seen. And he is witty, Lizzy. He can make me laugh." Kitty felt her face glow as she spoke.

"This is high praise indeed, Kitty. And you did not even mention that you share a great love for horses. I hope Fitzwilliam feels as fondly about me making him laugh. He was not very good at laughing when we first met."

They burst into peals picturing how austere and cold he had seemed then.

"Lizzy, he is such a fine man. He is wise and kind. And I have seen him smile more and more often. I believe he treasures you for making him laugh."

"Such is the magic of love, Kitty. If you have even one tenth the happiness I have found, you will have a glorious life indeed."

Kitty's thoughts wandered through notions about her dreamed-of elegant life with a dashing young man. She did not wish to let go that dream. Why should she? How many other young men were there yet to meet? Andrew had been only the first to catch her eye.

≈

The next morning Kitty settled at her writing desk, chose a quill, and began her letters.

Pemberley

Lady Drake,

My sisters and I would be pleased if you could join us for tea tomorrow at four o'clock. I hope to discuss equestrienne pursuits, amongst other pleasantries.

Yours sincerely,

Miss Catherine Bennet

Kitty pulled another sheet and dipped her quill again. Her pen flowed freely as she shared some of her recent adventures with Maria Lucas, her friend in Longbourn. When she had filled both sides of the page, she sanded and sealed the letter and then pulled out a third sheet. This one gave her pause as she considered how to address Princess Charlotte. Miss Elphinstone had used only initials to protect identities and secrets so she would do the same.

Derbyshire

Dear MME,

I am pleased to inform you and our esteemed mutual acquaintance of our safe return into Derbyshire. I hope this letter finds you well and enjoying pleasant summer rides in the woods and the countryside. My adventures in your locale and my honor in meeting both of you are amongst my most treasured memories. My wrist is nearly healed and I returned to riding yesterday.

Might I inquire about further discoveries regarding two gentlemen of our mutual acquaintance? One of whom you were instrumental in procuring an agreement from after a certain incident? I believe the parents of both of that party have now been informed, but I have not yet heard that a date is set. I shall inform you when the matter is concluded.

Regarding the other gentleman about whom you advised caution—by the time we returned to our first stop, his youngest brother and my friend had formed a serious attachment. He is presently in Derbyshire to meet her family. Need we have concerns on that head?

Your humble servant,

CB

Her correspondence completed for the present, Kitty set out to find Georgiana. As she approached the music room, her ears advised that her quarry was found. She peered quietly from beside the door to be sure she was not interrupting the lesson. Seeing only Georgiana, she entered the room silently and took a seat on the blue velvet chair. The light refracting through the large paned window behind Georgiana caused the atmosphere of the room to come alive with the notes being played. Kitty sighed and leaned back into the cushions with her eyes closed as the melody danced around her, enticing her mind to drift.

Her eyes flew open at the bang of a sudden dissonant chord.

Georgiana chortled. "Is my music so boring it puts you to sleep?" she asked, banging out a few more jarring chords.

"Georgiana!" Kitty said, gathering herself and rising. "Of course not, silly. Your music and the sunlight drew me into a place of pleasant repose, that is all." She shook out her skirt and arched her brow at her Darcy sister. "You play divinely, as you are well aware."

"Perhaps. When I am alone. It is playing, and especially singing, in company that sets my nerves on edge. I admit I am far more comfortable doing so now than I was before you came."

"I do not wish to interrupt your practice. Your music master has departed?"

"Yes, nearly an hour ago. I was practicing some new techniques, but I am finished now. What do you wish to do?"

"What do you say to a visit to Miss Lucy? It has been a few days since our return. I wish to follow up my friendship overture with action that will show her I was sincere. Would you like to join me in paying a call?"

"You are very kind, Kitty. Yes, I will call on her today, if you will join me in calling at Swan's Nest tomorrow. I am wild to know how things are going for Matilda and Mr. William."

"But Lizzy and I have invited Lady Drake for tea tomorrow. Could we go the following day?"

"I shall have to shore up my patience. But yes. Now tell me about this tea with Lady Drake."

The two joined arms and as they made for the stairway, Kitty apprised Georgiana of her hopes for the tea.

"That sounds very wise, Kitty. She is certainly the best choice in the neighborhood for a guide—a lady guide—in horsemanship, or in anything."

"Georgiana, that is not all I wish to improve on. I have a plan of several things in mind. Might I persuade you to teach me some of the skills of moving in higher circles? At Lord and Lady Matlock's, I would have been lost without your example."

"Of course. Oh, this will be fun. Let us ask the housekeeper for an elegant formal tea. And then later a very formal dinner—it has been some time since such a meal has been served at Pemberley. We must be in good form should Princess Charlotte herself come to call one day."

≈

Lucy received Kitty and Georgiana graciously when they arrived, but her smile was tentative.

"It is wonderful to see you both. May I ask the occasion for such a call?" she asked as she poured the tea.

"No particular occasion," Kitty replied. "I think our journey to Windsor increased my appetite for being more in company, and I wondered how you fared being back at Greystone. Will your mother be joining us today?"

Lucy frowned. "No, Mother has been quite exhausted and indisposed since the journey. She is not always in bed but she keeps mostly to her room." She looked at each of them with some apprehension. "I do hope she will not be ill the entire time. It is lonely here, and I am very glad you called. Father and Owen stay so busy with the estate; and of course Father oversees the care of Douglas as Mother is not up to that. And our vicar is retiring, so Owen has been obliged to take up some of those duties as well. I feel ... well ... I seem only to be in the way." Tears filled her eyes. "I do not know how I can be useful to anyone."

"Oh, Lucy!" cried Georgiana. "What a difficult situation. I should feel just as you do. In fact, that is often how I felt after my own father died. My brother had to take over everything. I know he was trying to spare me, but it left me feeling just how you describe, useless and rather a burden."

Lucy looked up, her eyes widening. "I had no idea! How long ago was this, Georgiana?"

"Oh, about seven years now. I was younger than you, and so felt even more useless. I was not even allowed to act as mistress of the household. Is your mother still trying to do those duties? Do you think that is too much for her? Perhaps you could be of assistance there."

Cocking her head, Lucy considered the idea.

"Well, perhaps there are some things I could do; but I have never been shown what to do here at Greystone. After my father died, we were always guests at friends' or relatives' homes. I would not know where to begin."

"Before my brother married Elizabeth, he spent a lot of time away from Pemberley. I had lived in London for some time, but after … well, after a time, I came to prefer Pemberley to Town, except during the season or if my brother was there. It was during that time I first insisted on being mistress, both in London and at Pemberley. I have known our Pemberley house-keeper all my life, and we are very fond of each other. She was of great help in teaching me the duties my mother had performed. I believe every estate does things differently—you know, they have different traditions—but how would you feel about talking to your cook or your housekeeper? Perhaps they are aware of which duties are most trying for your mother during her illness. I hope it is nothing serious," she said quietly.

Lucy looked quickly at Kitty, now aware that Kitty had not divulged their confidential conversation. With a smile of relief she replied to Georgiana, "My mother is not really ill. She is with child, and seems to be having a difficult time eating anything. She is tired and often tearful."

They looked at each other doubtfully. Kitty was the first to laugh at their situation.

"Well, it seems none of us have much experience being around a lady who is carrying a child. I was worried about Lizzy at first—before I knew—noticing some changes in her, but not suspecting … she and Mr. Darcy announced their news just before we left on our journey. So far, Lizzy seems to be faring well. That is the whole of my experience."

"And of mine," Georgiana said.

Kitty considered and then said, "What about asking your mother herself how you might be of help? Perhaps she is reluc-tant to burden you."

"I shall do it today. Thank you. This has made me feel less of a problem to everyone. Such kind friends you are."

Just then Mr. Wyndham appeared at the door. He bowed graciously to the young ladies.

"Welcome, Miss Darcy and Miss Bennet. I am sure Lucy is most happy to have company. I have been neglecting her since our return, but many quarters call for my attention. And tonight we host the Drakes for dinner. An occasion we all anticipate." He nodded at Lucy and winked. "I pray my wife will be able to attend; hopefully by resting all day she will have the strength to be hostess."

Lucy blushed and smiled. Then she addressed her father.

"We have been discussing the ways I might assist Mother as mistress of Greystone, whilst she is ... ah ..."

He gave Lucy a kind smile and picked up the conversation.

"Ladies, we are expecting a baby, if Lucy did not tell you already."

"How delightful, Mr. Wyndham," Georgiana said.

"That is wonderful news," Kitty said. "When?"

"Sometime in early spring," he replied. "About the time early foals arrive," he added with a chuckle.

"It will be a happy spring," Lucy said.

"Yes, the many challenges of late seem to be lessening," he said, giving Lucy a most particular look. "Well, I shall leave you ladies to chat. I have a tenant to meet with. Again, thank you for calling." He bowed and quitted the room.

"Have you seen Matilda and Julia since our return?" Lucy asked, taking another biscuit.

"No, we go there the day after tomorrow," Kitty said. "Tomorrow we host Mrs. Drake for tea. I wish to discuss some equestrienne activities with her. Have you seen the Drakes since our return?"

Lucy blushed again. "The Drake sons have called twice. Short visits, but a very nice diversion to my lonely days. I am so looking forward to our dinner tonight." Her eyes shone with anticipation.

"And how does your elder brother do?" Georgiana asked.

"Douglas? I do not really know. He seems the same as he did at Matlock. Confined to the chair. In a foul mood. Often he does not attend dinner. I know not how he spends his time." She shrugged.

"Well, you have an exciting evening to look forward to, and perhaps some new duties as well," Kitty remarked. "We shall depart to allow you time to pursue these."

"But, Lucy, do call on us as soon as you can," Georgiana said as she stood and reached for her gloves.

"I will be very happy to." She rang the bell for their phaeton and accompanied them to the door. "It was most pleasant to see you."

They were settling themselves in the phaeton when Owen came trotting up on his great grey. He slipped from the saddle and bowed.

"Miss Bennet. Miss Darcy. My father just informed me you were here. I am so sorry to have missed talking with you over tea." His eyes lingered on Kitty, so much so that she felt her cheeks warm and a glow radiate from within.

Georgiana looked between the two and smiled.

"How kind of you to take time to greet us, Mr. Owen. We hear you now have taken on the duties of the vicar?"

"Yes. Vicar Mosley retires soon and, as second son, that position will be mine."

"You shall be very busy indeed," Kitty said.

"Not too busy to enjoy good conversation—or to ride about the countryside. At times I find myself longing for company beyond family or equine." He gave Kitty a speaking look. "I imagine my sister will return your call. Perhaps I shall accompany her."

Kitty met his eyes but could not find words to say.

"You are welcome at any time, Mr. Owen," Georgiana said with an amused expression that went unnoticed by the couple.

His smile broadened and Kitty's heart beat faster.

"Give Mr. Darcy my kind regards," he said as he swung up into the saddle. He nodded to them and was off.

Kitty looked after him until he was out of sight.

CHAPTER TWENTY-NINE

"*M*rs. Darcy, you are looking well," murmured Lady Drake as she reached for a tart.

"Why, thank you," Lizzy replied. "I am feeling quite well now; much better than earlier."

"Quite understandable. It was so for me. I was almost too ill to ride for a few weeks, I remember, especially with my dear Christopher."

Lizzy spluttered into her tea. "Do you mean—excuse me Lady Drake—you continued to ride ..."

Lady Drake's countenance was sanguine. "But, of course. I was sensible about it. I took my cue from my mares. If one is accustomed to doing something, one should keep doing it until it becomes uncomfortable." She looked closely at Lizzy. "I am sure your lying-in will go well, Mrs. Darcy. You are an excellent walker and a practical, sensible young lady."

"I hope you are right, Lady Drake. My mother had no problems with any of we five. I pray it will be the same for me. Did you know my sister Jane recently gave birth to a son? Her first."

"No. How wonderful. And where do they live?"

"They continue at Hertfordshire for the present. But I shall not be surprised if in the near future they look for an estate to purchase elsewhere. She and I are very close, and her husband

and Darcy are thick. I believe they may cast their sights more in this direction."

"Well, I shall inform my husband. His ear is bent by many and if any possibilities arise, I shall get you word immediately."

"You are most kind."

Changing her focus, Lady Drake looked at Georgiana.

"Miss Darcy, my son Benjamin did nothing but complain whilst you were on your journey south. It appears he cannot do without your company. I do not know how he managed whilst he was at school. Thank goodness his schooling is now completed." She smiled and took a sip of tea. "Actually, I find him most companionable myself. Perhaps the time has come for a new chapter in his book?" She looked at Georgiana with an arched brow and an amused expression.

Georgiana blushed. "Oh, yes ... I do ... I enjoy his company very much. He is so kind and friendly, and can be very amusing ..." She faltered and appeared tongue-tied.

Lady Drake mercifully changed the subject once again.

"And my Christopher has been much subdued since the recent journey. We enjoyed a pleasant and significant dinner last evening at Greystone. I believe more is known than spoken of by some of those present, but I am bound to tell you he is engaged to Miss Lucy Jamison."

Georgiana and Kitty grasped hands.

"How wonderful!" they cried in unison.

"I thought you might enjoy that. Confidentially, I must admit that Miss Jamison has not been a favorite with me. But then neither has Christopher of late. He is ripe for change in his life. It is time he settles down to more productive activity."

She gazed off and for a moment appeared to be looking somewhere else entirely. She shook her head and said, "That girl has endured losses in her life and has lacked for sensible companionship, in my estimation, but I believe she may be able to win me over. In time." Her brows knit for just a moment, and then her countenance smoothed.

"The wedding shall be within the next two weeks. They are settling the date with her brother, Mr. Owen, who will offici-ate. A nice lad there. Wise beyond his years. Yes." She sipped at her tea and looked at each of them in turn, as if expecting replies.

"I am glad things have worked out for them," Lizzy said. "The two of them may be a bit ... volatile ... but perhaps when together, they will balance themselves out."

Lady Drake smiled and nodded. "Oh, and I expect Miss Jamison will call here soon. Young ladies are usually eager to discuss wedding plans with their friends," she observed and, eyeing Kitty added, "and she may be particularly eager."

After another sip of tea, Lady Drake said, "Now, Miss Bennet, I was most impressed with your riding for help at the time of the unfortunate accident. Not only are you a splendid rider, but you also appear level-headed. Practical. Not many young ladies would have so readily put their reputation aside to do the best thing in the situation, which was to ride astride. You have my admiration."

Kitty's mouth fell open. She glanced at Lizzy, who winked with one eye.

"I do not know what to say, Lady Drake. You are my model for a horsewoman and for a lady. I was not sure if I would lose your good opinion by—"

"Nonsense. Above all, a good horsewoman—or a horseman, for that matter—is practical. We do what must be done, what is safe, what is best. For the horse *and* the rider." She cleared her throat.

"I noted that Mr. Owen did not appear shocked at your ability?" She looked directly at Kitty with a lifted brow.

It would be useless to dissemble.

"He was not." She then told them the story of the day she and Johnny had come upon Owen and the broken-down wagon. She did not mention the beer.

Lady Drake looked at Kitty and then laughed heartily.

"Quite a pickle for a young lady to find herself in. I found myself in similar circumstances as a young girl."

She paused, then said, "Young Mr. Owen is a great horseman. Gives his father, and even Mr. Darcy, a run for their money. And a most respectable man he is. He will be a great match for someone with whom he can develop an understanding; someone

he can respect. A young lady who is bold, yet practical and kind."
She smiled in Kitty's direction.

Kitty could only blush and sip at her tea. This was quite direct.

"I did, however, think something might be brewing in another quarter. Well, well, we shall have to see what happens."

Gulping for a breath, Kitty screwed up her courage.

"Lady Drake, I have spoken with Mr. Darcy about being allowed to ride astride at times and about learning to jump fences, and even ride with the hunt or on a steeplechase. He recommended I ask you about such activities for a lady. He puts great store in your opinion on these issues."

"Does he?" Lady Drake laughed. "Mr. Darcy is clever in seeking the counsel of others, but wise—in this case especially—as he is not a lady. Hmm, so you wish to breach some of these tired rules imposed on ladies?"

Kitty set down her teacup.

"I do, Your Ladyship. Perhaps not publicly, except for the hunt. I cannot see what harm it might do in private. Why should anyone care what I do here at Pemberley? But I do not wish to disgrace Pemberley in any way. Pray, what is your opinion?"

Lady Drake looked deeply into Kitty's eyes.

"There is no disgrace in honoring one's true beliefs, Miss Bennet. Follow your own opinion, and listen to your own heart."

Kitty felt honored at the respect being shown her by Lady Drake, and returned her gaze with a newly-felt equanimity.

"The weather has grown quite warm of late," Lady Drake continued, "but I invite you to join me on a morning ride next week, Miss Bennet. And I would be happy to accept an invitation to watch you ride. Will you be taking lessons from Connor? Yes, I imagine so. An excellent teacher. Well, Miss Bennet?"

"I should dearly like to join you on a ride." She turned to her sister. "Lizzy, may I invite ..."

"Kitty, you are not a guest here at Pemberley. You are family. You may invite anyone known to us to visit you here." Lizzy smiled at her indulgently and nodded at Lady Drake.

"Oh, thank you. Thank you both! I shall ask Mr. Connor

when we might schedule a lesson. Oh, would it be too rude ... can I go now and ask?"

Lizzy raised her eyebrows at Lady Drake, who said, "My dear, it would be most practical to get it all arranged at once. Off with you! But do hurry back."

Kitty rose, curtsied, and was gone in an instant.

When she returned, Lady Drake's horse had been called for and plans were immediately settled for the morning ride as well as the observation of Kitty's lesson.

"You are so kind to indulge me, Lady Drake," Kitty said. "I am in your debt."

"Your sister is charming, Mrs. Darcy. I am impressed."

Turning to Kitty, she said, "If I had been blessed with a daughter, I should have wished her to be just like you, my dear. Or like Miss Darcy," she said, smiling at Georgiana. "Now *that* wish ..." She left off with her eyes twinkling.

"Give my regards to Mr. Darcy," Lady Drake said. "And let him know of my opinion," she added, with a quiet laugh. Her servant assisted her into the saddle, and with an elegant wave of her gloved hand, they were off down the lane.

Lizzy looked at Kitty with pride.

"Well done, little sister. You are grown into quite a lady. I am proud of you," she said with a mischievous one-eyed wink.

"Now I know we just had tea, but I am hungry again. I think I shall see what Cook has about that I might feast on until dinner. I cannot seem to go more than an hour or two without eating. Soon you two shall have to carry me up the stairs!" She laughed and made for the kitchen.

The young ladies linked arms. "Well, Kitty, your summer here seems quite successful, does it not?"

"Indeed it is. This has been one of the happiest times of my life, Georgiana. You and your brother and my sister have all been so good to me. And more happiness is yet to come—a baby, and at least one or two weddings. I am most fortunate."

Georgiana squeezed her hand. "Not any more fortunate than you deserve."

Kitty blinked back a tear.

CHAPTER THIRTY

A steady rain imposed a delay on the much-anticipated visit to Swan's Nest. Darcy was firm in forbidding the young ladies to go, even on horseback, until the road had at least a full day to dry. One evening after dinner the grey curtain lifted, revealing a rosy sun setting in the west. Kitty and Georgiana were filled with excitement, and Kitty was in no way averse to making the visit on horseback.

The young ladies set out just after breakfast. It had been more than a week since the four had been together, and Kitty and Georgiana were eager for information about the courtship of William and Matilda. The road was dried out tolerably. Johnny accompanied them on a younger horse he was schooling.

When the elderly Swan's Nest butler announced them, a wild clatter was heard on the stairs as the three younger Stapleton daughters raced to greet their visitors.

"Girls, girls, behave like the young ladies you are, please. I am sure Miss Darcy and Miss Bennet are not here to visit wild hooligans." Lady Stapleton motioned to one of the maids to take their bonnets and wraps.

A glowing Matilda came forward and eagerly grasped Georgiana's hands.

"My dear friend, I have a thousand things to tell you."

"Yes, yes, there is much to tell," said Lady Stapleton, "but let us save it until we are properly seated. Would you young ladies like tea?"

Georgiana responded. "We breakfasted just before departing, but a spot of tea would be welcome before the day turns warm."

Lady Stapleton gave directions to the servant and led the way to the drawing room. The girls rustled along in her wake—three eager to impart news and two eager to receive it. Kitty noted Julia's absence but would wait to inquire.

When tea was laid and the servants departed, Georgiana looked at Matilda expectantly.

Matilda in turn looked at her mother. Upon receiving a nod she cried, "Oh, Georgiana, it is the best of news. William and I are engaged!"

Georgiana leapt from her seat to embrace her friend.

"How wonderful!" Kitty exclaimed. "Though I cannot say I am surprised. His affection for you is obvious to us all. Where is he at present?"

"Oh, he and the squire went to a sheep sale near Grindleford. They get on marvelously. It is a good match by all accounts, and I am much pleased," Lady Stapleton said, her eyes dancing whilst her fingers flew with her knitting needles. "Yes, the squire and I are both pleased and thankful. Providence has provided well for this daughter." Her brows creased briefly.

"Is Julia unable to join us today?" Kitty inquired.

The gay mood in the room fell flat.

"Honora, if it please Miss Bennet, take her to Julia's room and announce that her friends are here. I fear she has not been very sociable of late. Perhaps you may succeed at cracking her dull mood, Miss Bennet."

"I shall try. I have been longing for her company." With that, Kitty followed Honora to Julia's room.

Honora knocked softly at the door.

"Yes?"

"Your friend Miss Bennet is here with me. May we enter?"

There was a shuffling within, then the door opened. Julia's eyes were red and her countenance troubled, but seeing Kitty brought a wan smile to her face.

"Oh, Kitty, I am so sorry to receive you in this manner."

"Do not think on it, Julia. Perhaps we can talk privately before joining the others?"

Honora curtsied, flashed Kitty a conspiratorial smile, and departed.

"You have heard Matilda's news?"

Kitty nodded. She knew not what to say and thought to let Julia speak first rather than guess at her friend's feelings.

"Of course I am happy for my sister. Things have happened for her as if in a dream. William has been steadfast and affectionate, and our family adores him."

"That is all very well," Kitty said, searching her friend's face. "I too am happy for them."

"But Kitty, so much joy paints my sorrow even darker. I have kept to myself to avoid casting a shadow on Matilda's happiness."

Kitty was silent for a moment, then reached for her friend's hand.

"Julia, I think your absence itself casts a shadow. Is there naught I can do to ease your pain?"

Julia made no answer.

"Have you had any word from Mr. Douglas or his family?"

Julia's eyes filled with tears as she looked up.

"Mr. Owen has called once, only to say there is no change in Douglas and that he remains angry and bitter."

Kitty's heart sank, but then anger stirred within her.

"Julia, just because he chooses to be so, why must you? Why cannot you detach yourself from him and all his problems? I know you loved him once. But he seems to be no longer that person. Can there be any love between you, as he is now? He cannot love anyone in his present state. It has not been *so* long since the accident. Perhaps, with time, things will change. Then you can begin again, or renew your love. Let him go for now, to find his own way. It pains me to see *you* suffering for something that *he* chooses to do."

Julia's shoulders shook with silent sobs. Kitty stayed for a time, sitting silently by. When Julia's sobs lessened she did not meet Kitty's eye. Instead, she gazed sullenly out the window.

"I am sorry if I offended you, Julia. You are one of my dearest friends. Do know that I will help you in any way I can, whenever you ask. I will go now." With that, Kitty rose and quitted the room, but the shadow of her friend's sorrow went with her.

As she made for the parlor, she wondered about Andrew. No one had mentioned him in all the excitement about Matilda's betrothal. Would he come for her wedding?

Once in the parlor Georgiana exclaimed, "Kitty, I am to be Matilda's bridesmaid!"

"That is wonderful! You have been friends for many years, have you not?"

"Indeed we have," Matilda replied. "We have known each other all our lives, but we became special friends when we were both about ten years old. Is that right?" she asked, looking at Georgiana, who nodded. "Julia has declined to participate in the wedding. I hope she will at least be present for it," Matilda said, a frown clouding her usually happy countenance.

"And when is the wedding?" Kitty asked.

"In twenty-two days!" Matilda exclaimed. "William and I thought it best to wait until after Mr. Christopher and Lucy marry, as they were engaged first."

More plans were discussed with great energy. Still no one mentioned Andrew. Kitty would say nothing that might dampen the family's present joy. She could inquire of Georgiana later, or perhaps of Julia if she saw her again before the happy event.

≈

The next day Georgiana and Kitty were lingering in the breakfast room when an early visitor was announced.

"Miss Lucy Jamison to see the young ladies," Wilson said.

"We shall receive her in the drawing room," Georgiana replied, hastily patting her mouth with a napkin. "And please send a message to Mrs. Darcy. She may wish to join us."

The butler bowed and moved off, and the young ladies made for the drawing room together.

In a few moments a breathless Lucy bustled into the room. Kitty and Georgiana hurried to meet her and all joined hands in excitement.

"You do look radiant today, Lucy," Georgiana commented. "Getting married must agree with you!"

"Oh, what young lady would not be this happy to be marrying the man she loves!" Lucy exclaimed.

"I am so pleased for you, Lucy," Kitty said, mustering as much enthusiasm as she could but catching a hint of apprehension in Lucy's expression.

"That is encouraging, Kitty. As I have no sister, and after our adventurous journey ..." here she gave Kitty a look that imparted her awareness of the secret ... "I should like to ask you ... I hope you will consent ... to be my bridesmaid?"

Hastily Kitty masked her astonishment with a smile.

"You honor me, Lucy. I would be delighted!" To her own surprise, she *did* look forward to fulfilling Lucy's wish. Kitty had never felt so needed by someone before.

Her eyes brimming with tears, Lucy embraced Kitty.

"Please, sit and tell us all the particulars," Georgiana said.

Hearing footsteps, they looked up to see Lizzy enter the room in an awkward manner.

"Miss Jamison, please forgive me for not being here to receive you. I came as quickly as I could, but I fear my speed is much lessened of late." Lizzy placed her hands on her expanding form. "I confess I was in the kitchen again—oh, the blessing of such an amenable cook!—and the stairs do take me some time."

They all rose and Lucy curtsied.

"What have I missed?" Lizzy said, making her way to a chair.

Georgiana spoke, her hands dancing to her words.

"Lucy has asked Kitty to be her bridesmaid. Isn't that exciting?"

"It is indeed."

"Oh, and I have this for you, Mrs. Darcy, from my mother." Lucy reached into her reticule and produced a parchment with a seal. "It is an invitation to my wedding and the breakfast. I do hope you can all come?"

"We will be honored to share your special day, Miss Jamison. You must be very excited."

"Oh, yes. Mother could not join us today. She does not feel well and gets in such a state ..."

"I do understand, Miss Jamison, believe me."

"Tell us about your gown, Lucy," Georgiana prompted.

"It is a very pale pink with hundreds of seed pearls. I love it. Now Kitty, what shall you wear?"

"I do have a gown in a darker shade of pink, more of a rose. Would that suit?"

"That would be quite lovely, Kitty," Lizzy remarked. "And will you go on a wedding trip, Miss Jamison?"

"We are still discussing that. His parents wish us to tour the Lakes, and I should like that very much. Christopher wishes to travel to the London and Windsor area, but I cannot care for it."

Lucy and Kitty exchanged a surreptitious look.

"I have always wanted to tour the Lakes," Kitty said. "I hope his parents prevail. I am sure you would both enjoy that."

As Lucy spoke, it occurred to Kitty she should write to Princess Charlotte with this information—the marriage was the condition for no further investigation of Christopher's questionable involvements. It would definitely be best that he avoid any shady connections in Windsor or London.

Hats, slippers, food, and other arrangements were discussed at length, and eventually it was time for Lucy to depart.

She had hardly left when another visitor was announced.

"Why, Mr. Owen, your sister has just left us," Kitty said. "Did you not come here together?"

"No. I had early business with Darcy and with the stable master. That is now concluded and I hoped to visit with the ladies of the house before I quitted Pemberley," he said, making a slight bow.

Wilson was at the door. "Miss Darcy, your music master has arrived."

"Thank you. I shall join him at once." She nodded to the others and whisked away for her lesson.

"May we three take a short walk?" Owen asked. "It is very fine out, not too warm yet."

"If we keep to the garden. That would suit me best," Lizzy replied as Owen offered his hand to help her rise.

Bonnets were fetched and the three made for the garden.

After traversing part of the outer path, Lizzy begged to sit in the shade of the spreading crabapple tree, but encouraged the couple to continue walking as she could still chaperone.

"Well?" Owen asked, looking quizzically at Kitty. "I know what my sister came to ask."

Kitty looked up at him and smiled. "I am happy to be her bridesmaid. It appears she *does* think of me as a sister."

"She does indeed. Thank you. Your influence will improve her," he said.

"Her mother-in-law will also support her I think. She is a woman of good sense."

"You are right," he said. "Common sense seems to run strong in those who are true horsewomen ... or horsemen, if I might flatter myself."

"Lady Drake described you as such the other day when she called. She supports my desire to ride astride and will watch my riding lessons as I learn to jump under Connor's tutelage. She thinks highly of him as well."

Owen simply nodded as they continued on the path, the gravel crunching under their feet.

"She and I hack out tomorrow morning. It seems female riding companions are scarce hereabouts. I shall be glad for her company. She is most interesting. I sense a wisdom ... or something ... in her that I can't quite explain ..."

He looked at Kitty. She could not decide if his expression was one of concern or contemplation.

"She *is* wise, Kitty. In the usual ways. And in some ... less usual ways. But of that you will learn as you further your acquaintance with her."

Kitty frowned at him. "That is rather cryptic."

"Perhaps. But you must form your own opinion."

"She thinks highly of you, Mr. Owen."

He colored slightly and glanced at her. "I am honored. She is rather an amazing woman."

After a moment he said, "If I may, there is one other thing I wish to address, concerning the wedding. I have a suspicion Christopher Drake is not wholly enthused about the event. Do you have any knowledge that might allay my concern?"

Kitty looked at him and sighed. "I do not. I have not seen

him since we returned. At that point he did not seem—as you put it—enthused. Lady Drake seems aware of some reluctance on his part. But she is determined he follow through and settle into a 'more productive life,' as she put it. He will not wish to be disinherited. And she is not a woman to be gainsaid, in my estimation."

"Well spoken, Miss Bennet, I hope you are right—about him going through with it. I think we all share a wish that my sister and he be married soon to avoid any possible compromise to her reputation." He glanced at her and she guessed his meaning.

"One thing may further reassure you, Mr. Owen—there is a royal interest in him following through with this marriage. There are those willing to turn their investigation of the 'investment club' in a different direction if he turns his life in a more wholesome direction. Their wishes are known to him and to others of us." She stole a look at him to see if he understood her.

"Ah, you are still in communication with Princess Charlotte then? That does set my mind more at ease. There are many forces encouraging him to do the right thing." He sighed.

"May I ask, will your brother attend the wedding? I assume both your parents will be there?"

"That remains to be seen. Douglas continues to be moody and unpredictable. Father is loath to leave him much alone. He has asked Darcy to give Lucy away in the ceremony if he cannot be there himself."

"I see. And you will perform the ceremony, am I correct?"

"You are. I have been ordained these two years, but a living was not yet available. Now that Mosley retires, I shall take over the parish. And I need not give up the horse breeding work with my father and with Mr. Darcy as a vicar. At present Father needs me to do almost ... well, his attention is much diverted by my brother. And with my stepmother now expecting ..." He trailed off, a frown darkening his features.

"He is most fortunate to have a son like you who can step in and do a fine job in his stead. It seems to suit you, more than your brother, to be the one to carry on with the estate."

Owen nodded. "It has always been so. Douglas is a restless

type, wanting to travel and have diverse activities. Sadly, he has never shown much interest in Greystone."

Lizzy beckoned to them.

"Mr. Owen, I fear my sister must return to the house. She is sensitive to the heat at present."

"Of course. We shall assist her at once."

≈

Later that day Kitty was handed a missive and recognized the writing immediately. She broke the seal and unfolded the page.

My dear CB,

Thank you for your letter advising us of your safe arrival. Please inform us of the status of the arrangement in which we were all instrumental. We hope it has taken place or will soon be concluded, that all parties complied to your satisfaction. We pray for their mutual happiness.

It surprised us to hear of a certain person's brother. Of him we have no news and have heard nothing suspicious. We wish that couple every happiness.

Regarding the gentleman under suspicion, those concerns have endured and increase. Remain on your guard. He appears to be in contact with the injured young man. The mission of our pact remains urgent.

We await word from you on the above matters.

Yours,

MME

Kitty let the paper fall to her lap, pondering the meaning of "endured and increase." Was Douglas in contact with George Cressley? Did Owen have any knowledge of this?

She would wait until after Lucy's wedding to respond to Miss Elphinstone. That way she could confirm Christopher and Lucy's wedding had taken place, thus concluding one part of the pact. She would apprise Darcy of the other situation immediately.

CHAPTER THIRTY-ONE

"So you ride with Lady Drake this morning?" Darcy said to Kitty, pouring himself another cup of coffee at the breakfast table. Lizzy sat at his right, nursing a cup of tea. Georgiana was gone, spending a few days with Matilda at Swan's Nest.

"Yes, I do," Kitty replied. "Might you have any message to convey?"

"None. But I will set you as far as the road and get you through that blasted gate again. I must have something done about that ... I hope you won't mind the company."

"I shall welcome it. It looks a lovely morning."

"It is. And I have a message from Lady Drake for you. She will bring two of her servants and a light lunch such as is fit for ladies. The group will return you to the crossroads by one o'clock, where either Johnny or myself will meet you and escort you home to Pemberley."

Kitty made no answer.

Darcy looked at her and frowned.

"Kitty, where is your mind? Did you hear me?"

She started and then grinned at him.

"Oh, yes I did. It made me so happy to hear you say 'home to Pemberley,' and be speaking of me. I *have* come to think of Pemberley as home—I hope that is not presumptuous?—and I got lost in the idea, like a dream."

Darcy's face softened. "I am pleased you feel at home here. I can hardly think of Pemberley without you now, Kitty."

He rose and downed the rest of his coffee.

"Can you be ready to leave in a quarter hour?"

"Yes, I am nearly ready now."

"Good. You may await me at the sweep. I will bring Cara down."

"Lizzy, I do wish you could ride with us," Kitty said, taking a final sip of her tea.

"Dear Kitty, riding on horseback is the last thing I would enjoy in this condition. Besides, I think it better you and Lady Drake be alone to forge a bond of friendship without my interference. You two have much in common."

"We do. I admire her a great deal."

"Good. Then be off with you. Darcy hates to be kept waiting, as you well know."

Kitty bent to kiss Lizzy on the cheek.

"You must know how very happy I am, Lizzy. Thank you."

Lizzy simply smiled and took another sip of tea.

≈

Darcy and Kitty made their way across the meadow, the grasses rustling as they passed.

"Kitty, I am glad you have this chance to better know Lady Drake. Having no daughters, she has long fancied Georgiana as a daughter ..." he glanced at her slyly, "which I wager will likely come to pass ... but you and Lady Drake have the foundation for a strong friendship. She is a fascinating lady. She has a kind of ... wisdom ... one does not often see."

Kitty frowned. "That is the second reference I have heard about her possessing a special kind of wisdom."

He looked over at Kitty as they trotted along the stone fence. "Who else—?"

"Mr. Owen. He said something similar."

"Ah. Only a few folks are aware of it or take notice of it. I am not surprised he would be one of them. There's a fine lad."

As they rode along, Owen's face was crowded out by her questions concerning Andrew. She decided to take a chance.

"Fitzwilliam, do you know if Mr. Andrew returns from Scotland for Matilda's wedding? Curiously I have heard no talk about it but did not think it proper to ask the family. And Julia ... well, Julia has not been in a state for talking much since the accident. I miss her company."

"I imagine you do. That is a sad affair for Miss Stapleton. I hope she can move past it. No, I have heard no news of young Mr. Andrew. The squire and I attend a cattle show in a few days. Perhaps I can make a discreet inquiry?" He hesitated a moment, and then gave her a curious look.

"I did not know if he left you with some kind of understanding. I am not so dull—I was aware of an attraction between the two of you."

Kitty looked straight ahead. "He has left me with no understanding; that is, he has not rightly declared himself. Although he almost did ... in a round-about way, at one time ... I had thought. It was a confusing conversation. I thought I might hear from him through Julia. That has not occurred. Not a single message. Not even a take-leave. I have had no news of him for weeks." This reality stung more sharply when put it into words.

Darcy dismounted to deal with the gate. Once they were through and he remounted, they resumed their ride to the cross-roads. Lady Drake's entourage approached from the south.

"Excellent timing, Mr. Darcy, Miss Bennet. What a glorious morning."

"It is indeed, Lady Drake," said Darcy with a salute. "In answer to your earlier message, either I or my servant Johnny—who is well known to Miss Bennet—shall meet you here at one o'clock. And now I am off to discuss with my steward a fencing issue—and a stubborn gate."

The ladies nodded, and he was off.

"Miss Bennet, we are for Avery Rocks today."

"I have not heard of it, Lady Drake."

"I am not surprised. It is little known amongst the population at large, though I cannot imagine why. I learnt of it as a girl.

A bit younger than you I was, spending the summer with my grandmother who lived somewhat south of the site."

They rode in silence some minutes, taking in the beauty of the surroundings.

Then Lady Drake remarked in a quiet voice, "There is a history and great wisdom in the land hereabouts, Miss Bennet. It is especially strong in the rocks and stones, as you heard Squire Stapleton say. They hold memories. Long memories. If you enjoyed our tales and discoveries at Benwick Castle, then you will appreciate Avery Rocks. And it is much nearer. I come here quite often. To ponder. To see. To dream."

Kitty listened with rapt attention. No one had ever shared things like this with her, or talked with her in such a way. What was this "unusual wisdom" Lady Drake was said to possess? Did she have special powers ... was she some kind of witch? A little tingle shot through Kitty's spine, but it was not an evil feeling. It was more of a thrill, even a recognition of sorts.

"Do you have any such special place, Miss Bennet? Perhaps found on a ride whilst growing up? You hail from Hertfordshire, am I right?"

"Yes, my lady. The only person in my family who went out into nature besides me was Lizzy. She was fond of long walks. As much to get away from the bickering ..." she blushed at her unintended revelation.

Lady Drake merely smiled.

"She appreciated the quiet and the beauty of nature, as I do. But I preferred to explore on horseback when I could, although my father did not approve of young ladies riding. There *was* one place, a cliff overlooking a small rill that became a torrent in the spring. Atop that cliff were large stones, some the size of a cottage, which hid a shallow cave. No trees grew there except one giant elm. It was near to Hadley's Woods. I sat with my back against that tree. I fancied I could feel its life and power coursing through me. I would close my eyes and listen to the endless song of the water and the happy grazing of the horse."

Lady Drake nodded and her warm eyes met Kitty's.

"I thought as much. I detected something different in you—a

deeper sensibility, a heightened awareness. It is somewhat rare, you know." She gave Kitty a keen look. "It is a gift."

Kitty had never thought of her sensibilities as a gift. Often they had seemed a burden when her fragile feelings were hurt whilst Lydia went about unscathed by critical comments.

They rode on in silence again, now single file on the narrower path. Kitty was grateful her studies over the summer now equipped her to better identify the trees and shrubs, wildflowers and grasses, and some of the rock types. The variety and beauty along even this common pathway were overwhelming. Her heart swelled. The world felt rich with abundance and possibilities.

The path began to twist and climb sharply. Trees lined the hills that rose high on each side of the riders, as if they were passing through a tunnel. In places the ground was still damp—the sun's rays had not yet topped the trees. The pungent smell of evergreens permeated the hollow. As they climbed, the evergreens gave way to outcroppings of stone punctuated by tufts of grass and late-season wildflowers.

Lady Drake turned in her saddle. "We are nearly there."

Soon they arrived at the summit. Large boulders emerged from hilly mounds. In some places groupings of stones stood in inexplicable formations. Kitty looked over at Lady Drake, who was smiling and breathing deeply as her eyes encompassed the vastness of the view.

The servants helped the ladies dismount and began laying out the foodstuffs and drinks on a rug nearby. Kitty and Lady Drake tended to their horses.

Lady Drake then walked to a large stone surrounded by several smaller stones set in a semicircle.

"Come, Miss Bennet, sit here with me a moment. This is the Seat of Vision."

Kitty joined. The stone was of natural form and shape, not hewn by human hands, but was somehow the perfect height and shape to seat two in comfort. They sat together taking in the sight of the valley below as it stretched into the distance.

"Would it alarm you, Miss Bennet, if I speak to you of some particular perceptions I have had?"

Kitty hesitated. "I do not know, my lady. I have heard you possess special wisdom, but I am not sure what that means."

Lady Drake tilted her head and looked at Kitty.

"I don't know about special wisdom. Perhaps. But I am gifted at times with deep sight into people or situations, and some foresight about future events. My grandmother said I have a very old soul."

They sat in silence again.

Kitty squirmed, wondering what she might hear.

"Your visit to Derbyshire has been quite propitious, Miss Bennet, am I correct?" Her voice was soft and warm.

Kitty looked at her and nodded. "Yes, it appears so, for me. I cannot speak to my effect on others. I have discovered there is more to value in people than meets the common eye. And that people may have reasons and motivations unknown to me—even unrelated to me—which might bear on their behavior."

"Interesting. Tell me more, Miss Bennet."

Kitty closed her eyes. "I have learnt I cannot foresee all ends, and that I do not need to. I am starting to comprehend my ability to manage situations—rather like on a horse. I cannot predict every move or event, but if my seat is sound I will remain in the saddle. An event that may appear tragic at first can sometimes turn out favorable—at least for some. And turnabout."

Her mind was a tumble of reflections, with the faces of Lydia and Julia and Lucy floating amongst them.

"I believe you have deep sight, Miss Bennet. A gift you are perhaps just now recognizing."

Kitty opened her eyes and looked up in surprise.

Lady Drake sat motionless beside her, looking far into the distance. She took Kitty's hand in hers.

"Look for changes in those around you, Miss Bennet. Changes you may not expect. Look beyond the obvious. Look deep, past what the eye can see. This is not unlike what we do with our horses. Not all communication is formed in words. There are some things we just know. Yes? Trust that. Do not let fear cause you to doubt yourself or what you know to be true."

A kaleidoscope of images whirled before Kitty's eyes—faces of those known long to her, and face of those newly met. Places from her past, and places newly discovered. She had to make an effort to focus when she heard Lady Drake speak again in a low, melodic voice.

"You care deeply for your family here, and your new friends. Miss Julia Stapleton stands at the edge of a precipice. You have perceived this. It troubles you. Miss Jamison has floundered long, since the death of her father, which caused her to lose her grandmother—her only voice of wisdom or reason, until now. And, as you know, your younger sister is beyond your aid. She must come to wisdom by her own path."

Kitty started. How could Lady Drake know about Lydia?

"As for Miss Jamison and Miss Stapleton, your role with each is powerful now, Miss Bennet; most especially in what you do *not* say and do *not* do. I see ahead a strong alliance that will serve the good of all. It is fortunate you chose to visit Mrs. Darcy at this particular time." She paused and closed her eyes; then went on.

"Beware of acting a part that is not yours to play. You cannot prevent all tragedy. As you have said, you cannot see all ends."

Kitty twisted the gloves in her hands. Her worries about Julia —and all the ways she had hoped to help but had failed—came bubbling to the surface. Her eyes filled with tears that brimmed over and spilled down her cheeks.

Lady Drake sighed and closed her eyes.

"Do not grieve. What you see are others on their path of discovery, which they must travel themselves. You cannot travel it for them. We each of us have our own path, our own destiny." Lady Drake patted Kitty's hand. "All of us wish to protect our dear ones from suffering, pain, humiliation; but at times we must step aside so they can find the sunlight and grow. It can be so with friends as well as family. Trust in Providence to show them the way."

"It is trying when a loved one chooses a rockier road for a time, like my Christopher." She clucked to herself. "Thankfully he is not as shallow as he appears," she said, the corner of her mouth turning up. "Nor is Miss Jamison. She has depths not yet mined, in my estimation. Their match has much promise."

Images of Julia and Lucy appeared again in her mind, and Kitty perceived a deeper link between herself and each of them.

Then Lydia's face appeared. It was a rocky road her younger sister had chosen. Lizzy had disclosed Darcy's role in bringing about Lydia's marriage—a marriage that Kitty had envied for some time simply because she too wished to know the thrill of a great romance.

Lady Drake's voice penetrated her thoughts again.

"Do not seek for that which you have already found, Miss Bennet, though it may not look as expected. Trust your feelings. Past sorrows have opened the doors to goodness and light. Follow the path of light and comfort rather than that of parade and pleasure. Is this new to you?" Lady Drake murmured.

"It is, my lady. I have been drawn by parade and pleasure, as you say. Yet it did not satisfy. This summer I have seen different views of love—deeper and broader and longer views. True partnerships. I no longer envy my younger sister. I no longer wish to be merely swept off my feet."

Who would be her partner on her life path? Andrew, so handsome and charming, made her feel important when in his company. Everyone knew him as a fine man, and on his arm she looked a fine lady. Was that enough? They had spent little time together. Immersed as he was in science, did he have any interest in such a partnership? She could picture him and his dazzling smile, but could not hear his voice. She heard, instead, a deeper voice of practical wisdom. The voice of a true horseman.

"Your place is here, Miss Bennet. I feel that. But one friend must depart to find a path of light. You will experience healing with a family member from afar, and see a growing sadness in the spirit of another." Lady Drake paused and drew in a long breath. "Your new friend at a distance can be trusted, but she will herself experience both great joy and great darkness." She shuddered and shook her head.

After a deep breath she opened her eyes and looked at Kitty.

"And you, Miss Bennet, have experienced only a taste of the joy ahead of you."

Lady Drake let go her hand and clasped her own hands in her lap. She smiled and then opened her hands to reveal a stone, smaller than a lady's palm, of deep red marked with veins of white. At Kitty's curious look she said, "My seeing stone."

Kitty stared at the stone and then at Lady Drake. A servant's voice startled her out of her thoughts, saying, "Luncheon is ready, my lady."

"Come, Miss Bennet. A little refreshment is surely welcome now. Today we shall dine with an unparalleled view, courtesy of Providence itself." A picnic was spread for them near a cluster of scrubby trees, which provided some shade but did not obscure the vista.

They spoke of lighter subjects during lunch. As Kitty made to rise when the meal was completed, she put her hand on a lump. She reached beneath the rug and drew out a stone, very smooth, swirled with greens and tans. Holding it in her open palm, she looked at Lady Drake, who returned a speaking look with the corner of her mouth turned gently upward. Kitty placed the stone in her pocket and smiled back.

Soon after that they returned by the same path they had come. After descending the heights, they ambled side by side along the more level road.

"I believe you and I, Miss Bennet, to be the leading horse-women in the neighborhood. May I count on you to join me once I deem the time ripe, to—shall we say—increase the girth of local minds about the style of riding appropriate for ladies?"

Kitty laughed. "Of course. I shall be the first to stand with you."

"Good. My husband supports us in this, as does Mr. Darcy. And, although he has not yet spoken, Mr. Wyndham will also agree. Squire Stapleton is eminently practical and his voice is powerful hereabouts. He admires your courage and will come to support us. It may take time, but so it always does for lasting change. I am glad to know we are comrades in this, Miss Bennet. And perhaps in other things as well?"

Kitty felt her face flush. "Indeed, my lady, my esteem for you grows the more acquainted we become. I have never known anyone old enough to be ... well, anyone not my own age ... who has such fresh, uncommon ideas. And who is grand enough to lead change."

Lady Drake threw her head back and her throaty laugh echoed amongst the rocks. "Grand, indeed. Some years back,

Miss Bennet, I was a girl much like yourself. Not grand at all. A plain young lady from an everyday gentleman's family." Then her eyes grew misty.

"Lord Drake has his own kind of wisdom. He saw depth and beauty beyond rank. We have a great respect and love for each other. One does not need to be grand to find true love and happiness. Always listen to your deepest self, my dear. Therein lies your wisdom."

To Kitty's surprise, Lady Drake turned to her and winked. With one eye.

CHAPTER THIRTY-TWO

A line of servants with umbrellas held aloft escorted Kitty, Georgiana, and a lumbering Lizzy into the carriage to attend Lucy's wedding. Darcy entered and closed the door.

"They say rain on your wedding day means good luck," Lizzy commented when they were all settled into the squabs.

"Then perhaps rain is the work of Providence for this young couple," Darcy said with a wry grin. "I believe they will need some luck."

"They do seem an unlikely pair," Georgiana mused.

"Not so," Kitty said in a soft voice. She looked at each of them directly. "I think they are much alike in that both appear shallow, but both desire something deeper. I believe together they will each become better than they were alone."

"What a lovely sentiment, Kitty," Lizzy said with a look of admiration. "I think that is the task of true love. I can think of one couple in which the man was greatly improved by the clever wife he chose, even against his better judgment." Her eyes twinkled and her dimple showed.

"Or perhaps choosing her showed he was far wiser than he knew." Darcy took Lizzy's hand in his.

The ride to the Drake chapel was short but merry, even on such a dreary morning.

≈

Kitty had never been a bridesmaid. She had attended only one wedding—the double wedding of her sisters Jane and Lizzy. When she arrived at the chapel, she smoothed her deep rose gown, adjusted her gloves, and checked the pins in her hair.

Lucy was all aflutter.

"You are absolutely beautiful," Kitty said as she straightened Lucy's necklace. Her dress became her very well. It lent an elegance to Lucy's figure, and with her hair swept up and sprinkled with tiny pink roses she looked every inch a lady.

Mr. Wyndham appeared and a smile lit his face at the sight.

"My dear Lucy, you have grown into a fine young woman. I am very happy for you." He offered her his arm then nodded at Kitty. "It is time."

After taking a trembling breath, Kitty led the procession the dozen steps to the altar where Benjamin stood attendance on his brother. Christopher's blue eyes seemed to see only Lucy as she came down the aisle. A sunbeam shone through the clerestory window, blessing the chapel with heavenly light.

Lady Drake looked up, then at Kitty with a knowing smile.

Kitty took her place near the altar and was drawn into the steady grey eyes of Owen Wyndham. A gentle smile played on his face. As he began to speak, she looked around. Lizzy gave her a wink. The world felt whole and complete.

≈

The skies had cleared during the ceremony, but the ground was still soggy as they entered the carriage and made their way to the great house at Greystone for the wedding breakfast. It was a small group at table—the Drakes, the Darcys, and the Wyndhams—minus Douglas. No one asked about him.

The company was cheerful, and Kitty was thankful to be seated next to Owen. His conversation was usually interesting and often witty, and his presence calmed her. She delighted in wit when it was not at the expense of others. Seeing the men enjoying a diversity of company, Kitty felt a touch of sadness for her father, who had been surrounded by only women in daily life —most of whom could not carry on an intelligent conversation, including herself. She and Lydia had been lost in a world of officers and flirtations. Kitty was relieved to have made her way beyond that.

A deep voice brought her back to the present.

"They seem happier than I might have guessed. What is your own opinion?"

She turned to Owen, who was eyeing the newlyweds.

"I have thought the same. Even the weather smiles on them. Before the ceremony, all was cloudy and gray. But that beam of light ... in the chapel ... I took it as a sign from Providence. I think they will be better together than either were alone."

When he turned back to her she remarked a light in his eyes.

"A sign of a true friend, Miss Bennet, to foresee happiness for others. Your kindness is not unexpected by me. I believe I know you that well."

Her whole body felt aglow. How was it that he, with his keen observations, made her feel so exposed yet so protected at the same time? She looked down at her napkin.

"You were the first in the party to be honored by the heavenly light, Miss Bennet. You looked quite ... divine." He shot her a look that pierced her deeply and then picked up his fork for another morsel.

She stared at the side of his head, stunned into silence. Still trembling, she managed to summon her courage.

"No one has ever described me in such a way."

The corner of his mouth lifted at her reply.

"I have not been a bridesmaid before. Lizzy and Jane were each other's bridesmaids at their double wedding. What a happy day that was." She spied Fitzwilliam watching his wife with admiration as Lizzy spoke with animation to those around them.

"Mr. Darcy is most fortunate in his bride. Your sister is sparkling and witty and kind. She looks very well."

"I agree. And how does your stepmother do?"

He looked at her and rolled his eyes.

"As you might expect. I believe she is quite well but her temperament is missish. I wonder if she is ever happy?"

Kitty gasped inwardly at this description. Her father had often called her missish. Looking back, she could see he had often been right. She was rarely happy back then. She gulped back those feelings and asked, "And your father? How does he do? He looks quite pleased today."

"I believe he is. The whole situation angered him at first. He has never admired Christopher Drake. Too arrogant, smug, irresponsible. Neither Christopher nor Lucy are like my father—practical and kind—so he does not understand them. But his vision is not clouded. He knows an unpromising horse can often be brought around. And with a friend like you, I see great possibilities for Lucy. I thank you for that."

Owen took another mouthful and chewed thoughtfully.

"Summer is ending, Miss Bennet. How long shall your visit continue?" He reached for his wine and turned to face her.

"I do not know. Lizzy said she would talk to Mr. Darcy, but I guess they have not decided yet. I dearly hope I may stay until their baby is born, and for some time after. It is odd, but I cannot imagine living at Longbourn again. Derbyshire seems like home to me now. It has grown on me, as have its people. But I do not wish to burden my sister." Her brow furrowed.

"I cannot imagine your presence ever being a burden."

"You flatter me, Mr. Owen."

"I speak as I see, Miss Bennet."

She felt unsettled again, fluttery and yet pleased, and hastily changed the subject.

"There is another wedding soon, you know. Miss Matilda and Mr. William. The day before Michaelmas."

"I knew they were engaged but had not heard the date."

"Georgiana will be Matilda's bridesmaid since Julia has declined. Oh, my heart aches for Julia."

He looked hastily away.

"I am sorry, I did not wish to bring up a painful subject. Things do not improve with Mr. Douglas?"

"No. And I appreciate your forbearance. Let us talk of it some other time."

The table was cleared and the bridal cake brought in, a delicate confection of flour, eggs, and candied fruits, shimmering with sugar.

Christopher sliced the cake with his usual flourish. Handing Lucy the first piece, he said with a bow, "A token of love for my beautiful bride." It was the same swaggering behavior, but with a new softness in his eyes, especially when he looked at Lucy.

Kitty and Owen exchanged a look of mutual understanding.

Georgiana spoke up. "Will you take a wedding tour?"

Lucy glanced at Kitty, but Christopher stood and spoke.

"I have been advised—indeed, convinced—by all who proclaim to love me that we should explore a region unknown to both of us. A mutual adventure seems an appropriate way to begin a marriage," he said with a lift of his brow and a toss of his blonde hair. "We shall tour the Lakes. This same region was explored those many years ago by my own parents on their wedding tour. However, if anyone has been there in more recent times, we welcome recommendations of sights to see or enchanting places to stay." He gave a little bow. There was hearty applause all around. "We leave two days hence," he said and then resumed his seat.

Soon the Darcy coach was called. Benjamin accompanied them out. He had not left Georgiana's side all morning. When would he declare himself?

Later that day Kitty penned another missive to her friends.

MME,

I am pleased to inform you and our esteemed friend that a certain gentleman was married here 22 August to a young lady of our mutual acquaintance, concluding an agreement between several parties. Two days hence they depart for a tour of the Lakes. The couple's chance of happiness appears greater than we have anticipated. I pray it will be so for the sakes of both parties and their families.

As to the other wedding, it is set for the day before Michaelmas. We anticipate the suspected brother will attend this event and we shall be especially observant and report anything untoward.

Your servant,

CB

CHAPTER THIRTY-THREE

*T*he summer drifted to its conclusion, days of rain alternating with days of sun. Kitty's time was filled with reading from her list, learning new tasks from Lizzy and Georgiana, and taking on the challenge of her new riding goals. Lady Drake came weekly to observe her lesson with Mr. Connor. Johnny also coached her in her near-daily practice. She and Cara were trotting cross rails and riding formations in the arena, but still enjoyed time on the bridle paths of Pemberley. Kitty rode astride unless they would be near the village.

One morning as Kitty approached the stable yard she saw another horse tied next to Lady Drake's. It was Owen Wyndham's, the very horse she had ridden the day of the accident. Johnny was just fetching the big grey as Kitty approached.

"Mr. Connor 'as a surprise today, Miss Bennet. Are ye up to a challenge?"

"If it involves horses, then yes I am. But what are you doing with Mr. Owen's horse?"

"He be your mount today, Miss. Mr. Connor says riding different horses improves skills. And Sultan here's an eager and scopey jumper."

Kitty's eyes darted to the arena. One cross rail was still set up, and the other three jumps had been raised. Her heart pounded with excitement.

"I shall join you at the mounting block in a moment, Johnny!"

His eyes sparkled back at her.

She slipped into a stall and pulled on the breeches and boots she now rode in, tying her skirt up to the side. She strode to the block, mounted Sultan, and was accompanied into the arena by Johnny. Her eyes opened wide. Darcy stood at the rail next to Lady Drake and Owen. She wasn't sure if she welcomed or dreaded such a large audience to witness her first attempts at jumping on a new horse. As Johnny adjusted her stirrups and the girth, she nodded at her onlookers. Johnny then joined them at the sidelines, and Mr. Connor began to direct the ride from the center of the arena.

Sultan had a long smooth stride and was a much bigger horse than Cara—a fact that had escaped her notice during the ride for help. Kitty gathered her reins and followed Connor's directions in warming up her own muscles; the horse's had been warmed up on the ride from Greystone.

"Sit back, Miss. Sit deep. This horse be needin' a stronger presence in the saddle than our little Miss Cara."

Kitty leaned back and pressed deep, keeping her shoulders back and down and her elbows at her sides.

"Heels lower and back, if ye please," Connor intoned, polite but forceful.

"There, there, yes, that's reet." The horse was moving at a long-paced walk, covering ground easily. "Now into a trot. There, aye, hands down and light. Like a feather, Miss."

The horse under her was full of fire. He was a great and powerful beast, but so far was compliant to her signals. He was eager to move out but did not challenge her.

"Now turn. Full circle, then a half, and change direction if ye please." The walk and the trot were repeated in the left hand direction.

"Now, trot the cross rail, if ye please."

Kitty directed the horse to the center of the cross rail. His stride was so long he did not need to jump it, he just lifted himself smoothly over whilst maintaining the trot.

"Aye! Aye, very good lass."

She smiled to herself. She felt at one with the horse, beautiful and strong.

"Halt. Turn on the front quarters. Aye. Now—slowly—gather him for the canter."

The gelding seemed to know the words spoken and gathered himself onto his haunches. He was most keen to move out! For a moment, Kitty was a little frightened. There had been no time for fright on the day of the accident when their mission had been so urgent. She could do this. Here. Now. A deep breath steadied her.

"Good, aye, breathe. Do not tighten. Sit deep. Now ask."

She moved her outside leg a little behind the girth and the horse collected into a smooth, rocking canter. It was delightful until he leaned onto the bit.

"No, no, when he leans, ye sit back and deep. Play the bit in your fingers. Distract him. Aye, back and deep. Now give that little cross rail a try. He'll canter over it."

She approached the cross rail.

"Two-point, if ye please."

Kitty lifted her seat slightly out of the saddle, shoved her heels down, and leaned forward, resting her hands lightly on the horse's neck—and they were over it, barely leaving the ground.

"Aye, ye've got it. Easy. Easy for ye both. Now that low jump. Use yer legs to keep 'im straight. Give 'im 'is head. Throw yer heart over the jump and he's sure to follow."

Her heart was in her throat. She pictured her heart over the jump. The horse engaged. Every sinew was taut and ready. His excitement mirrored her own. She played the bit in her fingers and leaned slightly forward, just out of the saddle in two-point as he lifted his front end. They sailed over the fence, flying as one. As he got all four feet on the ground, she sat back and deep again. His energy nearly burst beneath her. She had to squeeze with her legs and sit deep to bring him to a controlled canter. She was breathless with the thrill.

Looking at Connor in amazement, she cried, "Brilliant! We must do it again."

"Bravo!"

"Splendid riding!"

"Excellent, Miss Bennet!" came the cries from her onlookers. She glanced their way, flushed with pleasure. Then, of a sudden, a painful cramp shot through her lower leg. Keeping Sultan at a walk, she took her foot out of the stirrup to stretch her leg down at the heel.

"Miss Bennet?"

"A bit of a leg cramp, sir," she replied, wiggling her leg. "It will be better in a ..."

The gelding read her wiggling as a signal to speed up. He grabbed the bit in his mouth and lunged into a rather uncollected canter. Caught off guard, Kitty was lopsided, flailing in the saddle, her leg still in a stitch.

Deep and back! Breathe! She worked the reins to distract him but he had the jump in his sights. She pulled her other foot out of the stirrup for better balance. It would be dangerous to try to stop him now. She must ride it out. She lifted into two-point and they sailed over the jump. But she was still not centered and could not stick the landing, lost her balance, and at the next stride was flung to the ground.

Owen and Johnny were upon her in an instant. Darcy strode quickly towards her from the rail, and Connor calmly approached the horse to catch him.

"Miss Bennet, are you hurt? Miss Bennet?" All she could see were Owen's eyes, full of alarm. He reached for her hand and, as she began to sit up, cradled her neck in his arm.

"I do not believe I am hurt."

Owen looked to Darcy for direction.

"Kitty, are you sure?" Darcy asked. "Does your leg still hurt?"

She smiled ruefully. "I think the fall did away with the leg cramp. I am so sorry I misdirected Sultan. He is unharmed?"

Johnny helped her to her feet and Owen took the liberty of brushing some of the dust off her arms and back.

Connor stepped up. "Help her walk it off, lads. Let us see how she does." He had Sultan's reins.

"Mine's the blame, Sire. Pushed her too fast, I did. Larger horse, stretched her legs too much ..."

Darcy glared at Kitty, jaw set, eyes ablaze, fists clenched.

"There will be no further lessons until I—"

"Mr. Darcy." Lady Drake's calm voice interjected as she touched his arm. "Tell me, how many times have you fallen off a horse?"

"Me? I have not fallen for years. A man——"

"Pray, how many, sir? In your lifetime? Or even by Miss Bennet's age?"

All eyes were fixed on the two as they faced each other. Everyone present was younger than Darcy or in his employ and dared not challenge him. Everyone but Lady Drake.

Owen still possessed Kitty's elbow in a protective way, and she did not shake him off. His steadying touch was comforting. She held her breath.

Darcy scowled at the group and over at Connor, who held the horse and stared coolly back.

"The horse, Connor, he is unhurt?"

"Appears fine, Sire."

"Kitty. Please come here."

Owen kept hold of her elbow and stepped forward with her.

"No," Darcy commanded. "Let her walk unassisted."

Kitty looked at Owen and nodded her permission. He released her elbow and stepped back.

She took a deep breath and moved towards Darcy with a steady stride. When she reached him, in a measured voice she said, "Fitzwilliam, it was but an ordinary fall. I am unhurt. Riding a horse that was new to me—and especially me new to him—I should have been more aware. I was caught up in the excitement. It is a valuable lesson. Please do not prevent me?"

Darcy looked her up and down with detached precision.

"Your movements appear sound. Very well. I will not cancel future lessons, but we shall take things slower from here on. Agreed?" He addressed her, and then also looked at Connor.

"Aye, slowly; she being a young lass."

Kitty reached for Darcy's hand. "Thank you, Fitzwilliam. And now, if I may, I should like to ride the horse twice around the arena each way at a walk. I believe it will be helpful—for me and for him."

"A reasonable request, Mr. Darcy," Lady Drake said, blithely adjusting a glove. "I daresay it will soothe any muscles tightened by the fall, and reunite horse and rider in a pleasant way."

Darcy pursed his lips and they all waited. At last he spoke.

"Very well. Mr. Owen, you lead Sultan. I will take no chances in case her leg cramps again." He ran his hand over his head and said, almost to himself, "How could I ever face your sister if you were hurt?"

"Please do not worry, Fitzwilliam. I do this of my own choice, guided by my own wisdom."

Connor handed the reins to Owen and Johnny stepped over to give Kitty a leg up. Darcy offered Lady Drake his arm and escorted her back to the sidelines.

Kitty overheard Darcy say, "I prefer to limit our neighborhood events to pleasant ones if possible, Lady Drake. There have been enough accidents of late."

Owen sighed at the unwelcome reminder as he checked Kitty's tack.

"I am sorry, Mr. Owen. This whole episode is my fault."

"No, Miss Bennet. Sometimes things just happen. Horses, like people, can be unpredictable. It will do Sultan good to listen to a different rider. From now on I shall keep a better watch on him, and on you. Mr. Darcy is right. There have been enough accidents. Are you ready?"

She nodded and they circled the arena as she had asked. The session ended in quiet relief and a sense of thoughtfulness on the part of all.

CHAPTER THIRTY-FOUR

Georgiana had spent the past few days at Swan's Nest in preparation for Matilda's wedding so the Darcy party numbered just three in the coach as it rumbled down the road, rutted after several days of rain. The sun had graced them the last two days, but the unseasonable heat and the dampness were less than welcome with harvest underway.

Darcy tugged at his cravat.

"Whoever decreed weddings be held in the morning should be taken out and ... well, it is far too early to be forced to dress so fine." He continued to mumble and scowl.

His attitude irked her so Kitty attempted to change the mood in the carriage.

"I cannot wait to hear about all the excitement from Georgiana. I'm sure it has been a wonderful time for her and Matilda. They are very close."

"Indeed they are," said Lizzy. "I wonder how they will do so far apart when Miss Matilda and Mr. William remove to Reading. I suppose there will be a frequent and enthusiastic correspondence."

"Rather like you and Jane?"

"Yes. And as my confinement draws near, I do wish Jane could be here. Her presence is always soothing."

"I shall do my best to take her place," Kitty offered.

"You cannot take her place, Kitty."

Kitty and Darcy stared at Lizzy.

"Do not frown. You cannot take her place because you have *your own* place with me now, Kitty. I am grateful you will be here, and I hope you can stay some months after the birth to assist me —and entertain me with tales of your schemes and adventures."

"I shall not have much to tell. With no involvement in the local village and with no regiment as we had in Meryton, there are far fewer tales and schemes."

"And that is just as well!" Darcy exclaimed, and stared out the window again.

Lizzy's brow puckered. "My dear, what is it that has you so cross today? This is a joyful occasion—two young people very much in love with such good prospects for happiness. And the squire, your close friend, so pleased as well."

When he looked at Lizzy his expression softened.

"Yes. Perhaps you are right. You usually are. But this heat, the bumpy road—I worry for your safety and for our child. If anything should happen, I could never forgive myself."

Lizzy laughed softly and patted his hand, then put on a pert expression.

"Mr. Darcy. When have you known me to be in error on anything? I know perfectly well how I feel and what activities suit me. All this cantankerous grousing merely serves to upset my equanimity, sir. You would do well to cease it immediately." She arched her brow at him.

"Forgive me. I am so blind I cannot see I am making things worse. Tell me, how can I make it better for you, my dear?"

Lizzy pursed her lips and then said, "You should tell me one of your famous jokes."

He was nonplussed. "My ... jokes?"

Kitty and Lizzy burst into laughter.

"There, you see? I am much merrier now. Only your delightful smile could complete my joy."

Darcy smiled in spite of himself.

"Ah, I am now quite content. If *you* can but keep me out of excessive heat today, *I* can assure you of my health and happiness." She and Kitty snickered again.

Darcy rolled his eyes and gave the ladies a rueful grin.

The coach bumped and lurched its way to the Swan's Nest chapel. When they arrived, Darcy handed them out of the coach and then offered his arm to Lizzy. Fortunately there were but four muddy steps into the church and straw had been tossed down to provide a dry path.

Darcy and Lizzy stopped to speak with the squire. It was one of the few times Kitty had seen him without a pipe in his mouth.

Inside the chapel entryway Kitty spied her friends in the corner. Georgiana glowed in the lavender gown she had worn at Kitty's ball. Matilda was resplendent in pale shimmering green trimmed in lavender, her wild red hair captured in an array of ribbons and small flowers. The two young ladies fussed with each other's attire in between giggles.

"You must stop giggling!" Kitty admonished them, her eyes twinkling with amusement.

"How does my William look?"

"I did not look into the chapel, Matilda. Your sisters ... are they already seated?" She dared not ask if Andrew was with them.

"Julia is on the bench, just there," said Matilda, pointing to where her sister sat nearby quietly sketching.

Sketching! This was a good sign.

"Is she drawing you?" Kitty asked.

"I do not know."

Julia beckoned to Kitty, who quickly joined her on the bench near the door.

"Kitty, there is something I must tell you before we speak of anything else."

Then the squire entered. "Ladies, are you ready? Miss Bennet, you and Julia can sit together. Likely there is room with either my family or yours. It is nearly time." He gazed fondly at Matilda, who stood clasping Georgiana's hands.

"Julia, it must wait. We are holding up the ceremony."

The squire shooed them towards the center aisle.

"But Kitty ..."

Kitty linked arms with Julia and, to the squire's relief, they advanced into the chapel itself.

Lizzy turned and motioned for Kitty to join herself and Darcy. But there was room for only one.

Julia's sisters whispered and waved for her to join them in the only seat left in their pew.

Kitty patted Julia's arm, whispered "Later," and moved off to join the Darcys.

Julia shook her head and joined her younger sisters.

When Kitty turned to see Georgiana gliding past, a familiar pair of eyes captured hers. She gasped. There he was, across the aisle. Andrew Stapleton nodded at her. Kitty had to catch her breath. When had he arrived? Sitting next to him was a young lady in a lovely bonnet. As Andrew looked down at this lady, Kitty was shocked to see his gaze filled with obvious affection. When he whispered to the lady, a pair of large brown eyes met Kitty's. Before Kitty could react, everyone stood as Matilda and the squire passed by to the altar.

"Dearly beloved, we are gathered here ..." intoned the vicar, his voice a blur at the edge of Kitty's mind.

With great effort she kept her eyes ahead and on the ceremony. Her tumultuous thoughts proved less obedient. Who was the lady? And, more importantly, who was she to Andrew?

"... reverently, discreetly, advisedly, soberly, and in the fear of God;"

Perhaps the lady was a family friend?

"... into which holy estate these two persons present come now ..."

A cousin come from Scotland for the ceremony?

"Who giveth this woman ..."

The squire cleared his throat, stepped forward, and placed Matilda's hand into the vicar's, who placed it into William's.

"William James Cressley, wilt thou have this woman ..."

William's face was strangely solemn. With a firm voice and no hesitation he answered, "I will."

Matilda Serena Stapleton, wilt thou have this man ..."

Georgiana's eyes were brimming with tears. Matilda's were wide, yet a smile flickered at the corner of her mouth just before she said, "I will."

"... with this ring I thee wed, with my body I thee worship, and with all my worldly goods I thee endow."

William's rich baritone invoked the words after the vicar

spoke. Georgiana gave a little gasp as William placed his ring on Matilda's finger.

As all knelt, Kitty's eyes crept to Andrew, who supported his lady's elbow as they knelt together. Of a sudden, Kitty realized she was the only one standing and dropt to her knees.

"*... send Thy blessing upon these thy servants ...*"

Would Andrew now stay at Swan's Nest?

"*... ever remain in love and peace together and live according to Thy laws ...*"

Was he engaged? Married?

"*have given and pledged their troth, each to the other ...*"

Why had no one told her?

Wait. Perhaps Julia had tried.

"*I pronounce that they be Man and Wife together ...*"

Kitty stared hard at the newly married couple or, more accurately, stared through them. Her happiness for their new state was undeservedly subdued by her confusion about her own. Did not everyone expect Andrew to offer for her?

The vicar continued with prayers and blessings and Kitty went through the motions, her thoughts flying every direction, her heart askew.

The service ended. The couple made for the Registry, along with Georgiana and William's brother Charles, who had performed the ceremony.

How should she act towards Andrew now?

Suddenly Julia was at her side, taking her arm.

"Kitty?"

All Kitty could do was stare at her friend and appreciate what she had tried to do.

"We shall talk later," Julia assured her. "That is, if you wish it."

Kitty nodded and tried to mirror the happiness of those around her. She would need some time to think about all this. Had she misunderstood his speech to her, his very intentions? She left the chapel in a daze.

Darcy handed Kitty into the carriage, and she in turn grasped Lizzy's hands to offer support as her sister awkwardly tried to enter.

"I am rather like a chubby mouse trying to squeeze through a knothole!" Lizzy exclaimed.

Sensing her need, Darcy immediately called for the coach top to be lowered.

"There. Now you need not bend so far, my dear."

Lizzy's face was filled with love as the carriage made for the breakfast at the great house.

"No one could wish for a finer husband than you."

Kitty's thoughts were on Andrew. She knew not if she was angry or relieved.

CHAPTER THIRTY-FIVE

For a few moments there was no sound but the clattering of carriage wheels.

Kitty felt Lizzy's eyes on her but she avoided her sister's gaze.

Lizzy spoke first. "What a charming ceremony. Matilda is young but seems quite sure of what she wants. And her groom is certainly enamored of her."

"Matilda is not so young, Lizzy," Kitty said. "She is but one year my junior. Lydia was sixteen when she married ..." At Darcy's quick look, Kitty left the other name unspoken.

Darcy's voice was vehement. "Your sister may have had a wedding, but it will be no marriage of minds or hearts," he snorted. "These two today appear to have a connection of the heart, and they certainly have the support of both families." He frowned. "Age alone does not make a good marriage. The gentleman in Lydia's case will never be old enough for anything as rational as marriage."

Lizzy patted his hand.

"There is always hope," Lizzy said. "People do change, as you know."

Kitty stared out at the rocky scenery and thought how some change without a hint. Her mind's eye stubbornly dwelt on the vision of Andrew's smiling countenance as he escorted his lady from the chapel.

"I wonder when Mr. Andrew returned?" Lizzy asked no one in particular. "I don't recall any discussion of him traveling here, and it is quite a long distance."

"It *is* a long distance," Darcy replied. "And who," he said with a quick look at Kitty, "is the young lady he escorts?"

Kitty scowled and set her jaw.

"Do not look to me. I know nothing." She could not bear to face either of them, conscious that they both thought she had set her cap at Andrew from the very beginning of her visit.

The carriage pulled into the sweep and Kitty tried to reorder her scattered thoughts. Her main goal was to find Julia. She gave Darcy a brief smile as he handed her out. Spying Julia leading her younger sisters towards the house, Kitty made for there herself.

"Miss Bennet." The voice caught her completely off-guard.

She started, then whirled around to find herself face to face with Andrew—and the lady with the large brown eyes.

Kitty's voice faltered but she managed to say, "Mr. Stapleton," and drop a curtsey. The hammering of her own heart filled her ears. She strained to hear his words.

"Miss Bennet, how wonderful to see you again. We arrived just last night." He bowed. "May I present Anna Stapleton, my wife? Anna, this is Miss Catherine Bennet, sister to Mrs. Darcy."

Anna. Was that the name he had spoken before he left? So Anna and Scotland had won out. And what of Swan's Nest?

Kitty forced a smile. "Welcome to Derbyshire Mrs. Stapleton, though I am but a guest here myself."

"How nice to meet you, Miss Bennet. Andrew has told me so much about you, and his family, and everyone hereabouts."

"And how long shall you stay?" Kitty asked, hoping they would leave sooner than later.

Andrew replied, "Our plans are not firmly set. I had a letter from Julia that distressed me. I hoped you and I might discuss it? I am worried."

Kitty merely nodded, unsure how much he had told his new wife about his sister's situation.

"Ah, here is Julia now," he said. "I see you got the younger ones settled. You are very good to do that so Mother and Father are free to spend as much time as possible with Matilda. When do the newlyweds leave?"

Julia stared at him, confounded by so many comments and questions at once.

"Hello, Anna. Kitty. The newlyweds leave three days hence for Oakhurst with his brothers and the mares. After a rest, they will travel to the seaside for their wedding tour. Then they shall settle in Reading, where William's legal practice is located."

"So much traveling and change," Kitty observed.

Andrew laughed. "It is. But I believe Matilda is in great anticipation of both. She is ready for a different life."

Julia glanced sidelong at Kitty. "Georgiana has been asking for you. Come. Let us find her. Pray, excuse us."

As they walked away, Kitty whispered, "Thank you. I suspect I have discovered what you were trying to tell me."

"I am sorry. It must have been such a shock. It was so for all of us. We had no word he was coming until early yesterday afternoon when a messenger arrived. We did not know about ... her ... until he helped her out of the coach. Papa and Mama were quite shocked. I think everyone hereabouts had expected that you and he ... well, there had seemed to be an attraction ... but, oh, Kitty are you quite heartbroken?" She looked at Kitty intensely. "I did think, over the past few months, that your fancy might have turned in another direction?"

"Julia! You are a shrewd friend indeed. Wait ... are we really going to find Georgiana? Or was that a ruse?"

Julia laughed.

It was a relief to see Julia's countenance untroubled.

"Now *you* are the shrewd friend, Kitty! Let us take that path along the pond so we are not disturbed. We haven't long before the breakfast but we shall make of it what we can."

They walked a few steps in silence. Then Julia said, "Andrew did pull me aside briefly when he arrived to ask how you might take his news."

Kitty looked at her but said nothing.

"I told him I knew not, but that I was greatly shocked myself. He seemed disturbed by that, as he should be." After a few more steps, she said, "May I ask if he left you with an under-standing? I hope my own brother is not a scoundrel."

Kitty sighed. "Sometimes I thought he had nearly made me an offer. And he had confided concerns to me about how his profession might mesh with being master of Swan's Nest; but there was no understanding. Not really. Swan's Nest has no shadow cast on it, though my heart may have."

"And, Julia, your observations are ... not far off. Have others noticed? Andrew did capture my attention from the very start—how could he not!—yet somehow my heart remained untouched. I cannot explain it. I did still have some hope of things working out between us, but I am not sure why. We spent little time in each other's company. I do not really know him."

"And you have been thrown together a good deal with another young man of our acquaintance. One with whom you have the powerful bond of a shared interest."

Kitty blushed.

"Do not worry. It is not apparent unless someone watches you closely and knows you as I do. Even Georgiana may not be aware of it, she is so much in love herself."

Julia glanced back. The last of the wedding guests were going indoors.

"Make haste. We must not hinder the breakfast."

Kitty hurried alongside her friend. She hoped they would have time to talk later about Julia's concerns—and specifically about Douglas.

≈

The wedding breakfast was lively—which was no surprise to anyone—and the merriment went on for some time. Even the dampness and heat could not inhibit the spirit of joy present in the uniting of the happy couple, and the connection now made between the Darcy and Stapleton families, however far removed.

When some of the well-wishers spilled into the wooded area for fresh air and shade, Kitty was amongst them. To her surprise Andrew followed her, carrying two glasses of wine.

"Miss Bennet, perhaps we can talk now? There are two things

that concern me greatly. Talking with such a steady friend as you would greatly ease my mind. May I join you?"

Kitty was seated on a rustic bench in the shade of a large cedar. She slid over. "How can I deny such a flattering request?"

His eyes darted to her face, which she hoped was formed into just the kind of mask she had seen Lizzy assume in situations where anger or strong sarcasm might be felt but be inappropriate to express.

Here was the same charming Andrew with whom she had enjoyed conversations and flirtations in the past. But now, beneath the captivating surface, she saw a level of self-involvement not previously discerned. He was pleasing to be around. Had he been flattering her for his own amusement? Not as obviously as Christopher Drake had done on first meeting her, but she now sensed a similarity in their characters that had escaped her before.

"My first concern is for you, Miss Bennet, and how I may have set up expectations or hopes by my careless and self-centered comments to you when last we met."

"What can you mean, Mr. Stapleton?"

He gave her a speaking look. "I mean that everyone hereabouts, and perhaps you too, expected me to offer for you. I may not have made my meaning clear," he said, with a frown.

"As I remember our last conversation, you sought advice on how to combine your interest in science with your inheritance of Swan's Nest. Or does my memory fail me?"

He blinked a few times and looked away. Then, with his eyes on the ground he said, "No, Miss Bennet, your memory serves you perfectly. It is true. I was floundering. And in you I felt such stability and objectivity that, well, I could not help confiding in you. It was wrong of me to do so, to assume so much, and I apologize. I thought only of myself. I do not deserve to be called a gentleman!" He swallowed his wine and stared at the ground.

After a minute or two of silence, Kitty ventured, "And your second concern, Mr. Stapleton. Might you enlighten me? I know not how much time we shall have."

He glanced around. "Very well. My second concern is Julia. I am sure you are apprised of the whole of her history with

Douglas. My father reports he remains paralyzed and is angry and bitter. I have seen his anger. Julia remains true to him, and says he needs her love to heal."

"And do you agree?"

"Hogwash!" He punched his fist into his thigh. "He needs her money, not her love. He's a cawker and a lobcock. He has asked her to marry him, and is quite preoccupied with the amount of her dowry. I cannot like the situation at all, Miss Bennet. I believe he still gambles and remains involved with unsavory sorts, though I know not how. Blast! He does not woo her for love. But she cannot see it."

He turned to Kitty, his eyes full of what appeared to be genuine concern.

"What do you know of it all, Miss Bennet? What can I do that might help my sister? I have told Anna some of this, and she is most willing for Julia to come live with us until I am sent to the north of Scotland on an expedition. Would a few months away be time enough for Julia to see her predicament more clearly, do you think?"

Kitty sighed. "Mr. Stapleton, this is a great deal for me to take in at once. First, your concern for your sister causes my heart to be less inclined to give you a set-down for your own missteps with me. Second, I share your concern for Julia, as others do. However, since we returned from our journey south, Julia and I have not spent much time together, by her choice. Today is the first time I have seen her smile in weeks. Certainly I cannot speak for her. Perhaps she does not wish to detach herself. Does your father have an opinion?"

"I have not spoken to him of my desire to take Julia north. But he clearly has no intention of approving a marriage with the present state of things."

"If she will not go north, then nothing more can be done at present, Mr. Stapleton."

"But if they were to elope? I fear it greatly."

Kitty thought a moment. "Would the squire bestow a dowry in that case? The excitement of Matilda's wedding will be soon concluded. Perhaps in a few days' time something will change. How long will you and your wife be here?"

"We plan to say our farewells to Matilda and William when they leave, and our own farewells the day following if the weather agrees."

"Then let us hope I have more time to speak with Julia before you depart."

Julia and Anna approached. Julia carried her sketchbook.

When they joined the pair on the bench, Kitty said, "Andrew, have you seen your sister's great artistry?"

"I have not. I am sure Anna will also enjoy it."

Julia handed the sketchbook to her brother and said, "Please select one sketch as my wedding gift to you both. You will have a reminder of me whilst you are far away."

"Miss Stapleton, that is most generous of you," Anna said. "I am touched by such a personal gift."

The four spent some time paging through the landscape sketches until a scene was chosen. Julia did not show the sketches she had made of Douglas.

Kitty then looked around the group with a gleam in her eye.

"Mr. Stapleton, you have given *me* a gift as well, for which I owe you much gratitude, perhaps even my life." Kitty laughed as three sets of puzzled eyes turned on her.

"What you taught me about the moss—do you recall? That it grows mostly on the north side of trees. Surely Providence brought that memory to me in my time of need and prevented me wandering deeper into the famous Windsor Forest. Knowing about moss saved me. I was able to meet my rescuers with no real harm done." She proceeded to tell them more of the tale.

"Miss Bennet, you are an amazing young woman!" Andrew exclaimed.

"How brave you are," Anna said. "I am sure I should have sat down and wept in despair."

Julia's eyes were bright. She said, "I did not hear that part of the story before, Kitty. Pray, do tell my brother about Princess Charlotte now."

The rest of the celebration passed in pleasant conversation. Andrew now assumed a different position in Kitty's life. Her anger dissipated and she felt remarkably at peace.

CHAPTER THIRTY-SIX

*D*uring the hottest weather Kitty had taken to hacking out before breakfast, often with Fitzwilliam. But the day after Matilda's wedding he was unavailable so Johnny rode with her instead. The morning was windless under an overcast sky. The smallest noise carried through the dull air. Kitty and Johnny made their way along the edge of a bluff and were beginning their descent to the forest floor by way of a winding path when Cara's ears pricked up. Kitty checked the mare.

It was a carriage. Travelers were few on this road—it was only known by local people for the most part. Johnny reined in, and from their position in the trees they watched below.

Curiously, the carriage slowed, pulled to the side of the road, and stopped. Then, even more peculiar, a man leading a horse emerged from the woods below.

Kitty stifled a gasp. It was George Cressley. He looked up at the hill they were poised upon. Their movement must have been heard. Just then a doe and fawn leapt from the bushes below and ran across the road and up the next hill. She looked at Johnny.

His eyes twinkled with amusement at the lucky coincidence.

She pointed at the carriage, wondering whose it was.

Her jaw dropt when he mouthed back, 'Wyndham.'

They strained to catch snippets of conversation and watched as George handed an envelope and small package to the person in the carriage. Then George saluted and mounted his horse. As he rode off to the south, the recipient thrust his head out the window—Douglas Wyndham. After a round of maniacal laughter he hollered, "Drive on!" and the coach sped away.

Kitty turned this over in her mind.

"Johnny, could you see ... was there anyone else in the carriage?"

"Sorry, Miss, I could not see."

"Whatever would Mr. Douglas be doing out here? And meeting with Mr. George?"

"'Twas the Wyndham carriage, Miss, that I am sure. And their own horses in harness."

"This is all too strange. I must consult with Mr. Darcy. Let us return at once." She urged Cara down the path.

"Aye, but if I may," Johnny said, with some hesitation, "Mr. Darcy will not return from the north village until later today. Told us so himself early this morning. We are to have the coach ready for a dinner visit to Greystone at seven o'clock."

"Oh, yes, I had quite forgotten. We are for the Wyndham's this evening. Mr. Christopher and his bride have returned from their wedding tour so this will be our bridal call. Well, perhaps I can inform Fitzwilliam before we leave. He may know a logical explanation for what we have seen, but it is most unusual."

The air grew closer as they rode the lower path back.

"These clouds are full of rain," Kitty observed. "The air is so stifling I can hardly breathe. We shall walk the horses back."

Johnny scanned the heavy clouds above them.

"A storm would be a relief indeed."

≈

Upon her return, Kitty tried to put the troubling scene aside and concentrate on her daily tasks. Georgiana's master had come early for her lesson and the tones of the pianoforte drifted from the music room. Georgiana always practiced for some time after he left. Kitty joined Lizzy in the drawing room where they both worked at their stitching. Kitty was knitting trim to a cap for the baby. Lizzy was embroidering the Darcy monogram onto some soft baby blankets. They worked mostly in silence. Kitty longed to tell Lizzy what she had seen but did not wish to upset her sister in any way. The little talk they had centered on the two babies expected in the neighborhood. Kitty dared not speak of the possibility of a third.

Georgiana joined them for tea. All were looking forward to hearing about Christopher's and Lucy's journey to the Lakes. Georgiana was pleased she would see Benjamin again at dinner, though he called at Pemberley nearly every day. Both had abandoned efforts to conceal their mutual interest.

"Which gown shall you wear tonight, Kitty?" Georgiana asked, taking another bite of lemon pound cake.

"The day is warm and like to continue so unless a storm breaks," Kitty remarked. "Would silk be required, or could I wear my sprigged muslin with the blue trim? I believe the muslin will be more comfortable in this heat."

Lizzy spoke. "That should do very well, Kitty. Georgiana?"

"I, too, will wear a sprigged muslin. The peach, I think. And what of you, Lizzy?"

With a low, throaty laugh, Lizzy said, "I have only one dress suitable for calling that is full enough to fit around me at present. Luckily, the seamstresses will soon finish another dress, but for tonight it shall be the same green gown."

"Why do you watch the door, Lizzy?" Kitty asked, noting her sister's distraction.

"Oh, I was hoping Fitzwilliam would be back sooner rather than later. He did advise me that if he had not returned by seven, we should take the carriage without him. He and Mr. Sawyer had several stops to make today in the north part of the estate."

Kitty bit her lip. The Cressley party would leave the day after tomorrow. She hoped Darcy would have time to speak with her before dinner, and wondered what actions he might take. And if there would be time to take any.

The ladies retired to prepare for the dinner. When Kitty reached her room she found a letter on her table. She recognized Papa's handwriting and sat down, not knowing what to expect. Carefully she opened it.

. . .

Longbourn, Hertfordshire
  My dear Kitty,
  A reply to both your letters is long overdue. I have been giving much thought as to how to express myself. I have experienced somewhat of a change of heart and mind concerning some issues at Longbourn, past and present, and concerning you. I am heartily sorry for what I now see as my neglect in caring for you and your sisters—by my lack of planning and my lack of involvement. My own discouragement during that time does not excuse me from my responsibilities and I cannot forgive myself.
  I have thanked Lizzy for stepping in on your behalf. But she tells me that it was you who requested the visit to Pemberley; you who saw that things were amiss at Longbourn as far as providing for your future. I congratulate you on your clear-sightedness and your determination.
  My failure is a bitter pill to swallow. On the other hand, I can give myself some accolades for raising two wise and attentive daughters in Jane and Lizzy, who have risen on their own merits, and by whose attention I pray you will also rise. I am thankful it seems not too late for you.
  Your strength of spirit, as described by Lizzy and from what I have read in your letters, has surprised me. Your interests are those I would not have suspected, such as horses and science and drawing. Perhaps all the madness surrounding Lydia buried your ability to acknowledge and practice your desired pursuits. Your newfound companions—even those in high places—seem to join you in these and your letters reflect a respectable and remarkable young lady.
  You are correct, I am proud of you. Prodigiously proud. I look forward to hearing more about your activities and give you leave to remain at Pemberley as long as Lizzy and Darcy might agree. I hope you and I may spend a good deal of time together when I visit in the spring, or sooner, and I should dearly like to see you ride Cara.
  Until then,
  Your loving father

Kitty fell back onto the chair and stared out the window. Tears welled in her eyes. Her father had never spoken to her as an intelligent being, nor with any affection. She had hoped, from this visit, to gain Lizzy and Fitzwilliam's respect. She had not dared to hope for her father's. She was lost in thought until roused by Poppy to prepare for dinner at the Wyndham's.

Darcy had not returned as the ladies prepared to enter the coach. The clouds hung low. Nothing was moving in the outdoors and the thick air was heavy with silence; not even the chatter of birds broke the stillness.

"Bring a wrap and an umbrella," Lizzy cautioned.

"How can one be sociable in weather such as this?" Georgiana remarked. "The air is so thick I can barely breathe."

"At least it has not rained yet," Lizzy remarked. "Hopefully Fitzwilliam will be spared that inconvenience." Lizzy nodded to the footman, who then closed the door. A light crack of the whip set the horses off at a slow trot.

In spite of the stifling weather, a merry group greeted them at Greystone. To Kitty's surprise, Matilda and William arrived at the same time as the Darcy coach. And with them was Mr. George Cressley. Georgiana and Matilda went to each other immediately for an affectionate embrace, and then Benjamin strode up to offer his arm to his beloved. Mr. Wyndham and Owen had also appeared, both graciously aiding Lizzy in mounting the steps. Owen glanced back at Kitty with pleasure, but his brow lifted as George Cressley offered her his arm. All joined Mrs. Wyndham and the newlyweds in the drawing room.

Kitty noted the absence of Julia but was not surprised. Neither was Douglas in attendance.

"My parents send their regrets," Christopher said, addressing Mrs. Wyndham. "My father is not well today and my mother preferred to stay by his side."

Both Wyndhams nodded in understanding.

"And my parents have remained home with Mr. Alfred Cressley and my brother Andrew and his new bride," Matilda said. "As you know, they stay only a short time before departing for Scotland."

Kitty found she could think of Andrew and his wife with

equanimity. She stole a look at Owen, standing next to his father, and felt a rush of warmth.

William spoke next. "Thank you for inviting us, Mr. and Mrs. Wyndham. This is our first social outing as a married couple." He cast a devoted look at Matilda.

"It is a pleasure to host such a youthful group tonight," Mr. Wyndham replied. "You are all very welcome. But Mrs. Darcy, where is ..."

"Mr. Darcy will be along shortly. He rode to the north village today and was not back in time to ride in the carriage with us. I am sure he will join us very soon."

There was much news to be shared about the two weddings, and about one wedding tour just taken and another about to commence. Before even half of the news had been imparted, the group was called to dinner.

Just as they were assembling to go into the dining room, Darcy joined them. His eyes immediately sought Lizzy's; he smiled at her apparent wellbeing.

"I beg your pardon, everyone," he made a slight bow to the company, "for my lateness."

"You are most welcome, Mr. Darcy. Now our party is complete," Mrs. Wyndham said, smiling elegantly. "Let us go in."

They found their seats at the finely appointed table. Mrs. Wyndham obviously remained attentive to all things pertaining to dress and décor despite her present fragile condition. An enjoyable meal and pleasant conversation dominated the next hour and the company was most congenial. William proved an entertaining conversationalist and the party learnt much about him.

As the final course was cleared and dessert items set out, a servant entered with a note for Mr. Wyndham. He studied it, frowned, and then caught Darcy's eye.

"Pardon me; please continue with dessert. I have just received some urgent news. Darcy, will you join me for some fresh air?"

George, who was seated across from Kitty, colored and looked intently at his plate.

"Whatever can be so alarming, my dear?" Mrs. Wyndham asked, arching a brow. "Surely it can wait until later."

"No, it cannot. It concerns Douglas."

Kitty inhaled sharply and stared hard at Mr. Wyndham.

"A turn for the worse, sir?" asked Benjamin.

"No, nothing like that. Please do carry on. Darcy?" Mr. Wyndham rose and Darcy followed.

Kitty was flustered but knew what she must do. She leaned closer to Owen and said, "I too need some air. Would you accompany me?"

Owen's eyes grew large for a moment, but he recovered and obliged in a most gentlemanly manner.

"Pray, excuse us," Owen said with a bow.

They were only steps behind Darcy and Wyndham and could soon hear their conversation.

"Missing? But how?" Darcy paced in a tight circle.

"Douglas has taken to commanding the carriage for outings nearly every day. He says the fresh air benefits him."

Darcy looked at Wyndham. "Well, yes, that would make some sense."

"According to the stable master, he left unusually early this morning. His valet often accompanies him, and did so today. However, they have not returned. And when the maid entered his room just now to see if he wished dinner be brought up, he was not there. Most of his clothing was gone—along with all his medication and his wheelchair. "

At the sound of crunching gravel, Mr. Darcy whirled about.

"Kitty! What do you do here? This is no concern for ladies. Please, return to the house at once."

She set her chin. "I cannot."

Mr. Darcy's eyebrows flew up and his face reddened.

Kitty felt Owen grasp her elbow firmly.

"I have information that may be pertinent to this situation. Will you hear me?"

Mr. Darcy's face changed from rage to puzzlement.

"Miss Bennet, please tell us whatever you may know," Mr. Wyndham said, stepping towards them.

She looked at Fitzwilliam, who nodded. In spite of Owen's curious glance, she took a deep breath and began.

"This morning, very early, I was out riding with Johnny. I saw Mr. Douglas in a Wyndham carriage. Johnny recognized it, and your horses. It was near the place we once came upon you, Mr. Owen, when your wagon had broken down."

Owen nodded, then looked at his father.

"The old north road to Buxton, near where it crosses the path to the Manning estate."

Mr. Wyndham nodded. "Go on."

"We were up on the hill, unseen. To our surprise, the carriage pulled over and stopped. We were ready to ride down and see if they needed assistance but suddenly, out of the woods below us, Mr. George Cressley emerged, leading a horse."

"What?"

"In the woods?"

"Yes. I thought it very odd. And more so because, to my knowledge, the two gentlemen are not acquainted."

Mr. Darcy shook his head and frowned.

Mr. Wyndham sighed, his face sagging.

"Fitzwilliam, do you remember Princess Charlotte cautioning us about Mr. George Cressley?"

"I do now."

The others murmured at the mention of the princess.

Three pairs of eyes now focused on Kitty. "And this is not the first clandestine meeting I have witnessed involving Mr. George." She described the incident on the path at Oakhurst.

Mr. Darcy scowled. "Honorable connections would not meet in secret." His jaw clenched.

Mr. Wyndham then asked, "Miss Bennet, is there aught else you can tell us about this morning?"

Kitty searched her mind. "Just that Mr. George handed Mr. Douglas an envelope and a small package. Oh, and as Mr. George rode off, Mr. Douglas was laughing very loudly. A laugh of madness, I thought." She then turned to Fitzwilliam. "I had wished to tell you immediately, but you—"

"Yes, I have been gone. You have done right, Kitty."

Then he turned to Mr. Wyndham. "What do you make of it?"

Mr. Wyndham was shaking his head when a scuffling noise approached. Christopher and a stable lad were forcefully escorting Mr. George Cressley. Christopher shoved him unceremoniously towards Wyndham and Darcy. The lad departed.

"Ha! Shocked are you? I found this scoundrel attempting to saddle one of the horses. It seems he fancied a late night ride. In the dark, eh Cressley?" Christopher looked at the four surprised faces and then continued. "Just after you left the table, Cressley here was overcome with a coughing fit and made his excuses. Knowing him as I do ... or did ... I suspected he was up to no good and followed him. I have, unfortunately, had dealings with him in the past, although it was he and Douglas who were thick."

Mr. Darcy and Mr. Wyndham stepped forward as one.

"Explain yourself at once," ordered Mr. Wyndham.

George looked around the circle with his nose in the air.

"Perhaps he will be more eager to speak to the magistrate?" Mr. Darcy said, piercing George with sharp eyes.

All turned in surprise when Kitty spoke.

"You are exposed, Mr. George. Even Princess Charlotte is aware of your participation in the scheme. Things will likely go easier if you cooperate."

George Cressley looked at her, his mouth hanging open. Christopher and Mr. Wyndham also looked stunned.

"Come, cousin, speak. Silence cannot protect you now," Mr. Darcy urged.

George Cressley's demeanor suddenly altered. His face crumpled and he hung his head.

"My father ... is there some way he can be spared? And my wife ... with child ... I cannot endanger her." His pleading eyes searched Mr. Darcy's.

Mr. Wyndham said, "Perhaps Miss Bennet should be excused before—"

"No. I will not be excused. I mean no disrespect, Mr. Wyndham, but I have been instrumental in discovering evidence in this case and have even been directly harmed myself. My wrist *has* healed," she said, with an accusing look at Christopher, "but my dear friend continues to suffer heartbreak. I shall not be shielded." She crossed her arms in front of her.

All eyes flew to Mr. Darcy. He did not fail her.

"She may stay. I have been aware of her involvement for some time. Now, cousin, speak."

George then related his role in passing messages and money to Christopher and Douglas, usually to Douglas. Christopher corroborated this part of the tale and explained his own role as well. The three would meet at various watering holes for information dispersed by George—who also paid them—and then Christopher and Douglas would deliver the orders or money to others as they were directed.

"Who gave you these orders?" Darcy demanded.

Christopher responded first.

"I met only with Cressley. I believe that is also the case with Douglas, but I cannot be sure."

"It is so," George confirmed. "However, to gather *my* orders, each time I would meet with a different messenger in a different place. I do not know where the directions originated. I have some suspicions. I would see some faces repeatedly at the inns and at the racetrack, but I had no personal involvement with any one man in particular. Often it was simply an envelope left with an innkeeper."

The small circle pondered this information.

Mr. Darcy's face was drawn.

"This is a deplorable thing in which you are involved. Horses have been harmed. One has died, as has one jockey. George, whatever possessed you to keep company of this sort?"

At this point, George looked at Christopher and sighed.

"It all started during my last year at school. That is where I met Mr. Christopher and Mr. Douglas. We were a group of swaggering fools. Thought we could make some money by gambling on the races. I seemed to have a knack for picking winners, and I put all my winnings back into the races, betting more and more. But my luck turned. I was losing. My debts grew and I became desperate. We met a man who offered us money to deliver messages and, once we were trusted, we carried money as well. That is how it started. I cannot bear to have my father know how foolish I was. I continued to bet. But rather than diminishing, my debts have grown to an enormous figure. I don't know what to do. My father will be so disappointed. He might disinherit me. And my dear wife ..." He was so downcast he could not meet their eyes.

Mr. Darcy's face was stony.

Owen looked at Christopher. "And you, Drake, do you have gambling debts? Has my sister now become a partner to this?"

Mr. Wyndham looked aghast.

"I was a fool to become involved in any of this," Christopher admitted. "But, in a twist of fate, I was not lucky at betting. I rarely won, so I soon lost interest. I was bored here at home and thought the company around the racetrack all the crack—for a time. But I soon grew bored of them too. When I took Lucy to the races—sorry, Owen, don't come the ugly—I saw I was impressing no one. That was when I realized that was not the kind of life I wished to live. I was a pudding-head, as a certain royal person put it." He gave the group a wry grin.

"I decided I wanted out. I realized it was *I* who was boring. It was time to do something different. Through Lucy, I realized how fortunate I was by such a lucky birth, being a first son. Lucy needed me. And she was so devoted. The woman has the patience of a saint. Truly, I have now—at last—set myself a goal to deserve her, and Cedars. I have found luck at love far superior to luck at gambling."

Footsteps were again heard on the gravel. To their surprise Mr. Wyndham's butler approached and signaled to him.

After a few private words, Mr. Wyndham shouted, "What? How can he do this?" His back heaved. The butler bowed and made for the house. The group waited expectantly.

When Mr. Wyndham turned to them, his face was a contortion of fury and woe.

"It seems," he said in a choking voice, "that Douglas has made off with the strongbox from our safe."

"No!" Mr. Darcy exclaimed.

Owen's jaw fell. "Oh, Father!"

The group was shocked into silence.

Kitty turned. "Mr. George, have you any knowledge of Mr. Douglas' plans or destination? Did he say anything that might lead us to him? He has not been in his right mind for some time and needs help."

"He was in an odd state today," George said thoughtfully. "Not quite the thing. Looked dreadfully pulled. But kept laughing. A maniacal laugh. Frightful. I was glad to be out of his company. His valet was with him. The carriage did not follow me back south and east. But I do not know the roads hereabouts. I am sorry I cannot be of more help."

Mr. Darcy responded first.

"Thank you, George. That is of some assistance. Wyndham, can we send some searchers out at first light? Harvest has begun, but I can spare a few men. Certainly in a carriage he cannot have got far? Easier to trace than a man on a horse."

Mr. Wyndham's face drooped.

Owen looked at Kitty, and then spoke.

"Father. Let us return to the house. You and I shall withdraw to your den and work out something—a plan, a strategy. The guests are ready to depart now anyway."

Kitty nodded at him.

"If you wish, I shall stay too," Mr. Darcy offered.

Mr. Wyndham gave a weak smile.

"Thank you, Darcy. You are ever a true friend."

The Darcy coach returned as it had arrived, carrying the ladies but not Mr. Darcy.

CHAPTER THIRTY-SEVEN

*K*itty sat at her writing desk, quill poised, uncertain how to begin. After some moments of thought, she dipped her quill and wrote:

My dear MME,

I pray this letter finds you and our esteemed friend enjoying good health and happiness.

The couple of our mutual acquaintance has returned from their wedding tour of the Lakes. I believe that gentleman has gained command of his character and that the couple will do well together. He has actually been of assistance in the other issue of our mutual concern.

I am pleased to say that my friend has also been married to the brother of the gentleman you cautioned us about. The man under suspicion did travel here to attend his brother's nuptials and was, by a stroke of luck, observed by me—on my morning ride—involved in a clandestine meeting with our injured gentleman. When discovery seemed imminent, the first attempted to leave our area in secrecy, but was apprehended by our swaggering groom, who also made a clean breast of his own involvement and declared his regret of such.

My brother then forced from the first man a full confession. He does not appear to know the names of those directing the operation but did admit to recognizing a few faces that always seemed nearby when he received his orders. He has agreed to meet with one of your representatives, in confidence, to divulge what he knows. His gambling debts are heavy and he wishes to keep these from the knowledge of his esteemed father—my brother's cousin—with whom you are also acquainted.

The informant's wife is with child and her confinement approaches. He is loath to upset her. Should he fail to prove cooperative, please contact my brother, who will have strong leverage. My brother will send you the contact information for this informant by separate letter.

Unfortunately, the injured gentleman has disappeared. Searchers are being sent out as I write this letter. He has even stolen a substantial sum of money from his own father. His state of mind is not rational, nor has it been for some time, even before the injury. He is a deeply troubled soul. His family—you remember his brother who rescued me in the forest— grieves for him. If any of your contacts should become aware of the injured man's location, or have any news of him, please notify me at once.

Yours in friendship and alliance,

CB

She sanded and sealed the letter and prepared it for the post. She would remind Darcy of the information he must supply.

The day proved quiet as a gentle rain fell until nearly dark. Autumn weather had arrived. A crimson sunset gave Kitty hope that tomorrow she could walk outdoors with Lizzy, who grew fretful when confined to the house. She was large with child, and Kitty wondered if the predicted birth time might be off.

≈

Two weeks had passed since the disappearance of Douglas Wyndham. The carriage was discovered abandoned some twenty miles north. Kitty thought it curious no witnesses had seen a man in a wheelchair. The strongbox money had done its job.

Kitty and Georgiana called on Lucy every few days. The young bride seemed to bloom in her new role as wife. She and her husband were settled at Cedars, and Christopher had taken on the task of making improvements to the dower house. He had also come to Pemberley's library on two occasions in search of books on architectural design and landscape architecture, and had great interest in planning renovations for some of the buildings at the Cedars estate.

One morning whilst visiting at Pemberley, Lady Drake said, "My heart lifts at seeing my son step into his duties and inheritance with pride. He has an excellent eye for beauty,"—and here she nodded at Lucy, who blushed,—"but also a head for structure. Marriage has given him new purpose."

Kitty passed a tray of newly baked shortbread and Georgiana poured tea as Lady Drake continued.

"Benjamin, as you no doubt know,"—here she looked directly at Georgiana—"has made several trips to Matlock as he prepares to join his elder cousin's law practice. He, too, seems focused on a very specific future." She smiled at Georgiana over the rim of her teacup.

Georgiana colored. "I do hope he will be able to attend our Harvest Ball," she said with some concern. "It is a tradition my brother reinstated after he married. I cannot imagine a ball without Benjamin present."

Lady Drake lifted a brow. "A ball? Mrs. Darcy, that is a great deal to take on in your state."

Lizzy smiled. "Actually, Lady Drake, it is training for my sister. Kitty is in charge of the event as part of her education on managing a household. She of course has myself and Georgiana to consult, and my wonderful housekeeper."

"It has been challenging," said Kitty. "I have done nothing of the sort before."

"You will need those skills in the future, Miss Bennet. It is wise to learn from those who are experienced, whilst you can."

Unbidden, a picture of Owen and herself as master and mistress of a home caught Kitty off-guard and she felt color flame into her cheeks.

Lady Drake gave her a quizzical smile.

Had she seen the same vision?

Kitty fingered the stone she kept in her pocket.

≈

The spell of damp weather gave way to a crisp, lovely autumn. Kitty rode nearly every day. Those rides and the preparations for the ball were fair distractions from thoughts of Julia.

Lady Stapleton had come to call the day after Matilda and William departed for Reading. It was then disclosed that Julia had accompanied them. The newlyweds' home was large and they were delighted for Julia to make an extended visit.

Kitty was speechless.

"Swan's Nest is not the same, Mrs. Darcy," Lady Stapleton mused, staring past them and out the window. "Only the squire and the young ones for company. First Andrew—gone for we know not how long. And now both my elder daughters—one in joy, one in pain. Aye, but I must accept the will o' Providence. Perhaps Julia will find peace in Reading. Goodness knows she's had naught but pain these many months here, the poor lass."

Lady Stapleton had handed Kitty a letter that Julia wrote the day of the hurried departure.

Kitty could barely utter "pardon me," before she fled to her rooms. Once there she tore the letter open and read:

Swan's Nest

> *My dearest friend,*
>
> *Please forgive me for saying farewell in this selfish way. The pain of saying goodbye to you in person, added to all the other pain in my heart, would be too much to bear at present. I hope you can understand. It is impossible for me to find comfort in the familiar neighborhood. Memories accost me at every turn and I daily feel what I have lost, as well as dismay at the present unknown situation of one I love. My apprehension about where and when he might be found—if he is ever found—is overwhelming. I must remove myself. The entirely new place and situation in Reading will hopefully release me, at least for a time. I do not run from my problems, Kitty, but seek only a time and place for restoration.*
>
> *I beg you to write to me, especially about the happy events upcoming —the Harvest Ball, any romantic outcomes from that event, and of course the new Darcy and Wyndham babies.*
>
> *With fond regards,*
>
> *Julia*

. . .

Her eyes afire, Kitty tossed the letter aside and fled the room.

≈

Owen came to call one morning whilst Lizzy was resting and Georgiana was with her music master.

He and Kitty met in the drawing room. Making conversation, he asked, "How is Miss Stapleton? What do you hear from Reading?"

"Nothing. Nothing at all."

Owen turned to her in surprise.

"I do not expect to hear from her. I made no reply to her bird-witted note. I had nothing to say—at least nothing civil. How could she leave like that? Without saying goodbye? I thought she was my friend."

Owen rose and paced back and forth before the fireplace. His scowl suggested he shared her anger at Julia. But Kitty could not have been more mistaken.

"And what kind of friend have you been to *her*, refusing to respond? Refusing to lend support in a most difficult time? Miss Bennet, I would not have thought it possible."

Her eyes kindled and she raised her chin.

"What do you know of it anyway, Mr. Owen? If she is so special to you, perhaps *you* should write to her. It is, after all, your brother who caused her to leave."

She regretted her harsh words the moment she saw the pain in Owen's eyes. Looking at the floor in confusion, she muttered, "There was, after all, nothing I could do to ease her pain."

Owen walked to the window. After staring out for a time he returned and sat next to her. In a carefully measured voice he spoke.

"Miss Bennet, I ask that you consider what Miss Stapleton has done, and hold it next to what you have done."

"Me?" she asked, stupefied.

"Yes, you," he said quietly.

All Kitty could do was stare at him.

"Think what brought you here to Derbyshire to visit your sister. Was it not angst? Frustration? Did not painful memories—although of a different kind—surround you everywhere you looked? Did you not seek a setting of neutral ground? A place where you could be free of those memories for a time? A place to heal and start afresh?"

Kitty's eyes burned with insistent tears that she could not blink away.

"That is all Miss Stapleton seeks. A fresh start—with a lively sister to support her, just as you have here. A place where her memories don't stare her in the face at every turn. A place that will allow her to heal from all that has distressed her, and from troubles that occurred even before you came into our midst. How can you deny your friend the same solace you sought for yourself, and even now continue to enjoy?"

"I do not know what she wrote you, Miss Bennet, but I beg you to reconsider. Do not add to Miss Stapleton's pain. I believe —truly I do—" he said, looking her square in the face, "that you have a kind heart. Let it soften; offer comfort to your friend."

With a long last look, he strode from the room, leaving Kitty to sort a jumble of memories, feelings, and tears.

She returned to her room and found the letter. After a deep breath, she read it again, then pressed the letter to her heart as tears of sympathy for her friend spilled from her eyes—along with tears of regret for her own hardness of heart. She was struck by their similarity of situation. She, too, had been unable to find comfort in Hertfordshire where everyone associated her with Lydia. Yes, she did understand, most poignantly. A new place and situation was just what she had found at Pemberley.

Would she or Julia ever return to their childhood homes? What was it Matilda had said? *As ladies, we have always expected our entire lives to change one day.* Kitty had not given that serious thought then, but it rang true now. In leaving home, she and Julia had each made a powerful choice in pursuit of happiness. And each had a sister nearby for comfort. They were both very fortunate indeed.

She pulled out her writing desk.

CHAPTER THIRTY-EIGHT

*K*itty was restless in spite of all her new duties and interests. Nothing on her breakfast plate could tempt her.

Lizzy's face held a bemused expression.

"How are the arrangements coming? Are we ready for another ball?"

"We are. Though I admit I had no idea how much work went into such an event. I had thought only of the dancing and the gowns and having enough suitable partners." She leaned back in her chair and sighed.

"Then what is it? Why are you so agitated?"

"I cannot say. This fine weather beckons me out of doors."

Lizzy smiled languidly. "I do understand. I miss my own long autumn rambles this year. They have become, instead, short autumn waddles." They both laughed heartily. "Much much less satisfying; but I am determined to continue waddling for as long as I can, and try to appease myself with the picture of a healthy baby in my arms soon."

"Oh, Lizzy, are you at all afraid? Mama used to tell such dreadful stories ..."

Lizzy pursed her lips. "Any sensible person would, of course, be a little afraid. Are you not a little afraid each time you take a jump on horseback?"

Kitty nodded.

"But I am also practical. Babies are born every day and I daresay the majority of situations turn out well. Our family has a good record. So I shall hold to that positive view."

They sat in silence for a time, each lost in her own thoughts. Lizzy finished her tea and set down her cup.

"Well, Kitty, if the plans are all in hand, there is nothing to keep you indoors. Georgiana is in the music room. And Mr. Benjamin will likely be along soon for his daily visit. I believe he returned late yesterday from Matlock. Be off. Enjoy yourself. And take care to tell Mr. Connor where you will ride, so you can be fetched immediately should there be an emergency—such as a shortage of cakes!"

Kitty laughed and patted Lizzy's shoulder.

"I certainly shall."

≈

Johnny saluted Kitty as she approached the stable yard.

"Good afternoon, Johnny," she said, waving her hand in reply. "It is a fine day."

Cara nickered at the sound of Kitty's voice and trotted to the fence for a caress and a piece of carrot.

"'Tis indeed, Miss Bennet," he said with a bright smile. "I expected you at every moment. The arena today, or will it be a hack out?"

"I am in the mood to see rocks and trees today, Johnny. Are you available to accompany me?"

"Lemme ask Mr. Connor, but I think yes." He led a horse into the barn and emerged in a few minutes with Cara's halter.

"I can be spared for a few hours, Miss Bennet. Shall that be long enough?"

"That will be perfect. If I am not tired, I shall finish with some schooling in the arena, although Cara much prefers the bridle path."

"That she does, Miss; that she does."

He placed the halter on Cara, then Kitty opened the gate, stroking the mare as she passed through it.

"Will it be the sidesaddle today, Miss?"

"No. I have become quite spoilt, and much prefer the standard saddle. We are not likely to meet anyone on the paths. I shall join you at the mounting block in a moment."

"As you wish." His eyes danced merrily.

Kitty thought him in an especially good mood. But who could not be on such a lovely day? She pulled on her breeches in the darkness of the stall, tied up her skirt, and walked to the mounting block. Johnny held her off stirrup as she mounted, swinging her right leg deftly over the horse and settling lightly in the saddle.

Mr. Connor walked up, his eyes twinkling as usual.

"Where d'ye go today, Miss Bennet?"

She looked at Johnny. "I am not particular. What do you suggest?"

"Deer Hollow?"

Kitty nodded her assent and gathered her reins.

"Deer Hollow it is." Johnny patted the shoulder of a young stable boy standing near Mr. Connor and the child skipped off.

Mr. Connor stepped up and stroked Cara on the neck.

"Splendid, Miss. Have a lovely ride. And Johnny, keep a good eye out, lad."

"I shall." Johnny swung onto his horse, tipped his hat, and they were off.

The path to Deer Hollow led to the south. Johnny was always an agreeable riding companion and escort. At times he would lead; at other times he would follow. He could keep up a cheerful conversation if desired; but he was also sensible of the value of quiet reflection and seemed to enjoy that as much as Kitty did.

They spoke together as they rode side by side.

"Johnny, what does a young man such as yourself think of the Harvest Ball?"

"All are grateful for the ball being held again. 'Twas long a tradition, and I'm told greatly missed during the sad times of old Mr. Darcy's illness and that what followed. When the harvest is good, there is much cause for celebration—and relief."

"I have learnt that from coordinating with Mr. Sawyer and his wife for the event."

Johnny looked at Kitty with a quizzical eye.

"My sister put me in charge of the event this year. It is part of my training to become mistress of a house, should that ever happen. And, in Lizzy's condition, it would be trying for her to manage so much. I have enjoyed doing it." She fell silent for a moment and cast a keen eye on Johnny.

"But I was asking particularly about the dance. Do you often have dances in the village? Will your sister attend? And you—do you have a particular young lady you hope to dance with?" She flashed him a mischievous grin.

He tried to sound calm, but his flushing face gave him away.

"We do not often have dances. Sometimes after a wedding. Aye, now that my sister is back in health, she is most excited for this dance. 'Tis good to see her so happy."

Kitty looked at him expectantly; he had not yet answered her completely.

Johnny cleared his throat and his ears went red.

"As for me, Miss ... ah, well there may be one young lady ..."

"Aha! Good for you, Johnny. If you please, tell me about her."

Their conversation carried on as they passed through the orchard. Once below it, the path narrowed and Kitty was content to follow Johnny, relaxing to the rocking rhythm of Cara's movement whilst gazing at the scenery. Many of the trees had turned color, heralding the change of season. What trees might she be observing next year at this time? Not likely Pemberley's. A visit that long would surely impose too much on her sister's generous nature. But the idea of being back at Longbourn was unsettling so she pushed it aside. She would not let such thoughts dampen her enjoyment of this day.

After cantering westward in the sandy soil along the riverbank, they slowed and took a path to the right that wound upward into a heavily wooded area punctuated by rocky promontories and a few enclosed clearings. Deer were abundant at certain places on the estate. Deer Hollow was one such place. It was picturesque, being a large clearing surrounded by great timber. A craggy cliff snugged into the hillside on the north. Boulders were embedded here and there, providing seats to enjoy the view to the west and of the river valley below. The flattened grass showed favorite resting spots of the deer. Horses could graze contentedly whilst riders might be refreshed with a bite and a drink.

Kitty and Johnny were settled comfortably on nearby boulders enjoying the first of the autumn apples when they heard a rider approach. Kitty sat up straight and looked at Johnny, who continued to munch on his apple. Riders were not common on these paths. This was Pemberley ground.

"Johnny," Kitty whispered with some concern, "listen."

He met her eyes and looked towards the sound.

Kitty peered down the east path as the rider drew nearer.

"Johnny!"

He stood and tossed his apple core aside, then strode over to place himself between Kitty and the approaching rider. Kitty was ready to take cover behind Cara when the rider swept into view. Owen Wyndham it was.

Kitty's mouth fell open.

Johnny touched his hat and nodded.

"G'day, Mr. Owen."

"A splendid day, Johnny," Owen said, saluting him, then swinging off Sultan.

"And Miss Bennet, delightful to see you. What a fine day for a ride."

Kitty moved away from Cara and towards the men.

"Whatever are you doing here, Mr. Owen? We have never met with anyone on these paths."

He raised a brow.

"Well, except for you that one time ..."

"Ah, Miss Bennet, this is *not* a chance meeting. I came to call at Pemberley—having business with Mr. Connor—and planned to say hello to the ladies of the house. When he informed me of your whereabouts, well ... I hope my company is not unwelcome?" His eyes searched hers. When she did not respond immediately, he looked down, fingering his reins.

Kitty was stunned at his friendliness. They had not spoken since their disagreement about Julia's letter. With a little struggle she found her voice.

"No, of course not, Mr. Owen ... I mean, you are welcome to

join us. It is so unexpected, that is all. And I am not riding in proper style to be in company with a gentleman."

Owen shook his head and chuckled.

"Oh, Miss Bennet. I should be more shocked to find you *not* riding astride. Be assured, I do not think you any less a lady ..." His steady grey eyes claimed a strong hold on hers.

Kitty's heart pounded. She fumbled with her gloves to steady her trembling hands.

Owen glanced at Johnny. "Miss Bennet and I shall walk to the point. Might you stay with the horses? There's a good lad."

Johnny nodded, sporting a broad smile.

"Come, walk with me."

Not knowing what else to do, Kitty took Owen's offered arm.

"You are perhaps recalling our last conversation?"

She looked at him briefly but did not speak.

"Are you angry with me?" he asked. "Thinking I spoke out of turn? I can understand that. I did not give you a chance to respond, and I beg your forgiveness for that. But I stand by my words that day."

Those words still rang in Kitty's head.

"Mr. Owen, what you said that day left me most uncomfortable. And for a few hours I *was* angry with you for interfering in what I felt was not your business. But your words were honorable—true feelings from a true friend. Such must always be heard and considered. And after a time, my heart did soften. I wrote to Julia that very night and now await a return letter from her, if she can forgive my resentful neglect. I have known from the start that you consider her like a sister. You have protected her even from your own brother. The awkward position that puts you in is not lost on me. You have shown yourself a man of honor in many difficult situations. I have felt your friendship, and even your protection, since I first arrived, and am grateful."

Was she speaking too frankly? Would he guess her feelings?

They had reached the promontory where a great precipice jutted out. Owen motioned for her to take a seat on an obliging boulder and then sat next to her.

She spoke again. "I think I understand how you feel, Mr. Owen. It is painful to see people one cares for hurting each other. I grew up in that kind of household. My parents were constantly bickering; my father directed barbs at my mother that she often did not comprehend. As a child, I could do nothing. But you, as a friend to both Julia and myself—I'm sure you saw us as squabbling little sisters—gallantly spoke out to protect us both. And for that I thank you. This must be what it is like to have an honorable elder brother."

Owen shifted his seat and looked off into the distance.

As his silence stretched on, Kitty grew uncomfortable. Could he not forgive her?

At last he turned and said, "Miss Bennet, I must confess that what I have felt for you is not in any way a brotherly affection. Since first we met I have struggled to limit my kindness and curtail my affection to that of a friend because I believed your heart was attached to another. That, and only that, prevented me from declaring myself. As that man is now married, might I inquire after the state of your heart? Or is it too soon?"

Kitty's mind froze at this admission, but her heart did not. It was as if her heart had always known this. Her same heart that beat stronger and faster in Owen's presence, and caused her to tremble and gasp for breath when his eyes connected with her deepest being.

She squeezed her hands together.

"Mr. Owen, in return I will confess to you that what you say surprises me, and yet it does not. It is as if my head has been in a fog about you all this time, but my heart knew better."

He looked into her eyes.

"I was attracted to Mr. Andrew, yes. And for a time thought I was fond of him. Though he had captured my attention, for some reason he failed to capture my heart. Perhaps because his own heart was already bound to his present wife, even if he was unaware of that himself. He had spoken to me vaguely of a future that inferred my presence. I know that our union was expected by many hereabouts. When that fell out I was shocked and, for a little time, angry; but not heartbroken."

Kitty rose and walked back and forth at the edge of the cliff, gazing off to the west. She felt Owen's eyes on her as she paced.

"When my heart was not touched, I thought maybe that was

how love felt for adults. More somber. Logical. When I lost my beau at Longbourn to an heiress, my heart was definitely broken. But that was two years ago; it was a young girl's heart and he merely a young girl's fancy. I have changed a great deal, especially since coming into Derbyshire. Yet all this time I held on to an unexplainable hope that Mr. Andrew would return for Matilda's wedding and, with great drama, declare himself. Perhaps that was my vanity, or another girlish fantasy." Kitty lifted a brow at Owen. "You can imagine my shock when I saw him with Anna, and then learnt they were already married."

Owen nodded.

"While shocked ... and with my pride hurt a great deal at first ... after the wedding he and I talked about his situation, and then about his worry for Julia ... and as we spoke I again felt no connection of the heart. Only that of a friend, especially in our mutual concern for his sister. He had wished to take her back to Scotland you know, to remove her from here for a while." She smiled. "So you both recommended that for her, and she did end up doing just that, which—"

"Made you angry and resentful."

Kitty's eyes lit up. "Yes. It seems I have a problem of listening too much to my head and not enough to my heart. I did not mean to deceive or hurt anyone." She stopped before him and looked at him deeply.

He reached for her hand and pulled her down again to the rock. She sat, but he did not let go her hand. Instead, he enclosed it in both of his. A deep and satisfying warmth moved up her arm to her heart and flooded her body with an inexplicable mixture of peace and excitement. She was drawn to the light in his steady grey eyes that penetrated the depths of her being. He knew her. He understood her. He cared for her, and perhaps even loved her. There was a tender closeness between them, a certain esteem and regard. In return, she trusted him, felt safe with him, desired his company and regard, and valued his wisdom. She found herself not just willing but eager to partner him in life. She could not imagine a future without him. She loved him.

He looked at her hand encased in his.

"I know my family situation is ... unstable at present. Every young lady wishes a steady ... a more predictable—"

"Mr. Owen. You forget. I am not like every young lady. It is not your situation that I must trust. Situations will be forever changing. It is *you* I must trust. It is your character and your heart that must win me. And of those I am convinced I have seen the truth. And felt the truth, when I listened to my heart. I know your sense of honor and commitment. You live it every day. I feel I know you very well."

He slipped off the rock and onto one knee. Tenderly he removed her glove and placed it on her lap. He kissed her hand and looked into her eyes.

A sudden light flooded her being.

"Miss Bennet. Catherine. Kitty. You do know me. And I believe I know you just as deeply and as dearly. I cannot envision my life without you. Will you accept my love? Will you do me the honor ... will you marry me?"

The light within her exploded into a thousand crystals that surrounded them both. She reached out to him with both arms.

"Yes," she whispered. "Oh, yes."

Their embrace united the warmth of their affection, and a passionate kiss ignited a new urgency within.

"Let us go, then, and tell Darcy and your sister. He already knows my intentions."

"But my father ..."

He took her hand and brought it up for a tender kiss.

"Your father has given Darcy the power to act in his stead. There are no impediments. My own father will be thrilled. He admires you, both for your horsemanship and for your fine character. Oh, let us ride back now. Let us gallop with all speed! I long to share our news, knowing it will make so many almost as happy as ourselves."

They walked around the boulder to return to the horses, still holding hands.

Johnny looked up with the biggest smile Kitty had seen on his face. He scrambled to his feet and bowed, touching his hat.

Owen laughed, and Johnny joined in.

"What? Was Johnny in on this? Did he know your purpose for riding here today?"

"Well, yes, I must confess, I did take him and Mr. Connor into my confidence. You and I had much to discuss, and I was not certain how things would turn out. This plan has been in place since ... well, since Miss Matilda's wedding." His eyes shone and a smile played about his mouth.

She gasped. "I had no idea of—"

"I wanted time alone with you, so we could talk. In a place we both felt at ease—outdoors, near our horses."

She looked at him shrewdly and then smiled.

"You *do* know me well, Mr. Owen." She blushed at the thought of him knowing her much better in the near future.

It was as if he read her mind. He squeezed her hand and whispered in her ear, "I look forward to a lifelong and intimate romance with you, Miss Bennet."

Kitty's heart soared. Yes, this was how it should feel. Far beyond any novel read or flight of her own imagination. Greater. And deeper. She turned to embrace him and kissed his cheek. Then she faced Cara and bent her knee for a leg up into the saddle. When Owen handed her the reins she felt like the sun itself lived within her, burning with a steady glow.

Cara nickered her approval.

Kitty's joy was complete.

The ride back was one of merry abandonment and high spirits. When they arrived at the barn, Connor caught Owen's eye. Owen nodded with pleasure.

Kitty slipped her right leg over Cara's neck. Owen lifted her out of the saddle and lowered her slowly and lovingly to the ground. He grasped her hand and led her to the stable master.

"Mr. Connor, may I present my betrothed, a most unusual and admirable young lady, Miss Kitty Bennet."

Kitty played along and gave a great curtsey, pulling out the sides of her jodhpurs as if they were a skirt. Laughter filled the air and Owen embraced her with affection.

Once Kitty had exchanged her jodhpurs for her skirt, she returned to Owen, who was talking with Mr. Connor and Johnny in the dusty sunlight at the entrance to the barn. She could not help but admire him, in every way.

Kitty addressed the three of them.

"Thank you both—and my dear Mr. Owen—for the most surprising and happiest ride of my life."

Filled with gladness and gratitude, she embraced each of them, amused to see the color rise in their faces. Johnny had hold of Cara and Kitty moved to the side of the mare's neck, burying her face in the silken mane. She threw her arms around Cara and inhaled deeply of the horse scent she loved.

"My dear Cara, what a happy day this is." A few joyful tears spilled onto the mane of the beloved mare.

Walking the path towards the house, Owen observed, "You realize we have left a place of great comfort to us both—the outdoors, the world of horses—and will be entering the world of rules and propriety as we gain the great house."

"True," Kitty replied. "And yet, for all its magnitude and austerity, I have found a wonderful and unexpected treasure at Pemberley: my true heart. And a partner to share it with."

CHAPTER THIRTY-NINE

"What on earth is all this racket?" Darcy's voice boomed as he stood in the doorway where the ladies were lunching. His attempt to produce a ferocious frown was betrayed by his laughing eyes.

Georgiana ran into his arms.

"Oh, brother, I am so happy. I cannot believe my good fortune." Suddenly she pulled back and looked at him.

"Benjamin says you have given your approval. Have you? Oh, please say you have. I know you had wished me to marry a first-born son ..." She bit her lip, awaiting his reply.

"Who am I to stand in the way of true love?" He looked fondly at Lizzy and then at his sister. "Of course I gave my permission. How could I not? The young man will not stay away if he is within one hundred miles of you."

Georgiana hugged her brother and stretched up to kiss him on the cheek.

"It seems my harvest this year also includes two fine young men," Darcy said jauntily, pulling out a chair next to Lizzy. He sat down and gave her a quick kiss on the cheek. "I am a fortunate man indeed."

Lizzy looked at both the girls and smiled.

"The halls of Pemberley will soon ring with wedding bells."

"Benjamin's parents will call later today," Georgiana remarked as she reached for a sandwich.

Kitty said, "Mr. Wyndham and Owen will also call today. Mrs. Wyndham travels as little as possible now, but she may attend our Harvest Ball tomorrow."

"I cannot blame her for not traveling," Lizzy said. "The idea of rollicking around in a coach is most unappealing at present. I am lucky I need only waddle to the ballroom."

Darcy reached for her hand.

"My dear, you are as beautiful as ever; you are like a fully blooming rose."

"Thank you, Fitzwilliam, but be forewarned: this lovely bloom may also boast some thorns at present."

≈

As it turned out, Lizzy did more than waddle to the ballroom. She also managed to attend the Tenant's Ball held in the village. The immediate Darcy family, along with Kitty, Owen Wyndham, and Benjamin Drake were on hand to dance the first few with the villagers. After that they handed out baskets of apples, dried fruits and meats, nuts, and warm socks to each of the tenant families, along with bags of coins. A bountiful feast was later served to all. Kitty had not witnessed such generosity in the Longbourn neighborhood and marked it in her mind.

The Darcy party returned to Pemberley with only moments to freshen up before greeting their own guests at the Harvest Ball— the same families that had first welcomed Kitty to the neighborhood—and she could not help but reflect on the many changes in her life since then. She and Georgiana had now welcomed Lucy to their inner circle, but the absence of Julia and Matilda was felt strongly. The three young ladies did not want for partners all evening, but Kitty noted Lucy did not dance the livelier sets.

Owen appeared at Kitty's side as she spoke to Lady Drake.

"I hope Miss Bennet has shared our happy news?"

Lady Drake nodded.

"And you are not surprised."

Lady Drake laughed. "Mr. Wyndham, it is a match celebrated by the very stars. You have long known my opinion on this."

"Indeed I have, Lady Drake. And now, with your approval, I will sweep my future bride back to the dance floor."

Lady Drake nodded with pleasure. "May the spirits smile long on your love."

Earlier that evening the young couple had shared their news with Squire and Lady Stapleton.

"The whole neighborhood is alive with wedding bells," the squire had observed, his unlit pipe bobbing in the corner of his mouth. "Miss Lucy Jamison—now Mrs. Drake—started it, and joyful it is for all."

"And likely to give us several wee ones," commented Lady Stapleton, her eyes dancing in anticipation of little ones to tend. She had been waiting on Lizzy regularly, as had the midwife and the physician Darcy had engaged; both would take up residence when the birthing time drew nearer. They all looked at Lizzy and Darcy.

"Mark my words," said Lady Stapleton in a conspiratorial tone, "the Darcy child will be here weeks before that doctor predicts. Keep an eye on your sister, Miss Bennet. Five more weeks—tosh! What do men know of these things anyway?"

The ball was delightful but left everyone exhausted, none more so than Lizzy, who had managed to slip away to her apartments just after midnight. The next few days were quiet with no callers excepting the grooms-to-be.

A royal letter arrived for Kitty and she sequestered herself in the library to read it.

My dear CB,

Many apologies for the delay of this response to your helpful letter. Our affectionate friend has been 'secluded' in Brighton. I was not allowed to visit her until the day before I write this. Your information has been acted upon.

We are pleased that a once-dubious marriage has had such a good effect on the couple, and happy to hear of your other friend's nuptials as well. The questionable brother has been contacted and appears, so far, cooperative. We have hopes that those truly responsible for the scandal and injuries may soon be brought to justice.

Unfortunately, there is no news hereabouts of the injured gentleman. Please give our sympathies to your friend and his father. We will apprise you at once should we have any news.

We look forward to learning more of your happy adventures. How long do you stay in your present location? Our friend wishes you many lovely autumn rides. She may soon have happy news of her own.

Yours affectionately,

MME

Kitty read the letter with interest and reminded herself to impart the pertinent information to Darcy. And of course, she would write and share her own good news with her distant friends. She put quill to paper and penned a quick missive announcing her engagement and Georgiana's. Both couples were unsure whether to plan their weddings before or after the appearance of the Darcy baby, so no dates had been set.

≈

One October morning a few days hence, after the three Pemberley ladies enjoyed a light breakfast, Georgiana went to the music room for her daily practice. Kitty was languidly savoring a cup of chocolate and daydreaming about her future when Lizzy broke into her reverie.

Twisting slightly in her chair, Lizzy said, "Kitty, what do you have planned for today?"

"Oh, nothing in particular," Kitty replied, but then leaned forward and looked closely at Lizzy, alerted by an unusual tone in her sister's voice. "What is it, Lizzy?"

"Probably nothing, Kitty. Do not worry. But please, don't leave me today. I just don't feel quite myself. I am very restless and cannot get comfortable ..."

Lizzy's face had a faraway expression and her countenance was drawn.

"Of course I will stay with you, but shall I send for someone?

Can I get you anything?" Kitty tried to mask her concern but knew her sister could read her face.

Lizzy shook her head.

Just then Wilson appeared at the door with a bow to announce Mr. Owen Wyndham.

"Please, Wilson, ask him to come to us here in the breakfast room. And for the maid to bring fresh water for my sister."

Wilson glanced towards Lizzy, furrowed his brow, and hurried away at once.

"Oh, Kitty, I am not up to receiving callers this morning ..."

"I am sure Mr. Owen will understand. Now, where do you wish for you and I to keep company? In the music room? The drawing room? Perhaps Owen and I could help you—"

Owen strode into the room.

"Good morning, ladies," he said, "what a fine—" He stopped mid-sentence. "Mrs. Darcy, are you unwell? Shall I call for someone?"

Lizzy attempted to smile; the weakness of her effort was not lost on Owen and he glanced at Kitty with concern.

"No," Lizzy mumbled, shaking her head, "but perhaps you and Kitty can help me to the drawing room. I think I shall be more comfortable with my feet up."

"But of course. Come, Kitty, let us each take an arm. We two are strong enough to help you along, Mrs. Darcy. And walking does sometimes improve the discomfort from carrying ... well, it often helps mares when they are feeling restless and getting near to ... my apologies, I am certainly not comparing you to a horse, Mrs. Darcy, but ..." He glanced at Kitty for the proper words.

His awkwardness brought a smile to Lizzy's face.

"Walking is rhythmic and can be very calming, Lizzy." Kitty kept her voice low, exchanging a meaningful look with Owen. "You have always preferred walking to steady your mind. It will do you good."

They were making slow and awkward progress down the long hall when Lizzy grasped for Kitty's hand. A little cry of "Oh, no!" escaped her and she flushed crimson with a horrified look.

Kitty heard a splash and looked at the floor, feeling wetness through her house slippers. She frowned and looked at Owen.

His eyes were wide. "Her water has broken. Kitty, point me towards the room that is set up for the birth. Her labor has begun."

Lizzy whispered, "I am so sorry. I am mortified. You must leave at once, Mr. Wyndham. I cannot—"

"No, Mrs. Darcy. I will not leave you alone. I will stay until the doctor or the midwife arrives. All will be well. It is a good sign when the water breaks first." He glanced down at the floor. "And it is clear—also a good sign. Do not worry."

He reached around Lizzy to offer more support, pulling her arm around his neck.

"Mrs. Darcy, are any of the elder ladies of the house present this morning? The housekeeper? The cook? Anyone who has attended a birth?"

Lizzy looked at him wide-eyed and whispered, "No. Cook has gone into the village, and the housekeeper is there as well to tend her sick brother."

Kitty trembled. Her mind raced. Water? Labor? She had seen kittens born when she was a little girl. But the process itself had been lost on her—she had focused only on which one she would pick for her own.

Owen's firm voice penetrated her foggy mind.

"Kitty. Look at me."

She took a breath and stared at him.

"You must follow my directions. Listen. Go to Wilson. Tell him Mrs. Darcy is in labor. Doubtless Darcy has a plan of action in place for this. I hope ..."

Then Owen turned to Lizzy again. "Where is Darcy this morning? I am sorry to ask you so many questions ..."

"Swan's Nest. He and the squire were going to look—"

"Oh, yes, that stallion over by Froggatt. We must catch him before they leave. Kitty, when you find Wilson have him send for the physician and the midwife. And send the fastest rider he has to Swan's Nest to fetch Darcy here at once. Oh, and have Lady Stapleton come immediately." He paused, as if to put his thoughts in order. "Then send up a house maid. And a lad to start a fire. Tell Georgiana to handle things below stairs. Then return here to me—your sister will be easier for your presence. Now go!"

Kitty's eyes were large. She gulped, spun around, and raced down the hall.

After following Owen's many directions, Kitty returned to her sister, who now sat on a chair in the birthing room. Owen assisted the maid in preparing the bed whilst a young man started a fire. Kitty hurried over and knelt beside Lizzy, taking her hand.

"Tell me what I can do. How can I help you?"

"Just stay by me, Kitty." She gripped Kitty's hand hard as a contraction built.

Grasping Lizzy's hand, Kitty nodded and said, "Wilson has sent messengers out. The doctor and the midwife will be on their way. And Lady Stapleton."

Lizzy breathed deeply again when the contraction subsided.

"I shall be most relieved with Lady Stapleton here. She has attended many births."

"Yes, and she is especially excited about this one," Kitty said. "She looks on you almost as a daughter, Lizzy."

Lizzy merely smiled and closed her eyes.

Time seemed at a standstill as they waited for help to arrive. But it was not at a standstill for Lizzy, whose labor progressed quickly. The contractions were coming closer together.

Kitty looked at Owen in alarm. He pulled her near the door for a moment and spoke in a very low voice.

"No matter what happens, Kitty, you must stay calm. Like a skittish horse, your sister will look to you for comfort and reassurance. Can you do this? I understand it is more difficult with your own sister. But if you lose control, so likely will she. If you do not think you can manage, it would be better for her if you wait in the outer room."

"She is my sister. I will not leave her," Kitty said, pressing her lips into a determined line.

"Good. Now I must speak to her. I will give direction, you give reassurance. Yes?"

Kitty nodded.

He moved up near Lizzy's face, gently touching her shoulder.

"Mrs. Darcy, all possible help is on the way. I advise that you allow me to attend you until more experienced help arrives. But I do understand if you will feel too ... compromised ... by what I may see or have to do. I have helped deliver many foals, but no babies. Your comfort is of the highest importance. Things go better when the mother is comfortable. Shall I stay, or go?"

"Stay. Please stay. I care nothing for propriety at present. Only for the safety of our baby." She closed her eyes again to cope with another contraction. A few tears escaped and trickled down her cheeks.

Kitty had never seen Lizzy cry, except in anger or frustration, and her first instinct was to panic and to cry herself. But no! She must be strong for Lizzy. She cast about in her mind for what to say but could come up with nothing diverting, and simply said, "Don't worry, Lizzy. Remember what you said? Babies are born every day, and in most situations things go well. You are going to be a mother, Lizzy. A mother!"

Lizzy grasped Kitty's hands and nodded, and a bit of a smile returned.

"Move around however feels most comfortable, Mrs. Darcy," Owen encouraged. "The mother usually knows best."

Kitty continued to talk and ask Lizzy questions about baby names and anything else that might help Lizzy relax. Still, the minutes dragged and the halls remained silent.

Lizzy made for the bed and turned onto her side, no longer able to speak or look at anyone.

Owen had just positioned himself to assist the baby's entrance into the world when Lady Stapleton bustled into the room. She took one look at Lizzy and clucked.

"I see I am just in time."

Owen nodded.

Lady Stapleton leaned near Lizzy's face and whispered reassurances whilst stroking her hair. Then she moved to join Owen for the delivery.

"Now, my dear, you must push when I say, and *only* when I say. You are a strong, healthy young lady. We shall soon meet the youngest Darcy."

Kitty moved to her sister's face and murmured what encouragements she could think of.

The labor was hard but quick. With only a few well-timed pushes, Lady Stapleton's and Owen's voices cried out in unison, "It's a boy!"

The lusty cries of the baby were reassuring. Lizzy and Kitty were overcome with tears and laughter, relief and joy. Lady Stapleton cleaned the baby whilst Owen stayed to attend Lizzy during the final stage.

Boots were at last heard racing down the hall. Fitzwilliam burst into the room and rushed to Lizzy, his eyes flashing and his face contorted with alarm.

"Are you well? Are you in pain? Oh, my dear. The squire and I were halfway to ..." He glanced quickly around the room, astonished to see Owen. "But where is the doctor? The midwife?"

Lady Stapleton shushed him.

"Here now, Mr. Darcy, things are all in hand. I believe the doctor is on his way, but the largest part of the business is done, and done very well indeed." She walked over and handed him a tiny bundle. "Here be the wee one. Mr. Darcy, meet your son."

For just a moment, Fitzwilliam's jaw quivered. He knelt next to Lizzy, cradling the child between them. His eyes misted as he looked back and forth between his child and his wife.

"I cannot believe it ... it is so amazing ... are you sure you are well? And the baby—he is healthy?"

Lady Stapleton patted Fitzwilliam on the shoulder.

"Yes, yes, all seems to be well. The doctor should be arriving at any—"

A knock was heard and the doctor entered the room, followed by the nurse. With a quick look at the new parents cooing at the child, he puckered his brow.

"Well, I see nature has had her way once again." He glanced at Lady Stapleton. "Any concerns?"

"I believe all is well." She bent over and kissed Lizzy on the forehead and then retreated to the outer room.

Meanwhile, Owen had set himself to rights and now reached for Kitty's hand and led her out as well.

"We shall give the new family a chance to get acquainted," he said with a look of great pleasure on his face.

"How fortunate you were here, Mr. Owen," Lady Stapleton said, patting his arm.

"Providence, it was," he replied.

"Aye, praise be. But I am sure having someone of experience gave Mrs. Darcy some peace of mind, even if your experience is not with humankind," she quipped. Her eyes danced with merriment.

"An heir, and he looks to be healthy, too. The first of many babes in the neighborhood, I hope," she said, giving the young couple a knowing smile.

Kitty blushed as Owen put an arm around her.

"A fine hope indeed, my lady."

≈

Lizzy recovered quickly from the birth and had her hands and mind full of learning baby care from both Lady Stapleton and the baby nurse that had been secured.

One morning as Lizzy sat nursing the infant in the company of Kitty and Georgiana she said, "Well now, perhaps it is time to discuss wedding plans?"

The two exchanged an excited glance, but Kitty said, "Lizzy, are you sure you are up to such a thing so soon?"

Lizzy gave them a placating look. "I believe each of you quite capable of handling the plans. Meanwhile, I shall be planning a christening for young William here. Some guests for these events will need to travel and we must give them as much notice as possible. So, let us all commence our planning, shall we?"

And plan they did.

≈

After a lovely christening attended by family and friends, Georgiana and Kitty married their true loves in a double ceremony. There was satin enough to be sure, but that fact went unnoticed by those celebrating the happy bonds that further strengthened the ties between the Darcys, the Wyndhams, the Stapletons, and the Drakes of Derbyshire.

Many letters were sent bearing all the good news to friends and relations near and far, keeping the post in Lampton busy for weeks. Matilda and William Cressley were already located in Reading, and Christopher and Lucy Drake at Cedars. Now Benjamin and Georgiana Drake removed to an estate east of Matlock. And Owen and Kitty Wyndham settled into the vicarage near Greystone with Cara—a special wedding gift from Mr. Darcy.

≈

One day, some weeks after the wedding, a large parcel arrived for Kitty. She asked Owen to join her in the drawing room to cut the bindings. As she pulled away the wrapping and padding, the smell of fine leather met her nostrils. When she lifted off the last covering she beheld a beautiful saddle—not a sidesaddle!—with a gleaming brass plate fixed just under the cantle engraved: *"Catherine B. Wyndham from Princess Charlotte of Wales."* The accompanying note read:

My dear friend,

Your happy marriage is the brightest news we have received of late. It brought particular joy to our mutual friend who wishes to bestow the enclosed as a token of friendship. She hopes to tour the Midlands and the Lakes next summer, but as you know the plan is not entirely in her hands. So until we all meet again, we send our wishes for the health and happiness of you both, and our warmest congratulations.

Miss Margaret Mercer Elphinstone & Princess Charlotte of Wales

Owen put his arms about Kitty's waist and gazed into her eyes.

"I think you and Lady Drake need have no concern about your riding style now. This is as good as a royal decree."

THE END

THANKS FOR READING THIS BOOK!

Please consider leaving an honest review at such sites as Amazon, Goodreads, Barnes & Noble or other reader/fan page sites. Your review can help others decide if they, too, might enjoy this story about Kitty.

If you'd like to read more by this author, her upcoming works include: *The Pleasure of Her Company* (Mrs. Dashwood's story); *An Excellent Adventure* (Margaret Dashwood's story); *Love & Stones* (a contemporary Austen heroine's story).

ABOUT THE AUTHOR

SALLIANNE HINES is a fan of all things Austen, and is an advocate for animals, children, and simplicity. Her nonfiction writing has appeared in *Mary Jane's Farm, Seamwork, Mothering, Spin Off, Chicken Soup for the Soul*, and many more places. This novel is her fiction debut.

She is a lifelong horsewoman, parent of three, grandparent of eight, and shares her home with a boss cat and two dogs (who give way to that boss cat). They all live together in a little house on the prairie. Really. She believes we must each be the hero or heroine of our own story, and trusts it is never too late to do so.

CONNECT WITH SALLIANNE!

Learn about upcoming books and projects at her author website *www.salliannehines.com*. If you like, join her email list to receive occasional news, exclusive excerpts, updates, and offers.

FOLLOW SALLIANNE!

Go to Facebook.com/authorshineswrites or contact her through her author pages at Amazon and Goodreads and LinkedIn.

AN HISTORICAL NOTE

Princess Charlotte of Wales was married 2 May 1816 to her true love, German Prince Leopold of Saxe-Coburg-Saalfeld, who later became King of the Belgians. They lived at Marlborough House in London and at Claremont Park in Esher, Surrey with great and obvious mutual affection.

Kitty's journals do not speak of ever seeing Princess Charlotte again. Kitty did keep and cherish her invitation to the royal wedding but she could not travel at that time, being with child.

Sadly, Princess Charlotte died 6 November 1817, one day after giving birth to a stillborn son. Charlotte was twenty-one years old. The whole kingdom went into deep mourning. Leopold did not remarry until 1832.

Had she lived, Princess Charlotte would have become Queen. It is said she was the royal personage most beloved by the British people until the time of Princess Diana of Wales, who also was taken in death at a young age.

ACKNOWLEDGMENTS

So many people helped me along this publishing path. Many thanks to my beta readers, editors, and consultants: Allie Cresswell, Mikiya Goetz, Heidi Herman-Kerr, Cheryl Krutzfeldt, Jessica Lankford MS, and A.K. Paxton, for their eagle eyes and great suggestions. Special thanks to my daughters Elizabeth and Abigail, and granddaughter Mikiya who weighed in on blurbs and cover options; and to my son Dan who helped me keep my household in good repair as I wrote and revised.

Much appreciation to the members of my local writer's groups and the many online writing and publishing and Austen groups for their feedback and support.

I must also acknowledge Miss Jane Austen herself, who remains a powerful and timeless source of inspiration, comfort, and entertainment for us all.

Made in the USA
Coppell, TX
03 September 2020

36480814R00208